THE ROSAS AFFAIR

THE ROSAS AFFAIR
Honor, Abuse of Power, and Retribution
In Colonial New Mexico 1637–1645

A Novel Based on a True Story

Donald L. Lucero

SANTA FE

Sunstone books may be purchased for educational, business, or sales promotional
use. For information please write: Special Markets Department, Sunstone Press,
P.O. Box 2321, Santa Fe, New Mexico 87504-2321.

Book design ▷ Vicki Ahl ✧ Cover design ▷ Jen Lucero
Body typeface ▷ Bodoni
Printed on acid free paper

Library of Congress Cataloging-in-Publication Data

Lucero, Donald L., 1935-
  The Rosas affair : honor, abuse of power, and retribution in colonial New Mexico,
1637-1645 : a novel based on a true story / by Donald L. Lucero.
      p. cm.
  ISBN 978-0-86534-681-9 (pbk. : alk. paper)
  1. Rosas, Luís de, d. 1642–Fiction. 2. New Mexico–History–To 1848–Fiction.
I. Title.
  PS3612.U255R67 2008
  813'.6–dc22
                                      2008032778

WWW.SUNSTONEPRESS.COM
SUNSTONE PRESS / POST OFFICE BOX 2321 / SANTA FE, NM 87504-2321 /USA
(505) 988-4418 / ORDERS ONLY (800) 243-5644 / FAX (505) 988-1025

In Memory
of
The Grandparents
of
The Rosas Affair

Hernando Ruiz de Hinojos and Beatriz Perez de Bustillo
Alonso Varela Jaramillo and Catalina Perez de Bustillo
Asencio de Arechuleta and Ana Perez de Bustillo
Antonio Baca* and Yumar Perez de Bustillo
Francisco Gomez and Ana Robledo
Alonso Baca
Diego Marquez* and Bernardina Vasquez
Antonio Jorge de Vera and Gertrudis Baca
Pedro Lucero de Godoy and Petronila de Zamora
Matias Lopez del Castillo and (Maria) de Archuleta

*Those executed

A fearless soldier, ruthless in his methods, and avowedly anticlerical, Rosas entered New Mexico [in the spring of 1637] with two objectives: to place civil government and secular authority on a superior footing, and to profit from his governorship

—Gutierrez, *When Jesus Came the Corn Mothers Went Away*

The precise chronology of events [regarding the Rosas affair] from mid-1639 to mid-1641 is impossible to establish from conflicting testimony . . .

—Kessell, *Kiva, Cross, and Crown*

1

His Lordship the Governor

MEXICO CITY, KINGDOM OF NEW SPAIN, JANUARY 1637

A footman, acting in place of the duke's equerry, stood on the path below the garden. "All's ready, don Luis" he said to the man waiting on the tread of the terrace. "Do you wish for me to bring up the carriage?"

"A moment yet," replied the governor-applicant, Luis de Rosas, glancing at the landau awaiting him in the courtyard. A moment yet, he thought to himself, one further moment.

The day was bright and clear, crisp winter weather under a brilliant sun. Behind him, the eaves of the two doors leading from a series of palatial halls onto the red-tiled terrace were bright in the morning sun. The eave's porches of blue tiles and the walls up to the open-eaved roof were decorated with *azulejo* tiles and chiaroscuro frescos in the Italian design of fronds and foliage spilling from two-handled vases. Before him, his view swept over the walls of the courtyard to a high church and to the huge square façade of the viceregal palace almost transparent in the dazzling light. He could have walked to the palace, but protocol required that on this, his final meeting with the viceroy, he must ride in a carriage.

Rosas, who knew the importance of symbols, bore himself with dignity. He was clad in a rose-colored doublet of rich material worked with rows of silver crescents that sparkled in the sun. In full court dress sans hat, sword, belt, and spurs, his dark, bearded face bordered in a small ruff, he showed only slightly the marks of the pox that had afflicted him as a child. He appeared handsome and rugged with the type of masculine vigor appealing to men. Although sickly in childhood, and suffering all his life with gastric troubles, he showed no outward sign of these ailments or of the tertian fevers with which he was plagued and appeared to be in the peak of health. His medical problems had perhaps impinged on the development of his personality, however. Imbued with a considerable sense of his own importance—although he was, by all accounts, only the son of a merchant—he had been difficult as a child, sullen as a young man, taciturn and stubborn as an adult. Now often rageful and filled with arrogance, his measured bearing on this occasion, would, he felt, show the curious and expectant assembly he was about to meet, that here was a governor possessing presence and energy worthy of their attention.

Rosas knew it was imperative to arrive at the appointed hour. His actions would be observed from the instant his carriage entered the viceregal grounds. And when it did, as the lone occupant of the vehicle, he must appear to be in complete command of the moment. It was early, and, therefore, he waited. He stood at the top of the stairs examining the trappings of his horse, a prancing charger of the finest Spanish breed, waiting impatiently for him to spring onto his back. His horse would, instead, be led behind his carriage from the ducal palace where he had been staying while in negotiation with the viceroy, to the viceregal palace from which he would ride in triumph once he had the *cedula* (royal decree) confirming his appointment as governor of New Mexico. The preparations for his investiture were a pantheon of symbols, the symbols required of life—and death—in Spanish service. His 15 years of military service as a captain of *cuirassiers* (cavalry soldiers) in Flanders had taught him the importance of symbols. His attention to these, as well as his keen mind, had assisted him in his rise through the ranks, making him now the confidant and protégé to New Spain's new viceroy, the *Marques de Cadereyta*, a knight of *Sant' Iago* (St. James). Rosas, as one of the gentlemen in the viceroy's train, had come with the *marques* from Spain in 1635. Now, almost two years later—and following the payment of a considerable bribe—his patience in awaiting a lucrative assignment was finally to be rewarded. With a final survey of the duke's winter garden in which a myriad of rose bushes anticipated a welcome spring, he finished a mental tally of the preparations necessary regarding his horse and carriage.

"You may bring them up now," he said to the footman.

* * *

The defensive courtyard of the *Patio de Armas* into which Luis de Rosas rode was flanked on one side by the imposing stables of the viceregal palace containing 30 of New Spain's finest studs, horses constituting the viceroy's one obsession. In the stable among these beautiful creatures were the carriages and horses that had brought the members of the *audiencia* (high court). Opposite the stables, and completing two wings of the patio's surround, were the offices of the viceroy's staff. Making a tight circle at the center of the courtyard, Rosas's carriage made its approach to the palace, arriving square on.

Dismounting before a stone archway in a windowless façade, the governor elect was ushered into the building through its only entrance, a covered loggia or arcade beyond which were broad, open, double-doors, thickly studded and hung with iron. The walls of this gallery were decorated with a rich cloth of raised designs, Italian *broccatos* (brocades), and painted frescoes whose stiff, geometric patterns reflected European inspiration. A door leading off the entrance hall was held open by two liveried pages, one of whom politely asked Rosas to stand on the threshold of the room's carved and ornate doorway until he was announced. Waiting at the entrance as he had been asked, Luis stood beneath the doorway's stone lintel, observing the room's interior, and dwarfed by its majesty.

Inside the hall, amid a forest of garlanded pillars, palmers, armed with fronds of pine and willow, fanned air that was scented by sprigs of herbs and spices. Rosas admired with great interest the viceroy's brocade *baldachino*, a canopy that was erected above the viceroy's chair. This sign of royalty, the use of which had been denied preceding viceroys, was now being used to accentuate the fact that the viceroy, as the sovereign's deputy, ruled in New Spain in the king's stead. As Luis looked at the viceroy's banner of vermilion on a background of gold damask, he thought that he, too, would have one similarly designed and set out.

The crimson uniforms of viceregal servants, the dazzling short coats of heralds, and the violet jackets of attendants, all cast a regal glow on the walls of the reception hall. The room blazed with the brilliance of their raiments.

Standing beside the viceroy's chair was a master of ceremonies who briefly glanced in Rosas's direction before crying out, "Don Luis de Rosas, your Lordship!"

Rosas was ushered into the *Salon de Coronas*, a great reception hall distinguished by a *dado* (wainscoting) of *azulejo* tiles decorated with graceful blue and white designs, and a wooden ceiling, heavily beamed and decorated with radiant crowns. The viceroy, don Lope Diez de Armendariz, *Marques de Cadereyta*, a self-possessed gentleman with an animated look upon his face, rose from his chair. Twelve other men of honor, all beautifully dressed in their long black robes with ruffled sleeves, joined him in standing to receive Luis de Rosas. Rosas made a motion as to bend his knee.

The viceroy, gentle and pleasant to those with whom he had a close association, reached out with both of his hands and said, "We've no need for that, don Luis. Come. Come join us! We've been anxiously awaiting your arrival. May I offer you something to drink? A glass of wine perhaps?" He motioned for a servant. "It would be well to have something warm in your belly before meeting with these old men." The viceroy chuckled at the men standing before him who joined him in his laughter.

"Your health and welfare are all I ask, your Lordship, and if God will maintain these, I shall want for nothing more."

Elegant in bearing and comely in person, the viceroy was, as the king's representative, magnificently clothed and jeweled having been exempted from the canon prohibiting Knights of Santiago to wear anything but unadorned rough wool, although he was still obliged to say 15 Mysteries of the Rosary, daily, an imperative which he devotedly observed. He wore the grand, white satin robes of a Knight Commander of the military order of Saint James, his body concealed by the mantle's cumbrous plaits. With a bright, attractive face and deep-set dark eyes he had a remarkable presence. He introduced Luis de Rosas to each member of the *audiencia*, with special attention given to its president, Bishop don Juan de Palafox y Mendoza, royal troubleshooter and visitor general. For each member of the high court, he offered a brief resume of titles, lineage, and history in Spanish service. The viceroy then motioned for Rosas to occupy the chair of honor to his right. Rosas moved there, standing between the table and his chair awaiting the viceroy's signal for all to sit.

The visitor general, don Juan de Palafox, whose chair was directly across from that of the governor-applicant, eyed Luis de Rosas with suspicion. Naturally hot-tempered, impatient and proud—and even, perhaps, a bit contemptuous in his manner—he was, nevertheless, one of the viceroy's most trusted advisors, and he questioned the selection of this particular individual as New Mexico's tenth governor. The viceroy, Bishop Palafox knew, was a Spanish grandee who, ruling in place of the king, followed the simple and ancient theory of the "hungry falcon." This was the practice of placing comparatively unknown men into positions of leadership where their ambitions, plus their reliance upon and gratitude toward the individual who had bestowed the honor, could be counted upon to keep them productive and loyal. It was a method followed by Their Catholic Majesties, Fernando and Isabella, who, upon assuming their thrones, had kept tiny notebooks with the names of individuals they met throughout their travels who might be useful to them. The Catholic sovereigns often solicited the advice of these obscure individuals, ultimately inviting some to join their court. However, the sovereigns' appointees, like those of the viceroy's, had not always responded as expected.

And had it not been so with the viceroy's previous selection of governor of New Mexico? thought the visitor general. Was it not Francisco de Martinez de Baeza about whom the New Mexican priest, Antonio de Ibargaray, had been speaking when he wrote:

From the moment he became governor he has attended only to his

11

own profit, causing grave damage to all these recently converted souls. He has commanded them to weave and paint great quantities of *mantas* and hangings. Likewise, he has made them seek out and barter for many tanned skins and haul quantities of *pinon* nuts. As a result, he has now loaded eight *carretas* with what he has amassed and is taking them and as many men from [New Mexico] to drive them to New Spain, thwarting everything His Majesty has ordered in his royal ordinance.

Stiff charges, Palafox thought. Although loath to have others render such scathing judgments regarding one in royal service, he suspected that much of what Ibargaray had written was true. Martinez has proven to be little more than a drummer, he said to himself. We cannot have a repeat of his misrule. We must do a better job in selecting the new governor.

* * *

Distrusting both the Church and his overseas officers, the king, Philip IV, who had ascended to the throne in 1621, had established in New Spain three royal bureaucracies. Designed as somewhat autonomous but interdependent entities with a complicated system of checks and balances, these branches had ill-defined and overlapping jurisdictional boundaries with little definition as to how they were to share power. The first of these entities was the viceroyalty which wielded authority through a number of provincial governors and which administered in all matters civil and military. The viceroy, therefore, in selecting the governor of New Mexico, did not require the approval of the *audiencia*, the second of the three entities which constituted the district court of appeals. The third entity, the episcopate, the system of church government by bishops, was charged with ecclesiastical administration. The king knew that litigation among the three resulting from petty jealousies and jurisdictional disputes would check the power of each, while keeping him informed of affairs in the most remote corners of the Spanish empire.

* * *

Kind to his friends, cruel to his enemies, the viceroy was a man of practical skills. To assure that civil and military authority remained in his control, he sought the advice of others but ruled alone. Astute and unusually accurate in his judgment of men and other matters, he had the ultimate responsibility of choosing the new governor, and he wanted Luis de Rosas.

Looking around the room at the men who were gathered there the viceroy placed his right hand on top of Rosas's left hand and said, "*Senores,* as you're aware, don Luis and I have been meeting to work out the various aspects of his contract as governor of New Mexico, and I'm convinced that I have the right man for this assignment. But do not think that we're here for you merely to ratify my choice. I earnestly seek your advice and counsel in the selection of governor for New Mexico. And I especially request your assistance in the instructions he is to receive relative to the conduct of his office. In the Lord's name," he said, as he smiled at those before him, "I now ask for your advice and assistance."

Don Juan de Palafox, visitor general and president of the *audiencia,* whose velvet stockings and matching slippers were briefly visible beneath his black cassock, gazed about the room. He knew that it was his responsibility to set the tone for the inquiry, since few of the others would question the viceroy's choice in the selection of governor. If, therefore, his was the only voice the viceroy and governor-applicant might hear, he had to ask the questions the other members of the *audiencia* were reluctant to express.

The duo, Rosas and Palafox, observed one another shrewdly, each trying to deduce the thoughts of the other. The pause gave Rosas and the president time to evaluate the gap that lay between them and the *audiencia* members, time to advise one another as to where their advantage and security lay.

There was a long moment before the president spoke. "I wonder if you truly understand the honor and responsibility being placed upon your shoulders?" His intelligent eyes betraying his wariness of the viceroy's selection, he added in a contemptuous manner, "I wonder if a man of such meager experience can be truly aware of the difficulties he'll encounter as governor of such a remote province." He moved to the front of his chair. "There's an oft-quoted adage regarding the physical and political climate of New Mexico that expresses it well, don Luis," he stated, looking directly at the governor applicant. " '*Ocho meses de invierno y cuatro de infierno*!' Yes, eight months of winter and four of hell, for New Mexico is but a spare and unproductive land," he said, "blistering hot in summer and bitterly cold in winter. And although covered in abundant forests, its trees are not subject to forestation, for there are no roads or bridges. Communication is poor, and you'll be almost totally isolated, cut off from succor or aid." He paused, and then continued, "The land is colonized by an ignorant and vulgar people, don Luis, a people utterly obsessed with their rights and privileges. A vain-glorious people, bloated with a quite unjustifiable pride in the purity of their blood and in their nobility. You'll not be welcome among them, for they're uncourteous to strangers, regarding them with suspicion, if not with outright hostility. They live in mean dwellings, domesticated strong-houses with heavily gated doors reflecting a harsh way of life and built only for defense. These doors will not be opened to you, don Luis, for you'll not be welcome there," he repeated. "They're a tight-knit group," he continued, "so knotted up through intrigue and intermarriage as to form an intricate web of family relationships impossible to penetrate and difficult to unravel so that it's impossible to determine where their loyalties lie. It will be of no avail to speak to them regarding their obligations toward royal governors, for even their priests defy proper authority, administering the sacraments to the native converts—and to the faithful as well—in complete disobedience to the holy Council.[1] A colony of cousins, they're a troublesome and obstinate lot, don Luis, full of animus and deception, dedicated to land and family aspirations. They feel they can only count on themselves, and so distant are they from royal authority, that they'll not easily subject themselves to central control and will not participate in governmental affairs."

Palafox waited then, waited for his pronouncements to sink in and to be fully appreciated by the governor-applicant who sat there quietly, attentive to the cleric's words. After a moment, Palafox said, "I apprise you of these things not to discourage you, but to make sure that you're aware of the extraordinary difficulties you'll encounter as governor of so remote a province. Do you think you're ready for this?"

Rosas, who knew the importance of his answers, especially in gaining the approval of those who might be wavering in their support, waited a long and painful moment before replying, his words and tone then calculated to make the greatest impact. After a bit, he said, "I have served on the frontier and have lived the life of a soldier." Looking at Bishop Palafox straight on and then at each of the men spread about the room, he went on, "And being but a poor soldier, I consider my potential appointment as governor an exceptional honor and will accept it with justifiable pride, and with complete awareness of the burden being placed upon me."

The viceroy, who had been listening quietly, sat for a long time in silence, surveying the room. His eyes scanned the faces of the members of the *audiencia* looking for suggestions of approval or disapproval but seeing neither. He asked the president, "Perhaps you'd like to include questions regarding his instructions as part of your inquiry?"

His hands flat before him, Palafox pushed himself to the back of his chair. "Yes, I think that would be helpful," he responded.

The viceroy's instructions, previously developed in conjunction with the *audiencia*, filled seven pages of the book the president now laid before Rosas.

"These," the president said, "are only the most urgent. If appointed to the position of governor of New Mexico, you will be given more complete details before the departure of your train. Your primary responsibility upon assuming your post would be to re-establish royal command and authority by your personal attention to martial law," the president said in reference to the New Mexico colonists who seemed to be holding on tenaciously to a medieval dream. "You'll have to oversee the selection of a new *cabildo* (town council). At present, some of the councilmen are in confederation with brigands, while other members have intimidated some. We need representatives who are willing to listen to the suggestions we might make for the improvement of our northern kingdom. And we need priests who will allow someone other than their sacred selves to suggest them.

"Equal to that," the president continued, "is the re-establishment and expedition of Royal justice. In that regard, the governor elect will be required to conduct Martinez's *residencia*, the mandatory judicial review of one's administration. I'm afraid that we'll find much there that will be of concern to us. And we, of course, look forward to the determinations you might make. Are you equal to these tasks?" the president asked.

Rosas had heard of the passion with which the New Mexican colonists asserted their rights and their independence from royal authority, attitudes exacerbated by the apparent failure of his predecessor, Martinez de Baeza, to assert his control. "I know of these people and of their kabylistic tendency to divide themselves into clans, even into different tribes," he said, echoing a sentiment previously articulated by the viceroy in reference to the relationship of the early Iberians to the people of the Kabyl tribes. "Some have expressed this tendency as a matter of race, while I see it as an artifact of our ancient times, for they, like us, are shepherds by choice when they're not soldiers. Their psychology is that of wanderers who will forever fight central authority. Their natural tendency is toward disruption and disunion, which, I believe, can only be contained by the most vigorous, if not the most restrictive, exercise of authority. For no matter their protests to the contrary," he said, gazing about the room, "New Mexico is not a seigniorial regime in which its lords rule their lands and the tenants on them. New Mexico may be a nation of shepherds and remote beyond compare, a land where sheep are used in place of money, but in one way or another, and with the help of God, I will restore order and authority there and will punish those who are causing difficulty. Your Excellencies may be certain that in anything that involves His Majesty's service, I shall not be found wanting," he said gravely, again scanning the faces before him. "I'll do whatever's required to clean out the Augean stable you've described. And when all is said and done, the colonists will get what they deserve."[2]

These were the right words and the members of the *audiencia* smiled and nodded their assent. The bishop, who could wield a sword with both hands, determined to give his vote to the avowedly anti-clerical Rosas, but also to keep his eye on him. Looking across the table with solemnity, his long face, sharp nose, and high forehead, reflecting his gentle birth, he spoke politely and with sentiment, saying, "I have every faith that you'll do your work well." He then looked at the viceroy, nodded his head in agreement at the viceroy's choice, and speaking to Rosas directly, said, "You may now wear a hat."

The members of the *audiencia* stood and a great silence invaded the hall. Placed before the viceroy were the symbols of Rosas's office, his sword, helmet, and spurs. President and Bishop Juan de Palafox, who had risen from his chair with the others, walked around the table and with much gravity grasped Rosas's sword and belt and assisted the new governor in putting them on. Kneeling before Rosas, a page affixed the governor's long silver spurs to his high riding boots, while the governor, assisted by President Juan de Palafox, placed a small hat of crushed velvet upon his head.

After this was accomplished, the viceroy said, "*Senores y Caballeros*, Gentlemen, I give you don Luis de Rosas, military commander, captain-general, governor of New Mexico!"

Rosas knelt at the feet of the viceroy who had remained seated throughout his investiture. The governor's induction completed, Rosas removed his bonnet and laid it courteously in the viceroy's hands signifying, thereby, that he was the king's man. The viceroy accepted his hat and placed it aside. Then, putting his hands in the viceroy's palms, and swearing to defend his lord faithfully and to protect the New Mexican kingdom from its enemies, Luis de Rosas waited for what seemed an eternity for the viceroy's response to his gesture of vassalage.

"You'll meet with Fray Tomas Manso, *procurador-general* of the province, who is responsible for the missionary supply service and will proceed as he advises you," the viceroy said to Rosas. And then to the members of the *audiencia* who had remained on their feet, the viceroy said, "We will honor the governor's request to dispense with the festivities and entertainments this occasion would ordinarily require. Governor don Luis de Rosas has asked only that we share a glass of wine with him and that he be allowed to proceed with arrangements for going to his new home." Finally releasing Rosas from his grasp, he stood, raised the governor to his feet, and embraced him most graciously and affectionately. Wine was poured for all present. Several toasts were offered.

"We wish to hear of your progress as you go along your way until you are beyond sight and sound," the viceroy said. "Please make sure that we do so. Go with God, my dear Rosas!" He then gave the governor the kiss of peace and dismissed him from his chambers.

Several of the men with whom Luis had met followed the new governor through the heavy oaken doors of the viceregal palace and into the courtyard, ablaze in winter light. These so-called *hombres ricos* (the rich and powerful moguls), trim and haughty gentlemen carrying fluttering banners and Toledo blades, mounted horses that were now being brought to them. Their horses were caparisoned with silver-studded saddles, silver horseshoes, and bridles.

The governor's friend, the *duque de Segorbe*, at whose home Rosas had been staying while engaged in his many meetings with the viceroy, sprang from his own horse and held the governor's stirrup so that he could mount. Luis hesitated for a moment, his left hand grasping the pommel of his saddle, looking down at the gentleman who knelt at his feet. Theirs was friendship of convenience only, with little pretense of affection or loyalty, and the duke, Rosas knew, would throw him to the wolves if it provided the duke with an advantage. But that was all right, Luis thought, for I would do the same. However, this incredible gesture of humility, so uncharacteristic and unexpected of a royal knight, pleased him immensely. He had arrived in New Spain without position or prospects, and was now, with the duke's assistance, to be the ninth individual to serve as governor of New Mexico. He thanked the duke for his gesture, truly gratified that Segorbe had sought to put the stamp of importance on the event, for Rosas had only Segorbe with whom to share the proud moment. There was no one else.

Rosas lifted himself into his saddle glittering with gold gaud interspersed with red. The governor's boots were now adorned with the silver spurs, and he was girdled with a sword, its pommel of acacia wood wrapped in silver. On his head he wore the hat he had retrieved from the viceroy. Made by hand with the flora and fauna of his adobe kingdom sewed in with gold embroidery, it was one of the most important symbols of his office. He wielded a rod of holly in place of his lance as he and his small retinue clattered out of the courtyard.

* * *

On their return from the Zocalo, the central plaza around which the governor and the other members of his slight entourage had briefly ridden, Segorbe and Rosas retired to the duke's study where they sat before his blazing fireplace. The duke smiled at the fledgling governor, a man with whom he had fought in Flanders and with whom he was now engaged in the mercantile business in New Spain. The new governor, the duke knew, was in every way excessive, headstrong, and ambitious, one of the lowest grade, who, because of his successes in battle while in Flanders, had grown so proud and arrogant that he had become insufferable to his men. Glorying in the spectacle of battle where the prize goes to the bold and the brave, he had become coarse and dogmatic, lacking any of the refinements he had pretended to when he had presented himself at the viceregal palace. He was, nevertheless, the pawn in the duke's opening move or *gambito* in the duke's attempt to gain economic advantage in Spain's most remote Northern Kingdom. The viceroy, who had waited a long time before replacing Martinez as governor of New Mexico, had found in Luis de Rosas a ruthless soldier who would again assert civil and military control in the Northern Kingdom. This pawn, Rosas, the duke thought to himself, has reached the eighth row on the chessboard without being captured by a member of any opposing army we fought. He deserves this promotion, if not a "queening," then a governorship. Self-styled as a grandmaster in the game of political chess, Rosas might, as the king's knight's pawn, eventually have to be sacrificed, as Martinez de Baeza had been, in the crown's struggles with New Mexico's recalcitrant colonists and priests. Segorbe's gloomy prediction for Rosas was that he would not long endure among the New Mexican settlers. But while he survives, the duke thought, the governor's single-mindedness and strength of purpose, uncluttered by peripheral issues, can be counted upon to make both the governor and myself a sizeable fortune.

"Martinez is as good as dead," the duke said to Luis while grasping and ringing the small bell that sat on his table. "You may, in conducting his *residencia*, appear kind and benevolent while taking whatever you damn well please."

"I think I can do that," Rosas said with a broad grin. "I think I feel benevolence coming on. Almost like a seizure," he said with a satisfied smile. "Or perhaps it's flatulence, I don't know. I get those two mixed up," he added laughingly, as he requested another glass of wine from the servant who had arrived at the duke's summons.

The two men waited for the servant to leave before continuing their conversation regarding New Mexico. After a time the duke said in a more earnest tone, "You know, don Luis, the power is in your hands. Martinez will do whatever's necessary to save his worthless neck, pay whatever's required for a favorable report. He's as good as dead," Segorbe repeated. "And that being true, you may take the best animal in his herd." A short pause, then he went on, "The Indians of New Mexico are required to pay tribute and Martinez knows the business of *maize* and *mantas* and skins. He can be made to pass the business on to you. That's the way it is," he said emphatically. "You're to be paid two thousand pesos annually for your service as governor of New Mexico, hardly enough to get you there and to support you in anything befitting your position, and certainly less than the eight thousand you paid to secure the post. And, by the way," he added, pointing a long bony finger at the new governor, "don't forget that you owe me four thousand of that. We have to make a profit on our investment. And both the crown and the viceroy are prepared to tolerate our business enterprises so long as the sounds of weeping and wailing and the gnashing of teeth do not reach their ears. The decade of exemption for the Pueblos has passed," he added, "and a workforce in New Mexico, both unpaid and forced, is readily available. Your plan should be as we sketched it: to divide and conquer. It shouldn't be difficult, Luis. The colonists and Indians there carry either a candle or a club. Your goal should be as we outlined it, to castrate the colonists while separating both the colonists and the Indians from their priests. I look forward to receiving your *mantas* and skins when your *carretas* return with the wagon train," he said again, smiling, while reaching for a bag that he had placed beneath the table and rising to his feet. "I give you this as a token of our contract." The duke handed the governor a velvet bag in which a chess set had been placed. "To New Mexico!" he said as he raised his glass in a toast. "May it reward us greatly!"

2

Fray Tomas Manso and the Service of Missionary Supply

The governor dismounted from his horse in the shadow of the *convento* and proceeded to its gate, slapping at his thigh with the short whip he carried in his hand. Reaching the *porteria* (*convento* gate) of the walled enclosure, he tapped on it lightly with the butt of his crop, then more soundly, finally beating on its wooden staves with his closed fist. "Goddamn it!" he yelled, as the door opened to reveal a curious face. "Were you waiting for Father Francis's steward to announce my arrival?" he asked repeating a proverb often used in Castile. "You did expect me, did you not?" he shouted, as he rudely brushed by the *portero* (gatekeeper) who had opened the door.

"Yes, your Lordship," the servant responded meekly. "The fathers are at prayer. The walls are thick, your Lordship, and the cells are beyond the walls of the courtyard so that I did not hear you," he explained apologetically with smiling scrapes and bows as he ushered the governor into an inner chamber. "Fray Manso will be with you in a moment."

"In a moment," the governor muttered to himself. "Tell him that I'm waiting!" he said emphatically, slapping at his thigh.

Procurator-General Fray Tomas Manso, who was responsible for purchasing and stockpiling missionary supplies for the northern kingdom, finally appeared in the doorway, his eyes sharp, discerning. Having never experienced the manner in which he had been summoned, the well-respected friar stood there surveying the man who had demanded his presence saying, finally, and with ill-disguised annoyance, "Please come with me."

Fray Manso led the governor into the *convento's* interior patio and then to a storeroom whose lock he opened with a large key kept on a chain that was hanging around his neck. Flecks of dust floated in the sunlight as he opened the storeroom's huge oaken doors. Two 200-pound bronze bells partially blocked the entrance. Working their way around the bells, Fray Manso and the governor stepped inside.

Arrayed alongside one of the storeroom's inner walls were oil paintings of saints in gilded frames and several huge illuminated choir books which Fray Manso said contained introits and antiphonies for various saints' days. "These piles over here," Manso said of the mounds heaped against the opposite wall, "contain forty pairs of sandals; twelve large latches for church doors with their locks, keys, and ring staples; and one-hundred and twenty Sevillian locks with their keys for the cells, or private rooms for my brethren. Those other piles," he said, pointing to the back wall, "contain replacement parts, the supplies required for rebuilding our wagons, such as, spare axels, extra spokes, extra iron tires, and the tools required for their construction. And there is the equipment required for building a church, axes, adzes, small hand saws, long two-man saws, chisels, augers and planes, as well as the spikes, nails, pins, and tacks required to hold it together."

"What's in these?" Rosas asked, as he rapped on one of the many barrels arrayed about the room.

"The dry casks contain raisins, almonds, sugar, saffron, pepper, and cinnamon," responded Fray Manso, "while the wet casks are filled with olive oil, peach and quince preserves, syrup, honey, wine, and vinegar. And these, of course," he said of the damask vestments hanging from pegs on the wall, "are required by my brothers in their ministries. The colors alone should dazzle the natives," he said with a satisfied smile.

They walked about the room with Fray Manso dutifully showing and explaining the need for each object. The governor, largely silent but in deep thought, tested the heft of the metal goods provided, lifting one of the lighter ones above his head and then dropping it onto its pile.

"And how many wagons will we have?" the governor questioned.

"We'll have thirty-two wagons traveling in two groups of sixteen, two of the wagons allocated for your belongings."

"I'll need four wagons in addition to those I have," the governor said.

"That's impossible," Fray Manso answered abruptly, his patrician face and lined forehead now betraying his anger. "What you see here is the result of eighteen months of work," said the priest, brushing at the pale fringe of his hair. "We're the only regularly scheduled freight and mail service to the Northern Kingdom, and we only go every three years. I'm sure that you would not ask that the friars be denied food or clothing merely to accommodate you," he added in a haughty manner, while kicking at one of the large bells with a sandaled foot. "We can spare no more than two wagons," he stated. "Perhaps you can purchase some of the things you'll need from Governor Martinez. He may be happy to leave his possessions there so as to give him more room for the hides, salt, paintings, and *pinon* nuts he seeks to bring back."

"I'll not have cast-offs in my home," the governor said, "nor will I wear bits and pieces or hand-me-downs. You must remember that I have a distinguished station to uphold or imperial influence will suffer. Whose wagons are these anyway?" he asked angrily.

"Well, it's not all that easy to say," Manso responded while shaking his head. "Initially, the cost of each wagon and its sixteen mules was paid for by the crown. To be exact, three hundred seventy-four pesos and four *tomines*. But we're to assume the upkeep of the wagons and the replacement of mules, so is it a shared responsibility and ownership?" he asked with a shrug. "I don't know. But as far as I'm concerned, they're ours. They belong to the Custody."

"Well, I don't really give a shit who they belong to as long as I get my share," responded the governor in kind. "I must have at least three of your wagons and where you put these other things is of no concern to me. My equipment and gear will be on your carts when we leave," the governor said as they exited the storeroom.

Fray Manso placed the padlock in its hasp and did not respond, walking quickly through the patio and then down the hallway with the governor, leading him to the exit.

3

Francisco Gomez and the Baggage Train

The *fardage*, or baggage train, was composed of beasts and wooden carts, some of which contained the dishes, bedding, tapestries, and other possessions of the governor's household. It was spread out in the courtyard of the *Convento Grande*, the Principal House of the Holy Gospel, where Fray Tomas Manso was inspecting it.

The wagons—heavy, four-wheeled, iron-tired freight wagons drawn by teams of sixteen mules—were each capable of hauling two tons of equipment and merchandise. Inspecting the train with Fray Manso was Captain Francisco Gomez, a heavy-set individual with red hair, beard, and a flowing mustache, all streaked with gray, who, with a detachment of fourteen soldiers, had been sent from New Mexico to escort the governor to his adobe kingdom. A handsome man with light-colored eyes and a wound mark above his right eyebrow, Gomez was a natural leader and confidently assumed his responsibility for the train.

"He has everything on his carts, even, I suspect, stones for his *mangonel*," remarked Fray Manso shaking his head in disgust.

Before them, were seven wagons bearing the governor's personal things—his bed furnishings, garments, books and documents—tied up in hide-bound sacks or stored in chests. His kitchen, appointed with numerous pots and pans, was slung beneath one of his wagons. Two additional carts, which the governor had placed behind his personal wagon, contained articles of foodstuff and wine for the lengthy journey. Then came several canvas-topped carts burdened with baskets and

24

chests containing carpets and wall hangings for the governor's lodging. Twelve pack mules bearing the governor's table service as well as other household items were also burdened with a heavy oak table and its chairs, and a banquet service of twelve silver dishes and cups. Guards attended by several *alferezes* (ensigns) bearing the governor's armor and tack brought up the rear.

Gomez, a Portuguese soldier formerly in service to the Onates, and one who gave his first allegiance to the king's man whoever he was, said, "I'm sure that he'll become a more reasonable traveler as we go along."

"You think so?" Fray Manso asked with a smile.

"We can only hope," answered the 61-year old Gomez who had seen it all.

* * *

With the sun rising over their right shoulders, and with prayers rendered to God for a safe journey, the members of the wagon train set out. They rode aboard freight wagons, and astride saddle mules and horses, their faces set northward toward the mining town of Zacatecas. The whip-cracking muleteers on the train's 36 heavy, groaning wagons damned their mule teams and their misfortune at drawing this assignment. Assorted retainers, an extra team of 16 mules for each wagon, and meat on the hoof, brought up the rear.

Blas de Miranda, who, like Francisco Gomez, had been a member of several previous wagon escorts, was asked by Gomez to divide the train into smaller and more manageable units: two squadrons of eighteen wagons each, broken down into four nine-wagon divisions, with each squadron under the command of a wagon master. With the assistance of Nicolas Ortiz, who had also been a member of previous wagon trains, Miranda now made that division. The two lead wagons rumbling side-by-side flew banners displaying the governor's coat of arms, their teams distinctively caparisoned and wearing bells on their harnesses. The two young wagon masters, Miranda and Ortiz, rode beside their lead wagons, while Gomez, as *mayordomo* or conductor of the train, trailed behind.

"That man—Gomez?" Rosas asked of one of his aides, as they rode beside the governor's lead wagons. "What do you know of him?"

"Little," his aide responded. "Only that he's an *encomendero*, or 'estate holder,' one of the kingdom's most prominent soldiers, and the strongest defender of royal authority as vested in the governor. I think that he has no love for Governor Martinez," his aide continued, "yet Martinez can count on Gomez's loyalty until the day he leaves office, for that, they say, is the manner of the man." His aide, who was attending to his horse that had stumbled on uneven ground, continued, "Some say that he's an *alborayco*, the son or grandson of a Jew from Portugal forcibly converted to Christianity."

"And you know little of him, is that right?" the governor laughed. "With what you've told me I could either give him the kiss of peace or send him to the gallows. Tell him that when we camp at Queretaro, I'd like him to take council with me."

"Yes, your Lordship," his aide answered as he slowed his horse's pace to drop in with the rear guard. "I'll tell him!" he shouted.

* * *

At Queretaro, the first important station on their way north, they made their camp. Ringed about with mountains, Queretaro lay in a wide rolling plain, open during the day to the winter sun. On the move, with just a night's camp expected, the governor had only the canvas of his field tent erected within which he now sat, a velvet robe draped across his shoulders against the evening's chill. His servants entered and unfolded a day bed and draped it with several portable and lightweight *sarapes del campo*. These utilitarian camp blankets of natural dark-colored wool, striped with small bands of red, provided the only color in the canvas room. The servants then brought in a small writing desk, candles, a firebox full of radiant coals, wine and glasses. Also among their kitchen paraphernalia, were two large bowls, several spoons, a ladle, a kettle of soup and a tureen into which to pour it. The servants, having made things inviting with furnishings and food, removed themselves, pulling the flap of the tent closed behind them.[1]

In the last of twilight, Francisco Gomez watched the fog that back-dropped the encampment, hesitating at the entrance of the field tent before calling out and then lifting the flap. "Your Lordship," Gomez said in a verbal salute, "you requested I meet with you?"

"Don Francisco," the governor responded appearing at the door like a cowled monk with his robe draped about his shoulders. "Please, please, come in and add your warmth to my poor household," he said as he sat on one of the large cushions arranged about the canvas room. "And you may dispense with formal titles while we're on the road," he added as he beckoned Gomez to take a seat. "You may call me don Luis."

"I wouldn't be comfortable addressing you in that manner, your Lordship," Gomez responded, speaking politely, but without excessive deference.

"Governor, then," Rosas responded with some annoyance. "You may call me governor."

Gomez declined the bison robe offered him for warmth and waited for the governor to continue, thinking that the manner in which Rosas was looking at him suggested that he was disturbed about something. Gomez looked directly at the governor, trying to discern in Rosas's countenance the nature of his annoyance, turning over in his mind the many possibilities. He waited.

"I understand from Fray Manso that we'll be at least four months on the road, and I mean to make use of every moment of that time to learn the secrets of New Mexico," the governor said.

"And how may I be of service to you?" Gomez asked.

"I've been told that you're the most outstanding military official in the kingdom," Rosas said, further drawing his robe about his shoulders. "I don't say this to flatter you, but to tell you that I expect much from you—as one soldier to another."

"I'll do whatever I can to assist you, your Lordship—pardon me," Gomez laughed, "Governor."

"Soup?"

"Yes, please. May I serve it?" Gomez asked.

"This I can do myself," Rosas responded, as he ladled the contents of the tureen into two bowls and placed them side by side on the small writing desk before continuing. "This should compare favorably to your usual fare," the governor exclaimed, knowing that Gomez's typical food was the same as that enjoyed by his men: a scanty repast of one meal a day consisting of a small piece of meat, red chile, beans, and *tortillas* (*maize* cakes), with a cup of chocolate and a piece of bread in the late evening. "I have much to ask," Rosas continued, "but first, tell me a little about yourself. I like to know with whom I'm dining."

Gomez waited a long moment before responding. Clearly uncomfortable in speaking about himself, he stroked his graying mustache with the tips of his fingers saying, finally, "The facts are few, Governor. My origins are in Portugal. In Coina, five leagues from Lisbon. You may know it."

"Lisbon, yes, but not Coina," the governor responded. "A port city, I assume?"

"On the interior a bit," Gomez responded, "with access to the sea like Lisbon, but much smaller, of course." He waited before continuing, looking about the tent, choosing his words carefully as he said. "I'm the son of Manuel Gomez and Ana Vicente, both of whom died when I was a child. I was raised and schooled by my older brother, Fray Alvaro Gomez, a Franciscan in the *Convento Grande* in Lisbon and Commissary of the Holy Office. When I was thirteen," he went on, speaking deliberately "I passed into the service of don Alonso de Onate at the Court of Madrid. He was there pleading the case of his brother, don Juan de Onate, regarding don Juan's New Mexico contract. He brought me with him to Mexico when he returned there."

"And when was that?" Rosas asked politely, as the two dipped into their soup.

"It was in sixteen four or five," Gomez responded with uncertainty, "a year before I joined don Juan in New Mexico.

"Juan de Onate? New Mexico's first governor?" Rosas asked rhetorically.

"Yes, New Mexico's *adelantado*," Gomez responded regarding the honorific office Onate had held. "I first served with don Juan, and then with Governor Felipe de Sotelo, whom I also escorted to New Mexico. I've been in service to the office of the governor since my arrival there."

"As an *encomendero*?" Rosas asked. "As the recipient of an *encomienda*, one sworn to answer the governor's call to arms when requested?"

"Yes, one of thirty-five in the colony," Gomez responded. "My *encomienda*, good for three lifetimes in succession,[2] is at the pueblo of the Pecos," Gomez went on, giving no hint of the breadth of his extensive holdings which included New Mexico's best-watered lands, tribute from its most prosperous Indian villages, and access to trade.

"The entire pueblo?" the governor asked incredulously. "Was the entire pueblo given to you?"

"Not the use of native land or labor, Governor, but the collection of tribute as personal income. I am allowed to collect tribute from the entire pueblo of Pecos, except for twenty-four houses which are held by the *Maese de campo*, my friend, Pedro Lucero de Godoy. Also from two and a half parts of the pueblo of Taos, half of the Hopi pueblo of Shongopovi, half of the pueblo of Acoma except for twenty houses, half of the pueblo of Abo," he continued, "and the entire pueblo of Tesuque, although I receive services from the people there in lieu of tribute." [3]

The governor rubbed his hands together, looked at Gomez, raised his eyebrows, and blew between pursed lips. "And what do the other thirty-four have" he asked of the remaining *encomenderos*, shaking his head in disbelief.

"I won't attempt to justify the amount of tribute I've been allotted, your Lordship," Gomez said, flushing slightly and reverting to the governor's more formal title, "except to say that I've been deeply honored to have carried out many commissions for the governors under whom I've served. My services have been very generously rewarded, far in excess of what I deserve. There are, however, over forty thousand Christianized Indians living in forty-three pueblos in New Mexico, and the range of our responsibilities is enormous."

"And the tribute consists of . . . ?"

"*Maize* and a *manta* or animal skin, collected twice a year," Gomez responded. "The *manta* is a piece of cotton cloth six palms square, reckoned in price at six *reales*. A buckskin, bison hide, or a light or heavy elk skin of the same value, may be substituted for a *manta*," Gomez said, "with cloth and skins collected in May and a *fanega* of corn in October after the harvest." [4]

"And what do the Indians get for all of this?" Rosas asked.

"It's difficult to say, Governor," Gomez responded pensively. "As vassals of the crown they're required to pay tribute. And the king has granted us *encomiendas* for our pledge to defend the land at our own expense. Those of us who have been designated as *encomenderos* are to maintain arms and horses, live in Santa Fe, and respond to the governor's call to arms at a moment's notice. We ride escort, serve as guards, and command levies from colonists and Indian auxiliaries in the colony's defense. We like to think we make the kingdom a safer place to live, but in truth, your Lordship, I think the Indians get little from what we offer. We defend them from the *vaqueros* as best we can, but there are few of us, many of them, and millions of miles to cover. We assure the safety of the friars so that the Pueblos [5] are instructed in Christianity and in the ways of civilization, but, really, the Indians want little of that. They do not get much of what they truly want or need from Spanish authority."

"Are all the pueblos allotted?" Rosas asked. "My instructions say only that the crown has reserved the right to collect tribute from principal towns and seaports, and I know there are none of the latter there."

"Tribute from the native settlements has been conceded by the crown to the colonists themselves. Approximately sixty so-called 'units of 'entrustment' have been allotted during the past forty years," Gomez explained.

"There was a time, Governor, when the number of pueblos may have exceeded the one hundred and thirty-four named by Onate. These were small and large villages containing from twenty to seven hundred and fifty rooms, some with defensive walls such as at Pecos. But the Pueblos were constantly on the move," he explained, "uniting and then dispersing like bees in a hive. Whole tribes have disappeared, extinguished by warfare and by assimilation, some of the latter forced on them by us. In the fifty years from the initiation of the colonization by Onate to your administration, the number of pueblos has been reduced by two-thirds, so that now there are fewer than fifty of them left. Several of these pueblos are unassigned, but the fact that they have not been allotted undoubtedly means that they have little to offer in the way of tribute. Still, Governor, they're there. And they may be awarded by you to whomever you wish so long as your awards do not compromise the awards of your predecessors," he concluded, warning the governor by his words that he knew the authority under which he held his claims.

The governor looked at Gomez in deliberation, saying finally, "There's much to consider regarding these *encomiendas*, much to consider. Your thoughts and the information you've provided have been of considerable assistance to me. I'd like these discussions regarding New Mexico to continue as we go along our way." He waited a long moment before continuing, saying finally, "But please, finish your soup. Take the rest of it. I need something more. Something to deal with this god-damned constipation," he added while rubbing his distended stomach. "Would you like some more?" he asked, regarding the soup.

"No, thank you, Governor."

"When your work allows," Rosas continued, "I'd like you to dine with me."

"When my work allows," Gomez responded. Taking the governor's words and tone as a cue for his dismissal, he rose from his cushion, excused himself, and moved toward the entrance where he said. "You might have one of your servants find some *acacia*, *agave* or *algerita*, your Lordship. All of them are good for constipation. If they can't identity these plants," he added, "tell them to ask one of my men. Have them make a tea of it," he added as he left the tent.

4

On the Trail

ZACATECAS. THREE WEEKS LATER

"What's that ahead—Zacatecas?" asked the governor regarding the hump-backed mountain somewhat resembling a hog bladder which loomed on the northern horizon.

"The home of the Onates," Francisco Gomez responded, pointing to the promontory of *La Bufa* crowned by bare greenish rock. "Its mines, perhaps the best ever found in the Americas, helped to finance the settlement of your New Mexican Kingdom." He brought his horse up so that he was riding beside the governor. "There was a time, Governor, not so long ago," he continued, "when we could not have approached this *villa* without arms. The *Chichimecas*, or the dirty, uncivilized dogs, as we were prone to call them, were incredibly fierce warriors—cannibals even—who inhabited the deserts and *sierras* of this region just a short time ago. They're largely gone now," Gomez said, "killed or shipped off to the docks at Vera Cruz or to mines throughout the kingdom, men who've been changed from lions into hens. It's too bad," he said in rueful admiration. "They had much to admire, for they possessed courage inferior to no one, and before our arrival, they never knew slavery or servitude. We may see a few of those remaining in the market place or along the road, their bodies clothed now, and their voices stilled. We may see them, but they will not be the people they once were, for we took what they had and left them a sad and broken people with no interest in, or aptitude for, village life. They're neither civilized nor productive members of the Spanish community," he said as he reigned up at the train's approach to an obvious fork in the road. "Do you wish to enter the city?" he asked of the governor. "Your host here will be the local superior or father guardian at the *Parroquia de San Francisco de Zacatecas*. The *convento* itself, however, is in open country at some distance from the town, so that unless you wish to do so, we're not required to enter the city to visit the *parroquia* which is just down this road."

"I don't think it will be necessary to go into the city and I'll take advantage of the guardian's generosity as long as I don't have to do the stations," Rosas laughed, registering his dislike for visiting churches. We'll take advantage of the fathers' hospitality, but I'd like to be on our way again as soon as possible."

"As you wish, Governor."

SANTA BARBARA

Leaving the Custody of Zacatecas where its father guardian had sought to instruct Luis de Rosas about a governor's proper relationship to the Church, the party passed through Sombrerete and Durango. Trudging ever northward, the caravan finally crossed the Nazas, a fast, wide, deep, sediment-laden river, the color of rust, which raced through a broad, fertile valley below Santa Barbara. This was the jumping-off point for the New Mexican Kingdom. It was from this mining town, founded among the *Conchos* Indians by Rodrigo del Rio de Losa, that the most important New Mexican expeditions had embarked.

"The expeditions of Agustin Rodriguez and Francisco Sanchez Chamuscado, Bernardino Beltran and Antonio de Espejo left from this town, and Juan de Onate's second inspection was conducted here," Gomez said. "It was here, too, that his retreating colonists, when deserting the kingdom only four years later, sought shelter in the arms of *Nueva Vizcayan* authorities. This is where it all came apart for don Juan," Gomez added, "here in these mesquite groves, among these naked and poor Indians. I pray that, in your quest for an orderly and decent life in the New Mexican Kingdom, that you'll be more successful."

"Is there anything to be learned from all of this?" The governor asked.

"Only that New Mexico presents an incredible challenge for one who would attempt to govern it," Gomez said, "for New Mexico is not a castle, but an island, Governor, an island whose very isolation is seen by its eight hundred Spanish colonists as being to their advantage. Its governance requires maintaining a precarious balance between the wishes and needs of the clergy, the settlers, the Pueblo and Plains Indians, and Spanish authority, with each having incredible determination and will as deeply rooted in them as in any people. I would not presume to tell you how to conduct your office," Gomez continued, "but if one is to be successful in governing New Mexico, the needs and desires of the three estates must be kept in perfect balance with the promises and difficulties presented by the Indians. Neither Onate nor anyone else has been successful in achieving that balance."

"And you, Gomez, do you speak of yourself when you speak of the New Mexican character?"

"Yes, I guess I do," Gomez responded thoughtfully, "for I am, like you, a descendant of the Iberians, fearless soldiers who fought courageously but never learned to hold their shields together in combat. We learned, though, those of us from Spain and from Portugal, to fight together. Learned to hold our shields together in an impenetrable phalanx and have thus become among the greatest soldiers on earth. What we have not learned is how to live or work together as a people. And our independence and separatism, our stubborn refusal to be welded into a uniform dominion, are, perhaps, both our strength and our weakness. But our shortcomings, or what others see as our shortcomings, have made us who we are, and the qualities that are ridiculed as our faults are really the bases of our superiority. I was not a first colonist, Governor, not one of Onate's soldiers of fifteen ninety-eight or sixteen hundred, but I am one of them. So, yes, in terms of tenacity and will and pride, I am one with the New Mexico colonists and they are both the root of my successes as well as my failures."

Gomez was quiet for a long time, seemingly contemplating it all, saying finally, "This is the last measure of civilization we'll find before entering the wilderness. The country above Santa Barbara is referred to as 'The Beyond,' and you'll find little there. If you wish to correspond with anyone in the city of Mexico, or elsewhere, this will likely be your last opportunity."

* * *

Governor Luis de Rosas looked over Santa Barbara's extensive lands of mesquite and grass plains, a land bathed in the winter colors of sienna, gold, and burnt umber, viewing the many *arroyos* and verdant valleys of the foothills region leading to the *Rio Conchos*. He took his final opportunity to communicate with his business partner, the *duque de Segorbe*, and, also, as required, with his "Most Illustrious Sir," and with the *audiencia*, sending back with a returning caravan, his final notes. "Before me," he wrote to the viceroy, "lies a desolate land without convenience or refuge, offering every means of misfortune and peril. We will, nevertheless, keep our pace of ten or fifteen leagues a day and find our provisions along the way." And to the duke he wrote: "I see little of promise here, even my digestive difficulties have worsened. But perhaps things will improve as we go north."

DEL PASO

Trudging through sand dunes, the caravan continued northward along a route as ragged as the bed of a stream. Above *La Toma del Rio del Norte* (where Juan de Onate had, in 1598, first entered the new land) the caravan crossed the watercourse at a gorge the river had carved between two oddly shaped hills. The pass, referred to by the Indians as a "gateway" or "mountain gap" (the Spanish equivalent of which was "*Los Puertos*"), was, for the traveler of the period, the gateway north. Beyond "the pass," or "*del paso*," the train encountered a cascade of rapids. Beside the brown torrent were grassy banks in narrow strips, which at various intervals, spread out into small meadows with dense stands of emerald-hued willows growing along their edges. On either side of the river were rolling stony hummocks and higher knolls of naked earth.

* * *

In the opening days of the New Mexican spring, the train moved up the

35

east side of the Rio Grande Valley, its route devised so as to avoid soft and sandy ground and steep inclines. Lofty mountain ranges were strewn here and there both to the east and to the west of the river, with barren plains waiting just beyond the river's banks. The days were hot and a cloud of dust billowed behind their many beasts as the men of the wagon train rode along.

The river, offering appealing trailside marshes, coves, and pools, was a corridor for the millions of migratory birds the travelers saw as the birds made their annual relentless passage northward, moving from winter food in the south to their northern breeding grounds. Following the birds, the members of the caravan pointed the noses of their mounts northward and continued their journey.

* * *

At a bend in the river, five leagues above *del Paso*, they spent their first night at the *Ancon de Fray Garcia* where they went into camp. Here the scene changed. Over this stretch travel was slow and difficult for the ground was rough and they had repeatedly to skirt washouts and plough through marshes. On either side of the river ran ranges of barren hills. When they reached their tops they looked out upon a broad expanse of desolate plains edged on the east by the rugged peaks of the *Sierra de Los Organos*. Camping in turn at *El Estero Largo*, *El Estero Redondo*, the Pools of Fray Blas, *La Yerba del Manso*, and *Robledo el Chico*, the train moved forward.

EL PARAJE DE LA CRUZ DE ROBLEDO

At a point 22 leagues north of *del Paso*, in a bleak expanse offering little inducement to encampment, the caravan rode parallel to, but somewhat removed from, the river. The soldiers of the supply train stood in their stirrups, peering this way and that, obviously looking for something. "I promised my wife that I'd add a stone in prayer for her, so I must find it," Gomez said to the governor, regarding the stone cairn for which they were searching. "But you have no responsibility to come with me," he said to Rosas and to the men of the escort who rode beside his horse.

"We see it as our responsibility, too," said Blas de Miranda. "He may have been your wife's grandfather, but he was also the first colonist to die in New Mexico. It's important that we keep his memory alive." He, Nicolas Ortiz, Gomez and the governor broke away from the train and rode down toward a great, bare, roundish mountain on the west bank of the river.

"The original cairn was built almost four decades ago by Juan de Onate and one of his captains to mark a special place," Gomez explained to the governor. "Every year-and-a-half or so, as supply caravans pass though here on their way to or from Santa Fe, some of us who ride escort for the train do our best to rebuild it. It's incredible how much damage can accrue to a stone structure in such a short time," Gomez added. "If, in our passage, we didn't rebuild it, the cairn would soon lose its definition, its stones merging with those of the landscape. It would be lost."

"And who is the man we honor?" the governor asked as they rode across the rolling hills of a broad gap between the Caballo and San Andres Mountains.

"Pedro Robledo," Gomez responded, "an *alferez* in Onate's troop who died during the *entrada* of fifteen ninety-eight. A soldier from Carmena," Gomez said, "he was my wife's grandfather, a sixty-year-old gentleman, wearing mail and carrying the arms of Spanish authority who, with his wife and six children, came here as a settler. He provided four sons for the expedition," Gomez continued, "a number only equaled once as the largest number of soldiers provided by one family. The Indians at the pueblo of Acoma killed one son during the same year. We see the father and his family as symbolic of who we are as a Spanish colony," Gomez said, "and, therefore, we honor him."

Scrambling over rocks and through the tangles of brambles and thorns along the brown austerity of a wretched and miserable desert stretch, later to be known as the *Jornada del Muerto*, the Dead Man's Route, the soldiers of the escort finally found the gravesite. It looked very much like the so-called *Kuba Rumia* in Algiers, a curious circular stone monument said to be a Christian burial site, about which there had been much speculation.

"It's larger than I would have expected," the governor said, regarding the stone structure they had found.

"Four decades of stones," Gomez responded, "and the good wishes and prayers provided by the men of twenty-six trains. The site is known as the *Cruz* or *Paraje de Robledo*, the Robledo campsite. We'll rebuild the cairn for the settlers and soldiers of future trains to find and will camp here tonight."

* * *

Above Robledo, the river wound between steep banks intersected continually by transverse gullies. The gullies, whether shallow or deep, mired the wheels of their carts at every turn. Seeking better ground, the caravan left the river and continued northward.

OJO DEL PERRILLO

The members of Rosas's train rode through warm days beneath azure skies along the worn and tattered track of the royal road. Their course after leaving the river at Robledo took them through a seemingly waterless stretch of nearly 90 miles that would save them a day or more of travel. The lack of water and the choking dust brought them all—horse, man, mule, and foodstock—to the utmost limit of their endurance.

At one of the few springs the travelers found, they met a small group of Indians who, demonstrating their friendly intentions, knelt in the mud surrounding the spring, crossing themselves as a means of mutual recognition. Drawing their right hand from forehead to breast and then from shoulder to shoulder, they returned their hands to their mouths afterward signifying they required food.

"There are Christianized Indians here?" asked Rosas about the tattooed and painted Indians they found at the spring. "I've seen no churches or *conventos*. Are they members of a hunting party or nomads?"

"They're a Plains people, Governor," Gomez responded, "members of the *Jumanos* or *Rayados* whom we refer to as the *Apaches del Perrillo*. They live in three large pueblos which we'll find north of here near the pass of Abo, and, if people of the same tribe, in *rancherias* on the *Rio Colorado* far to the east. They come to the Rio Grande villages for purposes of trade," he said as they unloaded food from one of the wagons. "The friars tell of a miracle which occurred among these people," Gomez added continuing his discussion regarding the *Jumanos*. "Approximately two decades ago, as the friars tell it, the *Jumanos* were the subject of a supernatural conversion. The priests tell of visits by at least two nuns who were miraculously transported here from Spain for the purpose of preaching God's word and who assisted the friars in the Indians' conversions. One, a sister named Luisa de la Ascencion, an old nun of Carrion, had the power to become young and beautiful and to transport herself in a trance state to any part of the world where there were souls to be saved. The second nun, who was able to do much the same thing, was Maria de Jesus, the abbess at the convent of Agreda, who, the friars say, was carried here by the heavenly hosts. She was able to make several round trips in a single day."

"Do you believe any of this?" Rosas asked with a sneer. "That nuns can fly?"

"I'm not sure what to believe regarding these stories, Governor, so I've tried to suspend judgment," Gomez responded. "When *Custos* Salas, whom you'll meet at Santo Domingo, was at the Pueblo of Isleta, where he built the church and *convento*, he developed a special relationship with the *Jumanos* who came there to trade. They told him this story and Salas believes it. He went among them with another priest named Diego Lopez, and tells of the miracles of conversion they were able to achieve because of the work of these nuns. The number of conversions was so great that they had to baptize the Indians by swirling a fleece soaked in holy water over their heads. My brother would believe these stories without question," he said regarding the flying nuns, "but I respond better to fact than fancy."

"Then you believe the stories to be a fiction?" Rosas asked.

"I place the Indians' visions in the same category as the mirages one might see on the desert or at sea," Gomez responded, "those on the desert appearing as ripples on a lake ruffled by the wind, or of trees materializing upside down. I think the apparitions are like the so-called, *Fata Morgana*, the mirage of a city which my brother and I saw on the Strait of Messina. None of these images is real and yet they're there as plain as the nose on one's face. I think I'll suspend judgment until I know more."

The governor laughed at Gomez's statements regarding the Indians' visions while throwing food at the poor *Jumanos* who knelt before him attempting to pluck the morsels from the water before they sank into the mud.

* * *

Above the *Ojo del Perrillo* (Little Dog Spring), where the members of the caravan had found the *Jumanos*, the caravan continued its northward journey across a harsh, partially denuded landscape of awesome silence and immeasurable distances. It stretched before them, a desert plain with thickets of withered cactus and patches of wild pumpkin, the foliage of which consisted of long, sharp, arrow-shaped leaves, matted clumps of scrubby brush frosted over with silver and greasewood.

* * *

The distances from one *paraje*, or official campsite, to another were well known, for at some earlier time a soldier had been assigned the unenviable task of counting the steps or paces in each day's march. The camping sites offered in weary progression included *La Cruz de Aleman, Las Penuelas, La Laguna del Muerto, El Alto del Cerrillo, La Cruz de Anaya, El Alto de Las Tusas*, and *El Paraje de Fra Cristobal*. The last site metioned, located six leagues below the inhabited district, should have offered some promise of relief, but it did not. For above it—above the southern pueblos of Senecu, San Pasqual, Teypana, and Alamillo—the Rosas train still had to negotiate "*las vueltas.*" These were "the turns" where the river doubled back upon itself, making travel extremely difficult.

* * *

Above the turns, the caravan began at last to see daylight. The river, presenting sharply cut embankments, rolling hills, and a widening valley, now offered tiny, greening fields across its flood-plain. And, areas of Spanish habitation were also found. The train stopped briefly at the wine and brandy-producing vineyards of the Gomez *estancia* at *San Nicolas de las Barrancas.* Here the governor refilled the leather flask that was always with him. The train stopped for a lengthier period at the

Pueblo of Puaray to repair their equipment, badly damaged by the road, and by deterioration resulting from the arduous journey. Then it was on to Sandia, San Felipe, and finally, the Pueblo of Santo Domingo, the ecclesiastical capital of New Mexico.

5

Custos Juan de Salas and Santo Domingo

"We'll go ahead of the train and leave our livestock here," Gomez said in explanation of his plan to approach the pueblo with only the small contingent of individuals with whom he rode. "We're forbidden to have our livestock within three leagues of the village."

"Forbidden?" the governor asked. "Forbidden by whom, I'd like to know? I'll run my stock wherever I damn well please!"

"You could do that, Governor," Gomez responded as they rode along a ridge in the vicinity of the pueblo, "but it's one of the few rules we have that actually makes sense. We could take our animals into the village as you've stated, but then my men and I would have to spend our time here keeping our stock out of the villagers' fields. We'll take the wagons in, the ones carrying supplies for the missions, but it's best to leave the rest of the train here where the livestock can find other forage," he concluded as he, the governor, and Fray Manso broke away from the train and headed toward the village.

As the three rode toward the pueblo, set beyond clean gravel hills, its rich irrigated lands lying below in the valley of the Great River, Francisco Gomez lagged behind with the governor who was surveying the adobe village, viewing its corrals, its extensive orchards, and its produce gardens greening behind adobe walls.

"The pueblo might look like it's always been here," Gomez remarked of the village whose brown hulk loomed on the edge of the river, "but, like many of the pueblos on the river and elsewhere, it's been moved several times. This, I believe, is at least their third village," he said. "Previous villages built on the banks of the Galisteo and the Great River were destroyed by flood. And there's something else here which you may wish to make note of," Gomez added, pointing to structures which appeared physically and psychologically removed from the life of the village. "Notice the location of the churches," he said. "They're at least three hundred *varas* from the edge of the pueblo. They were placed there for strategic purposes," Gomez added. "It's a simple formula which you'll see repeated again and again at each of the pueblos you'll visit. The distance of the church from the center of the pueblo is in direct relationship to the resistance by Indians there to Spanish rule. As you can see, the Indians here are very resistant, and the structures themselves, their placement and fortifications, attest to the presence of enemies against Spanish authority both within and without the village."

Rosas nodded in understanding as he examined the three structures that rose before them. Adjoining the south wall of the principal church, a large structure with a central bell-tower and a balcony over its main entrance, was a modest multi-room adobe *convento*. Its rooms were arranged around an interior courtyard. A covered walkway encircling the interior of the enclosure secluded a *claustro*, or square court. On the west, the *convento* itself was of two stories.

Parallel to the main church and abutting it on the north was a smaller church with a window above a large doorway. Fronting the three parallel structures was an *atrio*, a walled and fortified enclosure of large size, which appeared to double as an exterior chapel and cemetery. Taking a large swig from his leather wine skin, Rosas and Gomez, dismounted and walked through the *atrio*, where they were met by *Custos* Juan de Salas, principal of the Santo Domingo church and *convento* and dean of New Mexico's ministry. An individual with an attractive face topped by a high forehead, he stood there with Fray Manso who had ridden ahead of the two men. Formal greetings followed, after which the four walked through the *convento's* archive room which was finished with wood—and, Rosas thought, set with remarkably fine furnishings—to a small table that had been placed in the patio by an Indian porter. Additional Indians, cooks, gardeners, and waiters, could be seen in the patio and through the open doorways of interior rooms as the Salas party, passing through a dimly lit labyrinth of passageways, made its circuitous way to the patio. Upon entering the interior court, they were surrounded by birds of every description, flitting over, underneath, and through the covered walkway, landing to eat seed that had been spread for them and for a beautiful wing-clipped parrot hopping happily about the flagstone court. A large garden, grape arbor, two peach trees, and a stone-lined well graced the southern end of the compound. Fray Salas bid the group sit on the chairs the Indian porter had also carried there.

When they were seated, Rosas provided the opening salvo saying, "Two churches and an *atrio*! You must have an enormous number of worshipers, Father."

"Yes, we do," Salas responded with pride, "we've been very successful in our conversions here and at our *visita* of Cochiti, and, also, among the *Jumanos* of the plains where our work was assisted by the Mother of Agreda. We use the *atrio* as an accessory chapel from which to administer the sacraments on Sundays and on other occasions when the faithful cannot be accommodated within the church."

"Facing the *mihrab*, I assume," Rosas remarked disrespectfully smiling first at Fray Manso and then at *Custos* Salas.

"Not Mecca," Salas responded, answering the taunt, "but God. Outdoor worship violates the idea of the mystical body of the Church, but it's what's required here by our circumstances." He smiled first at Fray Manso, and then at Francisco Gomez and the governor. "We've had to make many accommodations here," he added. "Undoubtedly, he said, speaking directly to the governor, "your Lordship will find that he must do the same."[1]

"I'll do whatever's required to place civil government and secular authority on a secure footing, even if I have to find a demented nun to assist me in my pursuits," Rosas said, smiling again but getting no response to his irreverent comments.

* * *

Bread and ripe apples, grapes, wine and fresh cheese were placed before them, the cheese taken from a box that was kept in the cool well where it was held in reserve, along with meat, milk, butter, and other food. They continued with their meeting in brilliant sunshine.

* * *

"I don't know how much you've been told, or what questions you've asked of Fray Manso as you've come on your journey, your Lordship," *Custos* Salas said politely, "so please forgive me if I repeat anything you may have already been told regarding our ministry." Determined, urbane, and politically cunning, the former *Provincial* of Jalisco and Michoacan—whose office was analogous to that of territorial governor—Salas had served his various apprenticeships well leading to his present position, to which he had been recently assigned, as custodian of his Order. He cleared his throat and began with the details of the Franciscan ministry, memorized for delivery to each of the dignitaries who came up the trail.

"Previously," he said, "the ecclesiastical superior in the colony held the title of *comisario*, which implied temporary authority only, delegated by our mother Province of the Holy Gospel in the city of Mexico. Fray Juan de Escalona, who is buried in our church here, held that title. We're set up differently now," he explained, while looking about the table at the three men. "We're now an autonomous unit, with a chapter, *definitors*, and our own prelate and father *custos*, or custodian, an administrator elected by the Holy Gospel Province in Mexico. I hold the titles of prelate and father *custos* now," he said, while chewing on a new apple, "but others in our Custody of St Paul, most recently Fray Esteban de Perea, who founded the mission of *La Concepcion* at the Pueblo of Quarai, and who presently serves New Mexico as agent for the Holy Office, have been previously honored—or burdened, I know not which—by these responsibilities."

"And how many priests are you now?" the governor asked, glancing at the cowled figures he saw throughout the courtyard.

"The Crown has agreed to subsidize the work of sixty-six missionaries, your Lordship, most of whom are now in place, grouped in twenty-five missions or *conventos*, spread up and down the valley of the *Rio del Norte* and in pueblos far distant from here."

"So why are you here at this pueblo, rather than in Santa Fe?" Rosas asked rudely, "is the *villa* so bad that you have to hide here?"

45

Custos Salas, who appeared to be censoring what he wished to say, waited a long moment before responding, seemingly looking for assistance from his fellow cleric.

Finally Fray Manso interjected, "The decision to separate our headquarters from those of the governor was made by our prelate, Fray Alonso de Peinado, more than two decades ago," Manso explained, "to establish Santo Domingo as the ecclesiastical capital of our adobe kingdom. It seemed best, I've been assured, to separate civil and religious authority here. It was, I think, the best solution to the difficulties previously encountered."

"Difficulties?" Rosas asked. "Of what difficulties do you speak?"

"Difficulties between Church and State," Salas responded. "Difficulties such as those presented by Governor Eulate in his administration of the kingdom," he said, while brushing crumbs from the table and then scattering them along the flagstone floor for the birds to eat. Salas waited for a long moment before continuing, careful, it appeared, to ensure that the Indian servants who worked around them would not hear his remarks. He continued then in a dark tone. "He was a petulant, tactless, irreverent soldier whose actions were motivated by an open contempt for the Church and its ministers and by an exaggerated concept of his own authority as the representative of the Crown. When I spoke with him regarding this—his authority as representative of the Crown—he said, 'The king is my patron.' The king is *my* patron!" Salas railed before catching himself and then continuing in a more guarded tone. "Can you even imagine one speaking in that manner?" he asked in exasperation. "He was a man more suited to operating a junk shop than to holding the office of governor!" No longer able to contain his anger, he exploded, "A bag of arrogance and vanity without love of God or zeal for His divine honor or for the King's. A man of evil example in word and deed, he did not deserve to be governor but was rather a hawker and a creature of his vile pursuits!"[2]

"Of what vile pursuits do you speak?" Rosas asked with undisguised interest.

"Of authorizing slavery, forced labor, and sweatshops," Salas whispered. "And he attempted to undermine the priests in their work

46

here." Continuing in a whisper, Salas added, "He said that we didn't work and that all we did was sleep and eat, while married men went about diligently working to earn their necessities. When I think of his words," he said sadly, "I think of my brothers, Fray Francisco de Letrado and Fray Martin de Arvide, who were killed by the Zuni just five years ago, and of Fray Francisco de Porras who was poisoned at Hopi just a year later. My priests did not enslave the Indians as he did," Salas said angrily, the volume returning to his voice. "Rather, they died in ministering to them. Governors Mora and Martinez were in much the same vein," Salas continued, "greedy and avaricious. Today, we hope for better," he said faking a confiding smile.[3]

"The pope is the head in Christian society," he said. "Authority flows from Christ to Peter to the pope, and from him, to us. The members of the clergy are, therefore, heads of the body politic and supreme over all provincial matters. We, as the representatives of the Custody of Saint Paul, see our roles here—those of the governor, the priests, and the settlers—as constituting a type of mystical body, with the governor and soldier-settlers as the arms and hands, which protect the Church from heretics and other enemies, and the Indians as the feet, which sustain and carry the weight of the entire body. We look forward to your assistance and cooperation in our work with the Indians, the provision of escorts, the loan of oxen to haul rock and dirt for the construction of our missions, and your condemnation of Martinez's misrule."[4]

* * *

What followed was a silence more damning than words in which Rosas seemed to be studying the birds and the distant mountains. Then he said in a measured tone, "We see our roles very differently, Father. I see the king as a warrior who carries two swords, one temporal, the other spiritual, the spiritual blade in the form of concessions of royal patronage[5] given to him by the pope almost 150 years ago. Therefore, it is he and not the pope who is the Vicar of Christ, a role that has been extended to the viceroy and through him, to me as provincial governor. Thus, jurisdiction over military, judicial, legislative, and commercial matters, as well as the administration of the Church, ultimately falls to me and not to you. But we'll see," he said. "We'll have to see." Then, changing the subject entirely, he asked, "And the Indians here at Santo Domingo, are they difficult?"

Salas waited for a long moment before responding, questioning whether he should further pursue a clarification of their roles, but ultimately deciding against that course of action. Instead, he followed the governor's lead in pursuing his discussion regarding the Indians. "The Keres of Santo Domingo are reputed to be the most difficult in the kingdom," Salas responded, "secretive and withdrawn from the surrounding civilization. Occasionally, they still make us *tortillas* from urine and mice meat, but we're getting used to the taste," he said, smiling at Fray Manso. "We cut their hair as punishment, but we've been unable to stop them from making bread in that manner, for mice and urine abound."

Observing the other three as they ate their cheese and drank their wine in New Mexican sunshine, Salas sensed that there was nothing more to be accomplished by their meeting, or by attempting to further crush the grapes, knowing the mash to be sour. He asked, "Would you like to see the church?"

On the outside of the principal church was a balcony formed by the projection of choir loft timbers and by the overhang of the nave roof. The balcony was available only through a small choir-loft window that was covered over with heavy timbers and barred from the inside. On the inside of the church the dimness of the nave was relieved by light provided by two small and inaccessible gridiron windows in which sheets of mica or talc had been set. These splayed apertures, presenting sloping or beveled surfaces, were placed high in the north wall. A transverse clerestory window also provided light. This was a source of illumination that was apparently of the friars' invention, for Rosas had not previously seen a window of this construction. This window was placed where the nave joined the apse, its blue-tinged light masked by the grime of time.

There was little decoration. An ornamented wooden bed molding, placed underneath the corbel course of the roof and upon which the corbels rested, was made of carved poles, laid end-to-end, projecting slightly from the surface of the wall. The molding, a rope motif patterned after the Franciscan cord symbolizing the vow of chastity, was ornamental and perhaps structural, too, serving to bind and strengthen the wall at its points of greatest load.

The sacristy was a modest room with a cupboard, a small altar, a rack for liturgical instruments, and a small fireplace. There was also an internal well four *varas* wide and over 40 *varas* deep, with a curb of earth and stone, and a wooden bucket sitting precariously on its rim.

In an anteroom near the front of the church there was a baptismal font built of adobes and consisting of a large *olla*, a wide-mouthed clay pot or jar that rose from the center of the earthen floor. There was little else, no pews, no hangings, nothing to burn.

What Rosas had toured was a fortress with thick, high, adobe walls offering no projections to hide an enemy. It had been designed to offer shelter but also constraint, to inspire feelings of well-being, calm, awe, or oppression, as the friars wished. The enormous space provided them with the capacity required to enhance their word, gesture, or the musical accompaniment of Catholic ritual.[6]

"One could hold out here forever," the governor remarked. Salas looked at him and smiled but did not respond.

* * *

"Are we to prepare accommodations here for the governor while the men of the supply train repair their wagons?" asked Salas's assistant.

Salas, who had found in the new governor an arrogant, irreverent, and uncompromising person, rather than the cooperative, if not actually weak and pliant individual he had hoped to find, said, "I wouldn't give him as much as an egg unless I was allowed to sprinkle it with ashes to dull his palate or dilute it with water to smother its taste. I don't know where they find these men, Father," he added in exasperation. "At least Governors Ceballos and Ossorio were admirals—even though we have no need for a navy here. But this one? What is he? A Frenchman from Auvergne? A Gavache from Gevaudon? God only knows! No wonder his wife and child deserted him while he was in Flanders," he said, repeating a bit of gossip he had heard from Fray Manso. "Perhaps he's a *franchone*, one of those foreigners who roams about Spain as a beggar, a peddler, a knife-grinder, or as a castrator of animals! No. We will not prepare accommodations. And if he rings the bell requesting entrance to the *convento*, Father, please pretend you don't hear him. Perhaps he'll go away."

6

Nicolas and Maria

"After we leave Cochiti and have negotiated the cliffs at *La Majada*," said Nicolas Ortiz to the wagon master, Francisco Gomez, "I ask for permission to ride ahead and to inform the senior judge and the members of the *cabildo* of our arrival."

"And to see your Maria, too, I assume," said Blas de Miranda, smiling knowingly at his friend who had presented his request to Gomez.

"I must admit that's an added incentive," Ortiz laughed, his large, luminous eyes glowing with delight. "But the welcome for a new governor is traditional," he added, further justifying his request, "and Antonio Baca must be told."

"Well, I'm sure he knows we're coming," Gomez said, "although the exact day may still be unknown to him. Today's Friday, is that right?" Gomez asked rhetorically, as he worked at rearranging the wood of their campfire with the heel of his boot. "We'll need your help in climbing the cliffs tomorrow," he said to Ortiz, "but once we've reached the *mesa* you may go ahead. Tell don Antonio that we'll be there within two days."

"I owe you!" Ortiz said.

"You owe me nothing," Gomez replied laughingly. "Besides, you'll be lucky if her papa doesn't shoot you."

Nicolas laughed at Gomez's remark, recalling these exact words as spoken by Blas de Miranda on the day he first met her.

* * *

In a stunning dawn, crisp and unblemished except for an enormous cloud hanging over the eastern mountains, Nicolas left his party on the *mesa* above *La Majada*, a sheltered place on the *Camino Real* (Royal Road) where shepherds with their flocks of sheep put up for the night. Riding ahead of the wagon train, which had just negotiated a series of black basaltic cliffs dividing the lower and upper regions of the Rio Grande, Nicolas, who knew how to press horses to their limit, bypassed the ancient lava beds of *quemado*.

Nicolas approached the Tano pueblo at *La Cienaga* (The Marsh), where the *Rio de Santa Fe*, a tributary of the Rio Grande, completes its underground course and again comes to the surface. There he struggled through a forest of bogs, their odors a musky redolence of cedar and mildewed grass. The bogs, widened here by beaver dams, were a series of tranquil pools clogged with logs, branches, brush, and rocks all plastered together, which his horse could not penetrate. I should not have tried to cross here, he said to himself, realizing that in his haste to reach the capital, he had merely slowed his progress. Backtracking through a jungle of thorn bushes and impenetrable willows, he finally regained the southern edge of the bogs and, above them, to the east, the Santa Fe River.

Following the cottonwood-bordered *Rio de Santa Fe* toward the royal *villa*, Nicolas rode across an alluvial plain, barren, rocky, fringed with coarse gray scrub, and rising to snowy peaks on this, the southern end of the *Sangre de Cristo* range. The pale peaks of mountains to the north, serrated and scalloped in their birth, gave to the region a sense of majesty and expanse. This was the part of New Mexico that had given to the kingdom its greatest challenges, its primal beauty, its demand of stoic endurance from its inhabitants. The sky behind the peaks was ugly, turbulent, with an occasional rumble of high thunder as Nicolas rode on.

Nicolas continued on across a sunlit landscape whose sagebrush land eventually turned into *pinon* and juniper foothills. Buzzards flying in tight circles above him glided on wings borne by unseen currents of air. Before him, he could see what the buzzards were contemplating, a dead coyote lying in the open before a stand of *chamisa* (rabbitbrush). While he watched, a large buzzard, its enormous wings outstretched to slow its descent, guttered to an ungainly landing beside the carcass. Suddenly, the seemingly dead coyote leaped to its feet, lunging at the startled bird that attempted to turn and take to the sky. The clever coyote leaped into the air and wrestled the bird to the ground where, with a quick bite to the base of the buzzard's neck, the coyote ended its struggle. Nicolas smiled to himself, thinking, you can never tell. Death leaps up when you least expect it.

Outside of the *villa*, which had been built on a sheltered bank of the *Rio de Santa Fe*, Nicolas left the woods that grew thickly alongside the river and rode toward the still uncompleted parish church. This occupied an entire block and was being built away from the plaza according to the king's ruling. Set within a half circle of carnelian-colored hills, it was the most prominent point on the eastern horizon.

The cultivated fields of *Las Milpas de San Miguel* (The *Maize* Fields of St. Michael) and *Barrio de Analco* were on the river's southern bank. Within the six *vecindades*, or *villa* districts on the northern bank a haphazard collection of low, flat-roofed houses were clustered around small fields and the royal palace. As he rode, he looked beyond the oxen, horses, and mules grazing within the defensive walls of *la muralla*, to the scattered ranches partially hidden among the eastern hills. Most prominent among these homes—which Governor Martinez had often referred to as the *casas de malicia* (houses of evil intent[1])—was that of Maria's father, Simon Perez de Bustillo. His home, a fortified and walled compound of over 20 rooms surrounding two enclosed *placitas* (little plazas) was one with the landscape. Among the rose-colored hills back-dropping the royal *villa*, were additional homes of the Baca and Perez de Bustillo clan. Grouped along the banks of the river where they huddled within their own adobe walls, they looked as through they had been positioned to parry an assault. Nicolas bypassed the path leading to Maria's home and rode down to the river that raged through a narrow gorge along a boulder-strewn canyon. He longed desperately to see Maria, but he had to inform her uncle, the *villa's* senior judge and leading administrator, of the impending arrival of the train.

SHELTERED FROM THE CENTURIES

The Baca home, situated among an extensive stand of spiny, tree-like cactuses, was a grand compound of many rooms. Sprawled along the southern slope of the canyon, Baca had chosen a spot outside the walls of the compound for the placement of a new cellar for his home. This is where Nicolas had first met Maria almost three years before.

* * *

Employed by Antonio Baca to excavate the *soterrano*, or root cellar, Nicolas had been working there with Maria's brother, Nicolas Perez. They had been digging among a stand of *cholla* (a spiny tree-like cactus) and saltbush, foliage that often marked the site of a prehistoric ruin. In the work they had accomplished, they had found an incredible cache of beautiful artifacts secreted within what had been a small niche in the wall of a pit house or ancient *kiva* (lodge house and ritual chamber). Providentially, some of the eroding material—stone, earth, clay, and crockery—had covered the bottom two thirds of the underground structure preserving from destruction what had been hidden. Their find was additional evidence for the presence of Indian encampments and villages along the banks of their river for over seven centuries. It was in an area which the *villa's* Tewa Indian informants had told the colonists was known as the "bead water place."[2] The Ortiz and Perez find, which, among other artifacts contained a Red *Mesa* bowl, a *Wijo* canteen, and several black-on-white pottery mugs, also included a perfectly preserved ceremonial jar containing a beautiful but fragile shell necklace. It was the latter find that the Nicolases had just unearthed when Maria appeared on the edge of their excavation.[3]

Dressed in a long, white, sleeveless dress, a short work apron, and boots of cordovan leather, she had stood quietly on the edge of their pit, a lovely silhouette against the sun. Although masking her appearance, the sun had, through the thin layer of homespun that she wore, revealed the essence of her beneath her clothing and Nicolas Ortiz was both embarrassed and disturbed by the fact that Maria's brother, Nicolas Perez, could also see.

Maria's brother had said, "You'd better get out of the sun," and she had responded by drawing the skirt of her ankle-length dress tightly about her long slim legs.

"Can I see it?" she had asked her brother in a question that was just short of a command.

"You might as well," responded her brother who knew that with his sister, to wish was to get what she wanted. "You will anyway," he said.

She took off her new boots and placing them neatly aside, jumped into the excavation where she knelt between the shirtless men. Although she appeared to be unaware of her surroundings as she carefully examined the shells that she held in her slender fingers, Nicolas Ortiz had been acutely conscious that she was there. Her skin was white and fresh and a mass of auburn hair toned with copper was piled high atop her head where it was held in place by a large pin. Hair too fine to be worked into her bun lay in ringlets at the nape of her long, white neck. She had hazel eyes, tending toward green, a lithesome flow of arms, and legs. He could smell her; feel the cool skin of an exposed arm touching his as they knelt in the moist earth. He could almost taste her, the scent of apples on her sweet breath. She smiled at him and he was filled with wonder!

Grasping his ankles and leaning back against his calves, he peered at Nicolas Perez, pleading for an introduction. When it came, Perez had said, "This is my sister, Maria." And when she looked up from the necklace and gazed into Nicolas's eyes, Perez said, "And this is my friend Nicolas Ortiz."

* * *

That's the way it began. Three years ago when she was 13. Under ordinary circumstances, he would not even have met a girl of her social class, yet he had not only met her, but had spoken with her and been immediately smitten. Unfortunately, he knew that she was quite unavailable to him.

But the 13-year-old Maria had vigorously pursued him, ignoring her father's admonishments that she was not to do so, seemingly unconcerned that Ortiz was an individual of meager prospects, a day laborer and ranch hand from Zacatecas, a guard and a member of the wagon escort.

Maria and Nicolas Perez de Bustillo, on the other hand, were "*hijos de algo*," the "children of a someone," individuals of gentle birth, which was first among the nobility's claim to precedence and leadership in New Mexico. They were the children and grandchildren of Simon and Juan Perez de Bustillo, two of New Mexico's original settlers who, upon completion of their decade of tenure as first colonists, had been given land and aristocratic titles as *hidalgos*, a royal designation which had been granted to them by the crown so that a memory would remain of them as first settlers. Both their titles and land, the roots of their social superiority over others in the colony, were jealously guarded by them and by the 15 or 20 other families who also held these benefices. Because of the differences in their social class, Nicolas Ortiz had not been allowed to openly pursue Maria. However, he had found that his friendship with Nicolas Perez, and his work among the wealthy and prominent Baca and Perez de Bustillo families, had given him ample opportunity to be with her. He would not be able to see her tonight, but tomorrow, after the wagon train had entered the *villa*, he would meet her in the woods above her home.

7

A Place as Parent

The riverside forest of cottonwood was full and cast a darkening shadow along the river corridor. In the groves the bottomlands were replete with the rich marish drift of the river, an earthy scent from which one could derive a sense of pleasure, place, and well-being. The sounds of the river could be heard far along the cottonwood passageway, its honeyed flow a roar and babble of fast water in dappled light.

The homes of several members of the Baca and Perez de Bustillo clan were clustered along the margins of the river where family members engaged in the common pursuit of ranching. Grazing in the foothills, and tended by herders from not one, but several ranches, were the families' cattle and sheep, the numbers of which were nearly doubling every 15 months. Sheepfolds and corrals to enclose these animals when not at pasture lay near the individual compounds.[1]

Above these homes and lost in the upper reaches of the crystalline stream was a *presa*, or rock-filled dam, diverting water from the parent river to *acequia madres*, one on each side of the watercourse. The *acequia madres*, or so-called "mother canals," were barely three feet wide and half that deep and were full of numbingly cold snowmelt from the 10,000-foot peaks in the distance. The gentle gravity-fed canals, gurgling slowly along their grassy banks, were hidden beneath tall stands of cottonwoods and lazy willows. Meandering past plots of beans, squash, chile, and alfalfa, the small streams splashed through creaking headgates on their ramble along the canyon walls. Although partially drained of their life-giving waters by their *parciantes* (ditch members)—all of whom were family members asserting their right to a full *derecho* (a share of water)—the small streams nevertheless returned sufficient amounts of water to the parent stream. The waters thus diverted were but a small portion of the full river. The main stream ran down through the canyon over a white-rocked bottom, with cottonwood, green willows, deep hay grass, and wild flowers growing in profusion along its banks. Evening primrose, fire- and butterfly weed, grew brilliantly among the sedges.

So slender and overgrown by weeds that it was invisible from a distance, the northern canal, and its lateral ditches, could be traced by the green ribbons of vegetation trailing them through the valley. Apple, peach, October pear, black plum, and apricot orchards grew along the margins of the river, and next to the orchards was the home of the Simon Perez de Bustillos. The adobe structure had grown through the years as the family had grown. All rooms faced inwards toward the security of its courtyards, its outer walls facing a forest of orchards as well as open country. A wide, double-doored entrance the depth of a room, led into it. The doors of this covered passageway, or *zaguan*, were barred and secured from the inside with a massive oaken beam.

Beginning with a series of rooms that had been built around a large, square patio and its well, the initial home, now almost 30 years old, had grown into a second house to accommodate the Perez children, as well as the many Indian servants the family had obtained. The walls of the rooms and compound, three feet thick and invulnerable to penetration, were built of huge adobe blocks, covered over with mud mixed with straw. The rooms' transverse rafters, or *vigas*, were made of heavy cedar logs, overlaid by aspen saplings (*savinos*), all of one size, lying close together in a herringbone design. By day, the rooms were cool and dim, illuminated by deep-set, tiny sheets of fused mica (known as talc lights). These windows, which were further covered by wooden shutters and Indian-tanned hides, or *gamuza* (chamois), were additionally shaded on the outside by the overhang of a porch. By night, the rooms were illuminated by candles and by the blaze of a fireplace in each room. The floors, except for those in the great room and kitchen, were of rammed earth. This was black earth mixed with fine sand and moisture and spread on the ground with the palm of the hand. The floors were then polished until they shone. The kitchen was a long room where the family's *criados* (servants) worked and where the family sat down to meals. Near it were larders and panaries, granaries and banks for dried fruits, *pinon* nuts, cider, both fresh and hard, applejack, round-bottom jars containing olive oil and wine, wheat and corn. The river house of the Simon Perez de Bustillos threw its high adobe walls around all the purposes and needs of its existence.

* * *

Maria fingered the edge of a trough-shaped wooden bowl and thought how much she loved it. Carved from cottonwood and smoothed by years of loving use, it was, she thought, one of the few things she had been given that had belonged to her maternal grandmother. Taking an apple from the *batea* (wooden bowl) and holding it in the fist of her left hand, she worked at it with a small knife, turning it around and around in a random fashion, holding the knife steady and at an angle, letting the blade do the work of removing the peel. She botched the job, however, which resulted in large chunks of the fruit lying on the table, and here and there, the green of unpeeled sections staring back at her. Her mind was obviously elsewhere.

"Where are you?" asked her mother, who was standing before an open cabinet. "You look like you're a million miles away."

"Oh, I was just thinking, Mama," she responded pensively. "Why can't we have a window there?" she asked as she pointed to the room's eastern wall. "Wouldn't it be nice to have light coming through that wall?" Leaning across a trestle-supported pine-plank table, she placed the apple on a wooden tray in front of the bench where her mother had been sitting, and dreamily took another from the wooden bowl.

Although the *cocina*, or kitchen was in many ways the richest room in the house, it was dimly lit for its patio windows, which were made of translucent, but not transparent selenite, were deep, and low, and shaded by the overhang of the porch. Against a wall stood three *armarios* or *tinajeros*, tall wooden cabinets (often called *trasteros*) with locked double doors whose upper panels were latticed revealing the wealth inside. Maria's mother was replacing dishes in one of these. "We're just going to have to give some of this away," she said regarding the dishes she was attempting to fit into the cabinet. On its wooden shelves, among the jugs and bowls that had been secured from the pueblos, were rows of white, crystal and green dishes. There, too, among the glassware and pottery, were a silver platter, several silver trays, and two silver dishes. Although treasured, the silver bore the little pits and dents of daily use, for to eat in the kitchen on silver was both don Simon's earthy simplicity and his pride.

"Don't you dare give them away, Mama," Maria said to her mother who had again taken a seat at the table. "I'm not like Catcha and Juliana, wanting only things that are new. I want the old things, too, the things they wouldn't have in their homes. I want them all. Not only the silver ones, but the other ones, too," she repeated, "especially if they were Grandma's."

"When you get married," her mother said, "I'll give you the silver ones, but not now. You may have the glasses if you want. Do you want to pack them?" she questioned as Maria's father entered the room.

"Hello, Papa, Maria said in a wistful voice.

"There's not going to be anything between you and Ortiz," her father responded sternly as he took a cup from one of the *armarios*. Then, sitting next to his wife with the empty cup in his hand, he said, "You're not to see him anymore! Do you understand that, Maria? You must remember that the men who work here or at the home of your uncle or other family members are not of your *calidad* and are not men with whom you're to have any contact. They have nothing to offer you," her father continued, as Maria looked at him apprehensively, unable to understand what she had done to provoke her father's comments. "Their only responsibility is to keep the required number of horses, for God's sake! And those without land may only earn three or four hundred pesos a year, hardly enough to feed themselves and their horses, much less raise a family. When the time comes," he continued, while waving off his wife who had attempted to fill his cup, "—and I don't know why we're even speaking of this now, for you're too young to marry—I'll find you a proper husband, one marked out above the rest, a Dominguez, or a Lucero, a Gomez, or a Chavez, a man with land, and livestock and a name!"

"You let both Catalina and Juliana marry a man of their choice," Maria challenged.

"Well, that's no different from what I'm telling you," her father responded, his dark features flushed red with annoyance. "I allowed them a voice in the selection of their husband, but I made the choice. Pedro Marquez—God rest his soul—was an *hidalgo*. His father and four brothers were also first colonists. He left your sister a widow at the age of twenty-five, but a rich one, Maria! A young widow with land and livestock at *La Canada*! She did well for herself under her husband's will," he continued, "getting back the whole of her dowry, as well as half of the amount to which Pedro had added. That would not have happened had I not chosen well. And your sister, Juliana," her father continued. "Blas may be a member of the wagon escort, as is your Nicolas Ortiz, but Blas has lands at Taos. I did well by her also," her father responded congratulating himself on his selection of proper mates. "I retained their honor and social positions by marrying them to the right men. You must not forget that," he said, while looking at Maria who was now silent. "That's who we are, *Hita*!"[2] he added in a more conciliatory tone. "We're members of the nobility. We can't allow others who have neither title nor rank to enter our group. When you become interested in a man," he said, "you must always ask, 'Do we marry them?' There's no use in your becoming interested in someone you will never be allowed to marry. There are rules about this sort of thing!"

Taking a deep and expressive lungful of air, he looked at Maria and smiled, reaching across the table and touching her hand. Then, taking a more affectionate tone with her, his youngest child, he said, "When you marry, Maria, your brother will become heir to our land. Your husband will provide your land. You'll be given Tula and your other servants and enough stock to start your own flocks and herds. You'll retain the right to a quarter of the *vigas* in our home, and some of the trees in the orchards will also be yours. But it will be your husband's family who will provide you with land." He pounded his empty cup on the table. "Before love, comes our name and reputation. That's the way it is. And that's the way it's going to be, in this house, and in this family, and don't you forget it!" he said as he rose from the table.[3]

"*Dios mio*, Simon!" Maria's mother exclaimed, "Why are you speaking to her like that? Hers is but a meaningless flirtation, *por Dios*! No harm can come from it! Would you not have her speak to the men who work here?"

"Yes! That's it exactly!" he bellowed. "I don't want her speaking to them," he said to his wife, in a strict and stern manner. "I want her to know her place. We would not have been allowed to marry had we not been of equal *calidad*. And so it will be with Maria," he said, glancing in her direction. "I don't care that she's judged Nicolas to be strong, or handsome, or ambitious," he said. "We must preserve the purity of our blood, and that's that!"

"Ay, God!" his wife said in exasperation, as her husband moved toward the door. "I'm glad you're riding out with Nicolas. I think that you need the air!"

Maria's mother waited until Maria's father had left the room before continuing, shaking her head and saying, "He's back, you know," she said in regard to Nicolas Ortiz. "Your papa said that he rode in last night."

"Oh, Mama!" Maria squealed. "Where? Where is he?" she asked, while opening the door and running into the *placita*.

"Come back here and calm down. You don't want your papa to see you like this," her mother said as she grasped Maria's elbow and led her back into the fire lit room. "He's not here, and I don't think your papa's going to let him work here any more because of the two of you. Nicolas came to tell your Uncle Antonio that the caravan will be here today. I'm sure that he's still involved with the train. But he'll be free tomorrow."

"Can we go down to the plaza to see the *entrada*?" Maria asked excitedly. "I'll go with Nicolas, or with you, or with anyone!" she cried while attempting to contain herself.

"Your papa and Nicolas will be among those who are riding out to meet the new governor," her mother said, "but we can walk to the *plaza*. It's a beautiful day!"

* * *

Maria and her mother, followed by a retinue of their Indian servants, hurried west along the path and road of the river canyon, and then north along the *villa's* one quasi-street to the plaza.

8

The *Adventus*

APRIL 18, 1637

The broad bogs of *La Cienaga* receded behind them as the members of the wagon train caught their first glimpse of the adobe village of Santa Fe just coming into view. Stream and fields stretched out before them to the mountains blue on the horizon.

To the outskirts of the royal *villa* they came: the departing governor, Francisco Martinez de Baeza, the *villa's regidores*, (councilmen) including its *alcalde ordinario* or *justicia mayor* (chief magistrate), its *Maese de campo*, (Field marshal) other members of the *cabildo*, and many of the *villa's* 250 citizens, all in gorgeous attire and arranged on horseback. Governor Martinez, about whom the young Fray Antonio de Ibargaray had so bitterly complained, was riding a white horse and wearing a *ferreuelo*, a short cloak without a cape across which was a *repostero*, a covering ornamented with his coat of arms. Governor don Luis de Rosas, whom the Spanish citizenry were here to meet, was similarly dressed, wearing a doublet of brocade, a small pleated collar stiffened in the neck with buckram, a flowing short coat, and tall boots of Cordovan leather. Before the kingdom's royal standard, a banner hung on a processional staff bearing the royal arms of Leon and Castile on one side and the image of Our Lady of Remedies on the other, Rosas rode uncovered, his baton in hand. His pages carried his damascened helmet, his carved Italian *cuirass*, his lance and his sword. Great salvos were fired from artillery and from a multitude of *harquebuses* (matchlocks). And like a ripple expanding in a quiet pool, the news of welcome spread in every direction from the *Villa Real de Santa Fe*.[1]

With the blue peak of *Picacho* Mountain looming before them, the two governors, Rosas and Martinez, rode up the long approach from the west. The men of their escort, wagons, horses and lumbering mules followed them. The two lead wagons flew banners, and their mule teams, specially caparisoned, wore neck bells. Amid the jangle of bells from the harnesses of the burdened mules, the train rode past houses interspersed among fields of corn, wheat, beans, and chile, past *La Cieneguilla* (Little *Cienaga*), along the *Calle de Agua Fria* (Cold Water Road), and toward the royal palace. Entering the southern end of the plaza, which was an open space of mud and dirt, Governor Rosas looked at the royal buildings of the *casas reales*, the governor's official residence. The adobe fortress displayed four defensive towers and buttressed walls fronting the north side of the plaza. He reined up, looked back over his right shoulder at *La Tetilla*, a peak which marked the terminus of the route he had followed along the 1,000-mile *Camino Real*, and then forward again toward the adobe fortress. Blowing between pursed lips, he said out loud and to anyone who might be listening, "My royal palace! My God, it's ugly! I had expected more."

A large group of gray friars (Franciscans) came in procession from the *parroquia* (parish church), which had, since 1628, been housed at the *Hermita de San Miguel*. They were carrying lighted candles and a large cross, singing hymns of praise and benediction akin to those with which they greeted the Blessed Sacrament on the feast of Corpus Christi. *Custos* Salas, holed up at Santo Domingo in a fit of pique, was not among them. The friars joined the men of the governor's escort who now stood in ranks in front of the royal palace. Once the friars were in place, the governor dismounted.[2]

Also standing in front of the royal palace along with the capital's 250 Spanish citizens, were many of its 700 or so Indian servants. Among the *Espanoles* were the *villa's* settlers with established households. These *vecinos*, or landed citizens, were individuals with full civic rights. In front of the *vecinos* were the *villa's* four *regidores* and the additional members of its *cabildo*, who had been with those who had ridden out to meet the new governor. Rosas was struck by the appearance of these men, 50 of whom bore arms. Wearing broad-brimmed hats, long flowing capes over brocaded doublets, and bloused buskins, they appeared to be rugged frontiersmen, yet were noble in their bearing and presentation. They think of themselves as noblemen, Rosas said to himself, noblemen who will soon be demanding their *fueros*, asserting their rights, and demanding their privileges. His reaction, although nothing but a knee jerk, was one which the Italian chess master, Giocchino Greco, would have supported regarding the opening stages of a game: "Establish a senior position so as to control the center of the board," Greco had written.

In a prominent place before the *casas* was the *villa's* most important official, its *alcalde* or *justicia mayor*, Antonio Baca. A civil official with judicial, executive, and legislative responsibilities, he held before him his diploma of office. Rosas waited a long moment before speaking, taking the measure of the man who faced him. Then, completely ignoring the so-called "ritual of courtesy," Rosas asked rudely, "Did you kiss it?" referring to Baca's document. "Did you place it upon your head as a token of respect?"

Baca, his mouth fixed, his expression restrained, withdrew his hand and said, "No, I did not, your Lordship. And may I introduce myself." It was not a question. "I am Antonio Baca, a *regidore*, *alcalde ordinario* of the *villa*, one who serves the province as *justicia mayor*, a councilman who holds an elective position. Our laws are based upon the principals of our ancestral government and our concepts of personal and familial worth and good conduct. Our common law has grown out of habit, custom, and the special rights and privileges that were given us to encourage the settlement of these lands. They are laws ordained by public sanction, rather than laws arbitrarily made by kings, viceroys, or royal governors. I am not, therefore, appointed by the governor, but am elected by my fellow citizens," he stated, ignoring the fact that he served at the governor's pleasure. "I offered my patent of office as a courtesy only," he said. "Do you wish me to withdraw it?"[3]

Rosas, who saw even in this first encounter, a battle from which he must emerge victorious, continued as though mastering a wild and obstinate horse. He twisted his features into a wry expression. "No! No, of course not, don Antonio," he said, while smiling broadly at the observing crowd. "You've brought it so far. Presented it so nicely. But you may give it to me later," he concluded in a patronizing manner, while again looking at the waiting crowd. Then, in a tone that suggested he was dismissing those who stood before him, he said, "I need a bath," to all, but to no one in particular. "Perhaps we may speak later," he threw out in Baca's direction. And then to one of his aides, he added, "Please see me to my quarters."

Baca could not be expected to take this slight to his honor without retaliation, especially since it was delivered by one whom he now firmly rejected as worthy of his respect. He said, "That was also our judgment, your Lordship. That you need a bath. Please remember that I offered my diploma as a gesture of friendship and with no strings attached. It will not be offered again. And as for speaking to us later? Well, perhaps, if we can work it into our schedule. We'll leave you now to attend to your toilette," he said as he turned to go, two fingers to the brim of his hat in a mock salute. Baca placed his patent within his brocaded doublet, remounted his horse and, with the remainder of the vecinos who had ridden out with him to welcome the new governor, clattered out of the plaza.

* * *

That evening, after the governor had successfully emptied his innards, the governors, Rosas and Martinez, walked over to a home on the plaza where the cabildo was holding its meeting. Told of Rosas impending arrival, the members of the council hastily adjourned leaving but their sheriff behind to greet him. "They were here, your Lordship, but now they're gone," said Nicolas Duran. "I'm sorry that there's no one left with whom you might meet. We no longer have a quorum."

"I don't need a quorum," Governor Rosas responded rudely. "I'm not here to transact business or to take a vote. Please tell the members of the council that they'll no longer be burdened with the task of apportioning land," he stated imperiously. "They may act as consultants in that regard," he said, staring pointedly at his predecessor, Martinez, "but from this day forward, the final determination regarding land apportionment of any amount will be made by me. Tell them that," he told Duran.

Duran, who knew that the *alcaldes* and councilmen had for 30 years been empowered by Governor Peralta and the king to apportion lots, fields, and 133 acres of land to each resident, stood there astonished, but said nothing.

Rosas made a cursory examination of the room in which the council met, and then, with Governor Martinez in tow, left the building.

It was an inauspicious beginning. Even Governor Martinez was appalled.

9

Maria's Well

They referred to the water source as "Maria's Well," not because she had discovered it, but because she cherished it and had made it her own. A seep in a country where water was magical, it was a tiny rivulet of spring water flowing gently into the river from a forested slope. Running first into a willowed pool, and then into the roar and babble of the river, it was the heart of a sylvan retreat where wild things peered through the pine and bracken, and where they came to drink. The pool, flanked by sprigs of watercress and with the stones that Maria had removed to enlarge it, was littered with the miniscule shells of fresh water clams.

Above the pool and beneath the canopy of trees, Maria and Nicolas Ortiz lay on a bed of pine needles looking at the clouds, and for one brief moment, the world consisted only of this sunshine-filled place on a hillside, among the juniper and *pinon* trees, overlooking the river canyon. In the far distance, smoke rose from numerous chimneys. People, unseen, but making their presence known by their muted whistles and shouts, were working in the fields just beyond the forest, irrigating, hoeing and tending to their flocks. Looking down on black and white magpies drifting lazily over greening fields, Maria and Nicolas could see the big cottonwoods lining the river by her parents' home which was itself shadowed by apple, plum, and apricot trees. The terraced hillside alongside her parents' home dropped sharply into the canyon, and from the front *zaguan* of the family compound, nothing blocked the view toward the west. The air was filled with the clean, sweet scent of the orchards and with the sound of water.

"I wonder where it comes from?" Maria remarked dreamily regarding the river. "From the mountains to the east, I know, but where, exactly?" she questioned as she lay looking into the sky. She was quiet then. He waited patiently for her to proceed, observing the fine, peach-fuzz of hair on her arms and shoulders, and sensing, rather than seeing, the roundness of her young breasts partially revealed in the gape of her blouse. Aware of her breathing and of the rise and fall of her chest, he dared not look at her as she rested there beside him.

Rolling onto her side, she sat up and drew her knees tightly to her chest, wrapping her arms underneath them and holding her skirts tightly about her legs. She looked at him and said, "Several years ago, just after you left, I was so unhappy that my papa let me go with him and the other men to take the sheep to the high country. We eventually had to come back when Nicolas broke his arm in a fall from his horse, but while we were there, we followed the river upward to cow paths flowing as brooks of snowmelt, each stream to a smaller one, going up and up to God knows where. I wanted to get to the top, Nico," she said, using one of the several pet names she used to differentiate him from her brother who was also named Nicolas. "My papa has a sheep station there," she explained, "a safe house where the *pastores* stay when they take the sheep to summer pasture. Someday I'll see it, and I'll find the beginnings of our river," she said reflectively. "I'm going to build a house there to look over this, the most beautiful place in the world. If a place could be a parent, Nico, this would be mine. This is where I belong."

"This is beautiful, Maria, but you should see Zacatecas or the city of Mexico. They, too, are beautiful. Different from this." he explained. "But with their own color and charm."

"I'm sure that's true, my Nico, and I want to see them, but I'd be very unhappy if I couldn't return here. Not just because this is the home of my parents and where my grandparents are buried, but because this place is in my heart."

"Then if you won't run away with me," he said, "we'll just have to devise a different plan."

10

The Controversial Fray Juan de Vidania

In a handsome wooden confessional erected upon a platform within the nave of the church, the air smelled vaguely of *punche* (tobacco) and ambergris. Nicolas, who knelt on one side of the small, enclosed space, waited for a small window to open.

Muffled voices from the other side of the booth told him that Fray Juan de Vidania was sitting between the two curtained enclosures hearing sins and giving absolution to the penitent with whom he was speaking. The voice he heard was that of an older woman, and, although he could not understand clearly the words she spoke, he wondered if the woman knew with whom she shared her secrets. He hoped that he had chosen his priest well—a reprobate, it was said, an unprincipled scoundrel, who might be willing to accede to his request.

"Say three Our Fathers and three Hail Marys," said Fray Juan de Vidania to the unseen woman who knelt on the other side of the confessional. "And now say an Act of Contrition and do not sin again!" he commanded, as he closed the small window on the other side of the booth.

Nicolas heard Fray Vidania moving about in his cubicle as he rearranged his seating. Then a prolonged silence ensued. Finally, a small window on Nicolas's side of the box slid open to reveal a wooden trellis behind which sat Fray Juan de Vidania, a transfer from the Franciscan province of Michoacan, and one whom the Franciscan Order had unaccountably accepted into its ranks after his expulsion from the Society of Jesus.

"It's Nicolas Ortiz, your Reverence," Ortiz whispered, using the priest's more formal title. "It's exceedingly important that I speak with you."

"And what is it, my son?" asked Fray Vidania.

"I came to make a request, Father, a request regarding Maria Perez de Bustillo," Nicolas said. "It's imperative that I speak with you," he repeated, "but not here, Father. I only came here because I had been told that you were hearing confessions. May I speak with you in private?" he asked.

"About what?" Fray Vidania asked, with a note of irritation in his voice.

"About a gift and a promise of love, Father."

Fray Vidania was quiet for a long moment, and then Nicolas saw the small door being slid along its waxed runners as the good father again covered the trellised aperture. Nicolas strained but could hear nothing more. Suddenly, Fray Vidania rose and stepped out from within the confessional, rudely brushed aside the curtain which had shielded Ortiz from view, and with his purple stole still prominently displayed against his gray cassock, demanded, "Come with me! I've heard enough sins for one day. These little old ladies dressed always in black, their sins are of little moment and will wait till tomorrow." He grabbed Nicolas by his sleeve. "A gift and a promise of love?" he asked as he and Nicolas walked toward the door leading to the office that Vidania had established within the *Hermita's* small sacristy.

"Yes, Father," Nicolas said. "I want to give Maria a gift, something she'll remember me by when I go on the wagon train. For when I leave, Father, I'll be gone for three long years."

They entered the office where Fray Vidania motioned for Ortiz to sit on a cushioned stool that had been drawn up for that purpose, the cleric himself taking a seat in a chair. Vidania, a gentleman of perhaps 50 years of age, lean and hard, and dressed in a drab cassock of enormous dimensions, gave the young Ortiz the once-over and then turned to his desk. "A *prenda* . . . a *prenda*," he muttered to himself regarding the marriage pledge for which he was searching as he rummaged around within the desk. Pulling out drawers and then searching within them, he opened and then slammed them shut one by one, saying, "You could give her a small piece of jewelry . . . or a medal or some such. I've got one here someplace. One of Our Lady. Silver. The weight of a silver coin." Shrugging and seemingly annoyed that he could not find what he was looking for, he said, "Or you could give her a poem. I've got one here." He felt around within his cassock. "A takeoff on a lovely Jewish ballad I found that I've been rearranging for just such an occasion," he said while taking from within the sleeve of his robes a folded slip of paper. Clearing his throat, he said, "The poem is called 'There Is a Beautiful Lady,' " He read:

> There is a beautiful lady,
> No one is lovelier:
> Her forehead is dazzling.
> And her hair is like brass.
> Her brow mother-of-pearl,
> Her eyes, the shape of almonds,
> are green,
> Her nose fine as a feather,
> Her cheeks are roses,
> Her mouth very rounded,
> Her teeth are pearls,
> Slender her throat,
> Her breasts, golden apples,
> Her waist small, her body
> Drawn fine like a cypress
> When she comes to Mass
> The church dances with light . . .[1]

He stopped then, looked at Nicolas and smiled, covering nicely the tinge of embarrassment he was experiencing—for had not his rendition been inspired by Nicolas's Maria? He put the folded piece of paper back into the crease of his sleeve and said, "Or you could give her one of these," pointing to a box full of rosaries. "They'd be fine," he tossed off with a shrug. "But I've seen your Maria, Nicolas," he said with a wide grin, speaking of the young beauty with the gaping blouse whom he had often seen kneeling on the stairs of the sanctuary. "She is lovely!" he exclaimed. "A jewel in herself! I think she should have something more, something better, something substantial." Fray Vidania, who liked to think of himself as an expert in matters of love, then knelt on the cold flagstones of his office floor and pulled out from beneath his desk a small hidebound chest. He opened it and very carefully unwrapped a copy of the *Traetatus*, a book of courtly love, which in his inglorious departure from the Society's motherhouse, he had stolen from the Jesuit library. "Nicolas," he exclaimed, while holding the gilt-edged book before him, "it's all here, devised by men who should know these things!" Taking the book, whose binding was laced and tied with a leather thong, he ruffled through several pages of the well-worn manuscript, leafing back and forth among the book's many folios, the parchment of the ancient vellum crackling beneath his touch. Finally finding the exact passage for which he had been searching, he said, "These are the gifts a gallant might make to his lady." He cleared his throat and read from the book:

> ... a handkerchief, a wreath of gold or silver, a brooch, a mirror, a purse, a tassel, a comb, sleeves, gloves, a ring, a powder box, little dishes, or any little thing which might be of use in the bath or in helping the lady to remember her lover, if it's assured that the lady is without a trace of avarice ...

"Avarice? Nicolas questioned. "I don't know that word, Father."

"Greed!" Fray Vidania exclaimed with great emotion. "Greed!"

"But it's not a *prenda* I seek, Father. She's to be my bride, not my mistress. She *is* referred to by her father as an *infanta*, or royal princess, but she knows nothing of greed."

"Well, then, you're a very lucky man!" responded Fray Vidania while replacing his cherished book within its velvet cover. "Have you asked for her hand?" he asked.

"That's why I'm here, Father," Nicolas said, "to consult with you regarding a gift and to ask you to marry us." He waited a moment before continuing, saying finally, "Her father has said that she's too young to marry and I fear what will happen to her in my absence."

"Has he denied your request? Um, dealt you the *calabazas* as they say?" he asked with a wide grin.

"I haven't made the request myself, Father, and I don't have parents here who might make it for me. But the problem is this," he said, leaning forward from his stool and speaking intently. "Maria's father, don Simon Perez de Bustillo, has three daughters and only one son. His older daughters, Catalina and Juliana, married well. His wish is to further cement the alliances he now has with other prominent families by arranging advantageous marriages for the other two, for Nicolas and for Maria."

"Like a feudal lord?" Vidania queried.

"Like an old colonist!" Nicolas said. "Like a *moradore* who, in contrast to an *encomendero*, does not have rights to Indian tribute and who must, therefore, maintain his superiority among the other colonists through marital alliances. I understand all of that, and I wish him well," Nicolas said with passion. "However, his ambitions for his children are about to affect me greatly. The impediment to his arranging suitable marriages for his two remaining children is that the kingdom is small and almost everyone's related. If Maria's brother, Nicolas, marries well, she may be allowed greater leeway in the choice of her husband. But if Nicolas does not marry into land and wealth, little or no consideration will be given to her wishes."[2]

"You're right in all of that, Nicolas," responded Fray Vidania as he sat back into his chair. "A misalliance for Nicolas Perez would lower the entire family's rating and diminish the possibilities of securing an honorable partner for his sister. And a daughter, especially one who's referred to by her father as an *infanta*, is always a potential liability, for don Simon or for any father. He must provide her with a dowry, stock, and money, which will detract, rather than add to his wealth. He may feel it best to send her to a cloister, or to dispose of her in some other manner as quickly and as quietly as possible and at minimal expense."[3]

"The law says any female may marry at age eleven, and since

73

Maria is sixteen, the age issue is merely a ploy. My fear is that don Simon will ask for a dispensation to marry her to one of her relatives, a cousin, perhaps, one who's a member of the nobility."

"But there are rules against that sort of thing, Nicolas. Such marriages are forbidden by Divine Law and are, therefore, ineligible for dispensation. I have a table here someplace . . . the table of Leviticus which outlines the prohibitions."

"But Leviticus says nothing about cousins, Father. They may be dispensed as close relatives."

"Yes," he said, "that's true. The exception is known as *pro honestis familiis*. Uh huh. Uh huh," he muttered to himself, seemingly contemplating it all. And then to Nicolas, he said, "You seem to be well versed in canon law, young man. Where did you get your information?"[4]

"From don Francisco Gomez, Father. His brother's a Franciscan priest."

"Well, yes, Perez could do that. Get a dispensation, I mean. Others have. And the members of the aristocracy think that they can do whatever they damn well please."

"My impediments are that I'm from Zacatecas and have neither land nor wealth. But I've taken the steps required to remove these barriers," Ortiz said. "I've petitioned the *cabildo* for residency so that I may obtain the *merced*, or grant of land, given to each *vecino*. I've yet to receive them, though—the residency or the land—and my request is impeded by my status as a member of the wagon escort, which only places me in the *villa* every three years. However, if I'm granted residency, I'll do whatever's required. I'll maintain my home here for the necessary ten consecutive years and request permission from the *cabildo* for the absences which may be required of me."

"It seems that you've a lot to overcome in your bid for Maria's hand," Fray Vidania responded.

"I do, Father," Nicolas said, "and my situation is further complicated by the fact that, although only twenty-seven of the thirty years have passed in which the *alcaldes* and councilmen were empowered to apportion land, the governor has taken that right away from them, giving them now the role of consultants only. So, if I'm to get the grant,

Father, it will have to be Governor Rosas himself who will award it." He waited a long moment before continuing, trying to gauge the priest's general attitude regarding his situation. Finding little in Vidania's face by which to make this judgment, he finally said, "I know of your great friendship with the governor and was hoping that you'd speak to him on my behalf."

"And why do you seek to marry her now?" asked Fray Vidania.

"To keep her father in my absence from marrying her to someone else," Nicolas said. "I've been told of your interest, and that of the Church, in aiding and celebrating marriages which are based on love, rather than on arrangement, and I'm here to ask you to speak to the governor on my behalf regarding the land. I also wish to make a further request."

Fray Vidania leaned back in his chair expectantly. He waited for Ortiz to continue, saying, finally, "Go on."

"I'm asking you to engage in a deception which will hurt no one, Father," Nicolas responded. "Maria will say that she has lost the flower of her virginity to me, and that her shamelessness will dishonor her father and family—even that she fears that her brother will take her life. And, if asked, you'll say that you married us to preserve her honor and to avoid public scandal."[5]

"Do you know her in that way?" asked Fray Vidania.

"No, Father. You would be acting on Maria's word."

"And Maria's father? What am I to tell him?"

"He will not be told that there's been a marriage unless it's required. And when I return, Father," Nicolas continued, "I'll come back a more prosperous suitor, with land and stock. Then Maria and I may have a proper wedding."

Fray Juan de Vidania looked at Nicolas Ortiz for a long moment before responding. He looked at Nicolas, handsome, well built, tall, intelligent, and well mannered. Then he said sadly, "But you're not of equal *calidad*, my dear Nicolas, and the marriage of an aristocrat and a peasant can only bring dishonor upon her family. In these matters, Nicolas, it's considered more dishonorable for one to marry below her station, than to have lost her virginity, or even to be with child. I'm not sure how I can make sense of this for don Simon. And why would I wish to do so?" he continued. "Why would I want to marry you? I have no love for her father, it's true. He spoke badly to the viceroy regarding the clergy, about me in particular, when called upon in the city of Mexico to give an account of state affairs here in the kingdom. Her father can go to hell, as far as I'm concerned," he exclaimed. "But why would I do something to further earn her father's enmity?" he asked. "What would I gain?"

"I don't offer you a bribe, Father, but a gift, because you know what I ask is just and good. For I'm not a peasant, Father," said the tall and handsome young man. "Not the son of a hangman, or a butcher, or a tanner, and my inequality to Maria is slight. My people were blacksmiths, and tailors, and shoemakers, men of decent and honorable trades. And I'm the son of a soldier, Father. Soldiering is also an honorable profession, and one in which our governor himself was engaged. My inferiority will not cause marked dishonor to her family. Her father and grandfather won their honor and privileges at the point of a sword, but the family's nobility is sustained through land. I'll obtain the land and will be her equal. And as for payment, Father, I'll give you whatever you wish. I will soon go to the city of Mexico which has the world at its doorstep, and I'll get you whatever you ask."

Fray Vidania then sat quietly for a long time, contemplating the ruse that Ortiz had outlined, scratching his beard and thinking, saying finally, "There's much to consider here. There are the banns. The marital investigation. Everything."

Fray Juan de Vidania and Nicolas Ortiz looked at each other across the span of a small desk with Fray Vidania considering his options. "Books?" he finally asked.

"Whether on the prohibited list or otherwise," Ortiz responded.

"And Perez may never know?"

"Only if required, Father."

"Then you pick the time and place and it shall be done," said Fray Vidania. "And don't let don Simon fool you, Nicolas," Fray Vidania continued. "He may say that he's a native of Mexico City, but he, too, is from Zacatecas. To hell with don Simon. Let him eat crow!"

"And you'll speak to the governor on my behalf regarding the land—meadow land for livestock grazing?" Ortiz asked.

"Be careful how much you ask for during one negotiation," said Fray Vidania with a tinge of annoyance in his voice. "The governor knows you, is that correct?" he asked.

"He knows me, Father. I was a member of his escort."

"Then I'll speak with him, although I wouldn't expect much to come from my intervention. He has his own ways in these matters, Nicolas. But I'll speak to him."

11

For Richer or Poorer

Following a shady trail in the windings of a riparian forest, Nicolas Ortiz rode parallel to an ancient riverbed. He rode hurriedly, up through a *bosque*, a forest of alder, cottonwood, and willow, and beyond that, as well, through *pinon*-studded hills on uneven ground. Finally, he stopped and dismounted.

The forest floor was spread with pinecones and an understory of roses, currants, and woody vines that grasped at his every step. He freed himself from these, looped the reins of his horse around the branch of a spare sapling and began working his way back down the trail he had followed through densely packed trees to a small pond where he hid himself among the brambles.

A scarlet flash, marking the passage of a red-winged blackbird, was briefly visible among the trees while the orange and gold crown of a black-headed grosbeak was visible on a perch of boxelders. Stalking the pond on impossibly long, slender legs, a great blue heron ruffled the water which moved in advance of his every step. All of Nicolas's senses were alert. He absorbed the sweet scent of pine needles and duff, the splendor of the boxelders turning red, the richness of the golden cottonwoods.

When he saw her riding up the trail, he took her for Fray Juan de Vidania, her appearance was so masked by a slouched hat and by the leather trappings of *gamuza* hiding her auburn hair and slim frame. God, she's lovely, he said to himself. He waited for her to dismount and tie up before revealing himself.

"Were you seen?" he asked.

"I made sure that I was," she responded. "I thought it best to have them see a hunter openly leaving the compound, rather than attempt to sneak out. They'll never even think to see if I'm gone."

"Are you sure you want to do this?" Nicolas asked cautiously. "I could still ask for your father's permission."

"And you know that it would not be given, my Nico," she said, her face lit by a radiant smile.

"He's right, you know, your papa," Nicolas said. "I'm not good enough for you. No one is."

"And you sound just like him," Maria teased. "He'd keep me tied up in a storeroom or put me in a convent if my mama would let him," she laughed. "But I'd make a horrible prisoner and a worse nun. I want to marry, Nico, and you're to be my groom!" Holding his hand, she looked around her in anticipation of Fray Vidania's arrival.

* * *

The nuptial service took but a few short moments: "Do you, *Senorita* Maria, take *Senor* don Nicolas, here present, to be your lawfully wedded husband as our Holy Mother Church commands?" And then the reverse. Nothing even remotely romantic or memorable about it. And when it was over—Was it truly over? Maria asked herself—the young bride questioned whether they were really married.

After Fray Vidania's departure, Maria and Nicolas retreated to the environs of Maria's well where, as children, she and her sisters had played at being wedded, at being nuns, and at commanding legions of *criadas* who would respond to their every wish. You could play at being a nun, even though you had never seen one and could not possibly have known anything regarding their behavior, but the wedding was special and could not be completely duplicated in play. The days and weeks of lavish preparations. The *prendorio* (betrothal). The wedding banquet. The parental blessings. The symbolism provided by the processionals, rings, and veils, all carefully orchestrated to provide the melody, beat, and time to the ancient ritual. This brief ceremony bore no resemblance to that. It felt like nothing, and Maria could not hide her disappointment.

They sat on their mat of *jerga*, a coarse wool carpeting which

Maria had thought to bring with her, their beautiful selves hidden among the tall grass and willows. Nicolas was shy, and unsure of how to proceed, for he had known but one woman before committing himself to Maria, and she was nothing but a *barragana* (priest's mistress) forced upon him by one of his brother's friends. That was lust, not love. And nothing like this, nothing like what he felt for Maria.

Nicolas leaned toward Maria and kissed her, her lips soft and pliant against his. He removed his lips from hers and brushed with the tips of his fingers her fluttering eyelids. The moment his lips were gone, she wanted them back and reached over to find them. She covered his lips with hers and he ground against her as he slipped his body over the length of her, and she pressed against him. He kissed her softly again moving his hand from where he had placed it below her breasts to the ties at her throat, yearning for the warmth of her flesh hidden beneath the cotton and leather trappings she wore. Maria, the nipples of her breasts hard and soft at the same time, responded by kissing him again.

Proceeding clumsily, her leather ties all but barring his advance, he fumbled with anglets at her neck and waist. Despite the tenderness and passion they shared, what followed was nothing but a series of awkward embraces. His fingers were useless against the barriers her clothing presented. She moved against him then. She started to help him by untying the leather thong at her throat when she became aware of the light as it filtered through the trees. She pulled away from him and sat up. He looked at her, his eyes wide and intense, but fearful, too, anxious that he had somehow offended her.

A distance was drawn between them as she said, "I know that we're married, Nico. Father Vidania has told us so, but it's got to be more than this. I've waited so long for this special day. I don't want it to be here or now. I want our first time to be in our own bed, with sheets of linen, plumped pillows, and a comforter of soft, fine feathers. Can you wait, my Nico?" she asked plaintively.

"I can wait," he responded. "I can wait until you feel it's right. I don't want to do anything you don't want to do."

"Will you do this for me, Nico?" she asked tearfully. "Will you do this?"

"I can wait, Maria," he said in resignation. "It's enough to know that you hold me in your heart."

"When it's right, my Nico."

"When it's right," he responded.

12

Difficulties at Jemez

"Do you have more bad news for me?" the governor asked the man who had just entered his small office.

"I'm afraid I do, your Lordship," his aide responded. "The garrison at Jemez, along with its priest, has been wiped out by the nomads, apparently, the *Apaches de Nabaju*. And the missionary at *San Jose de Giusewa* was also killed in the attack."

"How many men did we lose?" the governor asked, ignoring his aide's statements regarding the priests.

"All six, your Lordship. And the friars too," his aide repeated sadly.

"Well, we don't lose a hell of a lot by the death of two friars, for there seems to be an infinite number of them to send here. But we only have a limited number of men and the posts at San Diego and San Jose must at all odds be held as barriers against the nomads. Who do we have to send there?" he asked, looking up from the papers on which he had been writing.

"The simplest assignment would be to send the men of the escort, your Lordship. Some are working here while they await the train, but they may be easily diverted from their work."

"They're good men," responded the governor, who knew that the New Mexico colony, which had been carved out of a hostile wilderness, could only survive by its strength of arms. "Get them on their horses," he stated emphatically. "I want them there in a fortnight."

* * *

There's little to worry about," Nicolas said to Maria meeting her at Maria's Well. "I've heard that the walls of the church at Jemez are almost seven feet thick! We could hold out there with nothing but a *petronel.*"

"Then how did they get killed?" Maria asked, regarding the members of the squadron killed by the nomads at Jemez. "Is this not the second group we've lost there?"

"They must have been lured out from the behind the walls," Nicolas said, "We wont make that mistake."

"I don't want you to go!" she cried.

"I have no choice, Maria," Nicolas said. "I'm a soldier. I must go."

* * *

Clutching a shawl of white lace worn wimple-like with folds about her head, cheeks, chin, and shoulders, Maria and her Indian servant walked briskly against the evening chill alongside the river as it flowed down toward the village, and then along the ditch of a secondary *acequia* through fields of ripening corn. The church grounds and plaza, where three enormous cottonwoods were in full leaf, were still bathed in the glow of the setting sun. All was quiet, the *villa* uninviting.

A sentry, who had watched them approach the fortress, leaned out from his tower on its southern wall, eager to see more of the tall, slim, beautiful young woman who now approached the entry. The dry moat of a defensive trench and an *acequia* carrying water to western fields fronted the gate, a double-doored entrance the length of a room, wide enough for a wagon to pass through. Flanked by a pair of small cannons reflecting the prestige and power of the royal governor, the entrance could only be approached by a walled passageway and a rude bridge that Maria and her servant now crossed.

Gaining entrance through this covered passageway, they entered an enormous courtyard where Maria's servant was asked to remain. Maria was then shown into a small and Spartan office where she now stood, her servant on a long bench sitting just outside the door.

While waiting, Maria examined the tiny, square room in which she had been asked to wait. Its walls of post and corbel were covered with a strip of Dutch cotton cloth to protect the clothing of one who might rub against it. The ceiling, like the ceilings of the rooms in her home, consisted of *vigas* and *savinos* forming long, sunken compartments overhead. The floor of hard-packed earth was covered with *jerga*, and with the skins of bear, bison, and mountain lion. Long, plain benches were placed against two of its walls. A small, crude table, with two equally crude chairs, sat in the center of the room. A window of fused mica faced the interior patio. The fireplace was cold and appeared unused. The odors, not offensive but strong in the cool air, were of dust and dirt, of gypsum, animal pelts and earth.

A servant, who did not speak to Maria when he entered the room, lit its candles, worked in silence, and then left. When he had departed, Maria removed her *rebozo* (mantle). Refolding the garment into a large triangle, she replaced it on her head, its points crossing at her throat, the right point of which she threw gracefully over her left shoulder; the length of the fringe silently demonstrating the worth of the article and the wealth and position of its owner. And thus having stated her station relative to the governor, she waited.

Dressed in a jerkin of gray velvet festooned with colored flecks, the governor appeared in the doorway. He pressed two fingers against his lips in sincere appreciation as he observed the tall, slim beauty who stood before him, and gave a nod of welcome almost imperceptible in the dim light. "You asked to speak with me?" he questioned courteously and in a gentle voice.

"If you have time, your Grace."

"I can always make time for a beautiful young woman," he said. "I kiss the hands of your great beauty," he continued as he motioned for her to sit in one of the chairs in the middle of the cheerless room. "And what is it you wished to speak with me about?" he asked as he sat at the table.

"It's about one of your assignments, your Grace," Maria responded without acknowledging the compliment she had been paid. "You've assigned my husband to the pueblo of the Jemez, and he's to leave tomorrow. But he's been gone for three long years and we've had little time together." She chose to give this, rather than her fear of the

84

assignment, as the reason for her remarks.

"Your husband?" the governor queried. "Who is he? Is he known to me?" he asked.

"Nicolas. Nicolas Ortiz," Maria responded in a plaintive voice.

"I was not aware that he was married," the governor answered, "not that that would have necessarily made a difference in my assignment. He was a wagon master and a member of my escort from Mexico City, and I got to know him rather well," the governor continued. "A nice young man. Well thought of by those with whom he works. He never spoke of a wife," he added.

Maria, who had been clutching her shawl about her face, now removed it from her head, gathering it about her shoulders, placing her hands in her lap. She waited a long moment before responding, saying finally, "May I take you into my confidence?"

The governor looked at her, his shaggy eyebrows all but concealing his large eyes. A request to be taken into her confidence, he thought to himself. This is no ordinary girl. A rose, yes, but not one that would be easily picked. He pushed his chair away from the table and made a motion as if to rise, gathered himself up and then resettled in his chair but did not answer. After a long moment, Maria continued.

"I beg that your Grace give Nicolas a different assignment. My parents don't know we're married, and we've had no time together," she said.

"Your parents don't know you're married?" he asked incredulously. "How can that be? That's an enormous secret to keep from one's parents. And who are they, your parents?" he asked.

"I apologize, your Grace. I should have introduced myself before speaking with you. I think that I had hoped to get your approval for a reassignment without even telling you who I was," she laughed, her smile radiant in the candlelight. "I am Maria Perez de Bustillo.[1] My father is Captain Simon Perez de Bustillo. And my mother is Juana Baca," she answered.

"Are you related to our *justicia*, Antonio Baca?" the governor asked.

"Yes," she responded. "He is my uncle. A second father, really.

He's married to my father's sister, Yumar Perez de Bustillo, while my father is married to his sister. But I had not wanted to make this request on the basis of my family, but rather on my own," she answered.

"And when were you married?" the governor asked.

"Just yesterday," Maria responded. Father Vidania did it for us. I don't like to do things behind my parents' back, and I feel horrible to have done so, but if Nicolas had sought my father's permission, it would not have been granted. However, when Nicolas has acquired lands and herds, I'll tell my papa, and he'll feel different about Nicolas. My papa only wants my welfare."

"Well, your father won't find out from me," the governor assured her, "and your husband, Nicolas, will be given something safer to do, something that will keep him here a while longer."

"Please don't tell him that I intervened, your Grace. You know my Nicolas. He'd feel dishonored to have had his wife beg for something for which he himself would not ask."

"Then it will be our secret, and Nicolas need not ever know," the governor responded, as he rose from his chair.

"I will forever be in your debt, your Grace," she said, as she rose and grasped his extended hand.

"Perhaps we'll find a way for you to repay me," he answered enigmatically, as he drew her hand to his lips and kissed it. "Now go. Go to your Nicolas."

13

The Martinez *Residencia*

"They're insane. Completely insane!" Martinez railed against the priests. "And that damned Ibargaray may be the most demented! He'll tell you many bad things about me, Governor, but you must not believe him. I ask that I be allowed to accompany you to Pecos, so that you may see how he and the other religious behave. They want the Indians for themselves, and there's no compromise," Martinez said, "If you offer them a *celemin*, they want a bushel. No matter your concession, it's never enough."

"Well, I think that your suggestion that you accompany me is a good one," Rosas responded. "But before we go, I want you to tell me everything you know regarding trade."

Martinez, who knew that he had found a soul mate in the world of commerce, said, "The possibilities for trade with the Plains Indians are endless, Governor, and the pueblo of the Pecos is perhaps the most important in this. Indians come there to trade with the Pueblos and Spanish colonists offering mainly products of the bison, hides, jerked meat, and tallow, and, also, the skins of other animals, pronghorn, deer and elk. They bring salt, too, and their captives from other Indian nations upon whom they make war. The goods they seek are *mantas*, pottery, *maize*, turquoise, and bread, and, also, now that we're here, wheat, fruit, livestock, and iron implements such as axes, knives, spears and firearms. I don't think it's wise to make firearms available to them as the French do," Martinez said, "but I have a warehouse at Pecos in which I store the other things, *pinon* nuts, *mantas*, and leather goods, especially. And just before I was recalled, I opened a workshop here in the *casas* where Indian weavers and painters can produce additional goods. I mean to take the *pinons* and hangings with me when I return to Mexico City, but the warehouse and *obraje* are yours."

He waited then, wondering whether Governor Rosas would wish to hear the suggestions he, Martinez, might make as to how Rosas should conduct the trade. Presently, he said, "There are some things you should know about these people of the Plains tribes, attitudes you must display if you're to win their respect and admiration. They'll test you, Governor," he said. "Measure you as a man. You must go to the trading grounds at Pecos displaying both confidence and friendship. They must see you as protecting them from other tribes while they're there. You must sit down and smoke with them and permit their familiarities and, as is suitable, take part in their fun. You must come to know them, Governor, come to know the people of Pecos and the Plains."

"Then, let's go," Rosas said with enthusiasm. "We'll go to Pecos to see what it has to offer and to elicit testimony from Fray Antonio de Ibargaray and his cronies regarding your *residencia*. It should be interesting," Rosas said to Martinez with a wink.

* * *

Riding through a narrow passage 15 miles to the east of *La Cienaga*, the governors' party rode away from the *villa de Santa Fe* and toward the Pecos River Valley, a forested mountain basin nestled between the *Sangre de Cristo* Mountains and Glorieta *Mesa*. Approaching the Pecos Pueblo from the north, Rosas and the others could well see the site, a small ridge of red and buff sandstone rising above a forest of *pinon* and juniper, as well as, above fields of corn planted alongside a stream flowing through the valley.

Blessed with two year-round sources of water, the Glorieta Creek and the Pecos River, the Indian village, one of the largest in the region, was in a most advantageous position with productive fields lining both sides of a languorous stream. The watercourse wandering here and there, sometimes east and sometimes west, although unhurried in its movements, was in perceptible motion, a sliver of reflected light gleaming through the valley.

Crossing the stream at a small ford, the governors' party passed among some one-room field houses used by the Indians while tending their fields. The riders were to see many of these small structures as they continued moving southward toward a high and narrow hill on which the pueblo was built.

Along the center of the hill rose two distinct stone structures of four and five stories in receding tiers. Reddish-brown in color, they were mud-plastered quadrangles of over 600 rooms. A series of porches running along the second and third stories of each structure served as upper story passageways and as platforms where the Indians kept their arms, their bows, arrows, shields, spears and war clubs. Ladders leaning against walls and protruding from rooftop openings were everywhere.

A bulwark of flagstones, providing an oval-shaped defensive wall with only one opening, surrounded both the north and south pueblos. This shielded a spring and a few of the village's 26 *kivas* from the open countryside. The combined pueblo, formerly known to its Indian inhabitants as *Cicuye*, and now the center of a mighty city-state referred to as Pecos, gave its villagers a commanding view of the entire valley alerting them of anyone approaching from any direction. Wielding unimaginable power as a trading center, the pueblo, a fortress on a small *mesa* halfway between the Great Plains and the Rio Grande Valley, appeared well defended and invulnerable from attack.

Looming on the southern edge of the *mesa*, some 600 or 700 feet from the pueblo's southern wall, was a massive church. Reflecting the pueblo's size and consequence, the church, the greatest in New Mexico, was 150 feet in length and 55 feet in height and encompassed an area of 6000 square feet. With six bell towers and buttressed walls, some of which were 22 feet thick, the mission church, named *La Nuestra Senora de los Angeles de Porciuncula*, was a fortress. Its immensity was emphasized by the way it dwarfed the Indian shepherd who was leading his flock of goats back and forth within a long, narrow, new irrigation canal where the soil was being compacted.

Approaching the pueblo from the north, the riders had been

unable to see the mission's relatively small *convento*, an excellent adobe structure with a flagstone patio, a covered ambulatory, and a cobble-lined drain carrying water off of the *convento's* roof and into a cistern. Completing the *convento's* two distinct plazas were its workshops, corrals, stables, kitchen and refectory. There were, also, several sparsely furnished chambers, some with fireplaces, running alongside the church's southern wall. A kitchen garden with vegetables and medicinal herbs was on the south side. A low flagstone wall separated the kitchen garden from the *convento's estancia*, a small farm where sheep and cattle were corralled.

On the west, the friars' rooms and offices were of two stories. Here Fray Ibargaray had his quarters. On the second floor, looking back toward Santa Fe, was a *mirador*, or enclosed balcony, from which he watched the riders as they dismounted under some cottonwoods within sight of the *convento*, the sky a snarl of storm clouds behind them.

Gathering his gray cassock about him, the Basque, Fray Antonio de Ibargaray, a saintly and personable priest in his late twenties who was Guardian at the Pecos *convento*, took a deep breath and held it. Waiting expectantly for the knock, he now hesitated, wishing to appear neither anxious nor rude. On hearing the governors' vigorous pounding on the intricately carved door of the porter's lodge, the *convento's* business office and reception area, he pattered down the stone steps of a stairwell. He opened the door and said, "I welcome your arrival," in place of his usual greeting.[1] "And I think that it's well that you brought Governor Martinez with you, Governor Rosas. Please come in," he said, as he ushered them down a dimly lit passageway and into his study.

The room had for its furnishings a long, narrow refectory table so high that it could not be slouched over. Behind it, a chair had been placed. The remainder of the room's seating consisted of several cushioned stools and a splay-legged bench. A second chair was noisily brought into the room and placed beside the one that had been provided for Governor Rosas who drummed with his fingers on the top of his thigh, impatient, it seemed, to get on with his work. Fray Antonio de Ibargaray, and the seventy-year old lay brother, Fray Antonio Jimenez, sat on one side of the table, while the governors and their minions sat on the other.

Taking a deep breath, Ibargaray began. "May I offer you some chocolate?" he asked politely.

"We didn't ride here to drink chocolate," Rosas responded rudely. We came so that I could hear from you directly regarding the administration of the Honorable Governor Francisco de Martinez." He exchanged smiles with Governor Martinez. "I'd appreciate hearing what you have to say so that we can get back to the *villa* before it gets dark."

Prevented from airing his complaints regarding Governor Martinez in a more congenial atmosphere, Fray Ibargaray glanced at Fray Jimenez and then turned to Governor Rosas, "May I be blunt, your Lordship?" he asked glancing briefly at the sheaf of papers that lay before him. "Tell you of the governor's transgressions with no attempt to smooth them over? For there's no way of making light of them," he said. "No way to make them appear less outrageous or more commendable." He waited. Governor Rosas looked at him intently but said nothing.

Fray Ibargaray took out from among his papers a copy of the letter he had written to the viceroy regarding Governor Martinez. Then, using it as a guide and ignoring the presence of Governor Martinez, he said, "From the moment he arrived in New Mexico he has attended only to his own profit causing grave damage to all of the recently converted souls among the Pueblo Indians. He commanded them to weave and to paint great quantities of *mantas* and hangings. Likewise, he made them seek out and barter what little they have for many tanned skins and *pinon* nuts, taking those he commandeered from their fields and from the mission proper. As a result of his scandalous enterprise," Fray Ibargaray said now, looking directly at Governor Martinez, "he has loaded eight *carretas* with what he has amassed and plans to take the *carretas* and as many men as are required from here to drive them to New Spain, thwarting everything His Majesty has ordered in his royal ordinance. Thus," said Ibargaray, again addressing himself to Governor Rosas, "since Governor Martinez took office, not a single pueblo has been baptized. He has refused to lend support to the Faith," he said, pointing to Governor Martinez. "Instead, he has sought in every way possible to insult with the ugliest words every minister His Majesty employs here in his royal service to convert the natives. Likewise, he has sought by force and violence to use the citizens of the *villa* and of its *cabildo*, to make utterly untrue reports against us solely to discredit us with the viceroy." He stopped then, took a less rigid posture upon his stool and waited for the governor's response.[2]

Leaning forward on his right elbow, Governor Rosas cradled his chin between his thumb and forefinger, and maintained the posture he had adopted as he listened and studied Ibargaray's pronouncements and his every move. He then stood and walked to the small window of selenite that looked out from the father's study and into the patio and asked, "Commanded them to weave *mantas* and hangings? And how does that differ from your workshops? Are your products different from those sought by the governor?"

"They, too, are *mantas* and hangings, your Lordship, but the pueblo's land and its resources are the property of the Indians. We only hold them in trust. We use the production as a means of keeping the Pueblos here so that we may bring religion to them. But the care of the sick and poor has required that we reorganize the tribe's economy, teaching them woodworking, carpentry, and blacksmithing. The entire settlement with the church, *convento*, and all these activities comprise our mission."

"And the profits?"

"For the benefit of the mission."

"And how many Indians live in the *convento*," the governor asked, "working as servants, sacristans, cooks, porters, herdsmen, bell-ringers, interpreters, gardeners, and waiters?"

"And wood carriers and *maize* grinders, too," added Governor Martinez, pleased that he had something to add to the governor's inquiry.

"Wood carriers and *maize* grinders, too?" Rosas echoed. "How many men have you taken from their fields, Father? More than twenty? And how many do you employ as unpaid servants?"

"There are a few, your Lordship. Perhaps six . . . or twelve, most of whom, because of their duty to assist us in our work in the mission, are exempted from tribute. Some of them live in the *convento*. But their work, as well as the work of others, both men and women, is devoted to the service of the Church."

"Yes, yes, as both you and *Custos* Quiros have said in your letters to the viceroy. Do you have anything further to add?" Rosas asked.

Ibargaray rearranged himself on his stool without rising, his eyes dark with fury, saying, "Governor Martinez has not given us his support and he speaks very badly of us," he repeated angrily, sensing that both he and his fellow Franciscans were now on the defensive.

"And so on, and so on, and so on!" Governor Rosas responded mockingly. "Have you nothing good to say?" he asked as he stepped away from the window.

"There's more! There's more!" railed Ibargaray. "Have you not named someone to speak for the Pueblos themselves? They have much to say regarding the money he owes them for parchments and tanned skins, tents and *pinons*. Have you not named someone to protect them?" he asked again.

"I can well speak for them myself," Rosas responded. "They need no one else."

* * *

That evening, as the two governors rode away from the pueblo of the Pecos, with Governor Rosas promising to return, Fray Ibargaray, himself willful and headstrong, sat at his desk composing a new note to the viceroy. With his coarse and ill-trimmed goose quill pen he wrote,

> They behave as absolute lords, and there are no laws other than what they desire, for laws go as kings like, as they say. Not even the immunity of churches is honored. I pray that Martinez leaves the kingdom on the returning supply wagons and that Rosas goes with him.

14

The Egyptian Day

It was one of those unlucky days—September third—known as "Egyptian," and there was a commotion of leaves in the forest with killdeer, warblers, and siskin filling the morning sky. The birds, which had been becoming restless for some weeks, began forming long ribbons and wedges in the cloudless heavens. Finches, lifting off together like a burst of gunpowder, disappeared as they banked edgewise only to appear again with the next sweeping turn. They swirled like a huge plume of smoke over the harvested fields, their flight as foreboding as a flock of vultures encircling the fertile plain of the *vega*.

Maria took little note of this as she walked up the trail with her servant, a Plains Indian, who had been Christianized and raised as a member of the Perez household. Purchased for Maria when both she and the Indian child were six, Tula was an individual who shared Maria's bed and her every activity,[1] a confidant who now clutched a slender, narrow-mouthed jar beneath her shawl.

"We didn't ask how it was to be given," Maria said of the love potion Tula was carrying. "Am I to take it, or am I to give it to him . . . or perhaps to you?" she laughed. "Urine and mashed worms! Igh! *Dios Mio!*" she said, sticking out her tongue and shaking her head. "*Madre de Dios*, Tula. My Nico will never drink this!"

"He will if he loves you!" Tula said with confidence. "He'll take any of the powders or potions available at *Analco*."

"But this is an antidote for infidelity." Maria complained. "A potion designed to bring back a straying husband. How does that relate to my Nico?"

"If he loves you, dona Maria, he'll drink it if only to prove that he'll be faithful. Do you see him tonight?" she asked.

"I hope!" Maria replied. "We have so little time together, and then he'll be gone. *Por Dios*, Tula, I think I'll die without him!"

"Then I'll wait outside and tell you when he's here," Tula said

"Be careful," Maria said in reference to the jar Tula held beneath her shawl. "Hide it under the big rock at the well. I don't want my papa to see."

* * *

Told of Nicolas's presence in the great woods above the Perez compound, Maria entered the so-called "work patio," a shadow melting into other shadows. Quarters for the family's *criados* ran along one side of the compound while a blacksmith shop and tool house stood on the other. Closing the square were pens for chickens and a shed for milk cows. Climbing onto the rails of one of the enclosures, Maria was assisted by Tula onto to the top of the stable-yard wall, and Nicolas lowered her to the ground.

"I've got some bad news," Nicolas whispered as soon as they had moved away from the house. "We're leaving tonight, Maria!" he blurted. "We're leaving tonight!"

"Who? When?" asked Maria in alarm as they hurried toward her spring.

"Miranda and I," Nicolas said, "with Governor Martinez. We're leaving now!"

"How's that possible?" she asked. "The train's not scheduled to leave for several months."

"It will leave before the end of the week, and we'll wait for it below Robledo," Nicolas said, "a plan devised to get Martinez out of the kingdom before he can be arrested by the *cabildo*. You're to say nothing about this!" he cautioned. "You're to tell no one, especially your Uncle Antonio! Governor Rosas heard of the impending arrest of the former governor from someone in the *cabildo*, and, if the rest of the *cabildo* members were to discover that Martinez is leaving, and I was found to be the source, the governor would have me killed! You must not say anything!" he implored.

Hearing the anguish in his voice, Maria was silent for a brief moment before crying, "I won't let you go! I'm afraid!"

"Hush," he cautioned. "I have but a moment, Maria. Please let me speak." His eyes seemed to mirror more light than could have been produced by the star-filled sky. "You know our plans," he said. "I need not repeat them. I've asked your Uncle Antonio to tell you when the land has been granted. Do not think of it as three years, Maria," he said with more assurance than he actually felt. "Take it only as one day at a time, season by season, doing whatever's required to make our plan work." He held her hand firmly, his chin shaking with emotion. "Those stars, Maria, the three kings and the three Marias. They'll be in the east at the beginning of winter and will be found in the west by summertime," he explained with a catch in his voice. "Before they've made three turns in the heavens, I'll be back. I'll watch them each night, and I want you to do the same. It will bind us together until I return. I have something for you," he continued, showing her a small brooch with the tiniest possible emerald stone.[2] It was an emerald pin with the legendary ability to safeguard the virtue of its wearer. "Green to match the green of your eyes," he said. "Keep it next to your heart, and when I return—as a proper husband with land and stock—I'll replace it with a ring."

Maria grasped the brooch and held it to her breast, crying, "But I have nothing for you. I didn't know you'd be going so soon." She looked at Nicolas for a long time, praying to see his eyes that were now the color of a snow-filled sky. "Will you do something for me?" she finally asked as she began searching beneath the rock where Tula had placed the small vessel. "Will you drink this?"

"A love potion?" he asked, as he took the vessel from her hands. "I'd drink poison for you," he said as he removed the jar's pottery cover. Lifting the *penante* to his lips, he drank it, its sting muted by the pain in his broken heart. He held Maria in the darkness, kissed her softly, and then he was gone.

* * *

Rosas received more than 70 formal petitions of complaint against his predecessor. He combed the grievances leveled against Martinez at Pecos, Santo Domingo, and at Santa Fe, and selected only the most benign of these, which he then offered in his report to the viceroy in the form of a mild rebuke. Rosas then readied his carts for a southern journey. While he was composing notes to the viceroy and to his friend, the duke of Segorbe, a trade invoice was being readied to accompany his initial export of items for sale in *San Jose del Parral*. Listed on this statement were 50 pairs of knitted woolen stockings, 92 *varas* of *sayal*,[3] 122 wall hangings, 126 *mantas*, 413 blankets, 198 chamois skins, 900 candles, 57 bushels of *pinon* nuts, and 79 jackets[4] of various types.

And Martinez, with Blas de Miranda, Nicolas Ortiz, and Fray Tomas Manso among those in his escort—and with hounds baying at his heels—left Santa Fe in dishonor and returned to the city of Mexico.

15

A Plum to Be Picked and Eaten Off the Vine

"Well, I don't know about her," the governor said of his cook, Apolonia Varela, to the aides with whom he was walking. "She's the lamb everyone wants to eat, but off the bone, and then stop at the *acequia* to wash their hands," he said, slapping his thigh and laughing uproariously. "But that one over there" he said gesturing with a tilt of his chin at a young beauty who, with her Indian maid as her chaperone, approached them. "You'd want to take her home to meet the family!"

Uncomfortable with the demeanor of the approaching men, Maria considered reversing her steps and returning to the church. But then she thought, We've as much right to be here as they do. She grabbed Tula by her hand and the two of them walked directly toward the men, the governor and his aides moving off the graveled path to let them pass.

Maria's beauty and bearing had drawn the eye and interest of the governor. She and her maid had gone only a short distance down the path watched by the governor and his aides when the governor called after Maria, "*Senorita*, have you no word for your governor?"

Maria stopped and turned, hesitating but a moment before answering sweetly, "*Adios? Gracias? Que?*"[1]

I was hoping it would be "*Quando?*" or "*Despues,*"[2] or perhaps one of the four S's,[3] the governor thought to himself, responding with a smile.

Maria, who knew that she and the governor were engaged in some game, but was not sure of the rules, said, "I think *gracias* would be the most appropriate, your Grace."

Sending his aides on their way, the governor strode back to where the young women were standing. He eventually walked with Maria and Tula toward the *casas reales*, where he coaxed them inside for a cup of chocolate. Tula was invited to sit on a stool just inside the doorway of the spare office. Maria and the governor sat at a small table with Maria intently examining a Castilian *escritorio* or *papelera*, a writing desk, the only major piece of furniture in the room. Supported by high legs, the wooden chest was carved and inlaid with ivory and mother-of-pearl, and studded with worked metal. It was honeycombed with little drawers and had a drop-front writing surface upon which a game board was prominently displayed. "What are those?" Maria asked, regarding the game pieces spilling out onto the board from a velvet bag. "They're beautiful!" she exclaimed.

"Carved marble," the governor said. "I'd give you one, but that would break up the set. It's a game called *esches*." He rose from his chair and stepped toward the *vargueno*. "Don't you know it?" he asked, speaking directly to Maria, ignoring completely the presence of Tula in the room.

"I've seen the board and my father and uncles use it with men, castles, and horses, but not with pieces like this. Only men play," she said. "My brother has been taught the rules, but not me or my sisters. Is it like draughts?" she asked in reference to a game she believed was also played on a board with colored squares.

"Well, the board's the same, but there the similarity ends," the governor replied. "It's nothing like checkers," he laughed. "It's a royal game, one we learned from the Moors." He said the game was associated with wealth, knowledge, and power. "The board represents a battlefield in which two armies fight to capture each other's king. Let me show you." He returned to the table with the pieces and a campaign board made of soft leather. "I'll teach you how to play."

"I'd like to learn, your Grace, but we have little time before our mother is through with her confession."

"Well, then, I'll teach you the rules and when you have more time, you may come back, and we'll play. I may even let you beat me!" he laughed.

"I'll stay to learn the rules, your Grace. But your letting me win would give me no pleasure. If I beat you," she said proudly, while smiling at Tula, "it will be because I played better than you."

"Well, that squares and corners with me," he laughed. "I think I've found an able adversary!"

16

A Fit of Pique

1637: SOMETIME DURING THE FIRST YEAR OF ROSAS'S GOVERNORSHIP

Rosas stood in his *obraje*, a cheerless workshop he had taken from Governor Martinez where captured Apaches worked side-by-side with orphans and levies of Pueblo Indian laborers. Dark and dirty, the *obraje* had bare walls, no windows, and contained a weapons store for shield and *harquebus*, plus space for trade. "Can't they work any faster?" he asked his foreman regarding the Indians, some of whom were working on their hide and textile paintings and others at their looms.

"No, your Lordship! As the quantity goes up, the quality goes down. One has to make a determination as to which is preferred."

"Why can't we have both?" Rosas asked in exasperation. "It seems we should be able to have both!" he said emphatically.

"I've not been able to make it happen, your Lordship. It just doesn't seem possible."

"Well, then, perhaps we need another foreman. You can't blame the packsaddle for the ass."

"Or the ass for packsaddle," his foreman retorted.

"Are you getting smart with me?" the governor asked.

"No, your Lordship. I was merely trying to explain . . ."

"I don't want explanations or excuses, damn it! I want more *mantas* and hangings! See to it, or I'll have you replaced!"

Following the angry exchange with his foreman, the governor, who was accompanied by several of his men, made the short walk to the *Hermita* where Mass was already in progress.

The governor and his men noisily elbowed their way past a number of Indian men who occupied the low-ceilinged space beneath the choir loft at the rear of the church. They stormed up a passageway left free among the kneeling congregation until the governor reached his platform-placed canopied chair. His seat, an armchair of fine wood upholstered in crimson velvet with galloon and fringe affixed by nails of gilt metal, had for its seating, a red cushion with tassels at the corner.[1] Placing his hands in his lap, the governor reviewed the crowd expectantly while the good father waited on the bottom stair of a high rostrum for the noise to subside.

On this, the feast of St. Mark, New Mexico's former prelate, Antonio de Artega, ascended to the pulpit, a well-constructed wooden ambo set on the epistle side of the altar, where he began a sermon explaining that in all matters, civil and religious, the authority of the Church and of the pope were supreme. And since Catholic monarchs were children of the Church before all else, they were subject to ecclesiastical laws.

"Anyone challenging these laws is a heretic," Artega said.[2]

As Artega droned on and on about a subject with which Rosas completely disagreed, the governor spoke out loud to one of his aides who was standing behind his chair.

"Get me something to write on," he said in a stage whisper. "I want to send him a message." He pointed to Fray Artega with the tip of his tongue. Although the governor's communications were often set in ciphers and secret language, he wrote, quite pointedly: "No one wants to hear that, Father. Perhaps you should move on to a more pleasant topic."

Glancing briefly at the governor's note, Fray Artega threw it to the floor of the altar and continued on as before, speaking of lies, parsimony, and greed.

When the governor's suggestion was brushed aside, he shocked the parishioners by noisily jangling the coins he had brought for his donation. At this irreverent interruption, Fray Artega turned to him.

"What are you doing?" he asked. "Don't you know you're in God's house?"

At this, the governor rose from his chair and in a tone which suggested that he had intended to provoke this very response, said, "I'm trying to determine whether I should give these to you or use them for some more entertaining purpose."

Flushed with anger at the impiety of the governor's words, Artega demanded, "Please place them in the basket and leave the altar," at which the governor smiled and sat down.

Rosas then asked his aide for more paper and, as Fray Artega continued with his sermon, he composed a second note. "Do you not think that we have had quite enough?"

Ignoring the governor's scribbled question, Fray Artega, who had noted the governor's continual refusal of the Eucharist and his mocking statements regarding the other sacraments, continued his stinging rebuke. He suggested that one who behaved in such a manner must be a Lutheran, a heretic, or a Jew.

On hearing this, the governor became furious. He stood up, turned his back to the altar and shouted, "Shut up, Father! What you say is a lie!" Then, followed by his retinue of soldiers, he stormed out of the church, raging, "I represent the king, and the king is everything!"[3]

Stunned by this display, the worshippers who had witnessed this first salvo between the governor and the clerics left the *Hermita* in a daze, knowing they were in for trouble.

17

The Hapless Fray Antonio Jimenez

IN THE FALL OF 1638

"Ask him to pull his *carreta* into the patio," the governor said to his servant in reference to the armorer, Captain Gaspar Perez[1] who had just entered the courtyard through the palace's double gate. "I'll meet him there," he said starting down the corridor and into its enormous plaza whose bordering structures were three and four stories high.

"Have you finished them already?" the governor asked, as he walked briskly toward the small cart.

"I have," Perez responded proudly, "and they're some of the best I've made. Would you like to see them?" he asked, as he threw back the canvas. Beneath the cover were several open crates crammed with *belduques*, or trade knives. Modeled after the European peasant knife, these so-called "broad knives" were long, stiletto-like implements with bone handles. "They still need their sheaths," Gaspar said, "but we can have those made in a matter of days. Each one will have its own leather casing, fringed just the way the Indians like them."

"Oh, these are fine!" Rosas said appreciatively. "In fact, I think I'll keep this one." He indicated the bone-handled blade he held in his hand.

"You may, if you wish," Perez said, "but I can make you a better one, Governor. One with better steel and a brass boss."

"And the steel for these?" the governor asked. "Where did it come from?"

"From everything imaginable," Gaspar laughed. "Pots and pans. Griddles and shovels, scythes, and sickles. The latter are the best, of course, because it takes little effort to fashion a blade, but the secret is in the balance," he said as he took one of the knives from the box. "A well-fashioned blade made from a griddle or a hoe may be equally good. But the handle and blade, affixed with resin, beeswax, and a bit of sawdust, must be in perfect balance. Otherwise, you might as well be cutting with a stone. These are almost perfect," he said as he tested the heft of the one he held in his hand. "They've cost us nothing to make, but are worth a small fortune."

"They're perfect," Rosas said again. "Where did you learn your trade?" he asked Gaspar.

"In Flanders," Gaspar responded. "In Brussels, of which I'm a native. I learned my trade from my father and he from his. From horseshoes to armor, we've made it all," he said proudly.

"I was afraid we wouldn't have them ready for this year," Rosas responded, "but now that they're here, we can go to Pecos."

"As you wish," Perez responded with a shrug, silently questioning the wisdom of going to the trading grounds so close to the end of the season.

"Well, they do no good in my warehouse," Rosas responded, "and time is getting short."

* * *

As Governor Rosas and his entourage dropped down out of the mountains and viewed the broad valley before them, they were met by an incredible sight: Indians, many hundreds of the Apache nation leaving the pueblo of the Pecos after their annual visit. Some had been camped without cover under the eaves of the pueblo, while others had wintered nearby. Still many hundreds of others had, since August, been sheltered in tipis or tents made of tanned bison skins. They had camped in the open valley that spread out to the east. The mass was now on the move, their travois-saddled dogs and the few Indian ponies they had recently acquired, laden with the bounty of their trade. They formed long thin lines moving at trot-speed across the landscape.

"We can't waste any time," said the governor to Perez. "Have the inside chiefs meet me below the wall. And tell them to hurry."

Six Indians, representatives of the displaced warriors at the pueblo, were brought down to where Rosas had his cart. They were annoyed that they had been summoned, but interested, also, to hear what the governor had to say.

"I have a gift for each of you," Rosas said uncovering one of several boxes containing the Perez trade knives. "A knife and a proposition. Take these knives to the fields beyond the wall and trade them to the Apaches for slaves and pelts," he said to these men who exercised wide-ranging authority over all matters Indian. "If you do this, and are more successful than I would be if I were conducting the trade, I'll allow you to chose your own war captains as you did before the arrival of the priests." He hoped that by gifting the pueblo leaders, he would gain their loyalty and benefit from their labor. "But you have little time to make your decision," he stated emphatically. "I must have your word now!"

"We'll do this," said one of the chiefs, "but the *Vaquero* Apaches are leaving and may have nothing left to trade."

"There's time," Rosas said. "Perez," he bellowed. "You drive the cart!"

* * *

Seeing the governor's small cart being driven out onto the plains, some of the Indians stopped and returned to see what was being offered. They wanted the knives, but they had nothing further to trade. Rosas was furious!

"That son-of-a-bitch!" bellowed Rosas, regarding the Pecos guardian, Fray Antonio de Ibargaray. "How dare he allow the goddamned Indians to trade off everything they had before I arrived?" he bellowed.

"Did he know you were coming, Governor?" Gaspar asked.

"I told him I'd be back, goddamn it! Meet me at the *convento*," he yelled as he remounted his horse.

Leaving his men to eat his dust, the governor tore across the landscape. He rode wildly up the long slope of the pueblo's extensive trash mounds, over the wall of the *convento's* kitchen garden, trampling the leaves of fragile plants beneath the hooves of his mount. He dismounted, looped the reins of his horse around a brush-covered hitching post, or *ramada*, and began pounding furiously on the *convento* door.

"Where is he?" he yelled to the porter who answered his knock.

"Who, your Lordship? the *portero* asked.

"Who the hell do you think I mean, you stupid son-of-a-bitch? Ibargaray!" screamed the governor. "Where is he?"

"In the church saying Mass, your Lordship," answered the Indian neophyte.

"Well, tell him to get his ass over here!" the governor bellowed. "Over here right now! And tell him that if he's not here in five minutes, I'll go over there and drag his ass off the altar."

Told of the profane and insolent manner in which the governor had spoken, Fray Ibargaray left the altar and returned to the *convento* where a raging Luis de Rosas confronted him.

"Why did you let the Indians start without me?" he screamed.

"I didn't know you were coming, your Lordship."

"Didn't know I was coming? Then what did you think I meant when I told you that I'd be back? Or does that mean something different in Euskara?"

Ibargaray, who was not about to succumb to the governor's bullying, responded haughtily, "You didn't say when!"

"Well, you must be a stupid son-of-a-bitch!" the governor bellowed. "Did you think I was talking about next year? Goddamn it!"

The governor's men, who had followed on his heels, and were now standing in the porter's lodge or reception area, looked at one another in astonishment, appalled by the manner in which the governor was speaking to the priest and wondering what would follow. The governor stood looking at Fray Ibargaray, his eyes dark with anger. Then, in complete contrast to the enraged behavior he had just exhibited, he calmly stated, "I'm here on the king's business, and you have purposely impeded my work. You'll be put under arrest."

"But I can't leave," Ibargaray said. "The Blessed Sacrament is exposed."

"Then return to the church and consume it," the governor said, railing at this impediment being placed his path.

I can't," said Fray Ibargaray. "I've eaten and have broken the fast. I cannot consume the Host, nor can I go with you."

"What a bunch of shit," the governor bellowed, his face red with anger. "You'll come with me, or you'll pay dearly!"

Just then, the guardian's *companero*, or assistant, Fray Antonio Jimenez, the ancient lay brother who had been lurking in the background, came to the guardian's defense. Jimenez, made grotesque by a chronic case of conjunctivitis marked by a purulent discharge that often sealed his eyes, said, "Please do not speak to the guardian in that manner. What he says is true!"

"Seize him!" the governor bellowed. "Tie him to a horse! He'll go to the *villa* as my prisoner in the Father's place."

"But he's an old man, your Lordship, sick and unable to make the ride," Fray Ibargaray said regarding Jimenez who had begun to crumple and sag, as if emptied of life.

"Then take him and lock him in my storeroom," the governor said to his men, referring to the part of the *convento* he had taken from Martinez. "Keep him there under guard until the good father obeys my orders. He may then exchange his own freedom for that of the old man." He moved toward the door.

Father Ibargaray followed the governor to the door. "You're forbidden by the canons to confine one sanctified by the Church," he shouted after Rosas who had exited through the *convento* door. "I'm certain that before you've mounted your horse, you will have given orders for his freedom!"

Governor Rosas, who had thrown the skirt of his cape over his shoulders in preparation for mounting his horse, hesitated a moment, his left hand on the pommel of his saddle. He then took his foot out of the stirrup, and walked back slowly to the *convento*, where in the open doorway, he faced the priest. "The only cannons of importance," he said with deliberateness, "are those which I have—powerful, dangerous, and incredibly destructive, Father. You and your mission may yet experience them."

The governor's mount faltered in the darkness as he galloped off.

The news of the Jimenez imprisonment reached Santa Fe almost before the governor returned.

* * *

"What are you telling me?" asked Fray Domingo del Espiritu Santo of the soldier who had appeared at the door of the *convento* in Santa Fe.

"The governor," the soldier said in a whispered tone. "The governor has Fray Jimenez locked in a storeroom at Pecos guarded by four of his men. He's waiting to exchange the brother's imprisonment for that of Fray Ibargaray!"

"Can this be true?" the father asked incredulously, his eyes flashing.

"It's true, Father, but you must tell no one who gave you this news."

Without further discussion, the tall, well-built, Fray Domingo, who was a guest at the Santa Fe *convento*, reentered the priests' home, where he rummaged among the ecclesiastical accouterments that Fray Vidania had heaped within a trunk. Taking an altar cloth from among the many articles he found there, he placed several items within its folds, tied his articles into a small bundle, and walked to the *Hermita*. There, he stood at the altar placing before him a Mass book, a bell, and four candles which he lit from a taper he drew from the altar. His brow wrinkled in concentration, Fray Domingo first read the sentence of excommunication, then rang the bell four distinct times, symbolically announcing the excommunicants' "death." Finally, he blew out the candles, "snuffing out" the sinners who were now out of communion with the faithful. "*Vitand!*" he thundered in the vacant church. "The soldiers at Pecos are to be shunned until Fray Jimenez is released."

18

The Evil Counsel and Counselor

The governor strained, hoping to complete his duty before riding over to the home of the Casaus, but nothing happened. He cursed the malady that continued to plague him. Taking a deep lungful of air and holding it, he strained again only to be interrupted by a knock on the door.

"Don Luis!" his servant murmured, "your bath has been poured. All but the last pail. Do you want me to do that now?" he asked.

"No! Wait until I'm ready," said the governor with a degree of annoyance in his voice. "I'll tell you when I'm ready."

His attendant did not answer, but the governor could tell by the silence that he had left the hallway. The governor then returned to the task at hand.

Taking another deep breath and holding it for a long moment, he pushed. Strained. Held it, then strained again, only to receive another knock at the door. He had not heard the servant coming. Had he been there all the time? Lurking in the hallway? Listening?

"Don Luis," his chamberlain asked, "will you be needing your carriage?"

"Goddamn it!" the governor shouted. "Will you leave me alone? Leave me in peace! I'll tell you what I need when I call you to dump the pot!" he said regarding the handsome Sevillian chamber pot above which he sat.

His servant hesitated. Should he ask the governor about his horse? His clothes? A gift of wine or cheese, perhaps, for Captain don Roque de Casaus whose dinner invitation the governor was considering. The governor's orderly waited and then continued down the hallway. Stopped. And then returned to the door behind which the governor sat.

"Don Luis . . . "

"Goddamn it! Get out of here, or I'll have you garroted! I don't want to hear anymore from you!" the governor bellowed from behind his locked door.

Exhaling a mournful sigh, the servant walked down the hallway and through the open patio, returning to the kitchen. While he readied the governor's last pail of water, he contemplated the beating he would probably receive.

As the governor sat on his commode, straining, he contemplated the makeup of his two-seat box and thought about the invitation he had received from don Roque. He wondered about this man, don Roque Medon de Casaus, former treasurer of the *Santa Cruzada*, who had warned him of the impending arrest of the former governor, Martinez. He had more recently appeared without invitation in his study one night with his wife, a thin, matronly, Isabel de Lujan. They've probably got a daughter they want me to meet, he thought, a skinny, pockmarked daughter whose cranial hair will only be matched by that on her upper lip. He laughed to himself, thinking, This is not getting the job done.

* * *

His duty and job successfully completed, the governor rode over to the home of the Casaus, a site with a clear, spring-fed stream and a broad meadow that lay northeast of the plaza. The governor was seated in the splendor of his host's *gran sala*, a central chamber, lacking a bolt run, but connected by hallways to numerous other rooms. Gracing the perimeter of this room was an incredible array of furniture and equipment that included boxes, stools, and benches, but especially chests. The latter were all shapes and sizes, decorated in paint, ironwork, chip carving, marquetry, and inlay. There was, also, an enormous cache of travel chests, made of reed or wicker framework covered with rawhide, the materials of an itinerant merchant.

Sitting there with don Roque de Casaus, the governor nursed his second glass of wine, brought with difficulty and at great expense by the train of missionary supply. He steeled himself, expecting that dona Isabel would at any moment usher in another dinner guest, but there was none.

A crew of *genizaro* (detribalized Indian) servants waited to set out the dinner pheasant. Dona Isabel announced dinner by ringing a small glass bell that sat on the table. Then she rang it a second time, requesting that dinner be served, and smiled thinly at the governor.

Putting on airs, the governor thought, as he returned her smile.

At the ringing of the first bell, don Roque, whose tiny eyes were shaded by overhanging skin giving him an almost blind look, suggested that they move to the table. "I first came north from Mexico City as a soldier in the wagon-train escort of sixteen twenty-five," he stated, continuing a conversation in which he and the governor had been involved. "Brought Isabel and the children with me with the intention of establishing our home in the new settlement of *La Nuestra Senora de Piedad de Cerralbo.* However, four years later, I became the leader of another escort that reached Santa Fe. I sent back for my family as soon as I was able, and we've been here ever since."

"Eight years?" the governor asked.

"Give or take a month or two," don Roque responded.

"Then you know Gomez . . . and Lucero . . . and Baca?" the governor asked as they took their seats at the table.

"I know everyone in the colony," Casaus responded. "There are not many of us, and I bring the things they need on my wagons."

"What do you know of this Baca?" the governor asked Casaus who, like himself, he now knew to be an outsider. "I find him to be a royal pain in the ass." He looked at dona Isabel then, apologized for his choice of words and received a small gesture of the acceptance of his apology in return.

Don Roque, whose narrow, pointed nose, wedge-shaped head, and tiny ears looked grotesque in the candlelight, glanced at his wife and smiled and shrugged his shoulders. "He is," he said. "A royal pain in the ass, I mean. But I've learned to ignore him," he said to the governor.

"Well, I can't ignore him," the governor said. "He is, after all, the senior judge. A constant presence. Whatever business I have with the *cabildo*, he's there to annoy me!"

"Well, I can only tell you what's worked for me," don Roque responded. "He is from an illustrious family, Governor, and whether the spelling of his name is Baca or Vaca is irrelevant. He came to New Mexico with his father, Cristobal Vaca, a captain with Onate, and is the grandson of Juan de Vaca who may have been with Vasquez de Coronado."

"And I suppose he's related to Nunez Cabeza de Vaca too?" the governor asked mockingly.

"Well, to his credit, he's never made that claim, Governor," Casaus responded, "although he may have allowed others to make it for him."

"And if he is . . . if he is a descendant of Alvar Nunez . . . I find no major credit in that," the governor continued. "Nunez, as the shipwrecked treasurer of the Pamfilo de Narvaez expedition, might have been the first to cross the continent from east to west, but in his eight years of travel, he didn't know where he was, he didn't know where he was going, and he didn't know where he'd been when he got back! He may have discovered the Pecos, but he didn't discover the Great River and probably never even touched New Mexico!"

"Perhaps not, Governor," Casaus responded, "but it was Nunez's account of his wanderings that stimulated interior exploration. And as a castaway, a slave, a trader, and a medicine man, he showed such courage and determination to survive that he is an exemplar for all Spaniards. But as for Nunez having don Antonio as a descendant?" he said with a shrug, "I don't know. They may have had a common grandparent at some point in their lineage, but it's unlikely that Baca is a direct descendant, since Nunez, who was later appointed governor of the *Rio de la Plata* area in South America, never settled in either New Spain or New Mexico.

"From Martin Alhaja to *Cabeza de Vaca*," laughed Casaus, regarding Antonio's complete surname. "Head of a Cow! It's an odd appellation, isn't it?" he continued. "An odd name to be chosen by one ennobled. And, thus, we have the Vacas, or Bacas, as Antonio has it, formerly simple peasants who can now boast among their ancestors the likes of Alvar Nunez[1] and Pero Fernandez Cabeza de Vaca who was grand master of the Order of the Knights of *Sant' Iago*. There are many other *Cabeza de Vacas* as well who've held high and important positions and whose names have been placed on the roster of Spanish nobility."

"Martin Alhaja?" said the governor with a sneer. "It sounds like an Arabic name."

"It probably is," Casaus responded. "Perhaps the name of a *Mozarabe* family—a Christian family living among the Moors. Antonio's father, Cristobal, a captain among the Onate forces, was, like Francisco Gomez and myself, a leader of the wagon escort and functioned as syndic for the Franciscans. I respect the accomplishments of this family but have chosen to ignore don Antonio and the other members of his clan as the best way of dealing with them. They hate to be ignored and will eventually come to you," Casaus said, while fingering the stem of his glass. "And that's what I'm offering you, your Lordship, a means by which to ignore Baca and the rest of the *cabildo*." He explained that this was the purpose for their meeting. "May I speak openly?" he asked the governor.

"Go on."

"I have no ties here beyond those of my immediate family, your Lordship, and I must make my own way," he said deliberately. "What I want to ask you is to let me become your aide," Casaus said. "To provide you with eyes and ears in the workings of the colony and our town council of which I'm an *alcalde*. The members of the council drink from the same cup. Sleep in the same bed. Share secrets, your Lordship. Secrets such as those I was privy to regarding Martinez's arrest. And so it can be regarding everything," he said. "What I know, you can know. Our plans. Our strengths. Our weaknesses. Everything."

"And what are you asking in return?" the governor queried, glancing at dona Isabel, and wondering about the advisability of having this conversation in her presence. "I've learned that alms, although given freely, are most often offered as an investment," the governor said, taking a sip of wine from his glass. "What do you want?" he repeated.

"I would expect no payment for the information or assistance I provide, your Lordship. I'd only ask that I be protected in my work at the pueblos and that I be afforded access to trade."

"Preferred access?" queried the governor.

"Yes," responded don Roque, "and you may be assured that the *senora* would say nothing to anyone regarding any of this. She understands our place here among the other colonists and what we must do to exploit it. I'm a merchant and I have no loyalties to anyone besides my family," he repeated. "My only responsibility is to them and now to you," he said very deliberately. "You could, with my assistance, ignore the council," he explained. "What I'm offering is to be your man."

"And what would our arrangement be?" the governor asked.

"I'd work from the inside, Governor. Operate as a spy, as it were. Live underground until I was discovered. For discovered I would eventually be."

"And I would deny our relationship."

"Until it could not be denied any further," continued Casaus.

The governor pressed his fingers to his lips, considering. He thought of what Casaus had said regarding Baca and the other members of the *cabildo* and of the potential relationships dona Isabel might have among the wives of the royal *villa*. They probably know as much regarding the life of the colony, as do their men, he thought. The governor waited a long moment before responding. "You're asking for a lot," he said. "Asking for privileges second only to my own."

"Yes, your Lordship. But if we're lucky, and if we do our work well, it may be many years before you'll have to extend them."

Rosas looked at him for a brief moment and thought, This is true. I may never have to completely pay this debt. He said, "And what would we require by way of a contract, since nothing about this can be committed to script?"

"Our word only," Casaus responded. "Our contract would be our word."

Rosas waited still further, looking at dona Isabel and then at her husband and saying finally, "You may from this moment operate with impunity in your conduct of trade at Taos and at Picuris, be given every courtesy and remain free from punishment, penalty, or harm until our arrangement becomes known. I'll then give you preferred access to trade at those pueblos, but Pecos will remain mine. So be it?" he asked.

"So be it," Casaus responded.

As the governor rode off that evening, he realized that Casaus had made it possible for him to move even closer to his two main objectives for being in New Mexico: to place civil government and secular authority on a superior footing to religious authority within the colony, and to profit from his governorship. His orders were to put the foundering colony on a more secure footing and to consolidate the natives into fewer and larger towns. He was also instructed to encourage further colonization by the apportionment of land but to squelch further exploration unless led by himself. And, of course, he was charged with defending New Mexico against its enemies. He didn't need Baca to accomplish any of these aims. He would have to watch this merchant, Casaus, but Baca and the rest of the *cabildo* should no longer be a problem.

In this, too, Rosas began to establish a pattern in his governance of the colony. He chose to rely on those who did not belong to the spider web of New Mexican families, and to seek out those who had not been given *encomiendas*. He made it his mission to find those who had nothing to lose and who might seek to profit from their association with the governor. In this manner he hoped to divide and conquer.

19

The Ladies of the Altar Society

She sat there, very tall and stately, surveying the room. Fair and with extremely delicate skin, she gave the appearance of one who had experienced neither sun nor wind. She wore her white hair in braids coiled up like a crown around her head. A quilted, linen nightcap concealing the braids protected her head from the air, and her forehead was bound with a strip of black taffeta. Her pale countenance resulted from a week's bleaching achieved by wearing a face covering of white cascara, made from finely ground eggshells that had been dried in her outdoor oven and mixed with soaked rice and the nuts of melon seeds. The white of this so-called *"albayalde"* (a former cosmetic containing white lead) had then been applied to her face and neck with the tips of her fingers, resulting in a skin tone of an ashen hue set off by the red of carmine she had applied to her cheeks. She was Catalina Perez de Bustillo,[1] and she was an oddity even among the other women of the altar society whose own face bleaching was achieved by a mask made of bran and the crushed red spikes of the *Algeria* plant.

Plagued by numerous maladies, she had her servants grind roots and herbs into a paste, which she rubbed into her temples and the back of her head to cure her continuous headaches. These, she said, were caused by *aire en la cabeza* (air in the head). She slept in a room without windows, insisting that if she did not do so, she could feel the air swirling in the corners. And when not occupied with her cosmetics, remedies, or crocheting, she was involved with things of the Church.

She liked to think of herself as the founder of the group she surveyed, and perhaps she was. But many had been in it from the beginning, as had she. In fact, one would have been hard pressed to identify the beginnings of the altar society since had not the women of the colony been repairing altar cloths and vestments since the time of Onate? Still, she looked with an air of majesty, at the other women: her sisters, Ana,[2] Beatriz,[3] and Yumar Perez de Bustillo,[4] and her sisters-in-law, Gregoria de Archuleta[5] and Juana de Zamora.[6] We are the leaders of the colony, she thought of the small group, the wives or widows of the most prominent men in the kingdom. It was rare that they should all come together like this, rarer, even, that Petronila de Zamora [7] (wife of the *Maese de campo*), and Ana Robledo[8] (wife of the colony's most prominent soldier), would be among them. They were the ladies of a group officially known as the Confraternity of the Immaculate Conception, a lay organization to which practically all citizens of the colony belonged. The elder Perez de Bustillos, as the members of the core group, always arrived at the *convento* first to assure themselves of a "place at the table" where they worked on the Church's most important religious paraphernalia.

The rest of the ladies of the altar society, the women of the second tier, as it were (many of whom were the daughters and nieces of those at the table), sat on blankets or cushions in the middle of the floor. They usually worked on items of similar importance to those of their elders, but their articles could be conveniently held in their laps. Catalina smiled at her namesake niece, Catalina Perez de Bustillo,[9] the daughter of her brother Simon, and at the other women of the second tier, Catalina's sisters, Juliana[10] and Maria, and her other nieces, Isabel Santa Cruz,[11] Maria de Archuleta,[12] and Geronima Ruiz de Hinojos.[13] The rest of the village wives, if they came, would comprise the women of the third tier. They would sit on low cushions or *colchons*, folded mattresses placed around the walls, their sewing pillows held securely in their laps. Each knew her place and sat accordingly.

That woman sitting with Bernardina Vasquez[14] and Ana Holguin,[15] Catalina asked herself as she surveyed the room, is that Isabel de Lujan? Although her husband is an *alcalde*, he is, also, nothing but a merchant, an outsider, for God's sake! What's she doing here? We're the ones who pay the dues, provide the gifts, and donate the skins, hides, and livestock that pay for our activities. The women of the third tier, including the mousy dona Isabel, her hair pulled back tightly from her face, smiled back at her, deferring to this great lady who was, for many of the attendees, the colony's doyenne.

Arrayed around the perimeter of the large table were altar cloths and vestments, albs and almices, corporals, stoles and veils. Some of these were in need of washing and ironing. But that was not the job of those in the altar society; their assignment was only to embroider or repair. Some of the articles had been brought from the colony's outlying *conventos*, but most were from the ecclesiastical capital of Santo Domingo and from the *Hermita de San Miguel*, which was functioning as the *Parroquia de Santa Fe* until the Church and *Convento* of *La Asuncion* could be completed.

Placed in the center of the table among the priests' vestments and altar cloths was a small, wooden statue about a yard high of a beautiful woman standing on a pedestal and on a cloud out of which peered the chubby faces of three happy cherubs. The statue of Our Lady of the Assumption, which would later become known to the colonists as *La Conquistadora* (Our Lady of the Conquest), had been brought to the colony by Fray Alonso Benavides in 1625 and was the religious object by which the members of the colony defined themselves. Ancient, and certainly the oldest representation of the Blessed Virgin in the northern hemisphere, it had come into the care of Ana Robledo, whose husband, Francisco Gomez, had escorted Fray Benavides to the kingdom.

The daughter and granddaughter of first colonists, Bartolome Romero and Pedro Robledo, Ana Robledo had made care of the Virgin her primary responsibility. One aspect of her devotion was to mend or to make the clothing in which the statue would be dressed. Small, delicate-looking, and 37-years-old, Ana sat quietly at the table, her blue eyes examining closely all aspects of the statue's surface. The statue's carved, golden arabesque robes were those of a Semitic princess, but over these, the Virgin wore her traditional dress (or, on occasion, the graceful regal tunics and mantles of a medieval Spanish queen). Laid out before Ana were some of the Virgin's dresses. The statue also had over 30 pieces of jewelry, but Ana ignored these as she picked out the dress on which she would work. Having chosen her article, Ana looked up at Catalina Perez's sister, Yumar, who was describing the ordeal she had recently endured at Santo Domingo.[16]

"What an embarrassment, having to testify before a notary like that!" Yumar said, referring to the testimony she had been required to give in a trial of bigamy. "Made me wish I'd never gone near San Felipe. I tried to persuade Antonio to get me out of it, to make it possible for me not to testify, but either he was unable to do so or just didn't care. I don't know which," she said her face screwed up in annoyance.

"What were you doing in San Felipe?" asked the elder Catalina Perez de Bustillo who was scandalized by it all.

"Antonio and I were there for a christening," she responded. "I only remained in the church after the service was over because I'd been told that the baptism would be followed by a wedding. I just wanted to see who the fools were who were marrying on that day. For, as they say, 'Only fools marry in May,' " she laughed, repeating an old saw. "I just wanted to see their clothes, for God's sake! How could I know that the marriage I was to witness would be bigamous, or that I'd have to testify to having seen it performed? The Inquisitor read me the testimony of Captain Tome Dominguez regarding Juan Anton. Testimony taken at Quarai almost two years ago. Captain Dominguez testified that he'd been traveling between New Mexico and Mexico City the previous summer when at Cuencame, he learned by chance that Juan Anton had a wife there . . . a woman who worked at the inn where Dominguez had stopped. The inquisitors asked if I could witness his statement, which of course I could not, as his testimony had been given at Quarai. But what I could testify to was having watched the *mulatto*, Juan Anton, marry a Mexican Indian woman by the name of Ana Maria. And they were dressed very nicely, I must say. I only remember her name because it was the same as that of one of my servants. Oh, these priests!" she continued in complaint. "Sometimes I can't stand them. That Father Perea! Oh, my God! I had to go to confession to him because there was no one else there." Her face contorted in chagrin. "I told him that Antonio and I had been doing some things that I liked, but which made me a bit uncomfortable because I didn't know whether they were a sin."

"What sort of things?" Catalina asked her sister to the laughter of many in the room.

"Things! You know . . . things!" she said with the shrug of her shoulders. "I'm not going to tell you!" she stated emphatically. "Just things! They must be sins because I like them so much." More laughter.

"What did you tell him?"

"I told him some of the things," she said with another shrug.

"But how did you know what to say?" Catalina asked.

"He kept pressing me for the details."

"And what did you tell him?" asked Catalina through her laughter.

"I wasn't going to tell him the details about the real things, so I made a lot of it up!" Yumar said.

"You did not!"

"I did," she said, now through her own laughter.

"How did you know what to say?" asked her sister again.

"I have a good imagination," Yumar responded.

"And the things you made up," her sister asked incredulously. "Did you tell him the details?"

"I did, but I think he knew I was lying."

"Why do you say that?" asked Catalina, now fully attentive to Yumar's confession.

"Because of the penance he gave me," she said, nearly choking on her words. "He said, 'Say three rosaries and then three Our Fathers and three Hail Marys, but say the last one backwards.'"

The room was now in an uproar. Baskets rolling off the table and onto the floor. Fingers being pricked by errant pins. The group struggling to find the means by which to continue. Finally, one of the other ladies offered her own take on the priests, specifically on the tyrannical Father Isidro Ordonez.

"God, these priests!" said Ana Perez de Bustillo, widow of Asencio de Arechuleta. "Do you remember Father Ordonez? Do you remember the fracas he and the governor got into when the governor went to the *convento* to arrest him?" she asked the group, but specifically Ana Robledo. "Your father was with him," she said to Ana, speaking of Bartolome Romero, who was one of the men who had accompanied Governor Peralta to the priests' house. "Your mama—along with the rest of us—was crying because she was afraid that Father Ordonez would excommunicate your papa and the other men in the governor's escort. We had just gone into the church," she said referring to the women who had been with her on that fateful day. "We were just standing there," she again directed herself to Ana, "your mama crying, when Father Ordonez came in. He went right up to her and shouted, 'Shut Up!' Oh, my God! I thought I'd die" she exclaimed. "I nearly wet myself! Even Father Perez was appalled. Never had anyone heard a priest speak like that. And in God's house! And to your mama, for God's sake! She was like a saint."[17]

Ana was quiet for a bit, saying finally, "Oh, I remember. I was seventeen and that was almost twenty years ago, but the words and the way he spoke to my mama. I can still hear him. I couldn't believe that anyone could speak to my mama like that. It almost made me lose my faith in the Church. But then I came to see that these priests are just men. Many of them have no vocation. Some of them live with women, women whom Francisco refers to as the 'devil's mules.'"

"And what of their poverty?" Yumar asked, while picking up another vestment from the table. "It's supposed to be their 'first rule.' Complete poverty. Not only for the individual priests, but for the Order as well. I don't see it," she exclaimed. "They have enormous tracts of land, granaries filled with corn and wheat, and some of our largest flocks. *Conventos* all over the kingdom! And look at these vestments," she stated contemptuously, displaying the richness of the one she held in her hands. "And their paintings. And the things they place on their altars! They have everything!

"The governors, too," she continued, speaking to the other women regarding their domination by Spanish authority. "Most do what they want. Take what they want. Beat us to our knees! Look at Governor Rosas," she added, while looking around the room. "He even took for his own benefit the mule we were given to pay for our celebrations," she said in dismay. "I don't know," she said again, shaking her head. "I don't know why we have them . . . the governors or the priests."

A collective sigh, then. And all stood, the way their parents and grandparents had taught them, as *Custos* Salas entered the room.

20

Disease, Drought and Devastation

"I told them it was a mistake," don Simon said to his son, Nicolas, in anger. "Told those goddamned priests it was a mistake to invite the *Vaquero* Apaches into the *villa*, even if they had asked to see the statue of Our Lady. Goddamn them!" he said regarding the priests as he and his son, Nicolas, saddled their horses for their ride up the canyon to the home of Simon's nephew, Francisco de Anaya II. There, the Perez de Bustillo men had been told, a group of *Vaquero* Apaches awaited them.

"Of course, they're interested," he said to Nicolas. "Entranced, even. Who wouldn't be? Seeing her at night accompanied by a choir and surrounded by candles. Who wouldn't be fascinated?" he asked again as they lifted themselves into their saddles. "But do the priests think that it's only Our Lady that intrigues them?" he asked. "What about our defenses or the food we gave them? And not just the food we gave them here, but also what we gave them to take back to their people? Now, when the Pueblos have a barren year and they have no surplus to trade, the *Vaqueros* come here for a handout and to see what they might steal. I don't know," he said with a shrug, "those priests don't seem to understand that if these enemies are not kept at bay, they may yet overwhelm us."

As they dismounted, don Simon checked the pistol he carried in his belt, while his son, Nicolas, did the same. They did not draw them, nor did they take their *harquebuses* that remained sheathed in their horse bound scabbards.

Standing outside the Anaya corral with a number of other

Perez relatives were a *Vaquero* captain and eight or nine other Indians. Caddoan-speaking people, they came from three tipis of a *rancheria* located on the plains to the east. The *rancheria* encompassed eleven tipis containing perhaps 20 families. All of this was communicated by signs and by the few Spanish words the Indians knew which resulted in considerable confusion.

The group, which was led by a couple of older men, also contained five women and several children, two of whom were young adolescent males. The older males wore protective leather coats, known as *cueros*, and carried large leather shields and lances. The younger males, who were naked from the waist up, carried a bow in one hand and either a sword or a war club in the other. Their arrows, except for a single one that was affixed to the strings of their bows, were carried in a quiver on their backs. They were variously dressed in clothing fashioned from bison skins. The men, whose faces were painted with red ochre or other earths, had eyes that were highlighted with vermilion. They wore much adornment especially in their hair, which was braided and intertwined with imitation gold buttons, colored glass beads, ribbons, and whatever else they had obtained that glittered. The women, in contrast, appeared slovenly. Their hair was cut short which was, among this group, a sign of slavery and abjection. The women held back and allowed their men to conduct the trade. Those who spoke for the group seemed to be having difficulty keeping their stories straight. They had come from the *Cerro de las Gallinas*, they said, beyond the Sandias, or, alternatively, from the *Cerro de las Ceballos*, or from someplace else. They had come to warn the settlers of an attack, one said. No, said another, they were there peacefully, seeking food. They were eating the little cones of raw sugar (known as *piloncillo*) that had been given them by the Spanish men who eyed them suspiciously. The Indians wanted *maize* or other agricultural products but had essentially nothing to trade. Their harvest, they said, from what little they had planted, had been subjected to a drought during the previous season and a plague of worms that had ravaged their crops. They held their weaponry slack, looked at the settlers who stood in the mud before the horse corral, and waited.

Anaya asked the others, "Who do you think they are, *Faraones*

(Pharaohs)? Of what, the Sandias or the plains?"

There were shrugs from just about everyone in the Spanish contingent, with Simon finally saying, "Who in the hell knows who they are? They're probably thieving Indians who make their homes in the *Sierra de Sandia*. They are there to steal horses, and sheep, and cattle from the pueblos of Galisteo, Pecos and Santo Domingo. Bad, horse-stealing Indians," he repeated, regarding the nomads who surrounded the colony on all sides. "Thieves and murderers," he added. "Give them food and get them the hell out of here."

21

One is as Good as the Other

SOMETIME BEFORE OCTOBER 1638

"If they won't come to us, we'll go to them," Governor Rosas said to Gaspar Perez of the Plains Indians who traded at Taos, Picuris, and Pecos. "You've been there before, haven't you?" the governor asked regarding the lands to the east.

"Yes, several times, most recently with Captain Alonso Baca."

"Alonso Baca? Brother of Antonio?" the governor asked, pushing himself away from his desk.

"Yes, his younger brother," Perez responded. "Leader of the expedition to the east."

"Are there others who've been there?" Rosas asked. "I know of these Bacas. Root and branch. They spell out their origins so that all may know of their honor and privileges. Breathless with self-importance. Argumentative and pig-headed. I'll not ask one of them to lead me anywhere, for I have no interest in becoming indebted to them."

"There were others with us," Gaspar said of the Baca expedition. "*Alferez* Francisco Lujan and a friar of the Order of Saint Francis named Andres Juarez. There were soldiers, too, who accompanied the traders, but they're now guarding Jimenez at Pecos."

Rosas waited a long moment before responding, asking finally, "And Ibargaray, does he remain recalcitrant?"

"We've heard nothing from him, Governor, and Fray Jimenez remains under guard in the storeroom."

"Well, I've made my point," the governor said regarding the Jimenez imprisonment. "Send word to Pecos that Jimenez may be freed, given amnesty or some such. Then have his guards meet us at Galisteo tomorrow. We'll leave from there."

* * *

The old man, Fray Antonio Jimenez, who had been sleeping in his own filth, was cold, his eyes narrowed, sealed with a week of scrum. He heard the key turning in the lock and demanded, "Who's there?"

"It's Fray Antonio," Ibargaray responded. "You wouldn't allow the substitution of my imprisonment for yours as required by the governor, but now you're free."

"I don't want to go," Jimenez responded. "I've not finished my work."

"You must come with me, Brother," the father said. "Please come with me."

"A little while longer, Father," Jimenez begged. "One more good day and I'll have soiled all his *mantas* and hides! You may come for me tomorrow!" he said gleefully. "Give me some rotten food, so that I may finish my work, for if it goes in rotten, so it will come out. I'll be finished with my work tomorrow, and then I'll go."

* * *

Leaving Galisteo in the brilliant sunshine of this late October day, Rosas, and his party of slavers and traders, rode south parallel to the mountains, and then eastward toward the bison plains.

"Do you recognize the area?" Governor Rosas asked of Perez.

"Yes, the route here is well-known to me," Perez said. "It's not until we emerge upon the plains that we'll have any difficulty."

"And how far did you go . . . four years ago?" Rosas asked. "How far did Baca go?"

"We went due east from here," Perez said, giving a running account of his travels with Alonso Baca on Baca's exploration to the east. "We went through some extensive plains with very abundant pasturage, across the San Buenaventura, the Bagres, and the Magdalena. We traveled

128

almost three hundred leagues to a great river. The river had wonderful banks, and, although level, was so densely wooded that the trees formed thick and wide groves. There, we found a small fruit of very good flavor, the size of the wild pear or yellow *sapodilla*. The river contained an abundance of excellent fish, and although at some points it had good fords, in other parts it was extremely deep and vessels could easily sail upon it. It flowed due east, and its waters were fresh and pleasant to taste. The land there," Perez continued, "was fertile and much better than that through which we had passed. The pastures were so good that in many places the grass was high enough to conceal a horse. At that point, the Indians who accompanied us, *vaqueros* of the Apache nation, refused to let us cross over into the kingdom of *Quivira*. They were afraid to go any further, and, as our horses were spent, we thought it best to turn back. You may have heard of our time with the Apaches," Perez continued with a broad smile. "In order to assure those with whom we traveled of our friendship, we allowed ourselves to become a part of their nation. We slept with their maidens in the French manner of cementing relationships, and were made chiefs of their tribe. It was a hell of a job," he laughed, "but someone had to do it!" Governor Rosas joined him in his laughter, and they continued riding in an easterly direction.

Daily, as they rode across a treeless plain, they could see bison grazing in small groups wherever they looked. The plains, often parched grasslands with isolated patches of wild flowers, were now responding to a year of wet snowfall and abundant rain. There were flowers of a thousand different kinds, so thick that they choked the pasture. The yucca, or bear grass, was blooming to such an extent that it was no longer able to support its blossoms. *Playas*—wide-open spaces on the plains— were full of the white and yellow blooms of bull nettles, buttercups, and clover that filled the air with the scent of their blossoms. The tall spikes of evening primrose, goldenrod, horsemint, and Indian blanket intermingled with the yucca and sagebrush to create a kaleidoscope of color against the blue horizon.

Rosas sent an advance party ahead, the group returning each evening to tell what they found. One evening, as the sun was going down, the group returned with news of people camped along a small river that contained little water but was so overgrown with trees that its banks resembled thickly wooded mountains.

"They're the Escanjaques," Perez said, identifying the members of the encampment, "enemies of the Apaches with whom we trade."

"Do they not need trade knives?" Rosas asked.

"Of course, your Lordship, but it may not be wise to . . . "

"Do they not tan their skins in the same manner as the Apaches who come to Pecos?" he continued, looking at the remainder of his men who waited expectantly.

Perez, who knew that he was beating a dead horse, said, "Yes, and I'm sure their maidens are as sweet!"

"Well, then?"

"I'll tell the men they may set up shop."

Trading, once initiated, proceeded briskly with the commerce beginning that evening and continuing long into a second day. The articles used in trade by the Escanjaques consisted of dried meat, hides, and skins. The Pueblos and Spaniards used the leather good for clothing, sacks, tents, cuirasses, footwear and everything else imaginable. In return the Escanjaques received corn, trade knives, and *mantas*. While his men worked, Rosas spent much of his time under an oak tree, eating acorns and a roasted Castilian partridge that had been provided for him by his men. Presently, Gaspar returned to where the governor was sitting.

"There's a group of Apaches coming up the river," Perez said breathlessly. "Following game herds from one valley to the next. They don't seem to know we're here. The Escanjaques told me that they mean to attack them."

"And our men?" Rosas asked.

"They're still on the trading grounds," Perez responded. "What would you like us to do?"

Rosas wiped his hands on his trousers very deliberately, his thoughts seemingly somewhere else. Finally, he asked, "What do you see as our options?"

"We could alert the Apaches and advise them of the impending attack," Perez responded. "Or we ourselves could attack the Escanjaques or otherwise let them know that we're not supportive of their plan to attack the Apaches."

"Do you see those as our only options?" Rosas asked. "We may have sworn to protect the Apaches while they're on the trading grounds at Pecos. But have we promised them safe conduct? Immunity?" He did not wait for a response. "I think not!" said Rosas who was inflated by his own arrogance. "They are like the Opata of Sonora with whom I traded earlier this year. The missionaries want them for their souls, while I see them as good only for slaving or trading. God has placed this conglutination of aborigines in our laps for a purpose," he continued. "It seems to me a just war! We'll join the Escanjaques in their attack and take our share."

* * *

Governor Rosas, his men, their purchased and stolen hides and skins, and, also, approximately 100 *Vaquero* Apaches whom they had captured— a total approximating the number they and the Escanjaques had killed— were back in the *villa* before the first snow flew. Rosas put some of the captive Indians to work in his private textile workshop in Santa Fe. Others he sent to be sold in *Nueva Vizcaya*, where they were destined to work in the mines. The friars and the Christianized Indians at Pecos, who were soon to suffer the repercussions of the Rosas attack, were furious.

22

A Rain of Arrows

OCTOBER 1638

In the early hours of an October morning, before the nature of things was revealed in the darkness, Fray Antonio de Ibargaray watched as a Pueblo Indian staggered through the dead stalks of a Pecos cornfield. He walked uncertainly as though he had awakened from a fathomless sleep. When the Indian came closer, Fray Ibargaray could see the red of blood on the Indian's chest, and, when he fell, the shafts of two arrows protruding from his back. Ibargaray, who had just come from the church where he had been tutoring the Pueblo children in the "ways of civilization," ran back toward the church with the intention of ringing its bell in alarm. Then a rain of arrows began falling from the sky. My God, he thought to himself as he turned to face the onslaught, they're here!

Ibargaray watched in horrified silence as a small group of Apaches, their shields joined, their long spears held tightly to their side, walked in a calm and deliberate manner through the cornfield and toward the village wall. Marking out the pueblo's limits, the wall was too low for defensive purposes but served as a symbolic boundary between the village and the open plains. Suddenly, and with savage shrieks, the *Vaquero* Apaches who had approached the pueblo so deliberately began running up the pueblo's long midden slope, revealing, as they ran, the presence among them of three small children. Upon reaching the wall, with the Indian phalanx loosing arrows in every direction, three Indians

132

dropped their shields, and, holding the terrified children before them, slit their throats and threw their small bodies over the wall. Then, just as suddenly as the attack had begun, the Apaches withdrew from the walls and from the cornfield, disappearing into the great unknown.

Fray Ibargaray, who had watched the Indians' approach from the edge of the churchyard, thought of the many things he should tell the Pecos war captains relative to the safety of their village. But what he said to the one Indian male who came to him was, "Put them in the church."

"They will not go there, Father," the war captain responded. "The people of Pecos will not hide in the church while their village is under attack, for the Pecos pueblo is feared throughout the land and no one has been able to subdue it. I'll get some men and we'll follow them."

"You must not!" Ibargaray cried in alarm. "Tell your people that I'll send for our *encomendero*, Francisco Gomez, and some men. You and your men may go with them as soon as Gomez arrives."

"You may send for the *encomendero*, Father, but you cannot expect the people of Pecos to wait. The Spanish started this fight and now can do nothing to protect us. The *Vaquero* Apaches will be long gone before the soldiers arrive."

Fray Ibargaray, who knew the truthfulness of the Indian's words, and of his inability to keep the Pueblos from pursuing their attackers, sent an account of the Apache attack to Santa Fe anyway, requesting succor and aid.

* * *

"When?" asked an exasperated Francisco Gomez of the Indian messenger regarding the Apache attack.

"This morning," the messenger replied. "I came as soon as I could. Rode all day."

"We're always behind them. Eating their dust and trying to find their trail. We'll go, of course. Do what we can. But they'll be long gone by the time we get there."

* * *

Days later, Captain Francisco Gomez, leading a squadron of Spanish soldiers, and trailed by a small group of Pueblo Indians, ventured down the Pecos Valley traveling beside the parallel tracks of lodge poles.

Following the trace of this trail to the river, the trackers came upon one of the Apaches' newly acquired Indian ponies. Its leg was injured, and it was standing among a cache of Indian paraphernalia that the Apaches had apparently abandoned in their hasty retreat. Freeing the horse from its harness, the men resumed their march along the eastern bank of the river.

Farther down the valley, on a hillside to the west of the river, lay a number of pale, unidentifiable objects which gave the impression of a thick flock of sheep grazing in a pasture. Gomez crossed the river to investigate. The column continued on, reaching the site of an Indian encampment just below the place where Gomez had crossed. The camp was deserted, its fire beds blackened and cold. Debris littered the ground: blankets, soup bowls, horn spoons, and a grindstone. From three upright poles dangled three human heads bound together with leather thongs. Badly burned, the three were still recognizable as Pueblo Indian friends and relatives of the Indians who were with Gomez. One by one, the Pueblo Indians who accompanied the Spanish squad went aside and sat down, rocking to and fro, weeping and wailing.

Unmistakable fresh trails of lodge poles led toward the plains. Along their tracks, packs, travois, lodge poles, and utensils had been dropped or hastily cut loose. Everywhere the pursuers looked there was carnage. All of the Pecos Indians who had been residing in outlying houses tending to their harvests had been killed, and, to impair their spirit in the afterlife, their bodies horribly mutilated. The pale unidentifiable objects, which Francisco Gomez had found on the west bank of the river, were the bodies of Pueblo Indians. They were nude, had been decapitated and badly maimed, their entrails protruding from gaping wounds. Heads, feet, arms, legs, and hands had been chopped off. One corpse was found with one of Perez's trading knives driven to the hilt in one eye.

Gomez and his men followed the Indian trail at a gallop, hoping to see on the distant horizon a sign of the Apaches in retreat. They found, instead, a partially dismantled Apache lodge and inside, a dead warrior, handsomely dressed—as was the burial custom—wearing moccasins with ceremonially beaded soles. The soldiers burned the burial lodge. The Apaches, however, were long gone, fleeing across a stretch of devastation, swallowed up in the wide expanse of the Great Plains.

When the Spanish soldiers and their Pueblo Indian auxiliaries returned to the Pecos Pueblo, they were horrified to learn that the three murdered children were, in fact, Spanish and not Indians as was at first believed. One, a half-breed, was the three-year old son of Gaspar Perez conceived when the Spanish alliance with the *Vaquero* Apaches was cemented. The child's penis, severed and stuffed in his mouth, was still present when he was found, a chinstrap preventing its expulsion.

As Gomez and his men rode away from the Pecos Pueblo on their return ride to Santa Fe, Francisco de Salazar was heard to remark, "Assisting the Escanjaques in an attack against the Apaches! My God, what insanity! I wonder if the governor has any idea what he's done?"

To which Ensign Nicolas Enriquez responded, "I wonder if he cares!"

23

The Venerable Fray Nicolas Hidalgo

1638

"Oh, God, I love it!" Rosas shrieked with delight. "Oh, God! Would I love to see Salas's face when he hears this. Tell me again," he asked Casaus, with whom he was meeting in the darkness, "what did Hidalgo do?"

"These are not the first complaints that have been made regarding Fray Hidalgo, your Lordship, for the priests' influence and authority over the Indians is greatly weakened by the slightest departure from chastity on their part. Some complaints were made before you arrived, but apparently Governor Martinez didn't investigate them. The complaints are of rapes and brutal punishments, don Luis," Casaus said. "It's said that Hidalgo punishes those Indians he considers idolaters by castration and sodomy, emasculating the men by grabbing them by their testicles, twisting their genitals unmercifully until the man so punished collapses in pain. An Indian with whom I spoke, a male named Pedro Acomilla, said that Fray Hidalgo had twisted his penis so violently that he broke it in half. And, even more seriously, your Lordship, it's claimed that Fray Hidalgo had strangled an Indian man so that he could sleep with his wife!"[1]

"Fray Hidalgo? The venerable Fray Nicolas Hidalgo?" Rosas roared in delight. "You couldn't make this up! This is just too damn good!"

"There's more, your Lordship," Casaus continued. "There was at least two women with whom he was involved who made complaints against him. Both are Indians at the Taos Pueblo. One, was Isabel Yantula, the second Margita Tultamu. Both extremely ugly," Casaus laughed. "I saw them, don Luis! They looked like death warmed over! The first one said that Fray Hidalgo had fathered her four-year-old child, and the second, that he had fathered her one-year-old, and that Fray Hidalgo keeps both children at the *convento* where he dresses them as Spaniards! I was there when the pueblo's inside chief presented their testimony," Casaus said. "You now have this as a formal complaint."

"Well, I won't let this slip through my fingers like Martinez did," Rosas exclaimed. "I'll have Martin Barba go to Taos to investigate the matter before Salas has a chance to send Fray Juarez there for an Inquisitional investigation. I wonder if we have a medal or something we can give him?" Rosas commented, regarding Fray Hidalgo. "Something by which we may commemorate his achievements!" he roared. "Oh, God! This is too delicious! We'll use this to our own advantage, of course," he said through his laughter. "I'll send a note to Salas to congratulate him on the chastity of his priests."

24

The Governor's Lackey

JANUARY 1639

I assume that you've heard about the outrage at Taos," the governor asked Fray Juan de Vidania with whom he was sitting in the governor's office. "It's an outrage," he said in apparent disgust, "an absolute outrage! I want you to compose a letter as coming from the clergy to be sent to the viceroy regarding the immorality of your fellow priests. The pueblos are full of the friars' children! Do you not agree with me on this?" the governor asked Fray Vidania.

"Yes, yes, your Lordship," said the disloyal Vidania, who had gone over to the governor's side. "I agree!"

"Shocking! Shocking! That's what it is. And what has Salas done about it?" he asked. "What has he done about the gross misbehavior of his priests? Not you, Father, but the others," the governor asked, neither expecting, nor waiting for a reply.

"I, . . ."

"Nothing! Nothing! That's what he's done," Rosas raged. "I want this in your letter too. I want you to write about Fray Hidalgo and also about Fray Juan de Gongora," he said in reference to the subdelegate of the Office of the Holy Crusade, or *Santa Cruzada*, one of three ecclesiastical authorities with whom the governor and colonists had to contend. Gongora's responsibility to collect a tax, called the *Cruzada*, which was conceived initially to benefit participants of a crusade, but which had deteriorated into a method of supporting the propagation of the Catholic faith, was too much for the governor. The tax, as well as Rosas's dispute with Gongora over the legal immunities that *Cruzada* employees enjoyed, had sent the governor completely over the edge. He wanted Gongora stopped at any price. "I had Casaus question his authority before the *cabildo*, but that's not enough. Who's this Gongora anyway?" he asked Vidania. "Could he be from the family that gave us the bard of Cordova? Neither the poet nor this priest makes a damned bit of sense.[1] I want both of them, both Gongora and Hidalgo, driven from the kingdom," he said. "And on another note," he continued without pause, "to whom did Salas present his patent of office as all ecclesiastical officials are required to do? Not to me!" he said. "I presented my credentials to him at Santo Domingo when I arrived, but I've seen nothing of his. Therefore, as I had Casaus tell the council, we're not required to attend to his censures, or his interdicts, or his excommunications, or his threats of Inquisitorial prosecutions," Rosas raged. "For all I know, he's an artillery man! Say that in your letter, too!"[2]

Gathering himself up, he turned back to the game they were playing, "Now, where were we?"

"It's your turn, your Lordship."

"Ah, yes," Rosas said, as he looked over the chessboard. Picking up his king, he held it suspended above the board for some time before continuing. Then, very deliberately, he executed a compound move, his king two squares to its castle, the castle placed on the square the king had crossed. "There," he said, smiling at the good father.

"I don't think you can do that, your Lordship," said a cautious Fray Juan de Vidania who, as he corrected the governor, dared not look into his eyes. "The rules as set out by King Alfonso[3] say that you may only castle once during an engagement and, in any event, that you may not do so if either your king or castle has been previously moved."

"Is that right?" a smiling Luis de Rosas responded. "Well, I think I can."

25

The Reverend Fray Pedro de Miranda

NOVEMBER 1639

Fray Pedro de Miranda, a revered old man with a tuft of pale hair revealing itself beneath the hood of his thin cassock, was riding on a gaunt mule undecorated by caparison. His mule, long, lank, and consumptive-looking, bore the priest and his baggage, a single sack of dressed calfskin all rolled up in an undressed hide and a rude blanket that was fixed behind his saddle. His clothing, including his well-worn tunic, which he treasured as if it were a cassock of Florentine cloth, appeared thin and threadbare, cold against the season. It was an unbefitting garment to be draped upon the shoulders of such an august old man, but not surprising of one who would not allow himself the comfort of a fire in the forest where deadfall rotted on the ground. His presentation, as he carried only breviary and crucifix, plus bread and water for a single day, was a statement of the friar's penitental state to the soldiers who overtook him. It did not go unnoticed by their captain, Alonso Martin Barba. "Where do you go, old man?" he asked the priest who traveled without escort.

"To Taos," replied Fray Miranda indicating the northernmost mission. "I go to replace Fray Hidalgo," he said, his eyes directed toward the ground so as to shield himself from the gilt and glitter of the world.

"Aye, Hidalgo!" Martin laughed. "You've got some mighty big

pants to fill. Do you think you're up to it, Father?" he asked through his laughter, as he and his men rode away.

* * *

At Taos, always a center of disaffection and mutual mistrust, the location of the church of San Geronimo reflected the polar relationship that existed between the Indians and the Spanish priests. Martin Barba, in whom Governor Rosas had found a mule to be skinned at his pleasure, arrived at the pueblo ahead of Fray Pedro de Miranda who limped behind. By drum and bugle, Martin asked the inside chiefs of the Taos Pueblo to meet with him in the church.

Once the Indian leaders had assembled within, Martin said, "I bring you greetings and a message from the Honorable Governor don Luis de Rosas regarding the missionaries who reside among you. You're not to obey them, for they're a bunch of libertines, adulterers, and scoundrels. They only want you to provide them with free services while they're sleeping with your wives. Their magic may have worked at one time," Martin said, "but it's gone now, useless against the *Vaquero* Apaches who attack you. The governor knows that when the priests brought you Jesus, your corn mothers went away. He offers you his assistance in bringing them back."

The Pueblo Indians, who received these pronouncements, listened intently, eager to hear what the governor was offering. Martin continued, "If you'll provide him with more blankets and hides, he'll allow you to perform your dances as you did before the missionaries arrived."

* * *

After the Indians at Taos heard the governor's proposal, they contemplated their future, while Fray Pedro de Miranda, the modest and self-effacing old man who had been sent to Taos to rectify the sins of Fray Nicolas Hidalgo, carried his cross without assistance. He continued a series of sermons that he had initiated shortly after his arrival, scolding the Taos Indians for calumniating his predecessor. The Indians, who had not celebrated his arrival with the customary procession in which the Pueblos carried a large cross and lighted candles, now turned their backs on him. They left their pueblo in droves, refusing to hear any longer the

141

scorn being heaped upon them by the venerable friar. They asked him to leave their pueblo so that they could return there unhindered by his presence. But he would not go.

Eventually, however, even though Fray Pedro de Miranda remained in their village, some of the Taos Indians, eager to utilize the cache of corn that was stored there, decided to go back. On their return, a *cacique* (tribal chief) who claimed to be able to perform magic, told the Indians that he had built an invisible wall of stone around the pueblo that reached from the earth to the heavens. "We may now do as we wish, for the Spaniards cannot harm us," he said. "And should they attempt to breach the wall, I'll summon the darkness and destroy them." That was all the Taos Indians needed to hear.

DECEMBER 28, 1639

In the dead of winter, three days after Christmas, the Taos Indians rebelled, sacking their mission church, and killing two soldier-settlers and their priest, Fray Pedro de Miranda. A few days later, at the mission of *San Jose Giusewa*, some of the previously scattered Jemez tribes, who shortly after 1625, had been required to congregate in the settlements of San Jose and San Diego, killed their missionary, Fray Diego de San Lucas, left their village, and returned to their ancestral ways. The colony was starting to come apart and many blamed Governor don Luis de Rosas.

26

Bell, Book and Candle

Sweating and filthy from the trail, the fanatical and aggressive *Custos* Juan de Salas took off his habit and sandals. He put on sackcloth, and walked barefoot over the pea stones of the path from the new *convento* of *La Asuncion de Nuestra Senora*, directly to the equally new *Parroquia de Santa Fe*, where he passed the night in prayer. In the thin light of early morning, he left the main altar and opened the church doors. He stood just within the narthex or *portico*, which formed the entrance to the church, where rituals of excommunication were now performed. Leaning against the small altar there, he observed both Indian and Spanish members of the royal *villa* who stood within the *campo santo*, the holy ground consecrated to serve the *parroquia* as a cemetery. Stepping back into the interior of the vestibule, yet near the open doors where all might see his actions, he began the ritual of excommunication. Ten candles, one for each impenitent, were lighted, their wax dripped onto the stone altar, the drippings securing their placement there. He then recited the ancient formula of ecclesiastical censure:

> We exclude them from the bosom of our Holy Mother the Church, and we judge them condemned to eternal fire with Satan and his angels and all the reprobates, so long as they will not burst the fetters of the demon, do penance and satisfy the Church.

Then, taking the candles one by one from the altar, extinguishing them, and hurling them to the floor, he trampled them with a bare foot. Closing the bible with a resounding thud, he barred the doors to the sanctuary, while bells, pealing in the bell towers announced to the world the expulsion of the excommunicates. The name of Fray Nicolas Hidalgo and the others whom Fray Esteban de Perea had marked out for excommunication were affixed to the church door. And as it was unlawful to break bread or to speak with those excommunicated, it was as if they were dead. They were to be deprived of any dignity and were to be shunned.

* * *

As Governor Luis de Rosas walked out from beneath the passageway at the Royal Palace, he saw a pair of Indian women running along the *acequia* with firebrands in their hands. He thought they meant to set fire to the *casas*, but they ran by him on their way to the church. What are they doing? he wondered as he followed them. Reaching the church, he found several people standing within the *campo santo* watching the proceedings occurring just within the entrance to the church.

God! What is that lunatic doing now? he thought, as he watched *Custos* Salas trampling candles. "Who are they killing now?" he asked one of the bystanders.

Hearing that one of those excommunicated was Fray Nicolas Hidalgo, the governor walked to the *convento* of the Asumption and asked to speak to Fray Juan de Vidania. Shortly, a half-dressed Juan de Vidania met him in the hallway. "Take Hidalgo's name off your letter," Rosas commanded, regarding the letter to the viceroy that Father Vidania had been writing at his request. "Take his name off the letter," he said again. "Its presence there is no longer required."

"But you had judged him to be immoral," Fray Vidania said.

"Forget what I said," the governor responded angrily. "It's Gongora's tax and the seizing of intestate properties that's immoral!" he bellowed. He walked back to the doorway, looked out beyond the church, and turning, said in a more conciliatory tone, "Try to understand our actions here, Father. If they vilify one of their own, then we'll ask that he be beatified. And if they excommunicate him, we'll ask that he be made into a saint, setting out, as required, the miracles we attribute to him. What you've yet to understand, Father, is that an enemy of *Custos* Salas is a friend of mine."

144

27

The Excommunication of Sebastian de Sandoval

THREE MONTHS LATER

In the silence of the early morning when the moon was full, the sacristan at the church of Santo Domingo stood patiently at the side of the altar waiting for a kneeling Fray Esteban de Perea to complete his morning prayers. When the good father rose to his feet, the sexton, whose major duties consisted of cleaning the church, ringing the bell, and digging graves, approached him. "Are they to abstain from food during the whole or only part of the day, Father?" he asked in reference to Perea's Inquisitional prisoners. "And what are we to feed them?"

Leaning against the altar rail as he rose to his feet, the testy old Fray Esteban de Perea, whose propensity was to save cheese-parings and candle ends, answered with ill-disguised annoyance. "Those in the west cells may have a spare breakfast of red wine and tortillas," Perea responded, as he retrieved a stout willow from the altar steps. "Let them have that as their chief meal with perhaps a light collation in the evening. But do not give bread or wine to Sebastian de Sandoval. He's been singled out for special punishment. I want him to continue to be guided by the rules of a 'Franciscan fast' of only one serving of food a day, and that of *garbanzos* only. And not now," he added grimly as the two of them walked away from the altar. "I've got his day planned for him, and if he were to be fed now, the *garbanzos* would only be wasted."

Dressed in the official black and white raiment of an Inquisitional agent, a willow-carrying Fray Esteban de Perea, walked with the sacristan down a dimly lit corridor toward the door of Sebastian's cell. "Do you have the correct key?" Perea asked of the sexton who had tried several in a vain attempt to find the one by which to open Sandoval's door.

"Yes Father, it's this one," the sacristan responded, as the key turned in the lock. The door to the cell was then opened.

"Get up!" Perea roared, as he smashed the willow across Sebastian's thighs.

Looking at the wrathful Fray Esteban de Perea, but seemingly unable to comprehend what was being demanded of him, a senseless Sebastian de Sandoval merely stared at the raging priest. A strap with a noose fashioned at one end was brought to the cell by the sexton and put around Sebastian's neck. Forced, unclothed, from his mat, the ordinarily proud, erect, impassioned, Sebastian de Sandoval, was paying now for having slandered Fray Salas and the other priests. He was clothed in a hair shirt, wrapped in a long tunic of coarse serge, and dragged barefoot down a dimly lit hallway. Taken to an empty cell, he was made to lie on a pallet of cinders, and had squares of tuff placed beneath his head and feet. A prisoner of the Inquisition, he was now but a sack of humanity, a mean thing of skin and bones.

Having first insisted that he had nothing to confess, Sebastian de Sandoval, after days of punishment and humiliation, now said, "I've done nothing wrong, Father, and, although I do not wish to have a false confession against my conscience, I will bear false witness against myself, for I want this over."

"I don't want you to provide false testimony! Just tell the truth!" raged Fray Perea as he hit Sandoval on the soles of his feet.

"I've told you the truth, Father. What else have I to say?" Sebastian cried.

"Tell the truth!"

"I've done all that you say, Father."

"Tell the details!"

"Tell me what you want to hear, for I don't know how to say it!" Sebastian screamed.

"Tell the truth, damn it!"

"Oh, Lord, have mercy on me, a sinner," Sandoval replied. "Enough! Enough!" he screamed. "Please don't hit me any more. I remember what I've done. I'll tell the truth!" he implored, trying to collect his senses. "Bless me, Father, for I have sinned," he said, praying that Perea, after hearing his declaration of guilt, would absolve him of his transgressions. "It's been a month since my last confession."

"Liar!" Perea said as he again hit Sandoval on the soles of his feet. "It's been at least two months since your last confession, for no one would come near you!"

"Bless me, Father," Sebastian said again through his tears. "It's been at least two months since my last confession."

"And your sins!" Perea bellowed, "Tell Him of your sins!"

Sandoval, in a failing attempt to appease the raging Perea, continued, speaking of having incessantly slandered the priests, the leading citizens and their families. At the end of Sandoval's confession, the good father, Fray Esteban de Perea, former *custos* of the Franciscan Custody, and now agent of the Inquisition, conducted Sebastian de Sandoval to the area beneath the porch at the front of the church where sinners were normally punished. There Sandoval was made to kneel upon the path of pea stone as eager attendants tore off his external clothing and hair shirt to render his back to the *disciplina*, a knotted cord of rawhide with which he was to be scourged. A delegation of Indian novitiates, appointed by Agent Perea, then delivered each stroke as Perea's 12 were counted.

"Please, Father," Sandoval begged, "a horrible pain, beginning in my feet, has spread through my legs and buttocks. My body's aflame."

"Good!" Fray Perea responded. "Perhaps next time you'll think twice before spreading rumors regarding members of the *custodia* with the intention of doing harm to our name and reputation."

When the novitiates appointed to administer the scourging had completed their task, Agent Perea said, "Take him and tie his hands behind his back and have him lashed in the plaza at Santa Fe. And have him followed by a crier, so that all may know of his crimes. Put the *mordaza* in his mouth to enhance his humiliation." Perea indicated the gag put in a person's mouth to keep him from crying out. "Then bring him back here to Santo Domingo where he's to be imprisoned, and lash him in all of the pueblos through which you ride."

No one could have guessed that before the week was over, both Sandoval and Perea would be dead.

28

A Private Extinction

JANUARY 1640

"Could someone have thought they had my approval to do this?" a shocked *Custos* Salas asked regarding Sebastian de Sandoval. "When? How?" he shouted in indignation.

"They had him imprisoned in a room off the corral at the *convento* in Santa Fe, Father. He was tied securely, so he was not guarded."

"And?"

"And someone killed him, Father. Slashed his throat."

"Oh, my God!" Salas cried. "Do we know who did this?"

"The governor initially blamed it on our *regidore*, the *sargento mayor*, Captain Juan de Archuleta. But when the governor brought charges against the nephew of Antonio Baca, everyone could see that Rosas was merely attempting to use Sandoval's murder for his own political advantage."

"Is there anything to tie Archuleta to the crime?" Salas asked.

"Absolutely nothing, Father. Juan's father, Asencio de Arechuleta, was our syndic, and the governor knows of the family's loyalty to us. The governor had Archuleta arrested as a suspect, but due to the public's outcry regarding his imprisonment, the governor had to let him go."

"Then it was one of our own who did this," Salas said.

"I'm afraid so, Father. Someone, whether Indian or Spanish, who had access to the *convento* grounds."

"God! It could be anyone. What have we done, Father?" Salas asked one of the other priests as he paced the room. "What have we done?" he repeated in dismay. "And his body." The *custos* asked. "What did they do with his body?"

"They buried him in the church, Father. Near the altar where the priest stands. Fray Vidania himself chose the location."

"On holy ground?" Custos Salas was incredulous. "In an area set aside exclusively for the service of God? Is Fray Vidania insane or just stupid?" he asked. "Please, please, tell me what I've done to deserve Fray Juan de Vidania!" He paused, and then said through clenched teeth, "The body of Sebastian de Sandoval must be exhumed and buried elsewhere. Get my mule. I want to go to Santa Fe to speak to that miserable priest."

* * *

The *convento* office shook from shouts of indignation resounding from the adobe walls and rafters. "What was your thinking regarding Sebastian de Sandoval?" *Custos* Salas asked Fray Juan de Vidania. "You knew that that foul-mouthed slanderer had been excommunicated, did you not?" he asked. "How could you dare to bury him on holy ground?"

"I did it because the governor asked me to," explained Fray Vidania.

"And who is Governor Rosas?" Salas asked. "Is he the pope? Is he authorized to provide special dispensations regarding the Church?"

"No, Father, but he was so pleased when I spoke of him in my sermon that I thought it best to continue the good feelings by acceding to his request that Sandoval be accorded a burial from which he might enjoy everlasting life."[1]

"You did what?" asked an incredulous Salas of Fray Vidania. "What are you telling me about the governor?"

"I included a mention of him in my homily as he requested, Father, praising him for the peace he's brought to the kingdom. Was I in error?" he asked.

"Are you insane? Don't you know of the scandal he perpetrated at Pecos against Fray Jimenez, of his outrageous conduct toward the *Vaquero* Apaches, of his dark and dirty sweatshop, his slaving? Don't you

150

know any of these things?" Salas raged, the veins of his forehead showing purple above his brow.

"I thought . . . "

"You thought what, damn it? That if you lay down with the lion that somehow he'd become a lamb? Get your things! Get your things and get out of here! I want you to be ready to leave within the hour."

"Leave? To go where Father?" asked the dumbfounded Vidania.

"Picuris."

"But, Father . . . "

"But Father, what?" Salas asked dismissing Fray Vidania from the room. "What an idiot! What an absolute idiot!" Salas said contemptuously, speaking more to himself than to Fray Domingo del Espiritu Santo who was present when Salas pronounced Vidania's expulsion. Turning and facing Fray Domingo, Salas said, "You'll take over here, Father. And I want Fray Vidania in Picuris before three days have passed. Please see to it."

"Yes, Father," said the dutiful Fray Domingo, his hands clasped before his chest. "Are there any specific instructions, Father?"

"No!" an exasperated Salas responded. "He'll require no specific penance. Picuris is hard enough. Just get him there by Friday vespers."

29

Assignments and Reassignments

He heard Martin coming down the hallway and was aware of who it was even before his large shape appeared in the doorway. Rosas greeted him then, asking, "Well? Where is Vidania?

"I went to the *convento* as you asked, your Lordship, but he's not there," said Captain Alonso Martin Barba who, like a well-trained falcon, was perched by the governor's hand.

"Not there?" the governor asked. "We're to play chess tonight, just as we do every Wednesday. So where is he?" he queried.

"The *portero* told me that he's gone to Picuris, reassigned there by *Custos* Salas."

"Reassigned? How can that be?" asked the governor, barely able to comprehend what he was hearing. "You don't just reassign priests here and there without at least informing the governor!" he raved. "He knows of my great friendship with Fray Vidania, and he did this just to annoy me. When did he leave?" he asked.

"Just today, your Lordship."

"Then go after him!" the governor bellowed giving angry instructions to his aide who cowered before the verbal onslaught. "Take a squad of soldiers and bring him back! Go tomorrow. No, go tonight! I want Fray Vidania here by tomorrow morning."

* * *

"And where did you find him?" the governor asked Captain Alonso Martin Barba who had just returned to the *villa* from the northern territories with Fray Juan de Vidania in tow.

"The party with whom he was riding had gotten as far as Nambe before being overtaken by darkness. Fray Vidania, when I found him, was sitting in the outdoor chapel at the priests' house, contemplating the *zapatas* and eating a bowl of *posole*. He hadn't even taken off his cloak. He was I can assure you, very happy to see us."

"And now?"

"And now he's at the *convento* here with Fray Domingo del Espiritu Santo."

"Then take this note to the guardian and tell him that his services in Santa Fe are no longer required," he said referring to Fray Domingo del Espiritu Santo. "Tell him that Fray Juan de Vidania is back, and that one priest in Santa Fe is quite enough. And have him take this note to the father *custos* at Santo Domingo," he said as he rummaged about among the documents on his desk. Would you like to hear it?" he asked Martin, as he found among his papers the one for which he had been searching.

"As you wish, Governor," Martin answered with a shrug.

Reading from the sheet of paper he had taken from his desk, he said,

"Don Luis de Rosas, Governor of New Mexico, asks that his esteemed friend, the reverend father, *Custos* Juan de Salas, ecclesiastical superior of the Custody of the Conversion of St. Paul, accept this letter in the manner in which it is intended, etc. etc. etc!" Rosas skipped over his note's many ruffles and flourishes. He then cleared his throat, smiled at Martin, and continued:

It has recently come to my attention that a grave error has been made in the recent assignment of Father Domingo del Espiritu Santo as father guardian of the Santa Fe *convento*. My concern regarding this assignment stems from my knowledge of Fray Domingo's previous assignments as guardian of the *convento* at Pecos and as secretary for *Custos* Cristobal de Quiros. Each assignment lasted less than a year, the brevity of which could only be explained by his gross incompetence. In order to rectify this assignment, which I know must have been made without your knowledge or consent, and which I also know would reflect badly upon you, I have taken it upon myself to reassign Fray Juan de Vidania to Santa Fe. You may be assured that I made this assignment ever mindful of my primacy in ecclesiastical affairs as the representative of our king, who is patron of the Church, and of our viceroy, who is vice-patron. I am also acting on my own behalf as chief executive, legislator, and judge, as well as commander of the kingdom's military.

God keep you many years.
As always,

Don Luis
Governor and Captain-General of New Mexico

Villa, January 12, 1640

"Well, what do you think of that?" Rosas asked with a self-satisfied smile.

"I think that says it all, your Lordship," Martin responded.

"Well, not completely. Salas is not going to move him anywhere," he said of his friend, Fray Juan de Vidania. "I'm going to install him here as royal chaplain, and it is the priests who are assigned to the *parroquia* who will go!" He walked into the corridor from the room where he and Martin had been speaking. "Guard!" he yelled down the hallway. As if by magic, two guards appeared. "Go to the *convento* with the captain and secure it. Tell Fray Juan de Vidania that he's been assigned to the chapel in the east tower at the *palacio real*, and that everyone else is to leave the *parroquia* and *convento*. And tell Father Domingo del Espiritu Santo, and whomever else you might find there, that if they don't leave the church and *convento* immediately that I'll go there and will personally burn them down. And after you've thrown the priests out, I want you to lock the doors and bring me the keys."

* * *

At Santo Domingo, the *custos's* hands shook with fury as he read Rosas's

154

note. Shrieking in indignation, "How dare he meddle in the affairs of the Church! What's next? What's next?" he asked as he paced about his office. He saw the governor's reassignment of Fray Juan de Vidania as a *fait accompli*, however, but hoped to reverse the governor's orders regarding the Santa Fe *convento* and its priests. Accordingly, he sent a courier, riding among a cortege of mule-mounted priests, to Santa Fe with a patent for Fray Juan de Vidania as guardian at the Santa Fe church. He then reassigned the hapless Fray Domingo del Espiritu Santo to Santo Domingo.

30

The Embassy of the Fathers Bartolome Romero and Francisco Nunez

FEBRUARY 1640

Squeezing through the choir-loft window onto the balcony of the main church at Santo Domingo, *Custos* Juan de Salas stood in the gallery watching the falling snow. "I want everyone here by Monday, March first," he said to the messenger who had followed him. "Tell them that I've convened a council at Santo Domingo. Tell them to consume the Host, close their *conventos*, and come here," he said regarding his priests. "We must decide what we're going to do about Governor Luis de Rosas."

MARCH 1640

The priests and lay brothers who had been summoned to the ecclesiastical capital by Fray Juan de Salas met in the smaller of Santo Domingo's two churches during the first two weeks of March 1640. They prayed and took counsel with one another for what they feared might be their last winter in New Mexico. "What do you see as our options?" Salas asked the priests with whom he was meeting. "We've been subjected to slander and abuse, our authority has been undermined at every turn, and our persons threatened. Worse," he said, "the deaths of the Fathers Pedro de Miranda and Diego de San Lucas would not have occurred had it

156

not been for the governor's intervention in our work with the Indians. I have officially closed the *parroquia*, the *convento* of *La Nuestra Senora*, and the chapel of *San Miguel*. I have also excommunicated Father Juan de Vidania, but he doesn't even know it, cut off as we are from the royal *villa*. We've issued our manifesto, but we cannot remain as we are. What do you see as our options regarding the governor?" he again asked of his religious.

"The governor has said that he intends to seize you, bind you in a sack, and expel you from the kingdom," said Fray Antonio de Artega. "If he does that, Father, I'll go with you."

"And I, too, will go," added Fray Antonio Jimenez. "If the Father *Custos* is expelled from the kingdom, I'll go with him."

"Yes, yes," *Custos* Salas responded with a note of exasperation, "but have we only to run? Has our work here been for nothing?"

"We're acting as if we have no power here," shouted Fray Bartolome Romero who had come to Santo Domingo from his station at Zuni. "It seems that there's much we can do. We can, as we did last year, refuse to grant confessional absolution to anyone who does not sign a petition in our favor and against the governor. Those citizens who've followed us here will gladly sign it."

"But we tried that before, and few would sign," said another priest. "They may be afraid of our interdicts, but they're more afraid of the governor's."

"Well, I say that we try again," said Fray Romero, looking at the men who were seated upon the benches they had brought with them from the *convento*. "I'll lead an embassy to Santa Fe to meet with the governor and arrive at an amicable resolution to our positions. I'm sure that out of the eye of the public, and with calm deliberation, we may yet arrive at a just solution."

"If you're given permission to go to Santa Fe, Father, I'll go with you," said the aged lay brother Fray Francisco Nunez to Fray Bartolome Romero. "We can stay at the *Hermita* and meet the governor there."

"With your permission, Father," Romero said to the father *custos*, "we can send a message to the governor to that effect."

A FLOGGING: APRIL 1640. ON THE SOUTH SIDE OF THE RIVER ON THE SAN MIGUEL SLOPE

The governor was already there when the Fathers Romero and Nunez rode up. A driver was present in the governor's carriage. An ox cart with six soldiers standing around it was positioned before the chapel, now an infirmary, which had, during the recent past, served the kingdom as the *Parroquia de Santa Fe*. A structure of stone and adobe, its entrance, through a wide doorway in the base of a five-level façade, loomed before them. The priests hesitated. Respectfully greeted by the soldiers standing before the church in the golden New Mexico sunshine, however, they dismounted.

With some trepidation, the Fathers Bartolome Romero and Francisco Nunez tied up. Wearing traveler's spectacles and carrying sunshades, the priests waved lace napkins above their heads as they entered the chapel, its dim interior masking all from view. They found the governor lounging next to several stools he had found near the altar. He spoke first.

"Why are you in my city?" he demanded. "Didn't I close your *convento?* What is it about the word 'banish' that you don't understand?"

Fray Romero, who was standing nearest to the governor, said, "We brought you a paper signed by nineteen of our members and as many citizens, asking that we find an amicable solution to our conflict."

"And why would I wish to read the words of traitors?" the governor asked. "Of liars and pigs and heretics? Why would I wish to read their words?" he asked again, standing and reaching for the staff that lay on a stool beside him.

"Because he who sins and mends his ways commends himself to God," Fray Romero responded. The governor hit him with the rod he held in his hand, the rod flying up from the blow, chattering, until it resettled in his hand. He hit Fray Romero again, a vicious blow that nearly tore off his ear. He quickly struck him again, this time on his left shoulder driving Fray Romero to his knees. The governor then turned to a stunned Fray Francisco Nunez, who, at the governor's first blow against Fray

Romero, had raised his own arms in self-defense. The initial blow against Fray Nunez was across his unprotected chest, which took the breath from him. The second blow, which Governor Rosas brought down on the top of the brother's head, dropped him to his knees. The two beaten clerics, Fathers, Romero and Nunez, each bleeding profusely from wounds they had suffered upon their heads, attempted to rise. The governor raised his cane again, held it in the air menacingly, and then threw it to the floor in front of the altar where it clattered against the stairs. His anger spent, the governor threw the skirt of his cape over one of his shoulders and strode out of the chapel, saying to his waiting soldiers about the priests to whom he had given such a cudgeling, "It takes a little blood-letting to allow the learning in. Lock them in the *casas*. And I want this chapel destroyed. Maybe that will teach them a lesson."

31

Angry Words

OCTOBER 1640

"What did he call me?" the governor asked his aide concerning don Simon Perez de Bustillo.

"I wouldn't feel comfortable telling you, your Lordship."

"Well, I'm not interested in your comfort, or in your discomfort, for that matter, Goddamn it! I asked you what Perez said!"

"It was in reference to Juan Bautista Saragosa, whom you placed in stocks, and, also, in regards to the beatings you gave to Fathers Romero and Nunez," his aide responded, waiting a long moment before continuing. "He said that you might as well have beaten the ancient Fray Antonio Jimenez, or even the deceased, Fray Esteban de Perea, for that matter, poor individuals, old, and infirm, or even dead. Romero and Nunez were unarmed except for their rosaries. He said that you were a bully and called you a *sardesco*, a pony, rude or stubborn, a small ass."

"I know what it means, Goddamn it!" Rosas exploded. "In my own time and in my own way, I will make that Goddamned Perez de Bustillo pay for his insolence!"

AN INTERLUDE: APRIL 1641

The winter of 1640 in New Mexico had passed without major incident, the colony being far removed from the turmoil on the Iberian Peninsula in which Portugal was completing the final stage of its revolt against Spain. The settlers, unaware of this situation, looked forward to the spring of 1641 and the arrival of their new governor. While the colonists were waiting for the governor, however, a group of mounted soldiers were returning from the Taos Pueblo where they had collected Rosas's tribute. They encountered a group of citizen-soldiers coming along the snow-covered trace from the *villa de Santa Fe* and heading north. The tribute collectors' captain later reported to his governor:

"We came upon a small caravan of light wagons and horses, your Lordship. It was the Bacas and the Perez de Bustillos going to a christening in Cuyamungue, they said."

"Children as well adults?" Rosas asked.

"No, your Lordship. The elders only," the soldier laughed. "They said, ' Let the children take care of themselves.' I'm sorry you were not with us, your Lordship. You could have exacted retribution from Simon Perez de Bustillo for his insult. Perhaps I should have done it for you," he added with bravado.

"You've no need to be concerned for me," said the governor whose humiliation was magnified by the fact that others knew of it. "I've waited for six long months to exact my retribution. And when the time comes, I will, in my own way, get my due."

RETRIBUTION

"His Lordship is unable to see you now," said the governor's aide to Maria Perez de Bustillo who was again at the palace gate. "He asks that you return tonight and dine with him. He'll have a carriage waiting for you at the bottom of the hill on the canyon road."

Does he know that my parents are gone? She asked herself. Surely, he would not have made this suggestion if he thought they were in the *villa*. But so much the better, she thought, as she soaked in her tub of hot water to which had been added a few drops of lavender oil harvested from her Uncle Antonio's garden. Perhaps I can charm the grant out of him, she said to herself.

The room was in a jumble. Her parent's divan, a thinly mattressed double bed covered with a richly embroidered spread, was now further covered with the articles of clothing they had taken from a leather chest: *rebozos*, some of white lace, others of China silk heavy with embroidered scarlet and yellow flowers and a long red fringe. Still others were of silk that fell like water in solid colors, including black. A final one was of black lace with designs like the shadows of rose leaves. Also on the bed, were some of her mother's dresses, and some of her own, beautiful gowns with tight bodices and long sleeves, low necks and pinched high waists. Their spreading skirts were of heavy silk or satin, over which laces had been cascaded or looped.[1]

A second chest, a Spanish *hembra*, or bride's trousseau trunk of dovetail construction, was heavy with iron hinges, locks, and handles. It stood open, its contents strewn about the room. Among them were her mother's Moorish box of tortoise shell, ivory and teakwood from which Maria had taken a necklace and a small velvet-covered casket in which little votive images called *milagros* were kept. These silver images of cows, sheep, and body parts—arms, legs, and feet—were pinned to the clothing of the family's favorite saint as a perpetual request for assistance. Maria had chosen the representation of a sheep, and Tula had affixed it to the cloak of *San Lorenzo*.

"Will you put these back for me when were done?" Maria asked Tula. She stood before her *criada*. "Do you think this blouse is too big for me?"

"Bend over," Tula commanded. She surveyed the tall, beautiful, slim girl standing on a small, white hearthrug before the fire to keep her feet warm while dressing. "Um, I don't know," Tula said. "I can see from here to Pecos."

"Everything?"

"Everything. Even your toes."

"But I love this blouse," Maria said of the top made of bone lace, "It's elegant. I've loved it ever since my papa gave it to my mama."

"But it's too big for you. You can see everything when you bend over."

"Well, then, I won't bend over," Maria laughed.

"If you wear it off your shoulders like this," Tula said as she moved the top down, it will tighten it up a bit and make it less revealing. But you wont be able to pin your brooch on it, the material's too fragile."

"I'll pin it to my skirt," Maria responded, the hoops of which were now discarded.[2] "It will do very well there. I'm going to wear gloves and a jacket, too," she said of a brocade of beautiful threads all in white that lay on her parents' bed. "And a skirt of embroidered tabby."

"But your jacket is for the cold only," Tula responded. "You're not going to wear it through dinner."

Suddenly, Maria stopped in the middle of her whirlwind preparations. "Oh, God! What am I doing?" Maria exclaimed, "My mama would kill me if she knew."

"And your papa? He'd kill you, too. But he'd probably torture you first," Tula laughed. "Now get dressed. The governor will be waiting for you. You've got to go."

Maria dressed and then stood for a final inspection wishing that she had a full-length mirror by which she could see herself. A necklace of *aljofar*, small pearls of irregular shape, was placed around Maria's long, white neck. Tula fastened it, straightened Maria's skirts, and stepped away for a final appraisal.

"What do you think?" Maria asked expectantly. "Good?"

Tula, who knew that Maria had the sort of beauty that was best set off by rich simplicity, waited a long moment before responding. Examining Maria from her brocaded slippers to the top of her piled hair, she smiled. "Good. Very good!" she said to the beautiful 18-year-old, as she handed Maria her wrap. "Are you sure you don't want me to go with you?" she asked as she helped Maria into her *mantellina* and cape.

"To do what? Sit in the snow?" she asked. "I'll be all right. I've been there a million times."

The brooch, cherished but forgotten for this one brief moment, remained on her mother's washstand as Maria exited the room.

* * *

Bundled up in a light cloak with the folds of its hood held tightly about her face, Maria sat in the coach for a moment surveying her surroundings.

Suddenly, she tossed back the cape's hood with both hands and stepped from the carriage. The watchman lifted his candle lamp, and, in its glow, her auburn hair, much rumpled by the cowl she had worn as protection against the snow of a late spring storm, now fell in the soft, bronze waves of watered camlet about her shoulders. The hem of her long white skirts rippled over the unevenness of the flagstone floor as she wound her way along the *portico*. She appeared composed and magnificently self-confident as she entered the governor's study.

The room, so bare and cheerless on her previous visits, was now arrayed with tapestries on the wall and carpeting on the floor. The colors were mainly crimson and white, signifying joy and happiness—and sometimes, also, cruelty or innocence. And in the corner of the room stood a beautiful full-length mirror of Italian glass, as transparent as glycerin, so beautifully clear that Maria reached out to touch it uncertainly, half expecting to sense the softness of her own likeness being reflected back to her. She could see the governor standing behind her, surveying her with narrowly squinted eyes.

He had been drinking, and she could see that there was something wrong, his eyes dark and unseeing beneath thick eyebrows. He appeared addled, as if attempting to make sense of the world.

There were several courses: the main *manjar blanco*, an appetizing dish made of breast of fowl with rice flour, milk and sugar. And there were several glasses of wine. Maria was in the middle of her second glass, though she usually only had one. The conversation was light. She mostly listened. What did she know of the world? When dessert—flan with cinnamon sprinkled on top—was over, the dishes were cleared, the tablecloth removed, and the servants ushered from the room.

The governor discarded his short cape, and they sat before the fireplace in the chill of this late April evening. He pondered the flames flowing about upright sticks standing in the hearth. She sat quietly. Finally, she said in the sweetest voice she could muster, "your Grace, I have a request to make of you. She waited. And waited. And then, choosing her words well, she said, "I believe you know my circumstances. My husband will be home within a few months and he has still not received an answer from the *cabildo* regarding his petition for a grant. I know that you have the power to make this happen and I beg that Nicolas be granted an apportionment of land before he returns. Our future depends on it."

Tossing down the contents of the large glass of wine he had just poured, the governor swiped at his mouth with the sleeve of his doublet, stood, and walked around the table and over to her. She not so much heard as felt the pad of each footfall as he moved in behind her chair. Placing a hand on her bare shoulder—her *mantilla*, jacket, and gloves long removed—he ran his other hand down her arm. Stepping to the side of her chair, he curled his hand into hers and assisted her to rise.

She looked up at him, questioning. A *danza*? There's no music, she thought. He stood before her a long moment and then kissed her. She was both surprised and alarmed. Assuming the responsibility was hers, she said, "your Lordship. I'm sorry if I've given you the wrong impression."

He looked at her a long moment and then taking her in his embrace he kissed her again, placing both of his hands around her tiny waist, then sliding them down over the roundness of her hips and onto her buttocks. Drawing her to him, he kissed her hard but said nothing.

"Please!" she said, as she attempted to avert her face. "Please don't!" she said quietly.

"Do you think we play a game here?" he asked belligerently, turning her arm behind her back, turning her away from him, leaning her down across the table, she unable to rise.

"Please!" she whimpered in panic.

He slapped her hard between her shoulder blades. Once. Then again. The second blow with a closed fist taking her breath. After that, with her chest held flat against the table, he viciously thrust his free hand into her bodice, quickly squeezing each of her breasts, removing his hand to catch the hem of her skirts.

The rest was a nightmare. Fumbling to keep her skirts hiked above her waist, he removed her undergarments, opened his flies and forcibly entered her unknowing and unwilling body. His entrance was initially blocked, but he forced entry.

She begged him to stop, but her cries went unheard even by her.

He said nothing, his breath coming in ragged grunts like those of an animal in rut. The slap of bared flesh echoed in the candle lit room. There was searing pain. Fear and shame. And then it was over.

Although released from his hold, Maria was unable to rise, afraid of what he might do next. Her skirts slid from their place around her waist and fell to the floor. She could hear him behind her. The click of buttons. The rustle of cambric and Dutch linen. Moving about her like a cat, he walked to the door where he turned his back to her and said, "You may get dressed now."

Ignoring her pain, she replaced her underclothing, her hands, her whole body shaking uncontrollably. Her blouse was torn, her mother's pearls strewn across the floor.

Shrinking from him as though awaiting further attack, she waited for him to move from in front of the door, her only escape. He turned to her and said, "I'm sorry. I should not have done that, even though I was only exercising my *derecho de pernada*."[3] He took a step toward her and said, "But it's over and done with, and it will remain our secret. Neither Nicolas nor anyone else need ever know."

She refused to look at him, flinching from his approach and from his hand that he attempted to place on her shoulder. When he abandoned the doorway, she opened it and ran out into the covered walkway.

"I'll call for the carriage," he said.

She ignored him, walking quickly down the stone-flagged *portico*, her slippered feet, as in a nightmare, moving toward the open courtyard. Once there, she began running toward the gate.

"Put her in the carriage," the governor yelled to its driver, "and take her to wherever she wishes to go and don't stop until you get there!"

She refused to enter the carriage and was forcibly placed there by its driver and by the governor, who, following the carriage and its unwilling occupant, ran to the gate.

Clattering along a rough-packed road past the plaza and the parish church, generally following the route it had taken when it brought her to the royal palace, the carriage raced alongside the ice-clad banks of the river, a bleak, sad, leaden thing roaring in the canyon below. Crying for the first time, Maria demanded that the carriage stop, and when it did not, she leaped from it and disappeared into the darkness. The driver searched for her among the fractured shards of ice shelving, but she had hidden herself well. When he was gone, she removed her clothing and, screaming in the dark, stood in the raging stream, trying to wash herself clean of Rosas. Drying herself with an undergarment, she dressed, and, following the snow-covered path along the river, stumbled and staggered toward home.

* * *

"Your hands! Your elbows!" Tula shrieked in alarm. "For the love of the holiest Mary, dona Maria, what happened to you?"

"I fell!" Maria cried.

"You fell in the river? How did you fall in the river?" Tula asked.

"I don't know," Maria cried. "I fell! Get me some warm water so that I may wash myself," she said through her tears. "Take my clothes and burn them. And if you tell mama about any of this, I'll see that you're beaten! Leave! Please, leave me alone," she cried as she lay on her bed sobbing.

She had a pain in her head so severe she could not determine its location, and on her back she felt a coldness like the winds off the mountains, even though the sconce-held candles throughout her darkened room guttered toward the ceiling with an uninterrupted flame. The chill was followed by dry heaves and then by a period of profound sadness that Maria would be unable to shake either in the days following or ever after.

* * *

And Nicolas, somewhere on the trail between the city of Mexico and Santa Fe, and longing to see his bride, was soon to return.

32

In Antonio's Garden

SPRING 1641

"Why don't you come inside?" Antonio asked his brother Alonso, who was sitting in his courtyard.

"I can't. My boots are full of mud," Alonso responded, as Antonio's dog, bounding and barking in excitement, came out of the door.

"Then take them off," Antonio said to his younger brother. "Take them off and come inside."

"Why? So Yumar can see my toe?" he remarked, referring to the splintered toenail he had suffered when his horse had stepped on him. Alonso knew that his footless stockings would reveal his wound. "I don't think so," he laughed, while looking down at his boots that were curled and withered and caved in at the top. He held a hand down to the dancing puppy, who, clumsy and agile all at once, was asking to be held and petted while rejecting these at the same time. Alonso went down on his haunches, scratched the sides of the puppy's neck, spoke to him and "gentled" him. He put the puppy between his legs and ran his hands along his sides. He had grown, an indication of the dog he would become. "God, he's gotten big!" he exclaimed. When Alonso had first seen him, he was crying and peeing and shrinking from his hand. "I'll wait here," he yelled, as he came to his feet.

"Well, just a second then," Antonio responded, as his dog

reappeared at his side. "I'll be right out." Alonso had already taken a seat on a splay-legged bench placed, invitingly, under the shade of a tree.

Alonso looked back at the gate he had just entered. It had been opened to allow the entrance of a two-wheeled cart that was now being pulled inside. An Indian, a *genizaro* employed by Antonio as a servant, lifted the tongue of the cart with great effort, glancing briefly at Alonso as he struggled with the hay-laden vehicle.

"Can I help?" Alonso asked.

The servant did not respond, but Alonso assisted him anyway, helping him to raise the tongue of the cart so that it could be pulled inside. He then returned to his seat under the tree where he sat with his back against its trunk and waited.

In the deep shade of a cottonwood, one of three in Antonio's *plazuela*, he rolled the sleeves of his open-necked leather shirt up over his elbows. He had tied his horse beneath a tree on the outside of the courtyard and thought for a moment about the advisability of having left it there, for many horses were being taken from their corrals and fields by the "dirty Indian pirates" from the *sierras* who had begun to menace the colonists. But the presence of the servant and that of others working in the hay fields above Antonio's house should, Alonso felt, provide a deterrent to the thieves.

Flowers flanked both sides of the doorway where Antonio had greeted him, with additional blooms throughout the square. Long spears of purple penstemon grew within flowerbeds that lined the walls, while beneath the trees was a small treasure of clover with tiny yellow blossoms that gave his garden a wonderful scent. It is, Alonso thought, an island of flowers in the wilderness. The design of his *placita* had given Antonio a blank canvas upon which to create a place to relax, a meditative spot, an area to attract bees and birds and butterflies of every kind. He had brought some of the *cholla* growing outside the walls of his home inside, their pink flowers, on tall, slim stems becoming the centerpiece for his creation. To these he had added prickly pear bearing spiky rosettes of yellow and orange flowers and green leaves. Then, in response to Yumar's request that he provide her with the herbs she required for her well-being, he had added osha and the Mediterranean imports, sweet basil,

169

lavender, oregano and rosemary. The osha, Yumar had told him, was good for protection against snakes and, when placed in a medicine bag, would assist in warding off evil spirits. The basil, should it be required, was good for ridding a person of *susto* (shock or fright), and carrying it around in one's pocket would bring good luck. What she did not tell Antonio regarding the basil, as she secreted little bags of the miraculous ingredient within the lining of his clothing, was that it could also be used to return a straying husband to her spouse. It was also for Yumar that Antonio had planted the mint and lavender, in purple, blue, pink, and white which provided the ingredients she needed to make her "dream pillows."[1] He had finished—although he had told Alonso that a garden was never finished—with plantings of the gray and green foliage of stonecrop and of red yucca whose four-foot tall spikes were so loved by his hummingbirds. Irrigated with gray water reclaimed from his kitchen, or by the cold and clean water he drew from his well, Antonio's garden was a place of refuge.

The garden reminded Alonso of the plains of wild flowers he had encountered on his exploration to the east. Instead of the parched grasslands he had expected to find, the fields there were covered with flowers of a thousand different kinds providing a kaleidoscope of color to the distant horizon.

The expedition itself had served to remind Alonso of how differently he and his brother Antonio approached the world. In 1634, Alonso had led a company of Spanish traders out onto the bison plains. They had gone due east almost 300 leagues to the Magdalena (Arkansas River). They would have gone further, Alonso assured himself and crossed over into Caddoan *Quivira*, had not the expedition been prevented from doing so by the friendly *Vaquero* Apaches with whom they traveled. Alonso had asked Antonio to accompany him on that expedition but had been met with Antonio's usual response when asked to go exploring: "Let's secure what we have, Alonso, before searching for more." The old "bird in the hand" adage, thought Alonso, regarding Antonio's words, words that accurately reflected the instructions Governor Pedro de Peralta had received from the viceroy when establishing the royal *villa* in 1610. The viceroy had said regarding the colonists who had refused to build a village of their own that Peralta must not allow further exploration, "since experience has shown that greed for what is out of reach has always led them to neglect what they already have."[2]

While we might share a sense of purpose, Alonso thought—and I'm not completely sure about that either—our basic personalities are different, reflecting, perhaps, the traits of our fathers.[3] And aren't the differences in our personalities reflected in the way we wish to deal with the governor and with the priests? Alonso mused. Antonio wants to find legal means by which to remove them from their offices, while I just want to pull them down.

Antonio came out then, his dog, Albacar, entangled in his feet. Antonio, of course, said nothing to his overgrown puppy, for he could not reprimand or scold him because of love they shared. Antonio had found the puppy in a den created where the river had cut through the sedimentary slope. Here, in a cave carved out by the waters, the puppy had been hiding behind the lifeless form of his mother. Antonio had previously seen him with his mother and with five or six other puppies, the bitch moving them from place to place in her quest for warmth and shelter. They had disappeared, until Antonio, several days later, attracted by the puppy's small cries, had found him at the back of the small cave. The puppy had refused to come out and had to be extracted by Antonio, Alonso, and several of Antonio's men. Alonso had said, "He'll die of fright if we try to dig him out." To which Antonio had responded, "He'll die of starvation if we don't."

Albacar was an amber-colored puppy with a handsome face and enormous paws, his short coat soft and silky. Raucous and strong, he made his presence known by pressing up against Antonio's legs or ribs, whether Antonio was sitting with him next to the fire or lying beside him on the floor. Giving every appearance of health and vigor, he was in command of the *placita* (although he was not allowed to chase the hummingbirds). Unless Antonio accompanied him on walks outside the courtyard, however, he refused to leave the security provided by its walls. Drawn to Antonio like a magnet, Albacar now cocked his head and waited for Antonio to continue down the path. Talking to the puppy in a gentle, soft, and loving tone of voice, Antonio smiled at Alonso, then laughed, pleading, "Call him, or I'll never get out."

Antonio was dressed in leather trousers rolled up above his *teguas*, the hard-soled hide moccasins he wore when at home, and a leather shirt, his sleeves rolled up to his elbows. He was holding onto a bowl of *pinons* or pine nuts that he held in his left hand and two mugs of apple jack clenched in his right, the base of the two clay receptacles held firmly against the crook of his arm.

"Goddamn!" he laughed, as Alonso took the mugs from his hand. "Take these before I drop them. You'd think I could have made two trips— or that you could have helped me by coming inside!" They put the bowl and mugs on the top of a large cottonwood stump, a stub about two feet high that served the patio as a table. The stump was creased, furrowed, and decaying into a crumbly, brown compost about its edges, and Alonso was careful to select a flat and only marginally rotted spot on which to put the refreshments.

"Yumar says that she doesn't care if you track in mud, and that she'll easily find a servant to clean it. And that you should be happy that you have two good feet and boots to put on them. And that she wants you to eat with us," Antonio said happily.

"Ya? Well, I can just imagine how happy she would have been if I had come in my stocking feet," he remarked referring to the wool stockings he was wearing, the ends of which were pulled down under his heel so that the upper half of his foot was covered, but his toes were left bare.[4]

"How did you get so muddy?" Antonio asked, looking down at Alonso's boots where mud had oozed up along the sides.

"At the river. I got down to get a drink and sank in up to my ankles. Then I couldn't get out," Alonso laughed. You should have seen me. I must have looked like a dwarf. I was flailing around and looking for something to pull myself out with. I didn't want to yell," he said with a shrug. "What good would it have done anyway? You in your patio planting your flowers. If you had heard me, you'd have probably thought you were losing your mind."

"Well, I wouldn't have gone down there anyway," Antonio responded. "Maybe we'd have found you next spring. Look at him! Just look at him," Antonio remarked regarding Albacar who was lying at his feet. "Look at the way he sleeps." The puppy had his head nestled between Antonio's ankles, a large paw upon the arch of one foot. "Some part of him has to be in contact with me at all times. I suspect he thinks I'm his mama."

"Or maybe his papa?"

"Or both," Antonio shrugged. "You'd think he was glued to me!"

"And you wouldn't have it any other way," Alonso replied.

Then, with a sigh, Antonio responded, "No, I guess not. I think with the girls married and gone, I need something small to love."

They laughed and sipped from their mugs.

"Um. This is good." Alonso swiped at his mouth with the back of his hand. "This is really good stuff!" he said appreciatively regarding his drink. Taking a nut from the bowl in which Antonio had carried them, he cracked it between two of his front teeth. He took another one. This was one that had been roasted in an outdoor oven that enhanced its delicious taste. With his index finger and thumb, he searched for the exact spot on the shell where there was a raised portion, a seam where he might crack it open. As a child, he had, when the spirit moved him, cracked and shelled a handful of the delicious meats placing them in a copper mug until it was full before eating them. But now, as an adult, he was less able to wait, content, instead, to crack open and eat each pine nut, one at a time, as he and his brother enjoyed the *plazuela* at Antonio's home.

"And Yumar?" Alonso asked again, wondering why his sister-in-law had not joined them.

"She's inside with some of the servants," Antonio responded. "There seems to be a problem. Anyhow, something's going on, and she's trying to see if she can get it out of them."

"A problem?" Alonso questioned.

"Maybe," Antonio responded. "I don't know. But I'm worried."

Alonso studied his brother for a brief moment. Antonio looked concerned, his brow furrowed, his mind seemingly someplace else.

"It has to do with the Pueblos," Antonio continued. "A problem about which our servants heard in *Analco*. It just goes to show how stupid we are," he exclaimed. "We think and worry constantly about the *Vaquero*

Apaches and worry not at all about these other people who live right next door."

"The Pueblos?" Alonso questioned.

"Yes, the Pueblos," said Antonio shaking his head. "Their resentment is even deeper than we thought. Our servants say that the Pueblos are hoping that a leader will rise up among them who'll give us our due. Us, because we've taken their best land and because we pay them no respect. And the priests because they've destroyed their religious objects, burned and filled-in their *kivas*, and because they outlaw their ceremonies. The people of *Analco* say that the Pueblos are tired of putting the priests' houses in order, of sweeping and heating them, and of adorning their churches. And they say that the Pueblos hate the priests because the priests beat the Pueblo elders and shave their heads, humiliating and punishing their old men."

Alonso put his head back against the trunk of the tree and his feet out before him. He examined the mud on his boots, saying, "And all of that would be unbelievable if it wasn't true, even the part about our disrespecting them. Where do you think the Pueblos are going with this?" he asked his brother.

"I don't know," Antonio said in dismay.

"But it's not only the Indians who are tired of the priests," Alonso said. "Our *vecinos* hate the fact that we seem to be utterly dependent upon these men who have us by the short hairs. They initiate inquisitional investigations against us, demand that we pay public penance, and then excommunicate those among us who refuse their demands. Besides that, they want us to pay a *Cruzada* tax! Goddamn it!" he said, shaking his head. "What did we do to deserve them?

"And that God dammed Rosas," Alonso continued. "How much longer do we have to put up with him? When do we pull him down?" he asked, as he took another drink from his mug.

"Soon," Antonio responded reflectively. "Soon," he repeated.

Antonio took a handful of nuts from the bowl and plopped them into his mouth, cracking and eating them, shells and all. "I haven't got time to shell them," he laughed. "Well, I guess I have the time. I just don't have the inclination," he said sadly. "Maybe it's the weather. The heat. I

174

don't know. But I wonder where all of this is leading. We seem to be on a collision course, you know," he said to Alonso meaning the Indians' and the settlers' relationships with the governor and the priests. "All I know is that I have a job to do," he said, "to rally the militia and to take up arms in defense of the missions. And I know that all laws, human and divine, allow us to defend ourselves from attack—from whatever enemy or quarter. But I wonder where we'll be in five years?" he mused. "In a decade? Five decades? I know that you and I will be long gone, but I wonder if our children will still be here. I think that we're headed for a disaster."

33

A Scorched Earth

The governor now initiated a strange tactic. Aware of the enmity that existed between the colonists and the Franciscan priests, Rosas attempted to win the settlers' loyalty through a program of planned devastation directed against the Church. He started, absurdly, by robbing the friars' *conventos* and driving off their stock.

With mixed feelings about their priests who continued to make inordinate demands of them, the settlers nonetheless refused to abandon the clerics in their time of need. Thus, the smoking hostilities between the three estates were now blown into the blaze of a civil war. During the spring of 1641, a number of colonists took refuge with their priests behind the *atrio* walls at Santo Domingo which became their line of defense. Their numbers steadily increased as additional colonists deserted their farms, *haciendas*, and ranches and established encampments beside them. There was, in effect, a vast wilderness separating the colonists and priests from their governor, the wasteland extending along the Rio Grande River Valley which was now utterly deserted.

The colonists wrote letters to the viceroy and complained about their governor, but it was the priests who made the most noise. In addition to a public declaration by the clergy—20 of whom signed a document setting out their intentions, purposes, and motives in their dispute with the governor—the priests determined that no one who had pledged to make war on the governor should curse or blaspheme, though later, by their own revision, the *alcaldes*, captains, and clergy were freed from these restrictions. *Custos* Juan de Salas had, in addition, demanded that the governor reinstate all of the property he had confiscated, that he restrain his propensity to intrude in the business of the Church, and that he support the work of the priests in their conversion of the Indians. "Do you not know what we do here?" Salas had written, "We exist only to bring them to God!

* * *

"What would he have us do?" Salas raged. "Lead his horse through the streets? Scatter petals in his path? We'll do none of those things!" he said to the priests of his custody who, in their cassocks of milled serge, stood before him in their church of Santo Domingo. "We attempted to make our peace with him and he would have none of it," Salas said, looking intently at his men. "From the devil he came, and to the devil he must go! We've had it with Luis de Rosas!"

Salas's priests, most of whom were lean and hard from the rigors of their work, stood restlessly before him, shuffling their sandaled feet in anxious anticipation, waiting for one of their number to express their view. Finally, Fray Andres Juarez, former guardian at Santo Domingo, who would have willingly submitted himself to self-punishment and starvation in a bid to rid themselves of the governor, said, "We could stay here forever, Father, cowering behind these adobe walls while our children remain uncared for. Whatever the dangers, Father," he said, while kneading the knuckles of his gout-twisted hands, "we're prepared to sacrifice ourselves, prepared to suffer for Christ Jesus. And we have taken a vote. We are willing, in obedience to your wishes, to remain here, but we request that we be allowed to return to our missions. I know that you have personally advised me to stay here, but I beg to be allowed to go with the rest."

Fray Salas looked at the elderly priest, stooped with age and disease, a sick man, almost a cripple, who had been through it all. Coming to New Mexico in 1612 full of fervor for his ministry, he had later tried to desert his post in order to escape his *comisario*, the belligerent and tyrannical Fray Isidro Ordonez. In Ordonez's bid to wrest control of the colony from civil authority, he had imprisoned its governor don Pedro de Peralta. Also imprisoned by Ordonez—right here in the *convento* at Santo

Domingo—Juarez had spent four months in irons but was ultimately to outlast his superior in the adobe kingdom. Ordonez eventually returned to New Spain where, although reprimanded, he was absolved of sedition. The Father *Custos*, Juan de Salas, continued looking at Fray Juarez, a dedicated priest who had gone to the bison plains with Alonso Baca, and who, before being transferred to the mission at San Ildefonso, had, for 13 years, lived among the Pecos Indians. He had been most effective in his ministry there. In resignation, and in response to his men who wished to return to their missions, Salas decided that they could go and that, in deference to his wishes, Fray Andres Juarez could go with them.

"You may go back to San Ildefonso as you have requested, Father," Fray Salas said to Fray Juarez, "and the rest of you may also return to your missions. But know this, your Reverences," he said. "I have sought the intercession of Antonio Baca in our war with the governor, and requested that he, the son of our former *syndico*, take up arms on our behalf. I can protect you here, but I cannot protect you at your missions. You'll be in my prayers, Fathers, but beyond that, I can't offer you anything in terms of your safety."

"We'll be safe, Father, and we'll do our work well," said Fray Juarez, speaking for those priests who elected to return to their missions.

* * *

While *Custos* Salas was in conclave with his priests at Santo Domingo, Governor Rosas was conducting a similar meeting at the *Palacio de Casas Reales* in Santa Fe.

"They're unguarded," said Martin Barba of the missions the friars had abandoned in their retreat to Santo Domingo. "Their fruit is ripe and ready for the picking."

"Which pueblos?" Rosas asked Martin and the soldiers who were accompanying him.

"The pueblos of Nambe and Santa Clara in the north and Sandia and Quarai in the south, to mention but a few," Martin said. "The *conventos* are empty, your Lordship, the altars without priests. The priests' stock is wandering here and there without herder or guard," he said smiling. "How would you like us to proceed?"

Without a thought the governor answered, "Loot and burn them.

And should you find *porteros* there whom the priests may have left to guard the place, throw them out, no matter their age or circumstance. Then, while you're in the north taking Nambe and Santa Clara, go to San Ildefonso. The priests, in defiance of my authority, have fortified it. Take cannons there and turn it into a garrison. Also, if Fray Juarez is there," he added, "throw him out. I have a special hatred for that man."

"And what are we to do with the stock, your Lordship?" Martin asked. "The priests' flocks are some of the best and largest in the colony."

"Drive them to my ranch at Galisteo," Rosas responded, his eyes flashing, "then meet me at Santo Domingo. We've got to deal with the priests and colonists who are holed up there. I've had enough of their shit!" he continued, speaking about the priests, some of whom had been in retreat at Santo Domingo for more than a year. "Their ploy has been to remain in sanctuary at Santo Domingo until the colonists beg them to return to their missions, and now that a number of colonists have joined them in their refuge, they mean to stay there until I'm replaced. Their actions demonstrate an open rebellion against the Crown," he said. "They've thrown up earthworks and dug themselves in with ditches and *acequias*! I can't have those goddamned priests and treasonous colonists holed up there in defiance of my authority. I ordered the priests to leave the kingdom under penalty of fire and blood and I gave them three days to comply. But they've refused to pack their bags and are still here. Therefore, they leave me no choice. I'll take them into custody and send them south. And if they give me the least bit of trouble in effecting their arrest, I'll have them garroted. The stand at Santo Domingo is over!"

34

When the Enemy Flees, Build Him a Bridge of Silver

At Santo Domingo, the Great River flowed into a shallow loop, streaming over gravel islands that offered a panoramic view of the eastern mountains. Readily defensible gravel hills provided a bulwark or defensive wall fronting the pueblo and floodplain on which they lay.

Although the setting sun lay warm and glowing on adobe walls and roofs, the colonists' horizons were generally dark. Their dreams of living lives as noblemen, so bright and promising only a generation ago, now receded from view. Nonetheless, many of the colonists, including those that Rosas had stripped of their commissions and *encomiendas* or had otherwise wronged, had joined their priests in defiance of the governor. Feeling that right and justice were on their side, they filed into the main church at Santo Domingo with the intention of holding the kingdom's ecclesiastical capital against the governor until he was replaced.

In an atmosphere of fear and apprehension, the soldier-settlers stood out from beneath the choir loft looking up at their leader who was standing at its rail. They were meeting with their Senior Judge, Antonio Baca, in an attempt to convince themselves that they could hold Santo Domingo against any force. There, in light provided by the church's clerestory window, Baca's men looked up at Antonio as men are inclined to look at their captain awaiting his lead.

Baca, who believed that many of the governor's men would desert to his side when the fighting began, said, "As you're aware, the priests of the Custody of Saint Paul have come to us with complaints regarding Governor Rosas. There's much about their complaints that's real," he said. "But we must remember that in calling us to arms, and in asking us to defend them against an assault by the governor, they are really looking to their own welfare rather than ours. What they wish to do is assert their primacy in matters relating to the administration of the colony. Although they have called us to danger, they themselves will carry no arms, nor will they take on any load they may place on us. But that's the way of priests," Baca said, "for they're not soldiers. They're not soldiers," he repeated quietly, his voice trailing off. "Remember," he said darkly, "that while the bell-ringer may sound the alarm, he himself is safe in the belfry." He waited a long moment before continuing, seemingly weighing his every word and saying finally, "There are four conditions under which men may take up arms, draw their swords, and risk their persons, lives and fortunes: to defend the Catholic faith; to defend their lives or land; to defend their family, honor, or possessions; and to serve their king in a just war. At least three, if not four, of these conditions are present here. But do not fool yourselves by ascribing a holy cause to our actions. For we do what we do for our own honor and safety, and not theirs," he said gravely, regarding the priests. "And whether we succeed or fail, we will attribute it to no one but ourselves."

Whereas Antonio Baca's words were intended to set out the appropriateness of their war with the governor, the message provided by Antonio's brother, Alonso, provided them with the reality. Standing among the crowd below the choir loft, he had the ruddy complexion of the Bacas, further reddened by the sun. Although he was taller than his father, Cristobal had been he had the same thickset body as both his father and brother. He was of strong fiber and his bearing and stance were those of a soldier. "He's coming," he said of the governor. "He's coming with cannons, three from his cannon-of-battery at Santa Fe," he said as he glanced up at Antonio. "Guns made for battering down fortress walls."

"So how do we counter his move?" asked Antonio who had not anticipated this action.

"The governor told his men to establish a garrison at San Ildefonso," Alonso said, "and they're taking the remainder of his guns there for that purpose. I say that we take the guns away from him."

"Take his guns?" asked one of the men. "How would we do that?"

"Well, it won't be easy," Alonso said, "but he's only thinking of attacking us. He doesn't consider that we might mount a preemptive strike. He expects us to be cowering here behind adobe walls, awaiting his attack. I'm sure that it's never occurred to him that we might hit him first, or that we might use his overconfidence to our advantage. If we hit him when his men are crossing the river at San Ildefonso, I think we can take his guns," he said as he looked around at the men. "With a lightning force of men mounted on swift horses, I think we can get there ahead of them."

"How many men will you need?" asked Antonio who had begun to see that a defensive stance, rather than an offensive move, would ultimately end in defeat. "I'll give you as many as you need."

"Not many," Alonso replied. "The numbers are not as important as the will to succeed."

"Then I could as well give you one or seventy," Antonio responded, "for the men here are all of one mind when it comes to Rosas. I'll give you a squad of your own choosing. Yours may well be our most important battle. We must have his guns. Whatever the cost, Alonso, when the governor's men cross the river at San Ildefonso, you must be there too."

"And I will be," Alonso responded looking up at his brother. "And when we've taken his guns, I'll send word by Marquez."

AN ESCAPE FROM THE SLAUGHTER IS WORTH MORE THAN GOOD MEN'S PRAYERS

The colonists at Santo Domingo—73 of the 120 *vecinos* of the royal *villa*—worked to stiffen the walls of the *atrio*, knowing that the walls, no matter how high or thick, would eventually be destroyed if Rosas was successful in bringing cannons against them. They knew they had to counter his guns with guns of their own, but even if they were successful in taking the cannons away from the governor, they were unsure that Alonso could bring them to Santo Domingo before the governor arrived. The colonists, however, refused to speak of their predicament believing in the Spanish adage that "if a thing is not mentioned, it does not exist."

"I want the men kept busy," Antonio said to one of his captains who had joined him at the friars' *convento*. "Have them chip stone," he directed, regarding the making of stone cannonballs that were in many respects superior to cast-iron projectiles. "Keep them busy. I want to be ready when Alonso returns."

SUFFER OR STRIKE, STRIKE OR BE STRUCK

In the wee hours of the morning, while the moon still shone gold against a darkened sky, Antonio Baca received word from the north. "Set the board so that you have white," his brother wrote, "for you too shall have cannons."

"We've taken three from Martin Barba at San Ildefonso," said Antonio to his waiting men as he dismounted before the *atrio*. "Alonso will have them here before nightfall. Guns with their wheeled carriages," he repeated. "They're coming down the west side of the river. Once we've pulled them across," he added, "you're to drive heavy stakes in the ford and put boulders in the stream so that the governor cannot cross. He'll find another ford below this one, but his ride there will give us the time we need to set the cannons. Make sure that the governor doesn't cross here!" he repeated as he remounted his horse.

Once Baca's cannons had been dragged across the river and placed behind the *atrio* walls, the colonists worked to block the ford.

* * *

As he approached the village along the river from the north, and saw the men of Baca's contingent working in the stream, the governor decided to ride south along the margins of the river. When they found an abandoned ford, he and his men began crossing the river below the spiles. Dragging cannons, they rode in a rumbling mass toward the pueblo as the day turned into late afternoon and the afternoon into evening.

The preparations for defense at the pueblo were of many kinds.

While the men chipped stone and cleaned soiled arms, the Pueblo women wove a hempen cord by which to encircle their village. Then, as the friars had instructed them, they cut the cord into rush lights, taking them to the church for a blessing, and asking all the holy saints—especially the pueblo's patron, Saint Dominic—to protect them from the perils of an attack.

As night approached, the soldiers on both sides of the *atrio* walls watched the day move into indigo blue, then near black, in ominous eventide. A squall erupted over the peaks to the west, sweeping noisily across the valley, precipitating a deluge of rain and hailstones that beat upon adobe walls and roofs, smarting Rosas's soldiers who huddled without cover in the enveloping darkness. Confused by the failing light, the men outside the walls wandered aimlessly in the rain and hail, seeking refuge wherever it might be found upon a treeless plain, while those inside the *atrio* sought shelter within the church or below canvas-covered carts. At some point in the night, after intermittent showers of rain and hailstones, the tempest blew itself out. At first light, the world was sun-drenched but sheer and freezing, a thin, chilly dawn.

* * *

A lone rider approached the pueblo from the eastern reaches of the governor's encampment and was met by one of the governor's aides. The two men dismounted behind a gravel dune to shield their conversation from attentive ears. Hearing the news, which Martin Barba had brought from the north, the governor's aide sighed. "God! This is a disaster. What will you say to the governor?" he asked in dismay, then added, "Whatever you do say, and however you say it, Martin, break it to him gently. A bit at a time. Unpleasant news must be made known to him in bits and pieces. It's best that way," he said as he remounted his horse. "He may kill whoever informs him that we've lost the cannons. They were our only advantage," he said as he wheeled his mount. "He may now have no recourse but to parley with Baca. God! He's going to shit!"

Martin, who was readying himself to mount his horse, said, "I must tell him myself. It's my responsibility." But before Martin could inform the governor about the loss of the cannons, an additional rider, also arriving from the north, rode into the governor's camp.

"Am I to mark this day with a white stone or a black?" the governor asked the soldier who had arrived on a lathered mount that had clearly been driven cruelly over a great distance. The rider who had brought the devastating news about the cannons trembled with fear as he hurriedly dismounted and faced the governor.

* * *

While the governor was being told of the lost cannons, Antonio and his brother were withdrawing to the auxiliary church for a meeting as requested by Alonso. As they walked to the altar at the front of the church, Alonso said, "We have no powder, Antonio. The cart carrying their magazine and munitions overturned in the stream, and we lost it all. We were able to retrieve the ramrods and wormers, but the rest is gone." He grasped Antonio by his arm and continued in a whisper saying. "We can use the powder made for our *harquebuses* but it doesn't work well in the large guns. And we have no gunpowder beyond that with which they had charged the *pedreros*. Enough for one shot each," he said. "Niter and sulfur of excellent quality, but only a handful. We could make more, of course," he offered, "using *sal petrae* and the ash from willows we can obtain beside the stream. But we have no time for that," he said dejectedly. "I'm sorry, Antonio. I've failed you."

"Do they know?" Antonio asked his brother about the governor's men, his brow wrinkled in concentration. "Do they know that we lost it all?"

"I can't imagine how they could," Alonso said. "We had driven them off before we lost the cart, so they weren't even there when we crossed the stream."

"Well, we'll just have to play the board that's been set for us and beat the governor at his own game. I know how he plays," Antonio said, looking back at the door through which they had entered the structure. "His method is to win as many of the major pieces as possible with little attention given to tactics. But he forgets that it's the pawns that are the life of the game. And if we beat him it will be because ours was the superior strategy. Get a cart with a tarpaulin securely attached as against the weather to act as our gunpowder wagon. Bring it up to the wall. Then tell the men manning the cannons that I want them to fire a volley over the governor's head. Fire each of the cannons one at a time. Very deliberately. Ten seconds between each shot. Over his head and into the hills. With noise and spectacle! And after the cannons have been fired, I want the gunners to make a great show of recharging their beasts. The cannons may yet serve a purpose."

* * *

Once he had demonstrated to the governor that the guns taken from him were operational and were waiting impatiently to begin their destructive work, Antonio Baca wished that he could extend a challenge, to meet the governor in personal combat as in medieval warfare. That bravado, however, would have been unnecessary, for Antonio was, at that very moment, advised that a lone rider had come to the *atrio* walls where he had spoken with one of Baca's captains.

"He came with a message," the captain said. He was unarmed and under a banner of peace. He carries word from the governor who asks to meet alone with an unarmed Antonio Baca."

"What do you think he wants?" Alonso asked Antonio.

"I don't know," Antonio said with a shrug, "but we'll soon find out." He donned his cape.

"What can you expect of a man like that?" Salas queried. "He's ruthless, don Antonio, guided only by power and greed. A shameless liar you cannot trust. You cannot trust him don Antonio. You can't hope to trust him."

Hearing Salas's words about the governor and knowing them to be true, Antonio Baca nevertheless lay off his arms and mounted his horse, saying, "Whether he wears a cloth of silver doublet or armor, I've got to press our advantage. If not, all of this will have been for nothing. Alonso. If something should happen to me, I want you to lead the defense." He addressed his parting words to his brother.

"Don't let anything happen to you," Alonso responded.

Governor Luis de Rosas watched as Antonio Baca rode out from behind the *atrio* walls, without arms or escort, the skirt of his cape thrown jauntily over one shoulder like a shepherd's plaid. He watched as Antonio approached him and thought how ill advised his slight to Baca had been, for he now needed this man on his side. Both he and Baca

186

retained their mounts as though each expected treachery of the other.

A sickening cloud of smoke hung over the *mesa*, the atmosphere jagged and prickly with the nauseating stench of brimstone. A magnificent hawk, like a shard of tessera, winged silently across the grounds that separated the two encampments. Rosas looked up at the bird, watching it as it swooped majestically. He exhaled a great sigh, saying finally, "Has the kingdom grown too small for the two of us, don Antonio?" he asked as he leaned from his saddle. "By what authority do you do this?" he asked angrily. "You have treasonously taken up arms against me and stolen government property! What mischief is this?"

Baca, who had seized time by the forelock in his ploy regarding the cannons, waited a long moment before responding, his expression confident and his eyes flinty, as he surveyed the placement of the guns taken from Martin Barba. Setting himself firmly in his stirrups, he said in a loud, clear voice, "Barba! Your man Barba! We took his cannons and singed his beard. You asked about my authority," he remarked, answering the governor's question. "Do I need any other?" he asked, looking back at the row of cannons, their black open mouths leering over the *atrio* walls. "Remember that the king and His Lordship, the viceroy, are far away. Until they arrive, we will do as we please. And the mischief, Governor? The mischief is of your making. You pillage the *conventos*, and we'll raid your ranch. You take the missions' stock, and we'll sever trade with the Apaches. It will go on and on, don Luis, as long as you wish," Baca said darkly, "with no piece captured or pawn moved. Our stand here will be a passage of honor," he said. "Like the knights who undertook to hold the bridge of Orbigo against all comers, we'll hold these emplacements against you for thirty—no, for sixty days—or as long as it takes to turn you from the walls."

Rosas surveyed the fortifications thrown up in the pueblo's defense with a rush of disappointment. He had set up his cannons outside the walls of the pueblo expecting a quick and decisive victory, one that had to be accomplished before the arrival of the new governor. But now, the colonists were positioned to withstand a long siege and could do the same amount of damage to him as he could do to them. He had been advised by one of his aides to turn about and take himself and his soldiers out of danger's path. To establish a new line of defense, the aide had said, might be their best strategy. "We can always come back," his aide had suggested. Now, in fury, the governor contemplated his withdrawal from the field.

"I know what you do here, Baca, but you must remember that the game of chess has three parts: the opening, the middle, and the close. We may have reached a stalemate here, and perhaps this is a draw. But this is not the end," he said to this man whose defiance he had too long left unchecked. "Please remember, don Antonio," the governor said, repeating an old proverb, "that 'if the ram draws back, it's only to strike the harder.' We will, I'm sure, meet again."

"And I look forward to it, your Lordship. Whether in the field or in the courtroom, may we meet again."

* * *

Their parting represented a truce during which each man merely sheathed his sword. The metallic ring of their swords' extraction, however, would soon be heard anew.

35

The New *Custos* and Governor

SUMMER 1641

"It's all going to hell here, your Eminence," said Fray Salas to the incoming *custos*, Fray Hernando Covarrubias, as they knelt at the main altar in the sanctuary of the *Parroquia de Santa Fe*. "There was a time, Father, when the women of this *villa* would have been content to come to church in *picote*," he went on, as he assisted the elder friar to his feet. "Now, however, the most timid of them would be appalled to be seen in such meager trappings. They most often dress in *gamuza*, with their clothing of velvet and silk deemed impractical and packed away. But for church and for other formal occasions, they drag their finery out, and they are a scandal! Their dresses have tight bodices and low necks, their waists pinched and high. Their collars gape when they kneel to take the sacraments, for God's sake! Oh, we shield our eyes . . . but that can create even greater problems," he said in reference to the accident experienced by Fray Vidania who, while serving communion, essentially blindfolded, had dropped a communion wafer down the front of a parishioner's dress.

"You might think them rattlesnakes, your Eminence, if you followed the flow of their beaded tails. And the women of the Baca and Perez de Bustillo clan are the worst!" he said in dismay. "They were given places of honor here at the front of the church when it was dedicated two years ago, the year Antonio Baca again became *justicia mayor*." Salas and

Covarrubias seated themselves on one of the front benches. "Baca was out of office for a time, removed by the shenanigans of Governor Rosas who attempted to control the kingdom by balancing one faction against another. And then with the assistance of someone—some *cabildo* member it is believed—he rigged the *cabildo* elections to replace Baca and others with men eager to do his bidding and to earn his favor. But whether Baca is in or out of office, the women of his clan continue to sit here," he said, tapping with his knuckles on the *tarima*, the long, splayed bench upon which they were sitting. "Asserting 'squatter's rights,' they said. And now, with Baca once more serving as our senior judge, they again have a right to these seats and it's here that you'll always find them. They come in late, too, Father," Salas said of the Baca and Perez de Bustillo women, "so that no one will miss their arrival. They walk very tall and haughtily as if in command of the place, hoping that their mincing steps will give them a more regal bearing! They come in late, as I've said, expecting those who are sitting on the floor to part, as did the waters of the Red Sea, to create an aisle so that they might pass. They then drift silently to the communion rail, some even kneeling on the altar!"

"Is it as bad as you say?" asked Fray Covarrubias.

"It is, Father!" Salas responded, shaking his head. "Wait till you see them! Their husbands have been described by Governor Rosas as robber barons and malcontents, softheaded fools directing the actions of idiots. But they're none of that," he shrugged, "although cousins all, they may, in fact, be softheaded. But it's not only the Baca clan of whom I'm speaking, Father, it's really the whole bunch. What they are is *hidalgos*,[1] and full of pretensions!" Salas said regarding the colonists. "They completely ignore the examples of defense provided by the Pueblos who live in fortified settlements. In contrast to the Pueblos, the colonists live totally without protection in scattered ranches up and down the river valleys from Fray Artega's Senecu to Taos. But even those who live beside one another have little to do with the others if they're not of the same clan. Oh, they may borrow a cup of sugar or something to complete a recipe, but you'll never get one to tell the other what the recipe consists of, for everything is held as a guarded secret. They'll not join together for anything, except to go on a bison hunt or to ward off an attack. And

I think that they'll forever remain disjointed," he said. "They live in the glory of the past but with uncertain futures. Some, led by Baca, have taken up our cause in our difficulties with the governor. Rallied to our support at Santo Domingo. But who knows of their motives?" he said, shaking his head.

"Do you think we can count on them?" asked Fray Covarrubias about the colonists. "You appear to hold them in contempt."

"Well, it's confusing, Father," Salas said, "confusing. You see, it's not in contempt that I hold them, but at arm's length, for I don't trust them." The two priests rose from the bench where they had been sitting, walked to the tabernacle where they genuflected on one knee in the manner of the English reverence. The baptismal font, or *piscina*, which was present there, was filled with wild flowers and with water taken from the river, rather than from the church well on this special day.[2] After appreciating the display, the priests continued down the middle of the earthen surround to exit the church. Father Salas, speaking as an agent of the Inquisition, said, "But in addition to dealing with these difficult colonists, Father, there's much to be done here. First, the body of the excommunicant, Sebastian de Sandoval, must be removed from the church and buried elsewhere. I'd like for that to be done as soon as possible. And second, we must determine how to proceed with the excommunication of Fray Juan de Vidania, the one who went over to the governor's side. I demanded he come to Santo Domingo to defend his conduct while we were there, but he refused to come. So, I was forced to pronounce him out of communion with the Church. But he has not performed the penance I required of him."

"Then set him in shackles," said Fray Covarrubias in disgust, "and as a distinctive sign of dishonor, tie him to an ass with cart ropes with his face toward its tail. Parade him through the *villa*, so that all may know of his treasonous behavior. Then have him taken to Santo Domingo. I'll finish his punishment there. But enough of these sad duties," said Fray Covarrubias as they left the church, "we've a special Mass to celebrate."

* * *

In great state, the adobe church was alive with vibrant color and exotic sounds, so that all the senses were captivated: the brocade of the men's short capes and doublets, the filigreed delicacy of lace bodices, the luster of women's hair beneath their most cherished *mantillas*. The visual richness was enhanced by the jingle and jangle of scabbards and spurs, and the swish and sweep of silk and satin audible in the earthen surround as the Baca and Perez de Bustillo women took their seats.

The additional sound in the chancel—where the walls of the sanctuary were narrower than the nave of the church—seemed to be the warbling of a multitude of birds. The sound bounced from side to side within the adobe structure and echoed from the *vigaed* ceiling, fine, tiny warblings, and deep trilling tones. The note of the wood thrush and the trilling of the canary were particularly distinct.

The new governor, don Juan Flores de Sierra y Valdez, who was sitting with Governor Rosas on their platform-placed chairs, got up from his seat and walked to the front of the altar.

"Papa!" scolded his son who had been sitting behind his father's chair. "Come back here," he demanded as he moved to retrieve his father.

"Are those birds?" his father asked, looking up at the choir loft.

"No," Rosas responded, "they're boys." He meant to placate this old man who was there to replace him. "They're just boys," he repeated.

The new governor could not be constrained by his son who was concerned for his father's health and safety. He climbed the spare ladder leading to the choir loft. There, illuminated from above by the blue smudge of the clerestory window, were 15 or 20 small boys lying prone upon a floor of packed earth, each with a small basin two-thirds full of water in front of him, and with one or more short reeds, perforated and split in a particular manner. By placing one end of the perforated reed in the liquid, and blowing through the water, they imitated the notes of different birds most wonderfully. Flores lay beside them listening with joy. He was finally coaxed back to his seat on the dais set outside the sanctuary in the left transept of the church, and the service continued.[3]

A despondent Maria Perez de Bustillo, whose parents had recently become aware of her rape and resulting pregnancy, had been persuaded by them to attend the special Mass that was now being sung for the incoming governor. She was there with her sisters, Catalina and Juliana, her mother, and the other women of the Perez household. Fray Juan de Salas, agent of the Inquisition, began a long and reproachful sermon, a sermon that pierced Maria's heart, not because of Salas's eloquence, but because of the passion with which he said, "A virtuous woman is a crown to her husband, but she that maketh him ashamed is a rottenness in his bones." The Father's sermon seemed to echo her own thoughts about her circumstances. She felt he was speaking to her. She was sure of it. And so, she thought, was everyone else in the congregation, especially the women of the *cazuela*[4] who sat on the carpets or cushions that had been brought for them by their maids, their permission to sit finally announced by the tinkle of a small bell. The women of the *cazuela* came to church to see and to be seen and to gossip about the other people they found there. "I can't stay here, Mama," Maria cried as she stood to leave their bench. "I must go!"

Maria's mother with her two remaining daughters left the *parroquia* as soon as communion had been served, walking back to the Perez home among the lavender hills, returning along the same path they had followed into the village.

Juliana was the first to see her. Looking like a blanket discarded along the bank of the river, she was maimed and bleeding heavily from the wound she had inflicted upon herself. "I tried to kill myself and the baby, Mama. Please let us die!"

36

From One Regret to Another

"I thought it best to come ahead," said Francisco Gomez to a waiting
Simon Perez de Bustillo who was sitting beneath the *portico* at the
front of the Gomez home, anxiously awaiting Gomez's arrival. "We
got a late start and the rest of the train is far behind."

"Ortiz, too?" asked a distraught Perez who, since learning of
Maria's pregnancy, seemed to have lost his senses. He often sat in his
courtyard for hours staring at its walls. "Did you leave Nicolas Ortiz with
the train?" he asked.

"Driving a fine flock of *churros* which he purchased in Zacatecas,"
Gomez responded.

"He's not with you?" Perez asked again.

"No," Gomez responded, as the two entered the drawing room of
the main *sala* at the Gomez home. "The governor's ill, don Simon, and
I thought it best to come ahead. Is there something wrong?" he asked as
they pulled up their seating.

"Did you know that my Maria and Nicolas Ortiz are married?"
Perez asked Gomez. "Married Three years ago, when he was last here," he
continued. "Married to keep me from marrying her to another because
he knew I wouldn't consider him equal to her in social status," he cried.
"Married because he knew I was a stupid old man! Oh, God, Francisco!"
he cried striking his forehead with a closed fist. "What have I done? What
tragedy have I brought upon my Maria and upon my family by my pride
and by my sense of honor?"

Gomez, who did not fully understand what his friend was asking, just looked at the agitated Perez, searching for the words to console him. "They married without your permission?" he asked, just testing the waters. "What is it you plan to do?"

"It's not Ortiz I'm concerned about," Perez answered. "It's that *puto carbon*, Governor Rosas. Maria went to him with a petition for land for Nicolas and that son-of-a-bitch forced himself on her! Raped her and left her with child!" he bellowed. "It was my responsibility to protect her from violation, and I did not. But I'm a man of honor, don Francisco," he said drawing himself up to his full height. "A man of my word. And I promise that Rosas will pay!"

37

The Rosas *Residencia*

I NEITHER OVERTHROW, NOR SET UP A GOVERNOR, BUT AM AIDING MY LORD

A stranger might pass it unnoticed on his ride into the *villa*, a venerable cottonwood of enormous proportions that stood near the Indian pueblo at *La Cienaga* on the northern bank of the Santa Fe River. The tree, referred to by the New Mexican colonists as the "tree of lights," was an ancient arbor possessing, it was said, magical properties. Although the light that was said to have emanated from it had only been seen by a handful of people, everyone had witnessed its second "miracle." A smoldering blaze had been kindled in its crown by a lightning strike, and burned for many months, a plume of smoke rising from it toward the heavens until extinguished by a snowfall. The tree, which had reportedly demonstrated this miracle and which had withstood nature's wrath, had then, like the Gisors elm,[1] become a meeting place. It was a familiar landmark for rendezvous where area Indians[2] and Spanish colonists negotiated their differences. As Francisco Gomez rode up to the base of the tree, he saw the man who had requested their meeting, the man who had lately come to conduct secret discussions there on matters of policy just prior to official meetings of the *cabildo*.

"Could this be a more beautiful day?" Antonio asked Gomez as Francisco dismounted. "Could we have planned this better, don Francisco?" They folded one another in their arms, each making two quick little slaps on each other's shoulder. Francisco nodded in agreement but said nothing as they moved in beneath the shade.

Someone had pulled a fallen limb up to the base of the tree, and Antonio and Francisco now sat on it with Baca continuing in the same vein as before. "We have a new cast of characters," he said regarding the changing of the authoritative entities in the kingdom. "A new bill of players that should make our lives both interesting and productive. Governor Flores is here to replace Governor Rosas. *Custos* Covarrubias is here to replace *Custos* Salas. Salas is now an agent of the Inquisition. And Francisco de Salazar and my nephew, Juan de Archuleta, now serve the province as *regidores*!"

"And you are again *justicia mayor*," rejoined Gomez who wondered where Baca was going with all of this. "But could we have planned this better?" he asked with a shrug. "Well, perhaps not. But there is something about which we should be concerned," he said as he rearranged his seating upon the log. "It's Governor Flores," he said. "He's not well. The rigors of the journey were too much for him. He was seized at one point with a prolonged fit of vomiting, which I must say truly alarmed us. "We forced wine down his throat and were successful in getting him to bring up a large amount of corrupt blood and for a short time he seemed to get better. Perhaps, now that he's here, he may recover, but he's not a well man," Gomez repeated, his voice trailing off. "He insists, however, that he's well enough to begin Rosas's *residencia*, and he's to start today."

"To see Rosas held accountable for his administration will give me great pleasure," Baca responded. "But I'll try to remain an objective and disinterested observer."

"Do you think you can?" a smiling Gomez asked him.

"No," Baca responded as he stood from his place on the log. Then, brushing away bits of bark that were clinging to his breeches, he said, "Well, I didn't ask you to ride all the way out here for no purpose." He faced Gomez square on. "I thought it best that we speak here without fear of others seeing us at odds and seeking to profit from our seeming division."

He waited a long moment before continuing, hesitant, it seemed, to confront the matter that stood between them. Finally, he said, "It's about your relationship to Governor Rosas." Gomez, unlike Baca, did not claim nobility. He possessed, instead, something infinitely more potent—a magnificent life force and an unparalleled sense of loyalty to whoever represented the Crown. "Your support of him makes me very uncomfortable," Antonio remarked. "Uncomfortable because of my intention to bring him down." He waited then for Gomez to respond and, hearing nothing, continued. "And I can do that, you know, bring the governor to his knees, but you stand in my way, Francisco, and may be splattered by the blow." Baca waited, then looked at Francisco, and said, "Ours has been a friendship of many years and I love you like a brother. But there are many here who consider you to be an outsider." His enemies accused Gomez of being a foreigner, Portuguese rather than Spanish. "Don't let this issue—your support of the governors—further drive a wedge between you and those who hold that view," Baca warned. "We have a chance to do something different now," he said quietly. "To take command of the colony. Perhaps even to start again."

Francisco looked at him, silently questioning the meaning of Antonio's words. "What are you suggesting?" Francisco questioned. "That we forbid entrance to the kingdom? Bar our doors? Assert our independence? That sounds like sedition, Antonio. Mutiny. Even treason!"

"No," Baca answered. "Not independence. At least not yet. I'm asking you to think this out with me. To determine with me how we should proceed. We do it all Francisco. Have, with Lucero, total responsibility for the kingdom. I serve over local affairs, administer justice, and settle disputes over land and water. I supervise the use of Indian labor, rally the militia, and help the friars maintain discipline at their missions. The *Maese de campo* is the depository of the royal treasury, while you and he are responsible for the colony's defense. We serve his majesty without pay. We determine what needs to be done and place our lives on the line at every juncture while they, the governors, abuse the Indians, profit from their administrations, and dishonor us at every turn. Why do we need them?" he asked. "Am I missing something, Francisco?" he asked. "I fail to find a single reason for their existence. I'm asking you to think this out with me and, perhaps, use Rosas's *residencia* as a means for charting a new course. But if you can't do this," he implored, "please don't jeopardize your position here by getting in the way. And if you can't denounce him, then please say nothing."

Gomez waited for a long time before responding. "I understand what you're saying, Antonio," Francisco stated as he rose from his place at their seat. "But I can't do what you are asking of me. Can't abdicate my responsibility to the office of the governor. For it's the office I honor and not the man. I may speak to the governors regarding their policies, express my approval or disapproval of the anticipated results, and attempt to get them to abandon or to alter their course and direction as the case may be. But once they've made their decisions, Antonio, whatever those decisions might be, I see it as my responsibility to support and to defend them."

"But do you have to speak on their behalf, *mi bon compano?* Speak on behalf of Governor Rosas? You place yourself in jeopardy by your stance," he stated.

"I consider speaking on behalf of Governor Rosas my responsibility," Gomez answered.

"Well, you're wrong in this, Francisco. Wrong to tie yourself to the policies of these men who come and go like the seasons. We don't need them!" he exclaimed. "We've had eleven governors in just forty-three years and Ceballos twice. Less than four years apiece. They're here, and then they're gone. That's why the clergy ignore them," he said. "They outlast them. The clerics move in a circle from priest, to guardian, to *custos*, to agent of the Inquisition, to *definitor*, and then back again. Around and around. And it's only they and we who have a permanent stake here. The governors offer nothing. They take what we have and dishonor us. I'm asking you to reconsider your stance."

* * *

The plaza was a swath of noise and confusion. A crier, to the sound of a drum and bugle shouted:

> Let it be proclaimed that for a period of thirty days, any person with complaints or claims, civil or criminal, against his Lordship, the honorable Governor don Luis de Rosas, or his subordinates,

199

should appear before the honorable don Juan Flores de Sierra y Valdez, governor and captain general of this kingdom and the provinces of New Mexico, and castellan of its forts and garrisons for His Majesty. Your grievance will be duly noted, justice will be served damages will be paid. Thirty days! Thirty days!

Let it be proclaimed . . .

* * *

Crossing the plaza, the two men, Baca and Gomez, were ushered into the westernmost portion of the adobe palace where they were soon joined by as many of the *villa's* 120 *vecinos* as could be accommodated within the room. Other citizens who had not been able to enter stood beneath the latticed porch where they hoped to hear what was about to transpire within. Both groups stood, for there was little seating.

From outside the exterior doorway, where the unaccommodated *vecinos* were gathered, a *portal*, supported by columns and corbels, opened into an enormous patio. Within it were the compound's service utilities, its kitchen, bake ovens, forge, smelter, carriage house, warehouses, and stables.

On the inside, the room itself, a large, long antechamber often used as a ballroom, was finished in a glowing white plaster of *gesso*. Around the base of three walls, rising two feet above the floor, a *dado* in red had been painted as a shield for the pure white walls against the dust of the floor. Along the fourth wall, opposite the patio windows, was an unbroken bench made of adobe. On top of it, along its entire length, was a narrow piece of cotton cloth meant to shield the back and shoulders of the few who sat there.

The walls were over three feet thick and built of massive adobe blocks. The only windows were three small apertures facing the patio. The windows held sections of selenite and were shuttered with carved wooden panels hung from iron hinges. The floor, like the ceiling, was of hard packed earth. Black in color and polished by the bare palms of many hands, it was further covered with the woven black and white wool carpeting known as *jerga*. The panels of interior doors were made of bull and bison hides that had been tanned and painted so as to resemble wood. The woodwork, spare in this room as well as throughout the adobe palace, was rough and heavy. At the front of the room, before a wide, deep fireplace unused at the moment was a long, narrow table. Two large, well-stuffed chairs, covered with crimson, in which Governors Rosas and Flores were seated, were arranged there. A young man who had previously entered the room with the two dignitaries came forward and walked to the front of the room. There, Governor Flores's son, Juan Flores the younger, acting as his father's aide, read from a prepared statement:

> I, don Juan Flores de Sierra y Valdez, captain-general, and lord governor of New Mexico, have been charged with the responsibility of conducting the honorable Governor don Luis de Rosas's *residencia*, the standard review of an official's administration as required of one in Spanish service. I have, therefore, invited all who wish to provide testimony regarding the governor's conduct and affairs to meet here in the *villa* of Santa Fe on this day, and for as many days as are required, to assist me in making appropriate judgments regarding Governor Rosas's administration. I further wish you to assist me in formulating the recommendations that may emanate from these proceedings which will then be forwarded to the viceroy, his Excellency don Lope Diez de Armendariz, *Marques de Cadereyta*, and, ultimately, as may be required, to the *audiencia*, or high court of Mexico. I ask that all who have business before this body identify themselves, take an oath of fidelity, and present their testimony.

After a presentation of the speaker's *calidad* or social status (his age, ancestry, place of residence, occupation, religion, and authority over land, whether landowner or not), the hearing was opened with statements from the kingdom's leading citizens: its senior judge, don Antonio Baca, its leading military officer, don Francisco Gomez; its senior cleric, the former prelate and father *custos* of the Franciscan custody, now agent of the Inquisition, the venerable Fray Juan de Salas; and the departing governor himself, the honorable Governor don Luis de Rosas. An oath was administered to the four men during which they made the sign of the cross and swore to tell the truth in the name of God and Holy Mary.

A BABEL OF ACCUSATIONS

Baca, who was armed with a scathing bill of complaints totaling 61 specific charges, began by providing the context for the information Governor Flores was to receive so that exactly how Governor Rosas had threatened the colonists' way of life could be heard and understood. Speaking directly to Governor Flores, he said, "Our government, in a system devised when the colony was first established, is centered on the selection and service of four *regidores*, two of whom are chosen as *alcaldes ordinarios*, one of whom serves the *villa* as *justicia mayor*. The *regidores* were initially elected by our *vecinos*," Baca said, "the citizens among us who have full voting rights." Turning his attention to the larger group, Baca then said, "The *regidores* are no longer selected by the *vecinos* themselves, but are now elected annually by the incumbent councilmen. This system may seem strange to an outsider with no connection to the territory's Spanish population, but it has served us well, providing us with the continuity we require for maintaining our lands. Governor Rosas, in his administration of the colony, attempted to subvert this system by rigging elections so that men beholden to him would be placed in positions of patronage where he might profit from their control of our land, our water, and our pasturage." He walked to where Governor Rosas was seated. Looking directly at the former governor, whom he had not seen since their parley at Santo Domingo, Baca paused for a long moment before continuing, again addressing the large group who stood before him.[3]

"Governor Rosas was initially successful in subverting our rights," Baca said, "with great damage accruing to our *vecinos*, damage which will take us years to repair. He attempted, also, to control our commerce by appropriating our looms so as to monopolize textile production. He slaughtered, without compensation, a third of our cattle so that he could feed his slaves. And his raids against the Apaches have ruined the trade we had conducted with these Indians and have exposed us to their attack.

"Worse," Baca said, speaking directly to Governor Rosas, "has been the manner in which he has dishonored us. Dishonored our women. Ruined familial honor and reputation. Polluted our bloodlines so as to cause grave public scandal. He must be punished," he said quietly, shaking his head and blowing between pursed lips. "Punished, don Luis," he said speaking directly to the governor. "The code of *Siete Partidas*, on which the laws of the kingdom are based, states it well," he said, first to Rosas, then to those standing in the adobe room. "It says that these two crimes are equal: to kill a man or to defame him, for he who is defamed is dead to the good and honor of the world." He shook his head in obvious anguish regarding what was being left unsaid. "And so, as with a family, don Luis," he went on, again speaking directly to Governor Rosas, "If defamed, it must do whatever is required to restore its honor." Standing directly in front of the chair in which Governor Rosas was seated, Baca leaned against its arm and whispered in Rosas's ear. "You have said that we shall meet again, don Luis, and so we shall." Turning again to address the assembly, Baca said, "However, it's not my testimony that's of importance here, but the words of those who have been stripped of their commissions and *encomiendas* or have otherwise been wronged by Governor Rosas. You will, in subsequent testimony, hear from them as you wish," Baca said to Governor Flores as he relinquished the floor to Francisco Gomez.[4]

Gomez, who had been asked to represent those soldiers loyal to Governor Rosas, strode to the front of the room where he stood before the two governors and scattered assembly. "I speak to you on behalf of the soldiers of New Mexico who praise Governor Rosas as a military leader and explorer and who have asked that I provide His Lordship, Governor don Juan Flores, with the context in which Governor Rosas's administration has been conducted, a perspective which may be at variance with that previously presented," he said while looking directly at his friend, Antonio Baca. "You'll hear that the governor's wars against the Apaches have made us vulnerable to attack," Gomez said. "I wonder about that." He looked directly at the senior judge. "It seems to me that the Utes and the Apaches are no more troublesome now than they were before the governor arrived and, in fact, appear quite intimidated. The

Apaches' attacks on the Pueblos may result not from the governor's attacks on them, but rather from the epidemics of disease and pestilence the Pueblos have suffered in recent years. What is it now?" he asked, "twenty thousand deaths in thirty-six? And perhaps an additional three thousand just last year. They've been decimated! Their numbers have been reduced by at least a third—from sixty thousand to forty thousand souls in but a decade. The Apaches, too, faced with pestilence and drought, need the Pueblos' granaries and livestock. They see the Pueblos as depleted and vulnerable and, thus, they attack.

"And the friars," Gomez said, "they'll tell you that the governor's greed, his wars, and his excessive extraction of labor and tribute have precipitated revolts by the Pueblo Indians and driven them to apostasy. I question this assertion," he said. "The priests promised the Pueblos rain and protection against the wrath of God by disease and plague. They promised that if the Pueblos would gather themselves together in *congregaciones* and give up their idolatrous ways, that they would work their magic and make it rain. But there's been no magic and little rain," Gomez said. "The priests have been unable to fulfill their promises. The Pueblos, therefore, have found themselves with only two options available to them in their quest for survival . . . they can leave their pueblos and return to their nomadic lives or begin celebrating their ancient rites anew. The priests won't allow them to do either of these," he said. "They have this land so afflicted and exhausted with their threats of excommunication and other punishments that all despair. The difficulties between the governor and the clergy are easily understood," Gomez continued, "since the religious are the masters of our resources and conduct their business without benefit of a civil judge. The ecclesiastical judge they have merely throws the cloak of secrecy over their faults. And, as a result, the faults the clerics possess are not known beyond the kingdom, and they are not punished with more than a reprimand, should one even be handed down. And that doesn't hurt them in the slightest, for their ploy is a clever one," Gomez said. "It's to mire our governors in endless litigation in Mexico City, effectively leaving New Mexico without secular authority. New governors arrive every three years, while the administration of the Franciscans remains stable, its members moving from friar to guardian, from guardian to *custos*, and from *custos* to agent of the Inquisition or *definator*. In this way, the priests remain forever in charge and are the masters of the land and of its assets.

"But the governor doesn't need me to speak on his behalf since he can well defend himself," Gomez said. "I only ask that His Lordship, Governor don Juan Flores, remember that the clergy's complaints about Governor Rosas should come as no surprise. They entangled our first Governor don Juan de Onate, in a web of accusations until he was obliged to resign. They publicly humiliated and illegally imprisoned Governor Pedro de Peralta, finally forcing him from the kingdom. They have complained about every governor, for with them, it's a habit. I only ask that His Lordship remember that."[5]

Nodding to the two governors and then smiling at Governor Flores's son, who was known to everyone as Juanito, Gomez relinquished the floor to Fray Juan de Salas, who was to present the friars' case against the governor.

Fray Juan de Salas, former *custos* of the New Mexican friars, but now agent of the Inquisition, approached the front of the room. With ashes on his head and discalced but for a pair of crude sandals that he himself had made, he was strangely garbed in a formless vestment of sackcloth that had been crudely dyed a light blue[6] and gathered at the waist by a sisalian cord. Having previously appealed to the people of New Mexico to denounce anyone guilty of offenses against the Church, even suggesting a list of grievances to which they might refer, he had managed to compile a raft of complaints against Governor Rosas. At least 18 friars had responded to his request for a list of injuries, with each verifying and expanding upon the catalog Fray Juan de Salas had suggested.

"Governor Rosas has done many terrible things," he said. "He initiated numerous forays into Indian Territory under the pretext of waging a "just war" but really to obtain slave labor. His campaigns against the Plains Indians have resulted in disastrous retaliatory strikes by the *Vaquero* Apaches against the Pueblos and the colonists. He opened a workshop in the *casas reales* in which he placed unconverted Apache and Ute captives alongside orphans and levies of Pueblo Indians, all of whom worked there under conditions of servitude. On his visitation to the colony, which by law every governor has to make, he used the occasion to undermine our authority by promising the Indians they could choose their own war captains and resume their traditional rites and dances if they would furnish him with more blankets and hides. And he ordered the Indians not to obey their missionaries, which resulted in the deaths of at least two priests in my former custody.

"Worse," Salas said, the governor scolded my priests in public, and, on the pain of death, expelled them from Santa Fe. He savagely beat two of them who had asked to take counsel with him. And he sent a squad of soldiers to rob and to desecrate the churches my priests had been forced to abandon because of his tyranny. Governor, don Luis de Rosas is the devil incarnate and I'll prove it!"

Governor Rosas, who had been sitting quietly throughout the opening statements, stood and strode casually from his chair, walking to the center of the room where he stood squarely facing his audience. Directing his remarks to Governor Flores, he said, "The people of this colony are not to be trusted. That's why I protested my assignment here as governor, because of the bad reputation they have for mutiny and for seizing their governors. They'll tell you that I ruined the commerce the Pueblos conduct with the Plains Indians, and that I invited attacks against the Pueblos by those against whom I waged a 'just war.' They'll tell you that the Pueblos, without their lands and trade, have become as useless as stubble in a cornfield, there for no purpose but to be set ablaze. But why would I wish to do this?" he asked. "Ruin commerce? Invite attacks? I have no quarrel with the Pueblos! And the lies that you priests have told about me are an abomination," he said, speaking directly to the contingent of priests standing on one side of the room. "You've said that I follow the laws of Luther and Calvin, and that I have been practicing an odious idolatry with a goat! What stupidity! Those are lies! Lies!" he bellowed, while raging about the room. "You do this to tie me up in litigation," he said, speaking directly to Agent Salas, "and to further amass profits for yourself.

"The friars may have denied themselves food and clothing during the first campaigns of conversion, your Lordship," Rosas said, again speaking directly to Governor Flores, "but everything's different now. The town council of Mexico City has implored King Philip to send no more monks there, as there are more than sixty thousand without employment, providing nothing of worth, but living off the fat of the land. And so it is here," he said, looking again at the friars. "These thieves who have been stealing from the royal treasury by accepting subsidies for twelve to fifteen vacant missions, have, also, during my tenure, amassed seventy-five wagons of goods each weighing two-and-a-half tons. This, from a land so poor, amounts to more than exacting millions from Potosi. Their *conventos* are nothing but livestock operations and general stores that are owned by the friars," he shouted. "Besides all that, they've fathered a cadre of little bastards to provide them with a work force.[7]

"And I've undermined your authority?" he asked, pointing his finger at the priests. "Please tell His Lordship of the censures, interdicts, excommunications, and threats of Inquisitorial prosecutions you've used to subvert my authority and to alienate the *vecinos* from their governor. And tell him, also, that, while enjoying the quiet and ease of your cells and *doctrinas*, you've managed to disturb and afflict the land by keeping it in a state of continuous martyrdom. I'm sure that he will be greatly impressed by that. Or tell him of the paper you circulated, threatening to refuse confessional absolution to anyone who did not sign it in your favor and against me. I'm sure he will be greatly impressed by that, also. After all, he's only the king's representative in New Mexico and will probably not be concerned that all of you are traitors!"

With this, Rosas walked back to the front of the room where he addressed Governor Flores directly, saying, "I know with certainty that I'm not well-loved here, your Lordship, and that many of these lowborn people wish me ill. I despair of leaving New Mexico alive, for they can't allow the truth to go beyond the borders of the kingdom. They killed Sebastian de Sandoval, you know," he said, referring to the individual who had been killed while in the priests' custody. "Killed him for his mouth and for his alleged slander. They can kill others, too, your Lordship, for they've amassed weapons at their *conventos* in defiance of my authority and have sent soldiers and settlers to pillage my ranch. I live in continuous fear of their depredations. I startle awake at night, trembling like an aspen leaf, awaiting bugaboo, bugbear, or Baca. I want it known that if I'm found floating in the fetid pool of an outhouse, it was either Salas or Baca or one of their ilk who put me there. Please save me from them!"

"Good God! Enough! Enough!" Flores pleaded, as he grasped his son's arm. "That's quite enough for one day!" he said breathlessly, as he struggled to rise from his chair. "Enough! Enough!" he whimpered, as he limped toward the door. "Please, don Francisco," said the governor who stood on the threshold supported by his son. "A moment, please. Will you give me a moment, don Francisco?" He motioned for others to stay away.

Governor Rosas, who had taken his seat, observed the muffled dialogue between the governor and Gomez and wondered if it pertained to him. Others in the room also remained in their places. They had not been dismissed. It was quiet for a long time. Then, turning to the standing assembly, Francisco Gomez said, "The governor has declared this court adjourned until further notice. There's been enough for one day."

* * *

Governor Flores lay facing the wall, his visage shrouded with a piece of taffeta, his breathing coming in labored gasps. Pulling a chair up beside the governor's bed as he had been instructed to do, Francisco Gomez sat there and waited, observing the rise and fall of the governor's rib cage below his arm as Flores struggled to breathe. The governor finally twisted toward him, his face a portrait of despair, his eyes a blotch of reddened veins as he labored to face Gomez.

"I'm dying, you know, don Francisco," Governor Flores said hoarsely. "I must of necessity pass the torch to another. And there's something in this regard you should know," he said as he wrapped a soft coverlet about himself. "It's about the message I sent back to the city of Mexico when it appeared on the trail that my condition would not improve. In it, I resigned my position as governor, asking for an immediate replacement and promising to serve only until he arrived. But there's no possibility of that now," he said in a broken voice. "He will not arrive in time to take the mantle from my shoulders." He gasped, struggling to continue. "I've had much time to think about this, don Francisco," Flores said, "and to select the man best suited to serve as governor on an interim basis. A man trusted by everyone and strong enough to shoulder the enmity that will undoubtedly be heaped upon him when he takes the reins of office. For that's the nature of government, don Francisco," Flores said quietly. "A leader will be loved until he asks others to follow." Governor Flores then waited for a long moment before continuing, saying finally. "You are, as I've been told, the most outstanding military officer in New Mexico and have occupied every office of importance, including that of High Sheriff of the Holy Office. You are, therefore, well qualified for the highest position in the land. If I should die before my replacement arrives," he said, "I want you to serve as interim governor of the kingdom in full compliance with royal law. I'll make your appointment known to the *justicia mayor*, to the *Maese de campo*, to the members of the *cabildo*, and to the father *custos*."

Gomez was quiet for a long while, studying the governor, appreciative of his statements, but questioning his judgment. He asked, "Your son? Should not this honor be passed to him?"

Governor Flores groaned. "My son is not a soldier," he responded quietly.

"But I don't desire public rank," responded Francisco Gomez, who, in his tenure as special assistant to New Mexico's governors, had somehow escaped the dangers of privilege, of entitlement and greed and self-importance. He said again, "I don't seek this position."

"But you will not shrink from it," the governor affirmed.

"I'll do my duty as required, your Lordship," Gomez said quietly. "I'll do my duty."

* * *

"Do we have any news?" asked Governor Rosas of Flores's aide, as he sat quietly in the hallway with Francisco Gomez.

"The governor's asleep," the aide responded. "Each day he stirs less and less but has periods of lucidity. He's suffering from a fever, and we don't know what else to do."

"When he first became ill on the trail," said Francisco Gomez, who had been asked to the *casas* for a council, "we took his symptoms to suggest that he'd been poisoned. His body had begun to swell, chiefly one arm and a leg. His skin turned yellow and pustules began to break his skin. But we had noticed, also, that he wore his sword hung from a shoulder strap, rather than as a belt around his waist. And as this is the way those who suffer a kidney ailment may wear their arms, we began to treat his illness as resulting from this malady. Dominguez, who had taken responsibility for his care, bandaged him very tightly, including his toes and, also, his legs from his ankles upwards. We then gave him a balm—a potion made of oil, wine, salt, and rosemary—and forced him to vomit, and he seemed to improve. With Juanito's permission," Gomez said, "perhaps that treatment might be tried again."

* * *

On Friday Governor Flores's condition deteriorated. His son, Juanito, lay beside him in his father's bed, propping his father's cheek upon his chest, stroking his brow, and when momentary periods of consciousness returned, comforting his father with terms of endearment and struggling to hear his father's final words.

"What, Papa?" he asked.

"Pray with me, Juanito," his father asked. Then, in words little above a whisper, he said, and Juanito followed, "Jesus Christ, our Lord, who shed Thy precious blood for us, have pity on me, a great sinner."

Fray Hernando then asked if Juanito would like to "tell the beads" for his father and Juanito complied.

Throughout Saturday morning, the governor seemed better and spoke briefly, but his eyes and the constricted manner of his speech, which had been a feature of his condition since its onset, foretold the final setting. At some point in the afternoon, he slipped into a coma. Fray Hernando placed at the governor's bedside the small case and vessel in which he had carried the consecrated Host. Then, with a small basin of holy water, which he had obtained from the chapel of Our Lady in the east tower of the *palacio* where the soldiers recited the rosary of the Blessed Virgin, he began sprinkling the bed and its occupants, intoning, "*Asperges me, Domine, hyssopo, et mundabor.*"

With the coming of darkness, the governor's breathing became inaudible, then ceased altogether. His death came so quietly that Juanito, who had remained with his father throughout his agony, was unaware it had occurred. Fray Hernando, who had attended the governor during his final hour, said finally, "Don Juan is now with his Father, my son. He's gone."

Juanito buried his face in his father's beard, crying, "Papa, Papa."

Immediately, Francisco Gomez, now acting governor, was notified.

38

The Honorable Francisco Gomez

IN A PRIVATE HOME WHERE THE TOWN COUNCIL MET

When the members of the *cabildo* were informed of Governor Flores's passing and of the appointment of Francisco Gomez as interim governor, their mood became solemn, dejected. No matter that they ate from the same bowl, slept in the same tent, shared secrets with Francisco Gomez, they could not, they determined, allow this outsider—a Portuguese soldier, rather than a Spaniard—to serve as their governor.

"Who will tell him? And what reason will he be given?" Juan de Archuleta asked the other *regidores*, Francisco de Salazar, Juan de Herrera[1] and Sebastian de Gonzalez.

"I'll speak to him and tell him the truth," said a saddened Antonio Baca. "That we can't accept his leadership because of his support for Governor Rosas. But, gentlemen," said Baca who was about to put his shoulder to the wheel of a thankless task, "the rejection of his authority is not as simple as it may seem. It appears to me that our case against the governor may be weak. The Franciscans' pleas to the viceroy asking that Rosas be condemned for having encroached upon their privileges are based on facts that are easily demonstrated. He violated their ecclesiastical immunity by arresting their ministers. He again infringed upon their rights when he examined the case against

212

Fray Nicolas Hidalgo. However, our complaints against the governor may be more difficult to prove: that he seized control of our commerce, that he expropriated our looms to monopolize textile production, and that he slaughtered a third of our cattle to feed his slaves. We might say that because of Gomez's support of Governor Rosas we feared that he would continue the governor's policies. Perhaps we might then be pardoned for our refusal to follow his lead. However, our denial of allegiance may still be seen as an act against the honor of the government and one of its officers. I, for one, am not willing to withhold my allegiance to him in every aspect of his authority," Baca said. "If I receive an order from him as the leader of our military, I'll follow it, and I suggest that you do the same."

"But can we render our allegiance piecemeal?" asked Juan de Archuleta of his uncle. "Can we give him a bit here and a bit there, determine which orders we'll follow and which we'll ignore? Can we do this?" he asked again as he looked around the room.

"Our behavior may be seen as seditious," Baca said. "Seen as an act against the government. But we have little choice," he added. "We will not give him our complete allegiance, but we must accept his authority in military matters, for to refuse to do so, might truly promote a rebellion.

"Are we in agreement in these matters?" Baca asked the *cabildo* members. Receiving their response in the affirmative, Baca said, "Then there are two things we must do," he said solemnly, with the intention of putting his own plan in motion. "Governor Rosas must be arrested to keep him from leaving the colony before his *residencia* is completed, and we must move to seize his property, including his *estancia* at Galisteo, his foodstuffs and captive Indians, his hides and skins, wool and cotton cloth, salt and *piñon* nuts. Enough to pay for his *residencia* and for his trip south."

"I'll take responsibility for that," said the *Maese de campo*, Pedro Lucero de Godoy, "and I'll ask that Governor Rosas designate a person of his choice to assist me in the inventory and attachment of his property. I ask that the *cabildo* establish a fine of five-hundred silver pesos for anyone removing such property from the kingdom without permission."

"Does this put you in an awkward position?" Baca asked of his friend, the *Maese de campo*, who was newly married to dona Francisca Gomez Robledo, daughter of Francisco Gomez.

"It does," Lucero responded, "but it's Rosas against whom I must move, and not Gomez. And it's you who has taken on the responsibility of telling him."

"We must be careful," said a practical Juan de Archuleta. "Some of the governor's hides are of very poor quality. The bison hides and elk skins he has at Pecos are good only for sacks. We must assure ourselves that we have enough *mantas*, buckskins, and white and heavy bison skins to pay for the guards, shackles, food, and incidentals which will be required for his imprisonment."

"And there's something else we must take notice of," Antonio said, "for there is among us a Judas Iscariot who would betray our determinations and seek to profit from these events."

"What do you mean?" asked his nephew Juan de Archuleta.

"One who has been telling the governor of our every move. One who is responsible for our having to make many of our determinations in secret. I want a bond secured to rid ourselves of him," Baca continued. "May I have that in the way of a motion?" he asked.

"I so move," said Francisco de Salazar.

"So be it?" Baca asked.

"So be it," the men of the *cabildo* responded.

"Thank you," a smiling Antonio Baca said, leaving the front of the room.

* * *

His wife who had learned through the Ladies of the Altar Society that Antonio Baca had discovered his conspiracy to profit from the woes of the colony had forewarned don Roque de Casaus. At this very moment, he was on his way south with his wife and children. He hoped to escape before the powder keg that was New Mexico exploded.

214

39

A Family That Slays Together Stays Together

They were all there, Maria's father, brother, uncles, cousins and friends. Of the 14 men in attendance at the Baca home that fateful evening, 11 were related to Maria through blood or marriage. One, their leader and host, was the senior judge of the town council; two were aldermen; seven were captains; two held the rank of *alferez*; one, the only *encomendero* in the group, served the kingdom as lieutenant governor of the Sandia or *Rio Abajo* jurisdiction. They were the young Spaniards, the elite of the New Mexican forces, and four were slated for death.

Their discussion regarding the governor centered around two points: first, their right as they saw it to resist one who had abused his duties as governor of their adobe kingdom; and second, their right, in accordance with the wishes of the people, to slay a manifestly evil man, a point that was bolstered by the governor's excommunication. There were arguments both for killing him and for sparing his life, but in the end it was perhaps the argument of Nicolas Perez that ruled the day when he said, "We could support our case with many words, but, ultimately, both his crime and the method of his punishment are simple. The governor took our honor, and he must pay with his life."

The 14 were in agreement. "We've only to wait for Nicolas Ortiz," said the senior Perez. "He'll want a primary role."

A bond was then drawn up and signed by all present. Several others who had not been present at the meeting would sign later. Murder was not specifically mentioned, the matter vaguely phrased as their right to "take care of Governor Rosas by one way or another." The bond was then given to Antonio Baca who placed it in his doublet.

"And what do we give to the enterprise beyond our word?" asked Cristobal Enriquez.

"We have no need of money," Archuleta said, "for our task requires little in the way of wealth. But it must be 'all as one. All must give something to the venture so that their complicity is assured."

A WEEK LATER

Wearing hooded cloaks, Simon Perez de Bustillo and Antonio Baca walked to the Perez home, a house huddled beneath snow-bent pines growing along a ridge flowing to the west. They entered the compound through the open doors of the house's eastern *zaguan*, a walled and covered passageway through which they entered the main *placita*. The floor of the *placita* and most of the rooms throughout the compound, were of dirt, the exceptions being the hand-adzed wooden floors in the kitchen and grand *sala* that were on the southern side of the 21-room home.

In the great room where Baca and his host had often met, Perez had seemingly chosen his furniture and furnishings as a means of making a statement as to who he was. This grand *sala*, with its pine-plank flooring and walls of *gesso*, brought from deposits of gypsum that Perez had found near Cochiti, was the focal point for the beautiful home. Its furniture, dark and heavy, was placed in the center of the room, its many small and old mirrors reflecting the contents of the space back to its occupants.

The character of the main *sala* appeared to reflect that of Perez himself. Its chairs, which Perez had bought from departing Governor Francisco de la Mora y Ceballos, were of carved wood covered with leather. They were tapered and thin, their backs straight, their arms elevated and awkward. Perez, however, did not take his brother-in-law to the grand *sala*, opting, instead, for a room that was closer to his heart.

The minor *sala*, whose dooryard was immediately to their right as they entered the compound, had a corner fireplace in which a few upright sticks were burning, the fragrant scent of *pinon* and juniper hanging in the air. Two enormous six-board chests standing atop wool carpeting were positioned against the *sala's* northern wall. From this room Antonio could see through its open doorway into the main bedroom of the Perez home. A long row of boots, a pair for every task, stood in one corner. Although he could not see the bedroom's fireplace, which fronted its eastern partition, he could see its light flickering against its whitewashed walls.

The two, Baca and Perez, sat at a small table that, except for the two chests and an array of large, cushioned stools, behind the folding screen of a carpeted and elevated *estrado* (a room section, set for receiving and entertaining guests), was the only major piece of furniture in the large room. The table, on which a silver decanter, two dark blue drinking glasses, and a small dagger had been placed, was conveniently set before a *fogon de campana*, or corner fireplace, a ponderous iron poker standing by its side. In the same corner leaned a *harquebus* that was always loaded. The men took off their boots to which clumps of snow still clung. The scent of wet wool rose from the floor. Drinks were poured.

A large, upright candelabrum in which several tall candles were burning set off the pictures of various saints that were on the walls. These were retables or *retablos*, mostly, some of which were painted on Indian-tanned hides, while others were painted on small textiles. Other pictures, looking spare and unfinished, were painted on slabs of pine. *Bultos*, primitive statuettes made of wood, *gesso*, and cloth, depicting St. Francis and St. Lawrence, stood within shuttered *alacenas* (cupboards) on either side of the doorway. Antonio looked beyond the small statues and through the room's one window. It was snowing outside.

They drank on for a while, the two seemingly unwilling to broach the subject for which they were meeting. Antonio spoke first, asking after the health of his sister, Juana de Zamora Baca, to whom Simon was married; Simon asked the same regarding his sister, Yumar Perez de Bustillo, to whom Antonio was married. Twice brothers-in-law, they had many ties.

Simon then said, "The family's ready, Antonio, the Archuletas, the Varelas, the Hinojos. We await your word."

"And Ortiz," Baca asked. "When will he be here?"

"We hope to intercept him at the *Bosque de Isleta Paraje*," Simon said. "Maybe two weeks. Perhaps sooner."

Baca picked up the dagger, examining it for some time as though contemplating things unspoken. At length, he said, "I feel it's a bad wind for thrashing our corn. Perhaps we'll need a *montante*, rather than this." He indicated the dagger. "We should have a broadsword with large *quillons* requiring two hands."

"Why do you say this?" Simon asked. "What's wrong?

"It's my assignment. Gomez has ordered me to go to the Zuni-Hopi country on an Apache campaign," Baca responded quietly. Then with a great sigh, he asked, "Could it have come at a worst time?"

"Gomez?"

"Yes, Gomez."

"Do you think that this is just a coincidence, Antonio? I think that he knows of our plans and wishes to disrupt them."

"That is my determination, too. But both Alonso and I are required to go, and I want you to wait until we return. Wait until we can execute the plan with you."

"And if we cannot, Antonio, what are we to do?" Simon asked. "He who falls today may be on his feet again tomorrow," he said meaning Luis de Rosas. "He once sent in his resignation but the viceroy would not accept it. We can't let him be reappointed now."

"Well, if you must go without us, let Juan and Francisco lead," Antonio said. "Ortiz must play a prominent role, of course, but if neither Alonso nor I can be here, let Archuleta and Salazar lead."

40

The Encounter at Isleta

JANUARY 7, 1642

The Pueblo of Isleta, a village of wood and water, in the middle of the Great River, gleamed white in the moonlight, a radiant contrast to the lava flow remnant that rose like a little island from the flood plain on which it lay. Nicolas watched as an Indian youth splashed across the ford on a borrowed pony. The young man and his horse, wet from the spray they had kicked up in their frigid passage, sought the warmth of the shepherds' campfire, the youth asking, "Nicolas Ortiz?" When Ortiz identified himself, the Indian said, "I was sent to look for you by men who are waiting at the *convento*. The oldest of the men says that he's your father-in-law."

"My father-in-law?" asked an incredulous Ortiz whose lips were burned and fissured from his time on the trail.

"Don Simon Perez de Bustillo," the *portero* answered. "He and some other men are waiting for you at the *convento*. I've brought you this horse so that you may go there"

"I'll ride my own," Nicolas said, thanking the *portero* for the summons, and for his generosity in offering his horse. "I'll go there now," he said, more to himself than to the Indian servant who had brought the summons.

God! He knows! Nicolas said to himself as he forded the stream. But why are they here? He asked himself as he approached the church of

San Antonio de Padua. The priests' house, shaded in summer by a few bright acacia trees, was softened now by the shadowed outlines of these trees and by a walled garden. There were a number of horses stabled there. Nicolas counted them—12, no 14—as he rode to the *convento's* door.

Standing in the open doorway looking distant and forbidding was Maria's brother, Nicolas Perez. Without comment to his friend whom he had not seen in almost three years, Perez gestured with the palm of his hand for Ortiz to dismount. Observing Perez closely, Ortiz verified that his hands were empty, his dagger at his belt. He pressed his wrist against the cold of his own blade and dismounted.

"My papa's waiting for you inside," Perez said. "The priests have asked that you leave your arms here."

"And how am I to approach him?" asked the 24-year-old Ortiz, as he unsheathed his dagger, placing it in Perez's outstretched hand. "With caution?" he asked, his thin eyebrows and sharp nose prominent in his reddened face.

"With care," Perez responded. *"Estar contando las vigas."*[1]

Ortiz held his breath as he entered the *convento*, walking down a lighted corridor to a refectory with an office, spacious, exceptionally well lit, and nicely finished off in wood. It was here, Perez had told him, in the chapter room of the two-storied *convento* that don Simon would be waiting.

Ortiz stopped at the doorway amid a splay of light, surveying the extent of the white-walled room, looking for don Simon. The elder Perez sat silently staring across the table into a pile of blankets and a cache of parrot feathers he had brought from his home as gifts for the resident friars and their charges. He sat hunched over, looking downward at his restless hands. And when he looked up, Ortiz could see his lips thinned, his eyes darkened, his thoughts seemingly somewhere else.

Don Simon glanced at him and then away. His gaze then returned to Nicolas, his expression revealing his dire message. "Nicolas, my son," he said, "I have grave news."

Ortiz listened to Maria's father but was seemingly unable to understand his words. Maria? Governor Rosas? Raped? Pregnant? He held his hands before his face in anguish, joined his fingers in a closed fist and beat on his brow repeatedly, crying and moaning in deep despair. Then, through his tears, he said, as he staggered to his feet, "I must go. Maria needs me."

"Yes, we'll go, Nicolas," said don Simon. "But not yet. Not yet, my son," he said, his eyes tearing as if contemplating it all. "There's more," he finally said. "That bastard Rosas has a guard who will testify that Maria has for almost four years been the governor's mistress. That Maria is a notorious *barragana* who has had relations with all of the men of the escort."

"My God, don Simon! There's no truth in any of that!" Nicolas bellowed. "Even I did not know her in that way."

"Of course, they're lies," don Simon said quietly. "But I'll not have them attested to in a legal forum. Rosas's *residencia* has been postponed because of the death of Governor Flores. You were aware of his illness, I believe. The *cabildo* has arranged for Rosas's arrest to keep him from leaving the colony before his *residencia* is completed. It's members have, unknowingly, placed him in our hands. We must, therefore, move quickly, strike before the reinstitution of his *residencia*, plan our work well."

"Why?" Ortiz asked. "What are we to do, don Simon?" he asked angrily. "Merely curse him? Tie a scarf about his neck? Chase him into the wilderness? Those are not enough!" Ortiz raged. "I mean to kill him!"

"And you may kill him, Nicolas, but we must plan our work well," don Simon repeated. "It won't be easy to gain entrance into the *casas*, but when we get to the *villa*, we'll devise a plan." Gathering up his personal items, which he had placed on the table, he said, "I brought herders with whom you may leave your stock. We'll leave for the *villa* at first light."

"I won't wait," said an impetuous Ortiz, his beautiful, large eyes flashing with anger. "We may not be witches who can travel magically in a pumpkin, but I'll lead us over trails where we can find our way in the dark. I'm sorry, don Simon, sorry this has happened."

"It's not for you to apologize, Nicolas," the elder Perez said. "It was my responsibility to protect her purity from assault, and it's I who failed."

* * *

The three—with each trailing a string of horses—lifted themselves into their saddles. They left immediately, taking to the road at a gallop, embarking upon a long, arduous ride over mountainous terrain from Isleta to Santa Fe. Changing mounts repeatedly, they would ride continuously for 60 miles and arrive at dawn after a 24-hour journey.

41

Neither Excuse Nor Explanation

JANUARY 9, 1642

They had ridden with the wind at their backs along the trail and river course of the kingdom. When they arrived, Maria, who was in the final stage of her pregnancy, was sick with worry, worn with despair and hopelessness. For her, in her tragedy, there was no rest from regret or sorrow.

* * *

"Do you want us to go in with you?" his father-in-law asked Ortiz as he, his son, and son-in-law dismounted before the *zaguan* at the Perez home.

"I don't know," said Nicolas who was steeped in misery. "I want what's best for her."

"Then I think you should go in alone," don Simon suggested. "There's no need for her to have her father and brother also there to contend with. No, I think that it's best that you meet with her by yourself. She'll be in her bedroom," he said.

"And where's that?" Nicolas asked with a tinge of embarrassment and chagrin.

"The one door off the main *sala*," Perez answered. "And please, Nicolas," he said, "Take as much time as required. We can talk later."

The door opened to his knock, with a barefoot Maria appearing in the gloom. "Nicolas," she said tearfully, "I . . . "

"Shh," he responded quietly, putting a finger to her lips. "No questions or explanations," he whispered. "Not now. We can have that later."

* * *

But later was never to come, for Nicolas did not want to hear of it, or acknowledge it, or confront the dilemma facing them. His thoughts were like tassels of wheat in the wind, blowing this way and that without direction. He did not know how to think of it or how to correct the uncorrectable. Maria was pregnant with Rosas's child! He would be justified in killing the governor, but then what?

42

A Desperate Plan

"The governor's haunted by spooks and specters resulting from lack of sleep. He's striking out at every shadow," said Francisco Gomez to Fray Juan de Vidania with whom Gomez had asked to meet. "He goes about carrying a dagger to protect himself from assassins. He clearly requires your spiritual support and guidance, Father, and asks to meet with you."

"Oh, it pains me to hear that he's having so much trouble, don Francisco, but I can't see him," replied Vidania, while gnawing on a chicken wing with an abstracted air. "It is as I told your man, don Francisco. My new superior, *Custos* Covarrubias, has given me specific instructions regarding the former governor. I'm not, under the pain of a second excommunication, to provide him with sacraments or counsel or to have any personal contact with him. I'm sorry that he's still here," said Fray Vidania regarding the governor. "Some months ago I suggested that, unless he wished to live forever under the protection of an armed guard, he should leave the kingdom. But you know the governor," said Fray Vidania. "He wouldn't listen."

"Well, that option is no longer available to him," Gomez said. "A new governor has entered the kingdom. He's coming here from Santo Domingo. He'll soon be here to assume the burdens of my office. But Governor Rosas must stay until his *residencia* is completed."

"Well, I can't see him," Vidania said, wiping his hands on his worn cassock, "but I have something which may be of use to him." He walked from the office door to his desk on which a small silver box was prominently displayed. "Tell him that I keep a bit of consecrated bread in here as in a ciborium and that I suggested he keep it on his person until his fears are quieted." He waited a long moment before continuing, watching as Gomez carefully placed the silver box within the leather pouch he was carrying, and then, without comment, turned to leave. Vidania followed Gomez down the dimly lit hallway, finally grasping Gomez by his sleeve and saying sheepishly "Please ask the governor to return the box as soon as he's able. It doesn't belong to me."

* * *

The peaks behind them were black against the night sky as Alonso and Diego Martin Barba walked through the patio doors of a modest backyard. The fragrant flowers, trellised vines, and bushes of spring were withered now in the chill of this winter night, but they extended still to the walls of a welcoming home where the Martins were immediately ushered into its *sala*.

"I need your help," said Francisco Gomez to the men whom he had met at his door. "I need your help, and I must have it without our creating any noise or suspicion. We've got to take the governor from the *casas* and hide him somewhere," he said to the Martin Barbas. He motioned for them to sit while he, himself, remained standing. He said. "The *cabildo* believes that he's making plans to leave the kingdom prior to the completion of his *residencia*, and they mean to imprison him to prevent his escape. I need your assistance in removing him from the *casas* before they get the wind in their sails."

"And where did you think to hide him?" asked an incredulous Alonso Martin of Francisco Gomez. "Is he to sleep each night under a different roof? Take sanctuary in a church? Hide at one of the pueblos? I don't think so!" he stated emphatically. "Neither the priests nor the Indians want anything to do with him, so you can't hide him there. There's no place, is there?" he asked Gomez. He paused for a moment, rubbing his forehead, considering. He was known to the members of the *villa* as one of the governor's most ardent supporters. Trying to be helpful but cautious about the part he might play in the scheme, Martin waited a long moment before saying, "Perhaps my home." He glanced

226

at his son Diego. "Perhaps my home could be used," he repeated. "The members of the *cabildo* will never think to look for him there, especially since they know I'll be gone. Let us take him there," he repeated. "My son Diego here will take responsibility for him while I'm at Zuni on the Apache campaign."

Francisco looked from Alonso to Alonso's son Diego, and then back again, trying to weigh the soundness of the proposition being offered him, and saying finally, "I had thought to hide him at one of the sheep camps, but perhaps your suggestion is better. However, it's a gamble, don Alonso, a gamble that they'll not think to look for him beneath their chins. You may take him from the *casas*," he said to the Martins after some deliberation, "but he must be guarded night and day and kept from communicating with anyone." Gomez took a key from where it was hidden in a writing desk with nine drawers. Handing the key to the elder Martin, he asked Diego, "Can you do that?"

"Give me a chance to prove myself loyal," said Diego, while looking at his father. "I'll keep him safe until he can be moved farther, or until he leaves the kingdom."

* * *

Although it was considered an utter disgrace for a person of quality to ride in such a vehicle, the governor was placed on an oxcart where, hidden beneath a mountain of skins and robes, he was readied for his trip to the home of the Martin Barbas. As his cart rumbled through the *zaguan* of his adobe palace on its final journey away from the heart of the royal *villa*, he at last had time to think. Although his governorship had proven to be a thicket of thorns and nettles, his time among the brambles had prepared him for the political intrigues of his foes, armed him with the machinations of political chess in which he had learned to move the pawns on the board so as to avoid a checkmate. In the end, however, pawn promotion had become the dominant theme of his game, making his capture now a real possibility. In a final desperate attempt to avoid a checkmate, he was now to be hidden in the bowels of a private home, a move he could not possibly have anticipated even as recently as a week ago. How have I come to this? He asked himself.

* * *

"And what do we have here?" the governor asked, as his guards took him from his cart at the east gate at the home of the Martin Barbas. "Are you to secure or imprison me?" he asked Diego Martin who had met them there.

"The one might seem like the other, your Lordship, for is a keep anything but a jail?" Diego asked. "I'm to be the captain of your guard. My responsibility is to keep you safe and to deliver you to the new governor who will complete your *residencia*."

"Then you must do your work well, my friend, lest my blood be on your hands," the governor said, as he walked into the courtyard stiff from his uncomfortable ride.

"Take him to the *despensa*," ordered Diego referring to the room with thick adobe walls that was used for storing meat. "It may only be entered from the *placita* and its door may be barred from either the inside or out. Take him there now," he told the guards.

43

Dimly Lit But Full of Shadows

JANUARY 24, 1642

pproaching the Perez home in the moonlight, the *regidore*, Francisco de Salazar, rode up from the bed of the river. His horse was wet from the waters of the stream and from the snow, and it worked hard with its haunches, climbing up the near riverbank.

"Is your papa home?" Salazar asked Nicolas Perez, who had met him at the gate. "Is your papa here, Nicolas?" he asked again as he dismounted. "It's important that I speak with him."

"He's inside with Nicolas and Maria," the younger Perez answered. "I'll take you to them."

As Francisco and Nicolas Perez entered the fire-lit room, an angry Nicolas Ortiz was saying, "The doors of the *casas* are ready to be opened to us. We've only to pay the bribe required and find the correct passageway."

"But the story that he's imprisoned there is only a ruse, Nicolas," Salazar said as he removed his *gaban* and lay it across a stool. "The governor's not there," he said to the small group, as he stood warming his back at the fire. "He's been replaced there by Francisco de Anaya Almazan and by Francisco's son-in-law, Alonso Ramirez. He's been taken to the home of my father-in-law, Alonso Martin Barba," Salazar said, while knocking from his breeches the snow that clung there.

"And how do you know this?" asked Simon Perez of Salazar. "How do you know he's there?"

"Wives! You know how they are," Salazar responded. "Try as they might they cannot keep a secret," he said, slapping his leather-shod thigh and roaring with laughter. Averting his gaze from Maria, on whom his eyes had briefly lit, he said, "But I induced her to tell me what she knows regarding the governor, so now we know Gomez's plan."

"Now what do we do?" asked a distraught Simon Perez shaking his head in disbelief. "We had made arrangements to pay a guard to gain entrance to the Royal Palace, but the Barbas will not succumb to a bribe. Or will they, don Francisco?" Perez asked Salazar, "You know them a hell of a lot better than we do."

"They do pretty much as they please," Francisco said while taking a stool at the table. "My wife, Maria, does, too, as well as her father and the rest of her family. My old mother-in-law, also," he continued. "She did whatever she pleased until she was poisoned by Maria Bernal with whom old Alonso was having an affair," he laughed heartily. "But you're right," he said in a more serious tone. "Alonso's present wife, Francisca de Herrera, will bar the *zaguan* at the slightest provocation so that no one may enter."

"I can get us in," Maria said, looking at her husband, Nicolas Ortiz. "They'll open the gate for me, especially if the governor requires them to do so."

"I can't let you become involved in this," said Nicolas Ortiz. "It's too dangerous."

"But I am involved," said Maria who, although in the final stage of her pregnancy, gave little outward evidence of her condition. "This would not be happening if it were not for me. And there's nothing to be afraid of, Nico," she continued plaintively. "I know his mind and his heart," she said. "It will be as he taught me, an attack against his weakness. He won't be able to resist a defenseless girl arriving at the gate and asking for him. I can get in, and you can follow."

The four men were silent for a long time, attempting to devise a plan for ridding themselves of the governor and contemplating Maria's role in it. Francisco de Salazar, who knew that political, rather than personal, motives spurred some of the conspirators, finally said, "She's got to be involved, Nicolas. She'll be our cover. When you find her in his room, you'll be justified in killing him. Everyone will understand that."

Turning away from Francisco, Nicolas Ortiz looked from one man to another, from the strained face of his father-in-law, Simon Perez, to Francisco de Salazar, and then to his brother-in-law, Nicolas Perez. He was looking for direction, seeking an answer.

Nicolas Perez, who had been listening quietly as the others spoke, sat for a time in silence. Then he rose and moved to the fireplace where he picked up a pair of metal tongs that were lying there. Slapping them repeatedly across the breadth of his open palm, he said, "We can do this! We can convert the carriage so that it has a box with one of us suspended below the frame. Maria can arrive at the gate with a load of *mantas* in the back. They'll look through the blankets and, when they find no one there, they'll allow the carriage to enter the compound. Once inside the *placita*, the person hidden in the box can open the gate and let the rest in."

"Who will they be?" his father asked.

"Four of those who were to have gone with us to the *casas*," Nicolas replied, "Juan Ruiz and Manuel de Peralta, Luis Martin and Pedro de Chavez."[1]

"Is this an idea or a plan? It's too simple," Salazar stated emphatically.

"Well, what is a plan but an idea awaiting an opportunity?" asked the younger Perez. "And it is simple. That's why it will work."

JANUARY 25, 1642

Hearing the rumble of wheels on hardpan, a watchman peered over the gate as Maria drove her father's carriage up the hill and toward the Martin Barba home. Graceful and elegant, the former carriage of the bishop of Zacatecas, it had been brought by ox cart to New Mexico where it had been strengthened against the nearly non-existent roads with wrought iron brackets and fittings. These braced the carriage's slender wooden parts, as well as the corners of the small, narrow box that was now appended below its frame.

The darkness was magnificent. The mountains to the east, smudges of lampblack against the dark sky, were dimly lit but full of shadows. The pale image of a bird winged across the enormous disk of a full moon as minute snowflakes, like jeweled points of light, began to tumble out of the night's sky. Heartsick and weakened by apprehension, Maria caught sight of someone or something across the wash off the wayside. She peered hard into the darkness but sensed there was nothing in it and feared she was alone. Shivering slightly, she became aware of a chill greater than that which blew off the mountains. She held herself up tall as the leather-slung carriage rolled to a stop before the home's covered vestibule.

A small door recessed within one section of the wooden gate opened, and the guard, Diego del Rio de Losa, former secretary of the *cabildo*, who had watched the carriage approach in the moonlight, demanded, "Who are you?" He pointed his *harquebus* in Maria's direction. "What business do you have here?"

"I'm here to see the governor," Maria answered quietly.

"He's not here," Rio de Losa answered rudely. "He's at the *casas reales de Palacio*, where he belongs."

"I ask that you take him a message," Maria responded. "Please tell him that Maria Perez de Bustillo is here and wishes to speak with him."

"He's not here!" Rio de Losa repeated angrily.

"Well, perhaps I've been misinformed," Maria said. "But please, take my message to whoever is inside."

Rio de Losa was infuriated by her insistence, but unsure of what he should do. "Wait here," he commanded as he stepped back into the *placita*, closing and then barring the small door from the inside.

With her brother, Nicolas Perez, at her feet, Maria waited for the guard's return. When, after many minutes, Rio de Losa remained absent, Nicolas considered scrubbing the entire plan. Maria, however, would not allow him to do so. And so, like a Greek soldier secreted within a wooden horse, Nicolas remained hidden in the box mounted below his father's carriage.

With his left arm extended behind his head, and his chest and back pressed firmly against the box's roof and floor, his thoughts raced wildly. What If the guard puts his sword through the floor of the carriage? If that happens, I can't even defend myself, he thought in panic. What if he makes her leave the carriage outside? I've got to think clearly, he said to himself. I've got to be ready for anything. I can't make a mistake. Perez squeezed the hilt of his dagger more firmly with his right hand, looping the rim of the box with the fingers of his left hand to assist with his escape from the box. Whatever I do, he thought, as he waited to pull himself to freedom, I'll only have one chance to get it right.

Maria tapped with the heel of her boot on the floor of the carriage as a sort of warning for her brother who now heard the returning guard. Diego del Rio de Losa opened the small door in the gate and, unsheathing his sword, stepped through the opening and walked slowly to where Maria had brought the carriage to a stop. Holding his breath, Nicolas listened as Rio de Losa slowly flipped back the edge of each *manta*, very deliberately probing between the blankets with the point and shaft of his sword, satisfying himself that there was no one hidden among the cargo. Then, after making a cursory examination of the remainder of the carriage and looking very carefully beneath the horsehair robe that Maria had placed across her knees, he opened the gate of the *zaguan* and Maria drove the carriage into the interior courtyard.

"Where is he?" she asked Rio de Losa, as she dismounted from the carriage.

"He's in the *despensa*," he responded, pointing to a doorway beneath the *portico* at the end of the *placita*.

"Please take me to him," Maria asked, as she walked to the rear of the carriage where the *mantas* had been placed.

"There's no way to miss it. It's right there," Rio de Losa responded in exasperation, pointing to the roofed *stoa*.

"Please take me to him," she asked again. "I need your help in carrying the *mantas*."

"Goddamn it!" exclaimed Rio de Losa angrily. "Do you want me to carry you, too?" he mocked.

"That won't be necessary," Maria responded sweetly. "I know that you would not expect a lady to carry these by herself." She rolled and held a small bundle of blankets to her chest.

Nicolas Perez listened as Maria and the guard walked away from the carriage. He tensed but heard nothing further, and when he could no longer hear their footsteps, he began inching his way out of the narrow box. The amount of noise he was making in extracting himself from his wooden cocoon alarmed him, so he was overjoyed when, on opening the door to the *zaguan*, he found his five masked compatriots there awaiting him.

The interior of the *placita* was dark, the odors those of earth and corral. The vague edge of a door behind which a candle lamp was burning was apparent at the far end of the *portico*. Seated beside the door at a rough table against which two long benches had been placed was Antonio de Salas,[2] and a third guard, Juan Gonzalez, who, along with Rio de Losa, had been playing a game of *triunfo envidado*. They were now impatiently awaiting Rio de Losa's return. Salas and Gonzalez ignored Maria, as she and her *manta*-laden escort walked by.

Placing her cheek tightly against the barred door, Maria first listened, and then rapped with her free elbow. Her candle-lit face moved to the door's small window. There, a watchman appeared. His breath scented with onions and bitter herbs, he said rudely, "I think he's asleep." The door opened to reveal a poorly defined figure of a man moving from a reclining to a more elevated position on top of his bed. Maria stepped inside and found herself within a low-roofed vault. With an earthen floor and only a large chest, two stools, and a common bedstead as furnishings, the room was cold and cheerless, a cell for its lone occupant.

The governor reclined on one elbow with no movement, watching as Maria entered the candle-lit room. He was exceedingly quiet, but Maria sensed that he was in a stir of emotion. Agitated. Feeling between hawk and buzzard, as it were. He stood, his feet clad incongruously in a pair of velvet slippers, a small hat of crushed velvet upon his head. He stepped away from her, and then turned, his arms held out in front of him as if expecting to be shackled. His attention was focused completely upon her, but before she could utter a word, he said, "I suppose you've come to convert your advantage into victory."

Hearing the desolation in his tone, Maria was silent for a brief moment before responding, saying finally, "I brought you these. I thought you might need them against the cold."

Rosas made a gesture for Rio de Losa and the watchman to leave the room. Once they had gone, the former governor made a feeble attempt to kiss Maria on her cheek. Pressing her left hand hard against his chest to keep him from feeling the life beneath her cloak, she felt a hidden coat of impenetrable chain armor beneath his canvassed doublet. There was a tinge of harshness in her voice as she asked, "Surely, that's not for me?"

"No. It's not for you," he said quietly as he removed both the doublet and mail, and placed them neatly beside his unsheathed sword and dagger amid the jumble of chess pieces atop his bed.

"Do you play by yourself?" she asked of the chess pieces, making conversation, playing for time.

"No, I'm carving a set to take with me. Using my time here to some advantage," he responded wistfully. "I'm thinking that as long as the game lasts, each piece has its special qualities until put into the bag."

"Which is to the chess pieces what the grave is to life," she responded, looking at his thick and unkempt beard, smelling the scent of him, of someone unwashed, of sweat and leather and earth, and thinking him pathetic. Looking at this man whom she despised, she had thought that she would say something profane or final, but her mouth was dry, her voice muted. She stood for a long moment, regarding him in the candlelight with eyes full of anger—and pity—and then, wordlessly, turned and abruptly fled the room, slamming the heavy door loudly at her exit. The men outside the door drew back against the sound, flinching like frightened quail as the door slammed shut. Once outside the *despensa*, she began to run, crashing headlong into the masked men of her family as they entered the *placita*.

Nicolas Ortiz jumped over the stable's manure trench in an attempt to reach the door of the *despensa* before it was barred from the inside. He and Nicolas Perez reached the door at the same time, pushing aside the guards who were there, holding them at bay with the point of their swords until the others came up.

"I think he's asleep," said one of the guards.

"Well, between a sleeping man and a dead one," Ortiz responded, there's little difference.
Open the door!" he commanded Rio de Losa.

When Nicolas Ortiz entered the *despensa*, Governor Rosas was again lying on his bed. Without uttering a sound in evidence of surprise or confusion, he raised himself to a sitting position, a blank look on his face. Nicolas Ortiz, too, had thought of what he would say to the governor. He had envisioned pulling the governor's beard in a final assault to his dignity. But now, words failed him, and with no gesture sufficient, he merely said, "Pick them up," in reference to the governor's sword and dagger.

Paralyzed with uncertainty, the governor played for time saying, "But you have me at a disadvantage, Nicolas, with empty files and ranks. May we call this a draw?"

"We may not," said Nicolas Ortiz whose pride deepened and intensified with fury. "Your situation may be hopeless, Governor, but I won't allow you to resign. Stand and retrieve your arms," he demanded, pointing with the tip of his sword to the arms which lay on the governor's bed. "I don't want to kill an unarmed man."

Sweeping aside the chess pieces with the back of his left hand, the governor, with great care and deliberation, picked up his broadsword and dagger, arranging and rearranging them in his hands. Standing with his arms held out from his sides, Rosas made a quick feint with the dagger in his left hand and followed that immediately with a slashing blow with his right. The dishonored husband, Nicolas Ortiz, parried masterfully with the blade of his sword, then thrust once at the governor with his dagger, and a dozen times with his sword. The knot of assailants and their four prisoners who were standing in the courtyard felt the governor's ghost pass and all of them knew that he was gone.

44

The Initial Indictment

Gomez was the first to arrive, for it was he who had asked for the meeting. He stood there under the tree of lights watching Antonio Baca approach the meeting grounds. He wondered what he would say and how he would put his questions. It was the conspiratorial hour of five am, the morning coming up behind the mountains to the east. Baca was still in the saddle when Gomez asked, "And how are we to treat this? It's clear that Nicolas Ortiz was the perpetrator in the murder of the governor and must be indicted for his crime, but what of the rest? Do we even know who they are?"

"How are we to treat this?" Baca asked, echoing Gomez's question and wondering what response to give. "How am I to respond to that, don Francisco? And how am I to speak to you?" he asked, making no effort to mask the disappointment in his voice. "Our positions in this matter are very awkward," he said, as he dismounted and walked to where Gomez was standing. "You were appointed interim governor, and I serve the province as *justicia mayor*. These are positions that have historically been at odds with one another. One would have hoped that when the time came for us to fill these positions, we could have governed amicably, in concert with one another, to the betterment of at least two of the three estates. But I suppose that's not to be" he said sadly. "It seems we're never to see ourselves as working toward the same goals. But I want you to remember that I tried to behave appropriately, don Francisco. Tried to walk the line between a just war and a rebellion."

Baca sat then, took a small bag within which he had placed a bit of *punche* from a pocket on the inside of his doublet. But rather than roll it up as he would a cigarette, he placed a pinch of it between his cheek and gum, positioning it there very deliberately with the tip of his little finger before saying, "Alonso and I went on the Apache campaign as you asked to prevent confusion and disorder in matters military, and to prevent the sparks of anarchy from torching the fields, for once they've been set to flame, don Francisco, they're often impossible to put out." He waited then for Francisco to sit beside him, saying, "The members of the *cabildo* have assumed all interim governmental powers, so that, even though you've been appointed governor, I think that you should accede to our wishes and stay out of this." Expecting a response from Gomez, Baca waited a reasoned and careful instant before continuing, saying finally, "I've ordered Nicolas into custody and have asked him to surrender. As for the others," Baca said, "I know who they are, but I won't give them up." Rearranging his seating so as to face Gomez straight on, Baca said, "I was at Zuni when the governor was killed, and one might say that, as a *vecino* of the *villa*, I've done nothing of discredit to a man of honor, and nothing unbefitting my station as *justicia mayor*. But they'd be wrong, don Francisco. For in the consideration, if not the execution of the governor's murder, I'm as guilty as they are." He paused to give Gomez time to respond before continuing, saying, "I'll preside over Nicolas's trial, and will, as required, send his case to the city of Mexico for its final resolution. But Nicolas is not the responsible party here," Baca said, looking at Gomez intently. "He may have wielded the sword that took the governor's life, but in your heart of hearts, don Francisco, you know that we all killed the governor."

"Should you not recuse yourself then?" Gomez asked his friend. "Withdraw from these proceedings?"

"And who would hear the case?" Baca asked. "I can't ask anyone else to accept the responsibility. So I must do it myself."

45

Imprisoned

FEBRUARY 1642

The day dawned bright and sunny, one of those early February days when anything seems possible. On this day, attended only by her mother, her two sisters, and her beloved Indian servant, Tula, Maria gave birth to Lorenzo Perez. Unable to reconcile his feelings regarding her pregnancy, Nicolas had elected not be there at the moment of Lorenzo's birth, saying to Maria, "I go now to seek a final resolution of my case, and when I return, I'll make this right.' At his surrender, Nicolas could not have foreseen that the tragic events in the background would eventually lead to an even greater tragedy in the near future.

> *Quien mato al govenador?*
> *Santa Fe, Senor.*
> *Y quien es Santa Fe?*
> *Todos a una!*

As pale as one startled by a rattlesnake, Nicolas Ortiz had been pursued by Francisco Gomez and imprisoned at the *casas reales* by his Uncle Antonio. Now he was meeting with Maria's cousin, Francisco Lopez de Aragon, who had ridden the four leagues from his *Estancia del Alamo* (Cottonwood Ranch) to Santa Fe at his cousin's request. Lopez gave the accused prisoner, Nicolas, the news regarding Lorenzo's birth, asking,

"Why did you turn yourself in, Nicolas? Weren't you with the others at the safe house?"

"I was, but I didn't want to jeopardize their positions by remaining there. There's an indictment against me. But nothing has been laid at their doors. And I'm hoping that if I separate myself from them, they won't be charged.

"It's naïve to think so, Nicolas," said his friend Francisco who, with Nicolas, had been a member of the wagon escort. "They're accessories to murder before the fact. Some were participants in the crime. My guess is that they'll be charged and will eventually have to stand trial."

"Well, that may be," Nicolas said with a shrug. "In any event, I want my trial over and done with, and I want you to represent me."

"Do you think that's wise," Francisco asked, "given my relationship to Antonio Baca?"

"Antonio's son-in-law, yes, my dear friend, but my compatriot also," said Nicolas. "And as a member of the wagon escort, you may also be able to refute some of the accusations which will be made about Maria. You are my first and my only choice," Nicolas said earnestly. "I need you by my side."

"And what will your defense be?"

"That I killed the governor for violating my wife," he stated emphatically. "That I killed the governor so as to assure the end of his cruel tyranny. And that I killed the governor for placing us in jeopardy with the hostiles around us." He waited for a brief moment before asking, "Is not our situation identical to that of the residents of Fuente Ovejuna?" Ortiz asked rhetorically. "Remember the story of Fuente Ovejuna, Francisco? It was ruled by the cruel *comendador*, don Fernan Gomez de Guzman, and it was the home of Fray Andres Juarez who told us what happened. The *comendador* raped the virgin, Laurencia, and other innocents in his province and beat anyone who complained. The *vecinos* of Fuente Ovejuna killed him and were pardoned for their crime. So, is it not the same here?" he asked. "The governor took my honor and, by the authority provided me by unwritten law, I took his life."

46

Kill as Many as You Can

Beginning his journey in late December of 1641, Governor Alonso Pacheco y Heredia stopped at each pueblo and at each *visita* and *convento*, as he and his escort, Gaspar Perez and his men, very slowly worked their way up the Great River. Armed with special orders from his viceroy who had advised him to "kill as many of the dissident colonists as you can," Pacheco was also accompanied by Nicolas de Zamora, a native of Mexico City, who had signed on as the governor's aide. Without an official person to make them welcome—for the missions' priests were in council at Santo Domingo—they invited themselves in at each *convento* and were struck by the refusal of the *conventos' porteros* to answer questions regarding Rosas's administration. In mid-September, after a lengthy journey of nine months, they were to find out why.

Finally reaching the ecclesiastical capital of Santo Domingo on September 20th the governor was received amidst the ringing of bells. Governor Pacheco and his aide, Zamora, were ushered into a small dining room where, before a fine fire, they met with the good fathers, Juan de Salas and Hernando Covarrubias. New Mexico's interim governor, Francisco Gomez, who had ridden there from Santa Fe, was also present. Here, among a bevy of priests, Pacheco a large, balding, barrel-chested man was told of the death of Governor Rosas. "What kind of animals are these?" the governor bellowed. "Sedition! And mutiny! And now murder, for God's sakes! Who are the men who've done this?" he raged.

Interim governor, don Francisco Gomez, told the incoming

governor of some of the principals in the Rosas affair: Antonio Baca, Nicolas Perez, Juan de Archuleta, Juan Ruiz de Hinojos, Juan Ruiz Caceres, don Pedro Duran y Chaves II, and Antonio de Salas, all members of the Baca and Perez de Bustillo clan. He told them also, of Nicolas Ortiz, who, after his indictment and a trial that had continued intermittently throughout the spring and summer, was about to be sent south for a final resolution of his case. Governor Pacheco listened to all of this and began to craft a plan. The situation in New Mexico was much as the viceroy had advised him. Several of those about whom Gomez had spoken, were *"gente honrado y principal"* (honorable and prominent people) who would require a special hand. The rest of the individuals involved in the Rosas affair were *"primos hermanos,"* or first cousins, of the accused murderer, many of whom were also men of honor and social prestige. Governor Pacheco gathered the information offered him by Gomez and the priests with interest, but, also, with a suspicious eye, for the viceroy had warned Pacheco about these priests and Spanish colonists. He had said that the only way to deal with such individuals was to "use their pride and sense of honor as a torch and reduce them to ashes."

"And this Ortiz," the governor asked Gomez. "Has he left the kingdom?"

"I think his departure has been timed to occur before your arrival," Francisco responded. "If he's not now on his horse and riding south, he soon will be."

The governor waited a long moment before responding. He looked at the grim faces before him as he said, "If he remains in Santa Fe, I want him detained until I can speak with him. And whether he's there or gone, I want to meet with his wife. I have sealed orders regarding your fellow citizens." Pacheco directed his remark to Gomez. "However, I'll have to send Zamora back to *Nueva Vizcaya* and to Mexico City for special instructions regarding the governor's murderers."

Hearing that the governor's body had been carried on a board from the Martin home and buried in a corn patch where his soul and the memory of him might be relegated to obscurity, Governor Pacheco made his first major demand of the priests. "Buried in a field as if he were a Moor!" the governor exclaimed. "That cannot be! That cannot be," he raged! "I'd like for his body to be exhumed and for the governor to be given a proper Christian burial in the Santa Fe church."

"At the *Capilla de San Miguel?*" asked Fray Covarrubias.

"No! No of course not! Not the *capilla*," responded the governor with annoyance. "for that's but a chapel. I'm referring to the *parroquia*, the one you call the *Parroquia de San Francisco*. Close to the altar . . . at the foot of the *predella*. That would be the proper place for the burial of a governor," he said as he rearranged his seating. "Are there any major impediments to this?" he asked the priests as another log was put on the fire.

"Governor Rosas was in sin and died while under the pain of excommunication," answered Fray Juan de Salas, speaking in his role as agent of the Inquisition.

"And what will it take to put that aside?" the governor asked.

"We would have to have a Mass said for him," said Fray Salas, "a Requiem Mass with ritual aspersing and censing, after which prayers would have to be offered for his departed soul."

"Then it could be done?" asked the governor more as a statement than a question. "He could be sprinkled with holy water and perfumed with incense to absolve him of his sins. Is that what's required?"

"Yes, your Lordship, it could be done," answered Fray Covarrubias.

"Then, gentlemen, may I say this," the governor replied, casting his eyes about the room. "I will, in a few days, leave for the *villa* for the purpose of conducting a clean sweep and of establishing an administration of truth and reconciliation. The proper burial of Governor Rosas, as well as the restoration of his honor for himself and for his entire lineage, will have to be a part of this. Do you not agree that we need a new start?"

"Yes, that would be good," responded Gomez and the others.

"Well, then, if we're in agreement regarding this, I'd appreciate having the governor taken up in as decent and respectful manner as possible and his remains reburied in a military ceremony at the *parrochia* as befits a deceased civil official. I will then, when I reach Santa Fe, pay the governor the respect due him."

"In the spirit of reconciliation, your Lordship," said the father *custos*, "I'll see that it's done."

47

A Substitute Husband

Clutching a large shawl about her head and shoulders, Maria entered the *casas* alone, her father, in whose carriage she had ridden, intentionally detained in the royal courtyard by the governor's men. She was escorted down a hallway to the governor's office where Governor Pacheco met her.

Pacheco, who did not know what he had expected of the woman who had set this whirlwind in motion, looked at her and was struck by her appearance. Tall and beautiful, yes, but she seemed so vulnerable, so fragile beneath the heavy shawl which she retained as he invited, "Please sit down."

"I'd rather stand, your Lordship," Maria responded.

"But you will sit down as you've been asked," the governor stated.

Maria took the second seat at the small table where the governor was sitting. She held herself upright in her chair, betraying little of the discomfort she experienced at meeting with the new governor, and none of her feelings of dread and revulsion at returning to this terrible room.

The governor looked at her for a long moment, fingering the document he held in his hand and saying, "And we come to this."

Maria did not respond, for she did not know what the governor was speaking of, or what the paper contained that he was holding.

Then, sighing and taking a deep and dramatic lungful of air, the governor placed his left elbow upon the arm of his chair and brought

244

his left hand up to his lips. Holding his fingers there for a long moment, he finally said, "So you're the wife of Nicolas Ortiz and the daughter of Simon Perez de Bustillo?"

"Yes, your Lordship."

"Niece of our senior judge, Antonio Baca?"

"Yes," Maria responded.

"And the young man, Juan Ruiz de Hinojos, and the *regidore*, Juan de Archuleta, are your cousins, are they not? And Nicolas Perez, your brother?"

Maria did not respond.

Putting his elbows on the table and his chin upon his interlocked fingers, the governor sighed and said, "Well, It's clear to me now," he said. "Quite clear. We've only to make the final adjustments."

Maria continued looking at him, her face frozen in false composure, as he said, "We must now speak about your relationship with the governor. A nasty business. A nasty business" he repeated as he sat back into his chair. "You were the governor's mistress," he stated, looking at her with accusatory eyes.

"I was no such thing!" Maria responded in alarm.

"I have guards who will testify differently," said Governor Pacheco who again leaned to the front of his chair. "Guards who will say that you came here many times asking to meet with the governor," he said, picking his way through the evidence. "Guards who saw you dining with him, and who will say that you and he appeared to be on the most intimate of terms."

He waited then, and looked at Maria intently before saying accusingly, "You were observed, you know. Observed by the watchman who helped you from your carriage. Seen through that window there having relations with the governor."

In shock and humiliation Maria cried, the tears welling in her eyes, "I did not consent to that! I was forced!"

"Did you deny permission?" he asked.

"I could not speak!"

"*Chi tace consente*," Pacheco said. "Silence is consent. Did the governor know you were married?" Pacheco asked, continuing his interrogation. "Your father didn't know. Nor did anyone else. I have your father's sworn testimony to that. Did the governor know?" he demanded.

"I told the governor I was married when I first met with him regarding a petition for my husband," Maria responded.

"And you want me to believe that the governor sent your husband off on an assignment—as did the *Comendador* of *Ocana* and King David, for that matter—in order to have his way with you, and that you, of course, are the beautiful Bathsheba? Is that what you'd have me believe?" He looked at her contemptuously. "No! No! No!" he mocked. "The governor didn't know you were married! Oh, we won't absolve him of all blame," he said. "He knew that relations between unmarried people were illegal and constituted a mortal sin, but he didn't know that he was having relations with a married woman. He thought that your clandestine meetings with him resulted from your fear of your father."

"None of that is true," Maria responded, wiping tears from her chin where they had run.

"But that will be your testimony," responded Governor Pacheco. "Your testimony will be that you had an illicit relationship with the governor during the time your husband was gone from the *villa*. That it was consensual. That you occasionally received gifts and other favors from him in payment for your services. And that when you found out that you were pregnant, you concocted a story of rape because you feared that your father or brother would kill you."

"But that's not true! None of that is true!" she cried, her face wet with tears.

"You will testify that you were meeting with the governor at the Martin home when you were discovered by your husband hiding in a large chest underneath the governor's bed, and that you were with the governor when he was killed."

At this distortion of the facts, Maria said, "I had been there, your Lordship, but not as you say . . . I will not testify to that!"

Completely ignoring her protestations to the contrary, the governor continued, referring to the document he held in his hand. "My report will read that upon his return to Santa Fe, your husband, who suspected that you were having an illicit relationship with the governor, asked the *Maese de campo*, don Pedro Lucero de Godoy, to accompany him to the *casas reales* where they conducted a search, but that they were unable to find you there."

"The *Maese de campo*, who is indeed an honorable man, will not testify to that," Maria responded.

"That your Nicolas asked Lucero to file a formal complaint against you and the governor, and that, failing in his bid to accomplish that, he killed the governor out of frustration."

Enraged at the injustice of the governor's statements, Maria moved to the front of her chair and shouted, "None of this is true! You will not get any of us to say those things!" she cried.

"Please, please, *senora*," Pacheco said as he made a motion as though to rise from his chair. "You don't know me, nor do you know what I'm capable of. I'm the prince and I can make anything happen. I could, if I wished, require you to wear a distinctive badge upon your clothing, so that you might be easily identified."

"And I would not wear it!"

"You would, if I required you to do so," he said. "The kingdom's mine *senora*, I have control over the records, whether those of the *cabildo*, or my own. It doesn't matter what Lucero says regarding any of this. Perhaps his testimony won't even be solicited. The official record will be what I say it will be. Think of what's at stake here, my dear lady," Pacheco said as he rose from his chair. "What's of more importance?" he asked, "the governor's reputation and dignity, or yours? The lives of your husband, your uncle, and those of the remainder of your family, or your honor? What's done is done!" he said in disgust, moving from his side of the table and standing but a sword's length from her chair. "In wiping the slate clean, and in restoring the honor and dignity of the former governor, your testimony will be what's remembered and one has only to look at you to understand why the governor might succumb to his desire. You'll admit to what I've written and will swear to it before witnesses," he said regarding the document from which he had been reading. "That you committed adultery with the governor over a span of four years. That while the governor was enamored of you, you considered him nothing but your *cicisbeo*—merely a substitute husband. That you were with the governor when he was killed. And that no one has influenced your testimony. Respond well, my lady, and you may receive further kindness from me," he said, in a voice just above a whisper. "And as a reward for your believable testimony as I've stated, I'll issue a pardon for those involved in the murder of the governor, as it is within my power to do. You may, if you wish, see the pardons I've already executed for Luis Martin and Pedro de Chavez who were with your brother and husband when the governor was killed, as well as the pardon I've executed for Alonso Ramirez who has also been implicated in this affair. And when I have your signed statement regarding what I've read, I'll complete pardons for the rest. I only want this over!" he said, placing the document before her.

"May I confer with my father or with my cousin, Francisco Lopez, in this matter?" asked Maria who, in desperation, considered this, perhaps, her one final opportunity to save her Nicolas.

"No," he said. "Your Nicolas is on his way south. I must make an immediate decision regarding his apprehension, a decision to ask the governor of *Nueva Vizcaya*, don Luis de Valdez, to have him arrested. We've no time for conferences," he said. "I only want your signature on this testimonial as I've stipulated." He waited, and then asked, "Do you write?"

"Yes, I both read and write," she responded quietly.

"Would you like to read what I've read to you?" he asked politely.

"Yes, if I may."

"Your signature, please," he asked, as he pointed to the spot on the document where he wished it placed. "You will not regret this."[1]

48

A Bitter Harvest

Fall arrived gently, the golden swath of the river corridor a radiant contrast to the russets, siennas, and burnt umbers of the orchards. While the men cut grass and alfalfa for winter-feeding, Maria accompanied her mother to their meetings of the altar society, served the ladies wine and *biscochitos* (sugar cookies) when they met in her home, and, with her mother and the family's Indian servants, began preparations of food for long storage. They tied chile peppers into *riestras* and hung them out to dry, picked apples bruised from their fall from the trees, but still firm and hard, to use to make cider. They put the barrels of cider in the cool, stonewalled room of their *soterrano*, Maria directing their placement there but leaving the heavier work to the men. They cut apples and peaches in half, squash and meat into thin slices, the meat salted and hung on fiber ropes. They placed the sliced squash, peaches, and apples between loosely woven cloths and dried these in the sun. When all was ready, the dried squash (the so-called *tasajos de calabaza*), apples (*rueditas de manzana seca*), peaches (*orejon*), and meat (*cecina*) were loosely packed in bags of muslin and placed in the root cellar.

The preparation of beans and corn, however, gave Maria the most pleasure. The harvest of beans allowed her, in separating seed from their casing, to beat with a wooden rod the pods that had been placed on a clean, white canvas. She assisted, also, during the warm, moonlit evenings of the Indian summer, in husking and in removing by abrasion the corn kernels from their cobs. The separated kernels, along with the cleaned and aired beans, were then put in their respective muslin bags and placed in the cellar. Maria loved the transformation of corn into *chicos* because this allowed her to work far into the night, without having to think or reason. The change was accomplished by removing the ears of corn from their stalks when the corn was new and tender, its kernels stuffed with a creamy pulp. A fire was then kindled in a rock-lined pit that was otherwise used as a tanning vat. The pit, a hole about four feet in diameter and five feet deep, was in a sheltered place outside the walls of their compound. The fire was kept burning through the night. The ashes were then removed and a volume of water poured into the hole. The ears of corn were placed in the water and left to steam for many hours. In the morning, the ears of corn were removed from the water and hung to dry on the lines of fiber rope. When dry, the kernels, which had been transformed magically from raw corn into "*chicos*," were removed from their cobs and they, too, were placed into sacks and taken to the *soterrano* where everything was being separated for storage here at Maria's home on the river, or in the mountain fastness of the family's safe house.

* * *

Maria was in the kitchen helping her mother. The corn was in, most of it prepared and stripped from its cobs. The litter, stalks, husks, and gobs of corn silk, had then been taken to a refuse pile where they would later be mixed with the manure from the Perez corrals for use in their gardens.

She felt full of sadness and had a sense of foreboding. Despite her nature, which combined spirit and optimism with tenderness, she thought, I bet he's happy he's gone, leaving me to deal with Lorenzo and with the difficulties of our future all by myself. She wondered if he would come back, or if he would find a less complicated girl with whom to share his dreams. She hated herself for doubting him and caught herself up quickly, knowing that she could not give in to despair, that she would find her uncertainty overwhelming, with no sense of how her future with Nicolas and Lorenzo would end.

She looked for something to do, asked to take the corn soaking in a vat of limewater to the river, or at least to the *acequia* where it could be washed to remove the kernels from their husks. Her mother allowed her to do this but required that she place the corn in a large reed basket and that she go with Tula.

The sun was warm but the air chilled, the water within which they stood, frigid. Placing an edge of the basket into the glacial stream, Maria and Tula dipped and rinsed, dipped and rinsed, with Maria kneeling in the water and beating with tight fists the kernels that swirled within. She stood and looked at Tula, and Tula could see that she was crying. Tula attempted to remove the basket from the swirling waters, but the formless receptacle collapsed from her attempts, and retreated from her grasp. She looked at Maria, asking without words for her assistance. Their futile efforts were observed by the two Indian adolescents her father and brother had earlier seen with a larger group of Apaches near the upper corrals. The young men, carrying bows and with quivers on their backs, were now standing in the woods on the opposite bank of the river watching Tula's and Maria's every move.

Wiping at her face with the fringe of her blouse, Maria bent to grasp the curled edge of the basket, and she and Tula pulled on it. It had caught on an obstruction in the bed of the stream, however, and refused to yield to their demands. Tula fell, not so much in the water as in the mud of the slippery bank. And then Maria let go, let the basket empty itself of its hard-earned bounty. They watched as the huskless corn swirled downstream.

They walked back to the house, unaware that they were being observed by the two young men and went through the *cocina* where Maria's mother was working. She looked at them, wet and cold and splayed with mud. Tula glanced at her "mother" briefly but then looked away. Maria's mother curled her joined hands into a fist before her face but said nothing.

49

General Amnesty

SIX MONTHS LATER

Light was breaking, the earliest delicate glow of dawn showing behind the black granitic contours to the east. Francisco Gomez was lying in a deep sleep when he heard a heavy banging at his door. "The governor wishes to meet with you," the messenger said.

Putting on his clothes, and donning his hat and cloak, Gomez left his small house, which faced the corner of the royal plaza, and walked the short distance from his home to the *casas reales*. Here he was ushered into the governor's study where the two principal officials of the kingdom, Governor don Alonso Pacheco and the father *custos*, Fray Hernando Covarrubias, met him.

Governor Pacheco had been in Santa Fe for almost seven months conducting a posthumous examination of Governor Rosas's administration. There now seemed little time for niceties. The early morning hour begged for clear and brief communication. Gomez, his red hair catching the glint of firelight, was not invited to sit.

Governor Pacheco, did not know Gomez well, having had a distant, if not strained, relationship with him since first entering the kingdom. He looked at Gomez assessing him, saying finally, "When we met at Santo Domingo, I sent Zamora back for special instructions from the viceroy regarding the governor's murderers. Just last night

252

I received my instructions, and I wish to share them with you." He indicated the document he held in his hand. Again taking a long look at the man who stood before him, he said, "My instructions are to issue a proclamation of amnesty to all who took part in the war against the governor except for those specifically under indictment for the crime, with the understanding that they will lay down their arms and surrender. Those are my instructions, and I'd like you to make them known to the members of the colony."

"And why is this request being made of me?" Gomez questioned. "Surely the contents of your instructions would be better coming from you or from a member of your administration."

"Because you're a known quantity here, don Francisco, and are trusted by the other *vecinos*," the governor responded.

"And who issued the amnesty?" Gomez asked suspiciously. "Governor Rosas was the king's representative in New Mexico," he said, looking from one man to the other. "Surely, someone's guilty of something. Is it Ortiz only? He was acquitted at trial and is now on his way to the city of Mexico for a final resolution of his case. But the others, the other men who perpetrated this tragedy—what's to become of them? They're my friends. My kinsmen. My compatriots." He looked for meaning in the blank faces that appeared before him. "I can't offer them something that's not real," he said, the saber wound above his right eyebrow showing white in the firelight. "Something that's not been sanctioned by the highest authority. Something that will be rescinded once they've surrendered. It's their lives—and my honor—that are at stake."

"It was the viceroy himself who issued my instructions," Governor Pacheco responded with assurance. "Your friends have been put to the hounds," he said. "They must surely be tired of running. What we offer them is an exchange, an exchange of their confessions of complicity in the governor's murder for our amnesty. They may then stay here or leave the colony as they wish. You're to give this message of Safe Conduct or Royal Immunity to Baca and to the rest," he said, pulling a parchment from underneath a large book where it had been placed. Holding the document up to the candlelight he read:

You may return to your home as a friend and not as an enemy, with permission to come and go as often as you please, and to carry away things of your choice, for I offer you asylum, sanctuary, refuge, a shelter from danger and hardship and no harm may come to you, for I will punish the impeachment of your passport of safe conduct by a fine or imprisonment. I only wish to talk and to put this sad affair behind us.

"Can we believe this?" Gomez asked.

"Tell them that they may take this as a 'notice to appear,' which will be followed shortly by an order for their arrest."

"How much time do they have?" Gomez asked. "Their term of grace? Do they have the Inquisitional thirty or forty days?"

"Thirty days!" Pacheco laughed in amazement. "I think not! How much time do they need?" asked the governor mockingly, a dark look sliding across his face. Then, speaking very deliberately, he said, "Tell them that I'll give them a short while before they're formally declared outlaws and rebels with their titles, offices, and dignities forfeit."

"Anything else? asked Gomez sadly.

"I have nothing more to say."

50

Caught, Convicted and Condemned

JULY 19, 1643

Encomendero, don Fernando Duran y Chaves I, who was riding as a personal messenger from Francisco Gomez, dismounted within the courtyard at the *casas reales* where he had been told to inform the governor of the impending surrender of those involved in Rosas's assassination.

"I've been asked to tell you that my uncle, Antonio Baca, has coaxed the six men whom you identified to give themselves up on your promise of amnesty," said a breathless Chaves, who had apparently ridden from some great distance. "They'll be here tomorrow."

The governor, who was beside himself with joy, rubbed his hands together and smiled broadly. "What day is this?" he asked Fernando who was known to him as one who had accompanied the deceased Governor don Luis de Rosas on an expedition to the Apotlapihuas.

"It's July 19th, your Lordship."

"Then remember this day well, my friend," said Governor Pacheco. "Or better yet, remember the day after tomorrow as even more important. For on the 21st, I shall give you your *albricias* or *querdon* as a reward for good news, three molds of goat cheese to be taken once a year from my ranch at Galisteo for the length of my administration."

TELL ME WITH WHOM YOU WALK, AND I WILL TELL YOU WHO YOU ARE

The next morning, which was July 20th, *Justicia Mayor* Antonio Baca delivered to the *casas reales* the men of the conspiracy who had gone to the mattress in the mountain fastness of the Perez sheep ranch. The seven, Baca included, were soon joined beneath the *portico* of the interior court by Diego Martin Barba who arrived with a pistol at his belt.

"Are they all here?" asked Nicolas de Zamora, the governor's aide. Newly arrived from the city of Mexico where he had gone at the governor's request, Zamora, a man of 40-years of age, swarthy, and melancholy of countenance, now seemed to be distracted and troubled.

Baca noted this and was mildly concerned as he responded, "Yes, we're all here."

"And do you have the confessions you were asked to obtain?" a frowning Zamora asked the senior judge.

"Yes," Baca responded, handing him the documents.

"Then follow me," Zamora commanded as he led the eight men down a dark corridor to the western end of the palace. Here they were placed in the guards' room next to the chamber where Nicolas Ortiz had been imprisoned throughout his trial.

"Please remain standing," Zamora asked as he placed the men's documents among numerous others that were lying on a table. "The governor will be with you shortly," he announced as he left the room.

The rush-matted room, not grand, but one of the largest in the adobe palace, had for its seating a large chair near the front of the room and two splay-legged benches placed against each of its parallel walls. The small table on which the men's documents had been placed was in front of the chair. Covered with metal grates and wooden shutters were two, small, glazed windows placed high in an interior wall.

Looking very harsh and forbidding, the governor entered the guards' room. He was followed, shortly, by his aide, Zamora, who took a seat at the table. Addressing himself to the waiting men, the governor said, "Well, let me get a look at you." He walked from one man to another. "I've waited for months to know your faces. Not exactly what I expected," he offered, "although what I expected now eludes me. And your names?" he asked. "May I have your names?"

"Francisco de Salazar Hachero, *regidore* of the *villa*," responded Salazar who stood nearest to the governor.

"We can dispense with the titles," the governor responded curtly. "I just want an official statement as to who you are."

The men shuffled about, looking at one another before continuing: Diego Marquez, Cristobal Enriquez, and Diego Martin Barba. Then, the remaining four: Nicolas Perez de Bustillo, Juan de Archuleta, Juan Ruiz de Hinojos, and Antonio Baca.

"And these three are your nephews, are they not?" the governor asked Antonio Baca in reference to Nicolas Perez and the two Juans.

"Yes, I'm their uncle," Baca responded proudly, "The rest are my friends and compatriots."

"And the indicted murderer, Nicolas Ortiz, is he not also your nephew?" the governor asked.

"Acquitted, governor. Made clean of the crime because of the aggravating and mitigating circumstances under which the governor's murder occurred," Baca corrected, rearranging his riding cloak about his shoulders. "Yes, he, too, is my nephew," Baca responded.

"Yes. Yes," continued the governor, referring to Baca's correction. "Acquitted of his crime in proceedings during which he was defended by a *chicaneur*, a clever-talking lawyer, who, as it turns out, is your son-in-law and, thus, another cousin. And the trial was conducted by you! Is that not correct?" he asked rhetorically, looking at Baca and shaking his head. "It's interesting. Interesting, is it not?" He stood before his chair muttering, as to himself, saying: "He whose uncle is a judge goes to court with assurance."

Firmly clasping a sheet of paper behind his back, the governor then walked about the room looking at the earthen floor and then at the men who stood before him, saying finally, "My orders on assuming the governorship of New Mexico were to investigate the wrongs and injustices done to the king, to restore respect for civil authority, and to investigate the death of the Honorable Governor don Luis de Rosas." He looked at the eight, but especially at Baca, as he said, "I've spent the better part of the last seven months piecing together the facts of the governor's death and have concluded that the eight of you, as the leaders of the colony, are guilty of revolt, sedition, and murder, either as accessories before the fact, or as perpetrators in the death of the honorable don Luis. You're to be confined here by order of His Excellency Viceroy Juan de Palafox y Mendoza.[1] And I'm to get rid of you, and your relatives, and your associates, by an exemplary punishment, as brief and conclusive as I can devise. You're to be executed for your crimes."

"But these men returned to Santa Fe under the promise of royal immunity," said an incredulous Antonio Baca as though initiating a negotiation regarding their sentences. "And Instead of the immunity they were promised, they're being detained and are to be executed? What happened to due process?" he asked. "Their right to examine evidence? To face their accusers? To challenge the basic assertion of their guilt? What kind of justice is this?" he raged. "Are you ignoring the rules of honest engagement?"

"The viceroy told me that I'm to have you killed." Pacheco responded coldly.

"Were you not instructed to grant amnesty to all who took part in the war against the governor except for those specifically under indictment for a crime?" Baca asked. "Were those not your specific instructions?"

"I have signed confessions from seven of you, and you don't deny having taken up arms against the governor," he said to Baca. Then, looking at Antonio square on, he said, "I've read in minute detail the sworn testimonies of those who provided statements in Ortiz's trial. Some of them contradicted one another, while others provided self-incriminating acknowledgements of participation—and I thank you for those, don Antonio. They were very helpful," he said with mock politeness. Then, in an abrupt reversal in his demeanor, he said. "The indictments against the eight of you were obtained on the basis of those signed declarations and the admissions I obtained from other traitors. Would you like to review them privately, don Antonio?" he asked Baca. "I have copies of the originals right there." He pointed to the documents lying on the table.

Pacheco waited a long moment before continuing, stood as

though lost in thought, drawing a sheath of paper absently through his restless fingers. Then, looking at Baca, he said, "Well, there's probably no need for that. The indictments against you were sealed and known only to me, to be revealed at the proper time. What has been decided has been decided. What I've written, I've written," he said echoing Pilate. "You've been caught, convicted, and condemned. The warrants for your execution have been signed by me and are here in my hand."

Antonio Baca looked at Governor Pacheco and said, "Then your proclamation of amnesty was a trick to capture and execute us?" he asked shaking his head.

"Can Gomez be responsible for this?" asked Juan de Archuleta of his Uncle Antonio. "I can't believe that he would knowingly give us up."

"No, it can't be Gomez," Baca responded, "for no one is more honorable than he."

Baca was suddenly filled with an odd sense of serenity, the response of one who had resigned himself to the fact that he was soon to die. Recovering his composure and refusing to beg for mercy, he said, "We are alone, Governor, taken at a disadvantage, lacking anyone to plead our case. We are condemned by the words of men who've said what they've said out of fear of torture or death. However, we bow to your authority and ask you to remember that no Spaniard, by virtue of his honor, can be publicly flogged, or shamed, or exiled."

"And you cannot be hanged like common criminals," the governor added. "You must, therefore, be beheaded," he said spitting out their sentence and the manner of their executions. Gathering the documents from their place on the table, and then adding them to the warrants he held in his hand, the governor exited the room abruptly, leaving Zamora behind.

* * *

Sitting with the other condemned men in the guards' room, Baca went over the contents of his pockets and of the pannier he had removed from his horse when arriving at the palace. There was so little there. A few coins. A pomander case in the shape of an apple, within which, as a guard against infection, he carried an *Agnus Dei* (Lamb of God medallion). There, also, was a silver rosary that his wife had insisted he carry with him when he went to meet with the governor and a small muslin bag filled with what appeared to be sweet basil. So little, he said to himself with dismay.

"May we draw up testaments, or write farewell letters, or compose lists of what we have at home and to whom we wish our possessions to go?" Baca asked for himself and for the other men.

"No," Zamora responded.

"May we at least request Masses?" Antonio asked, a small measure of anger now creeping into his voice.

"You may make that request of the father *custos* when you meet with him tomorrow," Zamora said. "It will all be over tomorrow."

* * *

"Father Salas asked if they were to be burned, with Antonio Baca to be the kindling," said Fray Hernando de Covarrubias in a jesting tone.

"No, not burned," responded Governor Pacheco to the father *custos* who had come up to the *villa* from Santo Domingo at the governor's request. "Nor can they be hanged," he continued. "It's a matter of honor. They're not common criminals. Therefore, their punishment must be particularly dishonorable. They must be beheaded!"

"Beheaded?" the father *custos* cried in alarm. "Surely, you wouldn't!"

"Yes, beheaded," the governor said. "Not by a *vecino* here, of course, for we could not ask that of one of their own. By that man Suarez who followed me up the trail, the one I asked you to keep with Zamora at Santo Domingo until he was needed," he said, further identifying the man. "I could not house him here because of the questions his presence in New Mexico would raise. He's on his way to the *casas* now," the governor said. "Zamora returned with specific instructions from the viceroy as to how Baca and his men were to be handled, and Suarez is to be their executioner."

"Does he know of his assignment?" asked Fray Covarrubias with a shudder. "And how does one charge for such service?"

"Zamora brought him to the kingdom for the express purpose of carrying out the executions, and the fee for his labor is not great," the governor continued. "Thirty-two pesos and two *tomines* for the entire group. About the price of three saddle mules."

"Then this has been planned for a long time," remarked Fray Covarrubias.

"Yes, yes, for a long time," the governor responded. "Planned as the result of special orders given to me by the Bishop-Viceroy Juan de Palafox y Mendoza who considers your fellow clerics and the members of the Baca and Perez de Bustillo clan guilty of revolt and sedition. The viceroy may not have enough on Salas and the rest of your custody to punish them," he said as he looked at the record and certificates of sentence for the eight men, "but he has decreed that these colonists must die."

He waited then seemingly searching for words to continue. Finally he said, "I want you to know that it was not supposed to end this way. The viceroy wanted to restore order here but without resorting to further bloodshed. To accomplish this, he ordered me to investigate the governor's death and to send a secret report of the same to Mexico City for his review. He authorized me to grant a pardon, with or without limitations, as I saw fit, to any captain, citizen, soldier, or inhabitant of the province who had participated in the disturbances here either during or after Rosas' administration. Whomever I pardoned was also to be pardoned by the viceroy in the king's name. However, I was given secret orders of exception for Antonio Baca, Francisco de Salazar, the Lujanes, Juan and Francisco, and Juan de Archuleta, as leaders of the revolt and sedition, and anyone else I might find who had played a major part in the death of the governor. The individuals so identified were not to be informed of this reservation," he went on. "Rather, I was to find a way to induce them to go to city of Mexico so that the *audiencia* might make a final decision concerning their guilt. His Lordship felt that their sense of honor would induce them to go to Mexico to defend their conduct. But," he continued, "if I was unable to get them to go voluntarily, and they retreated into hiding, I was authorized to seize them and to send them into custody in *Nueva Vizcaya*. The viceroy also told me that if they were likely to be rescued on the way, and if I was assured of their guilt, then it would be better to get rid of them by a brief and exemplary punishment that would cause all the other malcontents to have proper respect for the royal name of His Majesty and his ministers.[2]

"But the situation here is most odd," the governor continued. "To give complete legality to the proceedings, I would have, under ordinary circumstances, been required to inform the local justice of the peace and other officials of the plan. But with the *justicia mayor* and two of the three additional *regidores* among the condemned prisoners, whom am I to notify?" he asked.

"The *Maese de campo*? Are you not to notify don Pedro Lucero de Godoy?" the *custos* asked.

"He's been recused from these proceeding because of his relationship to Salas and Gomez," the governor responded.

"The sheriff of the council then?" questioned the *custos* who was trying to be of assistance.

"Yes, that's good," the governor stated. "I'll tell Nicolas Duran. Then we can proceed."

* * *

Whistles, shouts, and the reverberations of hammering, could be heard outside the guards' room as a group of *genizaro* slaves worked to enlarge the platform of a scaffold already present in the courtyard so that it would accommodate eight men. The official time given to the condemned men for the preparation of their executions consisted of hours only. After a meal of blue cornmeal gruel and clear water, the eight were locked in the guards' room to await the new day.

JULY 21, 1643, LIFE FLEES LIKE A SHADOW

At dawn, after passing an anguished and sleepless night during which a fiery comet had roared across the northern skies, the eight condemned prisoners were taken to the little chapel of Our Lady in the east tower of the *casas reales*. There, they met briefly with Fray Covarrubias. The father *custos*, who was later to portray the beautiful weather as an indication that God had looked with approval upon the executions, insisted on administering the last rites to the condemned men, in spite of his being unsure even at this last moment that the governor would carry out his plan. Some prayed, and, although all were completely composed, they were given a small measure of bread and wine to bolster their courage.

At about eight o'clock in the morning, a thunderous knock was heard at the chapel door and the eight were told that the executioner awaited them in Pacheco's *Peralvillo* (execution grounds). The men demonstrated no signs of dread or anguish until told by Governor Pacheco, who met them at the door, that in keeping with the directions provided by the viceroy, the executions were to be held behind barred doors. The conspirators were to die unaccompanied by friend or loved one. There were to be no family members present to request a reprieve or stay of execution, no friend to observe their passing or to report to those who would wish to know the way in which they had approached their deaths.

Concealing his dismay and speaking impassively, Baca asked Governor Pacheco, "Is no one to be allowed to bid us farewell?"

"They would only upset you," the governor answered in what appeared to be a measured attempt to console his prisoners. "But I've asked your nephew, Captain don Fernando Duran y Chaves, to act as a witness. He'll be here to represent your family."

Putting aside the cloths, which had been given them to bind their eyes, the eight, some carrying the crucifixes or little prayer books that had been provided them by the father *custos*, entered the great plaza. Under an azure sky, they walked with immeasurable reserve, with courage, and with exceptional dignity.

In the center of the plaza was set a scaffold about sixteen feet square and two feet high, barely sufficient to accommodate the condemned men and their superiors who were about to enter it. Within the confines of the small platform were eight crudely constructed cottonwood blocks, each about two feet high. Also on the stage were two low stools that had been placed there to accommodate Fray Covarrubias and Governor Pacheco. Between the stools there was a large basket.

NO MANNER OF DEATH BRINGS SHAME IF IT IS SUPPORTED BY COURAGE
Alvaro de Luna[3]

Outside the stage and wearing their mourning dress was gathered a few spectators who had been extended the honor of observing the executions. They included Baca's nephew, Fernando Duran y Chaves I, the son of the deceased captain and *sargento mayor* (lieutenant marshal), don Pedro Duran y Chaves, whose wife, dona Isabel de Bohorquez, was Antonio Baca's sister.

Throwing the skirt of his cloak over his shoulders and retaining even in this terrible extremity great dignity and a grand *seignior's* mastery of himself, Antonio led the other prisoners up the three stairs following the governor and the father *custos* to their stools. He listened dispassionately while the warrant for bringing them to the block was read aloud. His look remained unchanged and, from the manner in which he listened to the commission, one might have thought that he was hearing a statement of his pardon, rather than a call for his death.

Antonio stood looking at the mountains to the east, at the barred doors of the *zaguan* to the south, and at his compatriots who stood at his side. They had defended the family and the kingdom against dishonor and the abuse of power by Governor Rosas and were now to pay for their "crimes." At Antonio's side were his nephews, Nicolas Perez de Bustillo, Juan de Archuleta, and Juan Ruiz de Hinojos; Diego Martin Barba, captain of Rosas's guards, who had failed in his duty to protect the governor; and his friends, Cristobal Enriquez, Francisco de Salazar, and Diego Marquez. Marquez's participation in the governor's assassination had been prompted by the murder of his nephew, Juan Marquez, former Treasurer of the Holy Crusade. It was alleged that Governor Rosas had ordered the killing.

Only 43-years-old, but worn from the strains of his position, Baca was old beyond his years. A large man, with long, dark brown hair that was beginning to gray, he had lived life in the saddle, in unending motion, sitting proud and elegant and in command of himself. He walked with a slight limp resulting from a fall from a horse that had occurred several years earlier. His eyes, still flashing wrathful indignation, were as passionate as ever. He was, in spite of everything, swift, burning, and zealous, but his countenance carried the mark of frustration, of blows parried and dreams deferred, of steadfast determination and stamina against the difficulties of his office. His clothes, selected by his wife, Yumar

Perez de Bustillo, who had sought to dress him nicely for his meeting with the governor, were of the best grade, without sword or scabbard, but beautifully worn, his turquoise-clad dagger, and dagger-sheath, hanging ceremoniously at his side. He was sensitive to the paradox of life in which time and circumstances had wrested the leading reins of the colony from between his fingers, and felt that it was fitting that he should go with the rest. He stood with his hands clasped tightly behind his back, waiting his turn.

An initial indication of distress was wrenched from the group when the executioner asked for Cristobal Enriquez's knife, for it was required that a condemned prisoner be beheaded with his own dagger.

"Your knife, please," the executioner asked politely.

The tall and well-featured Enriquez, pale, with hands shaking uncontrollably, tried but was unable to extract his knife from its sheath. The executioner, thinking that Enriquez was delaying the proceedings unnecessarily, struck the prisoner with his closed fist in the pit of his stomach. Amid the gasps and groans of Enriquez and the others on the stage, as well as many in the small crowd, the 36-year-old Enriquez, the son of first colonist, Juan Rangel, was driven to his knees, his knife forcibly taken from him. Walking behind Enriquez, the executioner grabbed him roughly by the hair of his head, forced his forehead down onto the block, and slit his throat.

It continued in this manner with the executioner working his way down the line of condemned prisoners until he got to Francisco de Salazar. Antonio Baca stood beside Salazar but refused to look at him, seemingly seeking something in the vast distance, something in his own mind. "Is this your knife?" he heard the executioner ask. "It is," Salazar said as he knelt and placed the knife in the executioner's hand. "Then it will be but a brief moment," the executioner said as he slashed at Salazar's neck.

Francisco began his prayer. "I believe in God, the Father Almighty, Creator of heaven and earth . . . "

"It will be but another moment," the executioner said politely as he again slashed across the base of Salazar's throat with Salazar's dull knife.

" . . . and in Jesus Christ, His only Son, our Lord . . . "

Cutting. Sawing. Salazar, who was ready to die with rage and spite but who was still very much alive pleaded, "For God's sake! Sharpen that thing and put me out of my misery." He struggled to regain his place in the prayer. ". . . Jesus Christ . . . Our Lord . . . born of the Virgin Mary." The executioner finally completed his task. He placed the severed head in the basket after which, the movement of Salazar's lips was still perceptible and continued to be so for many minutes after his death.

The executioner had asked, as was the custom, for the eight condemned prisoners to pardon him for causing their deaths. He had worked his way down the line of standing men, not one of whom had cried out in anguish or pain. And when he was through with seven, each head having been carefully placed in the waiting basket, he came to where Baca was standing. Fray Covarrubias asked Baca, as he had each of the other men, "Do you wish me to pray for you?"

Quiet for a long moment, Baca, who was now "*el hombre a secas*" (a man standing alone), was thinking of the blunt manner in which he had been told of his punishment, and that life—but a sliver of light between dark and dark—was now but a fleeting shadow. His thoughts, like the waters of a dappled stream, wandered from one memory to another, a slight, colorless snake of regret all but lost in a bed of white stones. He was imagining looking at his pretty wife standing behind the doors of his *placita*. Smiling. Petting his favorite dog. He was looking at his little garden set with fragrant flowers. At the priest's question, the image, like a specter in the moonlight, dissolved into thin air. Baca knelt down, held out his knife for the executioner to take, and speaking softly and without any bitterness in his voice, said, "Please tell my wife that I love her and ask that she take care of my dog." He looked up at Fray Covarrubias. "I commend myself to God!" he said with the same tranquil and unconcerned air he had previously displayed. He looked then at his nephew Fernando Duran y Chaves I who was standing on a bench near the scaffold and was thereafter silent.[4]

With the father *custos* kneeling down on the platform, praying loudly and seemingly forever, in a dogged attempt to place his mark on the proceedings, the executioner completed his grizzly task. A deft stroke severed Baca's neck, all but the least tendon, and, using Baca's knife as a saw, the executioner cut this. Baca crumpled upon the platform floor, only his nephew there to tell of his courage and of his gallant death.

Baca's head was given to Governor Pacheco who held it aloft, crying out, "So perish the king's enemies!" The head was given back to the executioner who nailed it to the projecting arm of the unused gibbet. Then, to the horror of the bystanders who crossed themselves over and over again, Baca's dog, Albacar, which had somehow entered the locked and barred plaza, placed itself pathetically below the detached head and could not be enticed away. At that instant, blood erupted from Baca's nostrils and dripped onto his puppy. It was about ten o'clock in the morning on Friday, 21 July 1642, and Antonio Baca and seven others were gone from this world.

* * *

The members of the colony treated the executions as murders with multiple victims. They felt both mortification and rage at the slaying of one who had served them as *justicia mayor*. As the town crier Jusepe announced the executions to a stunned populace, several *genizaro* slaves replaced the heads on the bodies of the executed prisoners, as ordered by Governor Pacheco. The head of Antonio Baca, which remained nailed to the gibbet, was the one exception. The bodies, their heads reattached, were then rolled inside woolen mats of *jerga* that were provided in place of winding sheets. The bodies, to be retrieved by their grieving relatives, were then unceremoniously laid out in the plaza.

Selected by Governor Pacheco to carry the grave news to his aunt, Yumar Perez de Bustillo, don Fernando Duran y Chaves I (who was later to be appointed an *alcalde* by Governor Pacheco as a reward for his various involvements in the Rosas affair) rode through the hills to the east of the *casas reales* and then across the river to the Baca home. His aunt, who had hoped that an exonerated Antonio would ride home in honor, had been alarmed by the news of his incarceration that she had received the previous day. Hearing nothing further regarding her husband and fearing the worst, she had gathered her daughters, Gertrudis, Ana, and Gregoria around her. Together, they were anxiously awaiting word from the Royal Palace when Chaves rode up.

Yumar received the grave news with shock and then with tears. She was at first unable to speak and appeared dumbfounded. But before grief could completely overwhelm her, she turned on her nephew, Fernando, like a ferocious beast, accusing him of attending the executions only to win the governor's favor. "Are a man's enemies the men of his own house?" she screamed at her nephew. "Get a cart and bring your uncle here. Bring him home, Fernando! Bring him home!"

* * *

Simon Perez de Bustillo, who was to drag out his days in bitterness and grief, tried, staggering, to carry his son from the plaza to the Perez home and was finally coaxed by those who accompanied him to place Nicolas in their cart. Driven to his knees by the barbarity of the execution of his only son and the others, he had suffered a blow from which he would never fully recover. Speechless and drained of comprehension, he was unable to console or comfort his wife, Juana de Zamora Baca, or his daughters, Juliana, Catalina, and Maria who were equally grief-stricken. Maria's child, Lorenzo Perez, now 16 months old, clung to his mother, attempting to comfort her while seeking her love and protection.

* * *

Later that day, while the families of the executed prisoners prepared their loved ones for burial, washing their bodies with *posca* (a solution of vinegar and water), and wrapping them in their capes, Governor Pacheco summoned the remainder of the town's *vecinos* to the *casas reales*. There he pardoned them of their crimes as accomplices in the governor's death, but ordered them to affirm their allegiance to the king within two weeks or suffer the death penalty. Crying in grief and in protest, the *vecinos* swore their allegiance before the head of Antonio Baca. Governor Pacheco then told them that he had ordered the traitors' property seized and declared forfeit. The proceeds from the sale of their belongings were to be used to pay for a peacekeeping force of 30 men to be enlisted that very day. "No Baca or Perez de Bustillo family member or friend need apply," he said.

* * *

Responding to the request by his nephew, Fernando, for assistance in the retrieval of his uncle's body, Alonso, who had been unaware of the executions, first rode to the central plaza and then into the courtyard at the *casas reales* where the executions had been conducted. Coaxing his horse to mount the scaffold platform, he reached up and took his brother's head from where it had been nailed. Then placing it in the crook of his free arm, he reversed course and returned to the plaza where Antonio's headless body had been placed.

Next, the scaffold and its bloodied blocks were burned, the ground around them turned over and over again with a garden spade and the turned earth mixed with the fire's ashes. Baca's dog, treated with a shampoo of *amole*, (yucca root) in an attempt clean him of his master's blood, was washed again and again, but red-tinged and mottled beyond recognition, it then became melancholy, refused to eat, and so wasted away and died.

* * *

Although other non-relatives had lost their lives in the murder of Governor Luis de Rosas, the tragedy centered on the family of the Perez de Bustillos. Yumar had lost her husband, Antonio Baca; Yumar's brother, Simon, had to bury his son, Nicolas; Yumar's sister Ana had lost her son, Juan de Archuleta; Yumar's sister Beatrice had to bury her son, Juan Ruiz de Hinojos. And, of course, Maria, daughter of Simon, was without her husband, Nicolas Ortiz, who, though acquitted of the crime of murder, had been detained in *Nueva Vizcaya* by its governor, don Luis de Valdez, awaiting final instructions from Governor Pacheco.

* * *

And now began the *velorios*, the death vigils. They were conducted in the candlelit courtyards of eight homes to assure that evil spirits were not given an opportunity to capture the dead men's souls before they fled their bodies. The vigils, conducted over two nights by a *resador*, consisted of the rosary and attendant prayers with *alabados*, hymns of praise to the saints.

JULY 25, FEAST DAY OF SAINT JAMES, SPAIN'S PATRON SAINT

On July 25th, after all family members had arrived from outlying areas, the caskets of the Baca and the Perez de Bustillo men were placed upon waiting wagons and driven to the main plaza where a crowd awaited them. There the people wept and prayed silently or aloud. Carrying out the custom of the nobility, four men, dressed in black down to the hoofs of their horses, functioned as the deceased's personal attendants and followed each wagon on horseback. A funeral procession composed of family members then walked behind the caskets as the wagons were driven to the church.

At the church of *San Francisco*, recently completed and still appearing new, the light was provided by funeral tapers, and the sound by a sad and dismal bell whose toll was achieved by a man in the tower striking the bell with a rock in each hand.

Family members knelt in prayer before the benches that the Bacas and the Perez de Bustillos had donated to the church. The women were wrapped and swathed in their skirts and gowns even in this terrible extremity. They looked elegant in the *mantonas* they wore in mourning and would wear again for Lenten services. They, along with their men who knelt to their left, watched in silence as Fray Hernando Covarrubias approached the biers that were lying two by two upon the earthen floor.

Large candles, which had been brought from the altar, were placed upright beside the coffins. The statues of St. Francis and St. Joseph had been taken down from their niches in the *reredo* as well, and placed on the altar steps where they could better see what was about to transpire.

"This is indeed a sad day," said Fray Hernando Covarrubias sprinkling holy water on the top of each of the four pine-clad coffins as he worked his way among them. "A sad, sad day," he repeated stopping before the small assembly. "May I speak for the governor in conveying his condolences?" he asked of his solemn and silent congregation. "He wishes he were here with you to mourn the loss of your family members, and he wants to assure you that he, too, mourns their passing. His absence is due to your request for a private ceremony. May I convey, however, his prayers and good wishes and assure you that he means you no harm," he said, his words echoing in the adobe void.

At this, the 75-year-old Alonso Varela, brother-in-law of the murdered Antonio Baca and himself a first colonist, struggled to his feet from his place among the kneeling congregation. He walked to the altar, interrupting the father *custos* by asking, "Sad? Is that all it is, Father?" He shook his head in dismay. Choosing his words carefully, and speaking without the stammer that sometimes impaired his speech, he said. "We were barely able to provide the requisite number of pall bearers from among our families for those who lie before you, Father, our numbers have been so sadly depleted." Then, sweeping his eyes across the black-clad assembly, he began to call out names. As he did, each man stood and walked to the altar. "Simon Perez de Bustillo, Blas de Miranda, Fernando Duran y Chaves, Agustin de Carvajal, Diego Santa Cruz, Matias Lopez del Castillo, Francisco de Anaya, Miguel de Hinojos, Alonso Baca, Antonio Jorge de Vera, Antonio de Salas, Francisco de Aragon, and my own family, my brother Pedro and his sons, Pedro and Juan. How many of us are there, Father?" he asked rhetorically, but in a sad voice. "Sixteen? Only sixteen of us left," he said. "But tell the governor this." The elder Varela shook his finger in the priest's face. "We're strong and resolute and will only require four, rather than six, bearers for each casket."

"And tell the governor who we are!" bellowed Alonso Baca, brother of the slain Antonio. He moved from where he had been standing among those who had been called to Varela's side. "We're Spaniards and Old Christians," he said. "Honorable men. *Gente de razon.* Rational beings who fully understand the implications of our behavior. And we're soldiers!" he shouted. "It's true that there are not many of us left, but there are enough of us to do what must be done. We'll bring charges against the governor for these murders, and if he brings arms against us in retaliation or reprisal, he will think us an entire army!"

* * *

After services at the church, the pine coffins were carried outside to the holy grounds, but only men would attend their burial. There, in the *campo santo*, the men dug the graves, scattered flowers and pine boughs, and placed heavy stones as markers upon the upturned earth. While the men accomplished these tasks, the women mourners walked to the home of Simon Perez de Bustillo, where they awaited their men.

* * *

The aggrieved relatives of the eight executed men filed criminal charges against Governor Pacheco. Five days later, on July 30th, Spanish and

Indian representatives from the entire province gathered in Santa Fe for a solemn High Mass, having been ordered by Governor Pacheco to do so under penalty of death. At this Mass, the Franciscan prelate, Fray Hernando Covarrubias and Governor Alonso Pacheco y Heredia pronounced their loyalty and obedience to the king and to his appointed representatives.

* * *

Striking out in every direction, Governor Pacheco next threatened *Custos* Hernando Covarrubias with expulsion or death if he did not give his approval to the exhumation of the body of Sebastian de Sandoval and to its reinterment in the Santa Fe Church. The *custos* complied, and Sandoval was for the third time placed in the earth. The governor then ordered the destruction of the Perez safehouse, a mean structure of stone laid up without mortar, but one that offered every means of security and defense. Finally, on the northern bank of the Santa Fe River, the governor turned with fury on the cottonwood spreading its shade over the meeting place of Indians and Spanish settlers. With ax and broadsword, his men fell upon its monstrous trunk. The colonists, awestruck, saw the gigantic colonial landmark crash to the ground, and they took it as an evil omen.

Bells were rung announcing the *Misas de ocho dias* (Masses of eight days) for the executed prisoners. Requiem Masses were said for the repose of their souls. Summer turned to fall, and soon the snows fell.

51

Treachery and a Rift

When Francisco Gomez received the message announcing the deaths of the accused men, he reacted as though he had been kicked in the stomach. He had given the eight his word, promising them amnesty in exchange for their confessions and had instead unintentionally made it possible for Governor Pacheco to execute them without a trial. "They testified against themselves!" he said aloud. And he, himself, had been purposely lied to. He now owed Pacheco nothing!

Summoned to the Royal Palace by Governor Pacheco, Gomez initially considered ignoring the governor's command but for the threatening tone of his words which hastened his response. Wretchedly despondent and sick with resentment and mistrust, he came into the governor's presence literally armed head to foot as against treachery. He was asked to take off his *cuero*, to put aside his arms and to eat with the governor. But he refused either to remove his weapons or to break bread. With bitterness in his heart, he asked, "Did you send for me?"

"Francisco, Francisco, are we to be enemies?" Governor Pacheco asked, coaxing Gomez to take a seat. "I have word, don Francisco, word regarding Ortiz. Please sit down and lay off your weapons."

"I'm only here because of the manner in which you issued your directive, your Lordship. Your words regarding my family."

"I mean them no harm, don Francisco," the governor said. "I

only meant to emphasize the requirement of allegiance to the king, to the viceroy, and to me personally," he replied with much haughtiness.

"You have my allegiance and that of the members of my family. But let all men know this for certain," he said. "If anyone harms a single hair on the head of any member of my family, I will be his enemy for as long as I live."

Without removing his sword or his dagger, Gomez sat at the small table across from the governor, steeling himself to hear bad news regarding Nicolas Ortiz, but stunned by what Pacheco told him.

"He was stopped enroute to the city of Mexico," Pacheco said. "Taken into custody at *San Jose del Parral* on the *camino real*, where he's to be retried by the governor of *Nueva Vizcaya*."

"How did that happen?" asked an incredulous Gomez, who knew that the governor of *Nueva Vizcaya* was functioning beyond his jurisdiction. The only law he could be following was that of the sword. "Ortiz's case, as one of substance, was to be forwarded to the city of Mexico for final resolution. In any event, he's not a *vecino* of Parral. By what right did the governor of *Nueva Vizcaya* take him into custody?"

"He was acting on my request," Pacheco answered. "I asked him in your name and that of *Alcalde* Lucero, to apprehend Ortiz. He was tried and acquitted by his own uncle, for God's sake! What kind of justice is that?"

"You did what?" Gomez asked in disbelief. "His uncle, as you put it, the *justicia mayor*, presided over his acquittal in a fair and just trial," Gomez answered. "Ortiz was at fault, of course. Guilty of murder in cruel circumstance, but deserving of leniency for the merit of the governor's death. The tribunal in Mexico City would have upheld his acquittal because Rosas took his honor! And a person without honor is as good as dead" he said emphatically. "And how did you advise the governor about the way a guilty verdict was to be handled?" Gomez asked. "I'm sure that advice was given in that regard."

"I requested that if Ortiz was found guilty in his trial there, I would be informed of this so that his property held in embargo here and entrusted to Captain Simon Perez de Bustillo might revert to the crown. I also requested that he be condemned and hanged, after which his severed head and sword hand would be displayed on the gibbet."

Gomez stood from his place at the table and looked directly at the governor wondering what manner of man sat before him. An uncrossable bridge now lay between them and a sharp suspicion of further treachery crossed Gomez's mind, as he asked, "And why are you telling me this? Why did you feel I needed to know of the success of your plans?"

"Because Ortiz, like Baca, went against royal authority, ignoring the rights of the government," the governor said. "Perhaps I was wrong in thinking you'd want to know this," he said feigning chagrin. "But I felt that you'd want to be informed that Ortiz, too, is to be punished."

52

Say Nothing to King, Rook or Earthly Man

While many of the ordinary colonists retired behind the walls of their adobe compounds waiting to see what would transpire next, Francisco Gomez was devising a plan.

* * *

Awakened by Tula from a deep sleep, Maria, who was trembling all over, now sat in her nightclothes before the fireplace in the grand *sala* of her parents' home, a quilt wrapped tightly about her slim shoulders. Francisco, too, was there. Looking very much like a man on a mission, he leaned toward her and said, "It was the last of October when they reached Parral. They had camped outside the village limits where they were set upon by some of the governor's men. Although Nicolas was initially successful in taking refuge in a church, he was eventually removed from the church by his Lordship, Governor don Luis de Valdez, who said that he had ample justification for the violation of your husband's immunity, and that he didn't have to wait to resolve the matter judiciously as required by the Church. Captured, Nicolas confessed under torture to the murder of Governor Rosas, and is to be executed. But, God willing, neither Governor Pacheco nor Governor Valdez will succeed in their plan."

"Oh My God! My God!" Maria cried. "What did they do to him?"

"It's probably best you don't know." Gomez responded. "The knowledge would only further disturb you."

"But I want to know!" begged Maria, who had listened with fear and trembling. "My imagination may be worse than the truth."

Hearing her plea and wondering how to proceed, a reluctant Gomez said, "Captain Andres Lopez Sambrano, who testified against your uncle and Nicolas at Parral, said that Nicolas's body was totally covered with bruises. His neck had burns from the application of live coals. His ankles were scabbed from the manacles in which he had been placed. And his knees had festering ulcers. Horrible wounds, Lopez said, sorry that he had played any part in Nicolas's trial. Do you want to know more?" he asked.

"Yes," she whispered.

"His knees were broken to keep him from fleeing. And his knee wounds are being kept from healing by his jailers who periodically reopen them by mincing his flesh with a knife," Gomez said to a horrified Maria. "We'll attempt to effect his escape, my child," Gomez said. "But if we're successful, you'll receive nothing but a sign. That will be the extent of our communication with you regarding Nicolas."[1]

"But what harm can it do if I know where he is, don Francisco," Maria asked plaintively, "whether in Spain or New Spain?"

"Because no matter how well a secret is kept, a hint of it will eventually become known to others," Gomez said. "And with Bishop Palafox now acting in place of the king, the *audiencia* functions like an Inquisitional court. They may torture you or the members of your family to learn of his hiding."

"Surely, they would not," Maria said. "Women and children have never been held accountable for the actions of their husbands or fathers or beaten to bare their secrets. But in any case," she said, "even if they did torture me, I'd never tell."

"And if you don't know, you won't be able to," Gomez said. "There's more at stake here than you and Nicolas, my child," Gomez said, gathering his cape about him in readiness to leave. "We must safeguard the lives of the men who will effect this," he said, rising from his chair and moving toward the door. "It will have to be enough for you to know that he's safe. There'll be no word," he said, as he exited the room.

"And I'll not ask for any," she called after him, as he disappeared into the darkness.

53

A Nicely Set-Out and Well-Provisioned Spanish Column

Pueblo Indians, who remained a subject of dispute between the priests, the colonists, and the Spanish officials, watched as a nicely outfitted and well-provisioned Spanish column rode through their pueblos on its way south. The larger portion of the Spaniards' adobe kingdom, built of scattered pueblos and valley retreats, lay behind them as the file approached Senecu, the southernmost of the mission pueblos. Here, the members of the group met with Fray Juan de Salas, who embraced each of the men happily, and then, as was his wont, bestowed unwanted counsel upon each.

"Don't go there," he said to Matias Lopez del Castillo, a Perez de Bustillo relative, regarding *Nueva Viscaya*.[1] "You may be riding into a trap. Don't you think it's possible that the governor told you of Ortiz's imprisonment knowing that you would attempt to effect his escape?"

"We thought of that," said Alonso Baca. "Thought, also, that even you might be in on the plot, for, as they say, 'he who knows not whom to suspect ends up suspecting everyone.' "

"Then please tell me nothing further," Salas said, directing his remark to Juan de Archuleta, son of the slain Juan. "We only seek ways to help," he said in regard to himself and to the father *custos*. "The father *custos* has, in this regard, imposed a fast to assist your brothers to atone for their sins. A fast on every Friday for three years, with abstinence from lamb or beef on Wednesdays as well."

Alonso could not believe the stupidity of these priests who thought that all of the colonists' problems could be solved with a prayer. He looked at Salas, censoring most of what he wished to say. "Do you think that will help, Father?" he asked mockingly. "That we starve ourselves when we most need our strength?"

"It's a penitential discipline designed to strengthen the spiritual life by weakening the attractions of sensible pleasures," Salas said.

"Well, at least you admit the pleasures are sensible, Father," Baca said as he mounted his horse.

As the members of the column rode away from the pueblo of Senecu, with the ground trembling in their passage, they watched as a group of hooded personages rode out of the pueblo, heading north. "Going about their nefarious business," Baca said of the Franciscan priests. "Although there is no tyranny like the tyranny of priests," he said to Gomez, "I think that the present coalition between the Crown and the Cross, their so-called 'real patronato,' will, in the end, kill both of them. But I love it when these priests make their incredible rules," said an angry Alonso who felt that Salas and Covarrubias had not intervened in the execution of the prisoners as they might have. "We thus know exactly what it is we must do to displease them. If it were up to them, we'd be leading the life of that madman, Mantua, sleeping in our clothes, and doing a thousand other penances to atone for who knows what. After we've helped Nicolas to escape," he said, "we'll eat meat whenever we damn well please!"

54

The Sign

The messenger had entered the church unnoticed, a dusky shadow beneath the choir loft. Standing among the Indians at the back of the church, he inched his way along the rear wall, slipping, finally, into an anteroom where he waited.

The room he entered, which was lighted by tapers that had begun their lives on the main altar, smelled of wax and incense, of adobe dust and pine. Presently, a small Indian boy, whose job it was to collect offerings from among the members of the congregation, entered the room. Startled as the child was to see an adult standing there in the shadows, he continued with his task of retrieving from behind an adobe altar, a long-armed offertory basket with which he was to perform his reverent duty.

Starting from the row of benches placed before the main altar and working his way down one side of the aisle, which the parishioners had created for his passage, the little Indian boy held his basket by its long arm before each congregant awaiting his or her donation. Without thought or attention, each member of the Perez de Bustillo clan placed a coin or a small linen bag within the basket, the tinkle or thud of his or her contribution the signal to the lad that the basket could be advanced. Maria, too, paid neither the basket nor the boy any mind, dropping a coin within, withdrawing her hand, waiting for the basket to move beyond Lorenzo and be placed before her mother. But it did not move. She gave it a cursory glance and then looked at the boy who stared at her in a blank-faced silence.

And still the basket did not move.

"Look, Mama," Lorenzo whispered, pointing to something within the basket. Maria looked inside. There, among an assortment of coins and linen bags, was a beautiful white stone the size and shape of a *cruzado* (a coin with a cross on the obverse side). With dread in her heart, a veiled Maria reached in and picked it up, curling it carefully into her tight fist. The basket and the little Indian boy moved on. She looked for the basket and the boy as soon as the service was over, but neither was anywhere to be seen.

After leaving the church, she examined the stone thoroughly, turning it this way and that, smelling it, and finally putting it into the pocket of her dress. Finding a cross etched across one face of its surface, but failing to find a message there, she now fell into a deep void of fear and hopelessness. She had known that Nicolas could not come home, yet she had remained suspended between doubt and hope that, by some miracle, this would occur. Now, however, she knew that Nicolas was safe but beyond her reach, and her dreams of his return vanished like dew in an autumn meadow.

55

Correcting the Uncorrectable

She had been a pawn in the honor system, her violation affording the governor a means to rectify an insult. But, whatever the circumstances of her defilement, Maria was now a wanton woman.[1]

* * *

It was said that a sexually shameful woman who had dishonored her husband or her father could in no way atone for her sin or avenge her honor. Only a man could do that. Maria had sent her husband and her brother and her uncle and a raft of male cousins on a vengeful mission, and, although a number of them had paid with their lives, they had been unsuccessful in completely restoring her honor.[2] Maria now took the only other course available to her to complete the task. She visited Fray Juan de Vidania.

* * *

The two women waited in the interior courtyard of the *convento*, ushered there by the *portero*, who had responded to their knock. Sitting now on the bench where they had been asked to stay, they waited as the shadow of a bell tower slid imperceptibly across the wall and then across their persons, eventually casting them in shade.

"What are you going to tell him?" Tula asked regarding Fray Vidania with whom they had asked to meet.

"The truth," Maria responded. "Just the truth."

There was not a cloud in the glaring sky. Birds sang. Defining their territory, Maria thought. She and Tula watched as a wren, fresh from its most recent foraging expedition, worked with a twig and a sprig of grass in its beak to build a nest in the ceiling of the covered walkway. Presently, the *portero* returned with the message that Fray Vidania was finishing his prayers and would be with them shortly.

Almost immediately, the good father followed, greeting them politely and asking, "May I help you?"

He seemed older than Maria remembered him. Wiser, too, she hoped. He held his hands before his face in the gesture of prayer. "Would you like to go inside?" he asked.

"May we meet with you in your office, your Reverence?" Maria asked politely. "We'd like to speak with you."

"You and . . . ?

"Tula," Maria responded. "She's soon to marry and will pass out of our care, but I love her and think of her as my sister."

Tula nodded to the priest at Maria's explanation, but said nothing.

When ushered into the office, the two women were invited to sit on the chairs provided by Fray Vidania as he closed the door. The room was cool, almost cold, an enormous contrast to the warmth of the blazing sun in the courtyard. The two women drew their shawls about their shoulders and waited for permission to proceed. Again, Fray Vidania placed his hands before his face and waited.

"Do you remember me, Father?" Maria asked.

"Yes, of course," he responded.

"You remember my Nicolas. And Governor Rosas. And the testimony I was required to provide regarding my relationship with him?" she asked.

"Yes?" he repeated.

"And of my dishonor?" she asked, waiting for a reply.

Fray Vidania looked at her sadly. "Are you asking to have your confession heard, my dear lady? Should this not be done privately?" he asked, glancing at Tula.

Maria waited before continuing, saying finally, "No, Father, for I've nothing to declare. But I've waited for two long years to make a request. Waited for Governor Pacheco to leave the kingdom. And now it may be presumed that Governor Arguello will silence me, as did Governor Pacheco. If this matter is not resolved truthfully, not only will I remain dishonored, but so, too, will the members of my family. I, therefore, request permission to present my case to the lord *custos* in his role as ecclesiastical judge, rather than to civil authority."

"Your case?" the priest asked. "What are you requesting?"

"To have the official register marked for deletion, Father. To have my honor restored. To tell the truth."

"But we have your testimony," he responded.

"And it's full of lies, Father. Lies I was required to tell in an attempt to save my family."

"And you wish to have your case heard by the father *custos*?" he asked pensively. "Well, that's not as easy as it may seem. A request for intervention by the father *custos* must be made in stages," he explained. "A written plea first. Then a statement. And if your written request is deemed worthy of further consideration, you will receive permission to meet with him and with the Tribunal. There are stages," he repeated.

"I'll do whatever's required," Maria responded.

"Well, then. I'll take your plea and statement and will present them at Santo Domingo before the judge ordinary, as you've requested," he said. "But please understand that I can promise nothing."

THE TRIBUNAL AT SANTO DOMINGO

They knelt at the altar, the four members of the Tribunal, Fathers Salas and Covarrubias, along with two officers of the *definatory*, whose duty it was to decide points of discipline and to advise the father *custos* regarding matters brought before him. There, also, was Fray Juan de Vidania who had asked to meet with the Tribunal in its deliberations regarding the requests for succor and aid made by members of the laity. Maria's request was not the only one the Tribunal would hear, but Fray Vidania had been successful in making it first.

After prayers at the altar, during which the father *custos* had requested guidance regarding the decisions the Tribunal might make, they took their seats at a long table where they readied themselves for their work.

Fray Vidania had nothing to do but watch them as they adjusted their seating, attempting to make themselves comfortable upon their small stools. Each had his own thoughts, looking pensive, or pious, or petulant. He smiled and might even have laughed, had not the proceedings been so serious. The father *custos* looked directly at Fray Vidania and in a tone suggesting he could proceed, said, "Father?"

His fanciful musing broken, Fray Vidania took out from within the bible he carried a sheaf of paper upon which Maria had written her statement and appeal. "This is in regards to a wrong inflicted by Governor Rosas upon one of our citizens," he said to the priests who were well known to him. "I was asked to present it to you as an appeal, to set the record straight. May I continue?" he asked the clerics who had now been joined by a notary.

Yes, yes, go on," said a curious Fray Covarrubias.

The chapter room was dark, illuminated by sconce-held candles placed in each of its four corners, and, also, by numerous candles arrayed about the table. Fray Vidania held Maria's statement up to the candle standing before him as he read:

> I am Maria Perez de Bustillo, native of New Mexico, daughter of don Simon Perez de Bustillo and dona Juana de Zamora Baca, wife of Nicolas Ortiz.

> My grandparents were Juan Perez de Bustillo and Maria de la Cruz and Cristobal Baca and Ana Ortiz, individuals, who, like my parents, were among the first *conquistadors* and pacifiers of the Kingdom, honorable individuals who served His Majesty for many years and ended their lives in royal service.

> I am an honest person. The good upbringing and prudence with which my parents raised me is publicly known in the royal *villa*. I have given no one cause to defame my honor or that of my parents or my husband.

It is my understanding that the law only punishes the seduction of a virgin. Please let it be known that my marriage to Nicolas Ortiz was unconsummated due to his absence from the kingdom. And that while he was gone, Governor Luis de Rosas, by means of absolute force, took my virginity without even the least bit of consent. Moreover, I made countless pleas, which were useless and had no other result than to quiet the fact of my ravishment, not so much because he was concerned for my honor, but so that his crime would not be discovered. I was effectively silenced because on no occasion are women who enjoy the state of virginity permitted scandal or involvement. I was silenced and would have remained silent to protect my honor and that of my parents and my husband, but time finally displayed my disgrace with a pregnancy from the said rape, and because of this, my parents charged me to declare, not without substantial shame, that the said governor (and none other) raped me in the manner I have described. He was killed by members of my family, punished for tarnishing the virtue that honorable and well-bred maidens customarily guard with great care.[3]

The father *custos*, Fray Hernando Covarrubias, who, with the other clerics, had been listening with interest to Maria's statement, interrupted Fray Vidania with the query, "And what is she asking for?"

"That we expunge the official record and restore her honor," responded Fray Vidania.

"God!" exclaimed Fray Salas. "Why can't they let this go?"

"When her pregnancy was first discovered, Father," Covarrubias continued, "did her father punish her by cutting her hair? I ask this to see how the matter was viewed at the time of its occurrence. Anyone can make this sort of charge two years later. It's the attitude and understanding of the woman's father or husband at the time of the discovery of the pregnancy that's important."

"I don't believe her father punished her," Vidania responded.

Salas, who had thought that the matter was of little importance, sat back in his chair, pressing the knuckles of his left hand against his chin in contemplation. "Well, it seems to me that there are conflicting values at issue here," said Fray Salas to the men who listened intently. "Men of honor are to enforce female purity in a wife or daughter and to protect it from assault, while other men enhance their honor through the conquest of another man's woman." He scanned their faces. "It's a delicate balance, isn't it?" he asked. "One that can't possibly be achieved. My own sense is that this young woman has that unfortunate frailty to which all of the feminine sex is inclined. And that while her husband was absent from the kingdom, the governor invited her to adultery. With the governor dead, the circumstances that led to her pregnancy cannot be proven one way or the other."[4]

He waited before continuing. "Is there not another matter to be set before us regarding the governor?" he asked while rummaging around among the inkhorns, pens, *arenilla*, and sheets of paper on which a transcription of the proceedings was to be written. "A matter regarding one of his female servants . . . an Apolonia Varela or some such . . . Ah, here it is."

"But Father . . . " complained Fray Vidania who railed at having Maria's appeal diluted, if not corrupted, by coupling it with another.

"No! Wait, Father!" Fray Salas interjected, interrupting Fray Vidania. "This is very interesting," he said, rising from his chair. Stepping around a cider press, which for some reason had been left in the middle of the room, he walked to an array of shelves hanging along one of its walls. "This is not the first petition the Varela woman has placed before us," he said, as he looked among the items of his former custody, the religious paraphernalia mandated for each priest: his flasks, lanterns, cruets, funnels, plates, vessels, and a mold for making altar bread, all in tin, and under lock and key, and a metal coffer in which to carry them. "It was a couple of years ago," he said. "Her complaint . . . the complaint of the Varela woman . . . was that Governor Rosas had forced her to marry a Juan Bautista Saragosa against her will. She said Saragosa had agreed to the marriage because the governor had kept him in the stocks for several days and had told him that if he did not marry her, he would have him whipped and gibbeted. The governor's servant, his cook, I believe, said that she agreed to marry Saragosa because she feared the governor, knowing that he was an absolute lord and that, with or without the law, he trampled on everyone." He continued his search among the items on the shelves.[5]

"Egh," he said in annoyance at the manner in which Fray Covarruias was keeping his shelves. Their were veils and goatskin covers as well as blue and scarlet cloths covering sweet incense, anointing oil, and olive oil. Olive oil! What in the hell is olive oil doing here? Bugia and scotula and palmatoria! As if there wasn't enough junk on these shelves, he's got to have olive oil, too! he muttered to himself, as he rustled around in annoyance.

"Ah! Here it is! Here it is," he repeated, obviously pleased at having found the document for which he had been searching, as he again took his seat at the table. "Yes," he said. "She was the widow of Julian Escarraman and was asking that her marriage to Saragosa be annulled because although married against her will and at the governor's insistence, the governor continued to demand intimate favors from her."[6]

"And what is she asking for this time?" queried Fray Covarrubias.

"She's requesting ten sheep . . . one string of chilies . . . four bushels of corn . . . and a white cotton bedspread with a black and yellow fringe which, she says, the governor had promised to give her."[7]

"But these are two very different women, your Reverences, and their complaints are as different as night and day," said Fray Vidania in chagrin. "One is a servant who was apparently being compensated by Governor Rosas for her sexual favors, while the other, an alleged rape victim, is a member of one of the most prominent and honorable families in the kingdom. Their appeals, the appeals of the two women, cannot be judged in the same manner," he said, as he brushed with the back of his hand at the fringe of his hair.

"And the Perez woman," asked Fray Covarrubias for a second time. "What is she asking for . . .?"

"That the truth of her statements be put into the official record and publicly proclaimed on the next major feast day," said Fray Vidania. There was silence then, wonder at the audacity of it all, contemplation.

The father *custos* finally said, "Well, nothing will save her from the public dishonor and scandal that she's probably already suffered, and the burden of proof, should she wish to pursue further inquiry, will be on her and on her family. She'll have to produce witnesses who will testify to her good conduct and to her virginity. Does she want to do that, Father?" he asked of Fray Vidania.[8]

"She has a witness, Father," responded Fray Vidania. "Her *genizaro* servant, known as *La Tula*, was there when she returned scratched and disheveled from the governor's apartments. Her servant later found her crying and cleaning her genitals with a blood-soaked cloth."[9]

"She could have been doing that to solace her evil," Salas remarked. "Governor Pacheco said that she roams the streets alone at night, going from house to house." He looked at the other men, saying, "I've seen that woman. She's too beautiful for her own good."[10]

"But beauty itself is not corrupting, Father," responded Fray Vidania. "In fact, Our Mother, from whom the Perez woman takes her name, was beautiful." He waited and looked at the men arrayed around the table, sensing that the hearing was not going well for Maria. Knowing that these were likely the final words he was going to be allowed to speak regarding this matter, he said, "Maria Perez de Bustillo has lost not only her honor, but also her self esteem, her good name, and her reputation, which, up to this time, had been acknowledged by all. Therefore, on all counts, this Tribunal must favor the person and honor of the *senora*. Her status and name are well known in this kingdom, for she's a Spaniard and the child of noble parents and grandparents to whom the king conceded special privileges. The Tribunal must do what it can to restore her honor, for she's the daughter of a family held in high esteem, reputation and good name. Do what you must," he pleaded, "so that she can return to her parents with her status and honor redeemed."[11]

Fray Covarrubias just looked at him blankly then turned to the other men in the dark room. "Well. I'm not quite sure what to say," he remarked, as he rearranged his seating. "But it seems, in any case, that our decision would be irrelevant." Addressing the members of the Tribunal, he went on, "We can order compensation in the way of an endowment for one who is requesting monetary or other damages for a wrong perpetrated against them, but our decision in this case would be irrelevant," he repeated, looking at the members of the *definatory* who nodded in agreement. Then, with a great sigh, he concluded, "Please tell the Perez woman that we dismissed her appeal under the branch of the mootness doctrine barring the Tribunal from deciding on a case when no practical consequence would flow from its decision. Tell her that her appeal has been denied."

* * *

It didn't matter. And it probably wouldn't have mattered, whatever the Tribunal had determined, for the women of the *cazuela* had taken testimony and had arrived at their own conclusion. It was the verdict of public opinion that the family's honor, the honor due the Perez de Bustillo family, had been cleansed and restored by its response. For "blood was the soap of honor," and Nicolas Ortiz had been justified in killing the governor. But they were unwilling to make the same judgment regarding Maria, for her dishonor, they insisted, somehow tarnished them all. She was brash and haughty and, yes, shameless, they determined, because she had not lived in seclusion, had had too great a familiarity with Governor Rosas, and had presented herself without discretion or timidity around men. Governor Rosas may have used her improperly—engaged in the "dry loves," for all they knew—but she had, by her own behavior, contributed to her defilement. They had it by her own testimony, for God's sake![12]

For Maria's part, she knew that her intentions had been honorable and said that it was irrelevant what others might think. But of course it was not irrelevant. And she felt this most strongly in their treatment of Lorenzo.[13]

56

Tokens of a Life Just Begun

SPRING 1645

The snow-clad mountains were crimson in the rising sun. Slope after slope of wintry pines filled the horizon, their boughs weighted with rose-tinted snow as the quiet morning broke over them. Above Maria's home, the spring lambs were being made ready to take to the high country. Some had been rejected by their mothers but had then been accepted by other mothers whose own lambs had been born dead. These gamboled about their adoptive parents wearing the scented fleece of a deceased lamb. To these were now added a smaller herd of goats whose responsibility was to act as leaders and, also, where required, as nursing mothers for orphaned lambs.

The sharp-rising sheep pastures were still ice-covered and unyielding, their peacefulness barely disturbed by the bleat of sheep and goats and the tinkle of their bells. The goatherds and shepherds, tall, gaunt *genizaros* and their mounted and armed escorts, looked to the mountains for signs of the spring melt.

* * *

Maria, who had planning her journey for some time, looked at the mounds of items on her bed: cookware, specialty items of food, bedding, candles, strike-a-lights, coils of rope, an *harquebus* with its accoutrements. She looked at the clothing, hers and Lorenzo's, and placed hers in piles by order of priority: leather footwear, woolen stockings, leather and canvas trousers and shirts, hats for warmth, gloves. She looked at Lorenzo's, too, and smiled. Much of what Lorenzo was taking was already on his back, in the canvas knapsack that had been made for him by his grandfather, and, also, in a tiny kit bag, which his grandfather had told him was to hold a soldier's or traveler's personal effects. Lorenzo had placed his treasures in it. Insisting on packing the knapsack himself, he was now wearing it, the large rectangle of the canvas pack hanging unceremoniously to the top of his boots. He wore it during the day as he stomped around within the corral, drilling with a *harquebus* he had fashioned from a tree branch, and then at night, he took his haversack to bed.

* * *

Maria folded her skirts tightly about her legs and, with her back placed firmly against the frame of her lavender-scented bed, sat on the floor. Although covered with the coarse, woven, black and white carpeting known as *jerga*, the floor was cool against her buttocks and the backs of her legs. Pulling to the floor some of the items that had been on top of her bed, she placed these between her legs and began the job of rolling and packing, placing the finished articles within a canvas bag. She had chosen her seating at the side of her bed to catch the good light from one of her two patio-facing windows. The light, however, had to travel through sections of selenite that were shadowed with carved wooden panels and the overhang of the porch roof, making it diffuse and hueless. Leaning back against the frame of her bed, she thought briefly about opening her patio-facing door but quickly abandoned the idea. An open door, she thought, might provide more light but might also bring unwelcome company. Faced with this prospect, she elected, instead, to leave the door closed and to light some of the candles in her room although the effort to accomplish this seemed overwhelming. It would require her to get up, put the candles in their holders, light them, and then place them in various locations where they would provide the best light. Do I want to get up? she asked herself. Deciding against this prospect, she shifted about onto her knees, reached up, and drew to her breast a candle and one of the many strike-a-lights that were lying on top of her bed. This device, an early tool for fire making, was one that had been given to her by her brother. The fire-making implement, housed in a leather case, was a piece of trimmed flint made to be struck against a hard stone or a pyrite to produce sparks. The case, which she opened, also contained a piece of steel, two pyrites, and a bit of quick tinder. It had been given to Nicolas on his thirteenth birthday, but she had cried so much because she had not received this cherished gift, that he had willingly given it to her. God, he was so solicitous of my welfare, she thought, as she dumped the contents of the case into her hand. So willing to do whatever was required to make me happy. She cried then, her tears becoming sobs and then mournful cries. She struck the pyrite pieces together in a minor frenzy of fire making, but only produced dull sparks. She did this over and over again until the pyrites, through fracture and decomposition, lay in useless pieces upon the floor. Laying aside the candle, which she had also taken from on top of her bed, she returned to her task of folding and packing and wiping at her tears. And she thought about her plan, a plan that had unwittingly been given to her by Tula.

Tula had told her a *genizaro* slave had escaped from her master at Taos. Hiding in one of the carts of the supply train, where she had concealed herself under a heavy roll of bison and sheep pelts, she had remained undiscovered until the second day of the four-day journey. The wagon master had then been unable to make arrangements for her return to Taos until the train arrived at the *villa*.

I could do that, Maria had thought. I could hide among the cargo of the returning supply caravan. She knew she would eventually be discovered, but the wagon master would have to take her at least as far as Parral. Her cousin, Francisco Lopez de Aragon, who would be part of the wagon escort, would help hide her and, after a short life as a stowaway, she would come under his care.

The plan itself was simple, for there were only two possibilities. She could go, or she could stay. Go to Zacatecas where she could look for Nicolas's people and, perhaps, find out from them where he had gone after his escape from Parral. Or she could stay in New Mexico and with Lorenzo make a life here. One course was dangerous, the other bitter. She had tried to devise other schemes, but in the end the plan was this: She would go in search of Nicolas, leaving Lorenzo with her parents until she and Nicolas had established a new home. She would then return for Lorenzo and take him there. Going to the sheep camp is merely a diversion, she thought, a diversion that will give me the time I require to get to Francisco's. But how will I accomplish this? she asked herself. How will I get Taton to let me return without an escort? She did not know.

* * *

They were not going as one party. Those selected to repair the safe house were going ahead. Don Simon's principal overseer, Taton, whose additional responsibility was to guard the few women in the troupe, commanded them. Francisco Lujan, who was now at the Perez corral where the food stock was being loaded, would, with his string of pack mules, follow the initial group that was leaving from the upper canyon home of Francisco de Anaya II. The shepherds, with their large flocks of four-horned sheep and the main supply cart, would then wait for a week or so before setting out. Lorenzo, Maria, and her *genizaro* servant, Tula, along with the other women who were to function as camp cooks, would accompany them. It was a simple plan and well thought out, and it all went to hell.

* * *

The morning was crisp, with a deep fog lying in the river valley. The high bald on the mountains before them loomed skyward. Maria, who was accompanied by Lorenzo and her father, had ridden up from the main house. They followed an Indian child who was leading an ox cart laden with supplies. The task of Maria and her father, in addition to bringing a water bag to Lujan, was to assist in the packing of the sumpter mules.

Balancing the final sacks of shelled corn on either side of the packsaddle, Simon helped Francisco cover this final load with a straw mat, and after tying it down, stepped away. Francisco, his knee braced against the mule's side, pulled on the lash rope until it was taut, his pack-mule breaking wind in annoyance.

"Whew!" Simon said fanning at the air with his hat.

Lujan laughed as he mounted his horse. Then, of its own mind, his horse responded to something on the wind, jumping and stepping all at once. It gathered itself up and broke wildly into a run, crashing headlong into the corral fence. The initial blow, which had shattered a rail, was not great. However, Francisco's horse appeared dazed, the life seemingly blown from its body as it fell in a mangled heap. It tried to regain its feet, and seeking only to escape, rose on uncertain legs with Francisco still securely mounted upon its back. As it rose, the horse caught Lujan's leg, impaling it upon one end of the broken rail. Screaming in pain, Francisco was helped back to the house where he would be nursed and put on the mend, but he was not able to accompany the party from the upper canyon that was now headed toward the distant hills.

"I can go, Papa," Maria said. "I can catch up to them."

"And be the only woman there?" her father asked, just shaking his head.

"Taton will be there," she said. "He's with the rest." She pointed to the small group of mounted men visible just beyond the forest. They were on the crest of a distant hill whose slope was purple and scarlet with anemones, the windflowers of spring.

"Well, you can't go," he stated emphatically. "It wouldn't be safe. I'll get one of the men who was to have gone with the sheep."

"And they'll be long gone, Papa," she said of the initial group. "With their food here."

"It doesn't matter," he said. "It wouldn't be proper for a woman of your *calidad* to be there alone with a bunch of men."

"I'll be with Tula."

"When? In two or three weeks?"

"I've known these men all my life, Papa. They're like brothers to me," she choked, with the sense the term implied. "I can catch them and Tula will be with the others. I'll be all right," she said.

"No! I don't like it."

"You can keep me here, Papa," she cried, "force me to stay. But it will accomplish nothing, for I'm going to join them in a few days." She looked at her father and then toward the hills. She began to cry. "I'll die here, Papa. Waste away. I have to find some purpose for my life."

He looked at her, then, the tears in her eyes matched by those in his. He peered at her intently, knowing that he would not be strong enough to alter her course. "And Lorenzo?" he asked.

295

"He'll stay with you for now, and then he'll go with Tula."

Her father looked at her and then back at her three-year-old who was playing among the sheep in the corral where they stood. He said, "You may go with them, *Hita*, but only if you go now so that they're not so far ahead. Catch Taton and he'll be responsible for you."

Maria mounted her horse and rode back quickly to the house. She went to her room where she dressed in her leather trappings of *gamuza*. She gathered her hair, put it within her hat, and pulled her hat down tight about her face. And then, without speaking to her mother who she hoped would be in her own room, she emerged with a bedroll wrapped in an undressed cowhide within which she had placed some clothing. Additionally, she had a pair of saddlebags stuffed with more clothing, a leather-bound journal, a *gaban*, and two additional blankets. She had looked at the other clothing on her bed and decided that what she was carrying would be sufficient. With this, she put spurs to her horse and, without taking leave of anyone in the household, rode back to the corral where she accepted her father's assistance in attaching to her saddle's rigging dee, her bedroll and blankets. "Did you say goodbye to your mama?" her father asked with sadness, knowing that the two of them could hardly speak to one another; Maria and Lorenzo were constant reminders of her son, Nicolas, and how things might have been.

"No," she said sadly, knowing that her mother would have sensed in her appearance, the hint of a plan. She stood there with her father, he looking back over his shoulder at Lorenzo who was running toward them through the mud. "Are you sure you don't want me to send someone with you?" he asked.

"By the time another packer would get here, Papa, they would be long gone," she said, regarding the lead party. "I'll catch them by noon. It will be all right."

Lorenzo, who was now standing beside his grandfather, said, "I don't want to stay here, Mama. I want to go with you."

"You can't, Lorenzo," she said, suddenly unsure of her plan. "You must stay with your *abuelos* until Tula comes. You'll be safe here," she reassured him as she stepped away.

He looked at her quizzically. Then, seemingly suspicious of

her explanation, he said, "I want to go with you, Mama." He said in a plaintive voice.

"I'm going to the mountains to find the beginnings of our river, Lorenzo. You can come later."

"Are there bears there?" he asked his mother with the wonder of a small child.

"Yes . . . I don't know . . . yes, there are bears there," she said, as she mounted her horse.

"I wont be afraid, Mama."

Riding a saddle horse and leading a string of mules, she looked back at her small child standing there in the mud with her father, looking puzzled and scared, his chin trembling. She had not been aware that she was holding her breath until she was choked with a sob. Dismounting and tying up, she walked halfway back to where Lorenzo stood with her father and stopped again, her arms out before her, her face working upon itself. Before her father could speak, she said, "My brave little boy."

Looking at her father, she said, "The water, Papa. I almost forgot it." She indicated the leather bag of *gamuza* that was still attached to her father's saddle.

"I'll get it," her father said, as he bent over to straddle and then slip between the rails that separated him from where his horse was tied.

As her father did so, Maria removed the knapsack from Lorenzo's shoulders. Looping the straps of the haversack onto the horn of her saddle, she lifted Lorenzo to his place behind the saddlebows and mounted herself.

Her father worked at the ties that held the bag in place. I did my work too well, he said to himself. There was no need to have put a knot in it. Then, sensing rather than seeing Maria as she lifted herself into her saddle, he looked up, puzzled, but alarmed as well. "You can't take Lorenzo," he stated emphatically.

"And I can't leave him here," she said, as she turned her horse toward the gate. Giving her father no further time to argue or to complain, she said, "When the rest come, Papa, send Tula with the clothes." She and Lorenzo left the corral. Her father watched them through the railings as they picked their way in a careful and cautious manner down the steep slope toward the river. He watched them until they disappeared into the trees. Then, making a decision, he turned toward the house, thinking, I've got to get my *harquebus*. I'll be damned if they're going alone.

* * *

The world at the river was a twiggy haze. Steep, forested banks flowed toward the bottom of the canyon whose waters were swift and deep; the waters close to the banks were shallow but in perceptible motion. The morning sun, its light diffuse and hueless, glanced off the waters, deepening the shadows on the bark of the trees. Deep hay grass, wands of willow, and butterfly weed lined the banks.

The fog lifted from the waters of the stream as Maria and Lorenzo rode on toward the mountains beneath a canopy of mist and grayness. A cobalt sky was all but hidden above blackened branches. The light was low and shadowed, masking much that was around them as they came out from beneath the dense cottonwood shade that sloped toward the river. The air here, burdened with moisture, was rich with the scent of humus and duff. Riding but a short distance through lush willow groves, they stopped and dismounted at her spring on the boulder-strewn banks of the *Rio de Santa Fe*. The borders of the pool itself were carpets of miniature lichens, white as ermine, and soft and compact as the fleece of a lamb. There was still snow on the ground, especially here in the deep woods where the sun had yet to completely melt it.

Maria shivered involuntarily while grasping the top of Lorenzo's pack. "Did you pack your *gaban?*" she asked, as she fumbled with the straps of his knapsack, struggling to open it.

"It's on top," he answered, as she opened the flap.

"Here, then. Put this on," she said, handing him his coat.

"It's too warm, Mama."

"Lorenzo," she said warningly, as he put it on. She left the haversack open and hanging below her stirrup.

Brushing the snow from a large, flat stone, Maria took from her saddle bags the tokens she had determined to leave behind: a rosary of acorns, the shells of a necklace now restrung onto a leather thong, the small emerald broach that had been given to her by her Nicolas.

"What are you doing, Mama?" Lorenzo asked as she placed these items at the center of the stone.

"I'm burying my treasures, *Hito*," she answered.

He looked at her with no understanding of the ritual she was about to perform, but with a desire to participate in her odd plan. Finally, he said, "Me, too."

Retreating to their horse where his haversack hung, he reached down deep within it where he had buried his kit bag, a small leather sack secured with drawstrings. Opening it carefully, he took out a chess piece that he now held in a tight fist. Standing before her, he unfolded his small hand within which he held a miniature horse carved, it appeared, from soapstone. He handed it to her saying again, "Me, too."

She looked at him, wondering where he had gotten the chess piece, and for one agonizing moment, feared that somehow it was one that had been carved by his father. Holding it carefully and turning it over in her hands, she determined that it was from a set that had belonged to her own father. She accepted it from him and placed it alongside the other treasures, and they began to build. Things to leave behind, she said to herself. Things of the past that have no place in our future. There by a cascading stream in the windings of the forest, they worked to build a small cairn of stones, an internal core made with those rocks Lorenzo brought her, and then an outer shell of much larger stones that she gathered herself.

* * *

As they performed this odd ritual, the two adolescent Indian males who were again at the river, scouting among the settlers' corrals for horses they might steal, observed them. The Indians watched as Maria placed Lorenzo upon her horse and then mounted herself. Guessing that the adult rider and young child would cross the river at the upper ford, they strung their bows and began working their way, silent and unseen, along the opposite bank of the river, looking for a convenient place to conceal themselves.

Leaving their cherished items within the cairn, Maria and Lorenzo entered the river at the ford just above her uncle's home. The cold, black water swirling about the legs of their beasts failed to mask the white-rocked bottom of the streambed. They picked their way through a stream of boulders, the babble and splash of the river here contrasting musically to the roar above. She held the reins of her horse tightly against Lorenzo's chest and held Lorenzo even more firmly against her own. Halfway across the wide ford, Maria drew rein and sat there, seemingly contemplating the snowy banks on the other side. It was a wildscape, a *bosque* of cottonwood and willow, where daises, blue flax, and penstemon were beginning to break the surface. She stayed there for a long moment, out from beneath the canopy of trees, bathed in the glow of morning light. She looked up at the sky, then, coming to a decision and kissing Lorenzo on the top of his head before turning her horse. Well, we can't go with Francisco, she thought. It would be hard enough for me alone to hide in a cart, but I could never do it with Lorenzo. But perhaps it's for the best. Whatever my difficulties living here among the others of the *villa*, this is our home. Leading their string of supply-laden mules, they splashed back across the stream to their cairn to retrieve what they had hidden there.

* * *

The young braves had planned to shoot Maria at the moment of her greatest vulnerability, when she reached the deepest part of the stream. But they had let that moment pass, the moment at which they would have had the greatest advantage. Coming out from their hiding places within the woods, they raised their bows and waited for a clear shot at their retreating quarry, but the packsaddles and burdened beasts blocked their view. With their initial plan foiled, they threw their bows aside and ran into the water, unsheathing their knives as they ran.

The water was shallow where they entered the stream, and, although it quickly got deeper as they ran, they were able to reach Maria and her service team in an instant. They had come up behind her so fast that Maria was not even aware of their presence until one of them grasped the halter of a trailing mule. The second youth then splashed up alongside her horse and grabbed onto its reins. This boy attempted to pull Maria from her saddle but was encumbered by his knife, which kept him from completely grasping her clothing. The reins were being wrested from Maria's grip, but she managed to hold on. Failing in his attempt to unseat her, the young brave grabbed Lorenzo.

Lorenzo looked up at his mother's face and saw it paper white and contorted in agony. He cried, "Mama!"

Desperately, Maria held on to Lorenzo. She kicked at the young brave, screaming at him in fury. "Let go!" she cried. The brave held onto Lorenzo's haversack as he fell into the stream. Anger and fear washed over Maria in spasms, making the figure of the one who held onto the reins of her horse seem out of focus. The youth, who was trying to regain his footing, pulled at Lorenzo's haversack and at the reins of Maria's horse and refused to let go. Squealing in fright, its neck bent down and around, her horse spun in a tight circle, trying to rid itself of the unwanted appendage that hung at its side. Lorenzo's haversack finally came loose from the saddle and fell into the stream giving the Indian youth one less thing to hold on to.

Maria reached across her body with her left hand, and with one smooth motion pulled her *harquebus* from its sheath. At the same time, she released the reins of the mules she had been leading, freeing them to go where they might. Followed by the young brave who had been holding onto their reins, the mules ran toward the shore where they waited within a stand of trees cropping grass.

There was a moment of stillness, and then a fury of motion, as Maria fired at the figure below her feet. At the sound of the report, her horse, its ears pinned to its head, took the bit in its teeth and attempted to break toward shore, but the Indian youth, uninjured by her single shot, hung on. Although he was being flung about like a rag doll, he continued to try to pull the child, or Maria, or the horse's cargo from their places on the horse's back. Maria sawed at her horse's reins to check its motion, and spurred him at the same time, just trying to hold on.

* * *

Splashing through a small, icy stream, Maria father came upon Lorenzo's knapsack lying in the water of a tiny rivulet. He threw himself from his horse, crying in despair, a sound so full of pain that it was as if it were coming from something inhuman. Running, crying, falling, he searched the stream and the near woods but found nothing more. Wet from the waters of the stream, he climbed upon his horse and rode like a man possessed along the margins of the river, toward the mountains and the high bald. Then he heard the shot.

Her father came upon them quickly. He knew that it was Maria and Lorenzo, even though they were too far away to identify. The water below the hooves of Maria's mount was a froth of motion, as she kicked and screamed like a caged animal at the person below. Lorenzo's large, brown eyes were wide with desperation as mother and son slid from their places upon their horse, and fell into the stream. And then Maria saw her father.

Simon charged straight at the figure he saw below Maria's horse, his *harquebus* held before him in a one-handed grasp, and then he fired at the menace in the churning water.

* * *

The world fell away below the hooves of their horses as the men of the vanguard reached the top of the slope. The snow there was now marked by their tracks as they dismounted upon flat ground. They tied up, and while some gathered stones by which to build a fire pit, others gathered deadfall in the woods.

Taton was puzzled. Lujan should have caught up to us by now, he said to himself. While his men worked to build a fire, he walked back to the ledge they had crossed on their climb up the steep slope. From his perch he could see far into the valley below, a small rivulet of snowmelt at his feet. There, he could see some riders, a mule team or a mounted escort, he could not tell which. "Ah, Lujan," he said aloud. As he scanned the crocus-filled meadows below him, his senses were acutely attuned to what was occurring around him. Peering into the distance, he listened to the clink of the bed-stones in the stream as it flowed down the slope, to the call of the birds in the forest as they searched for mates, and to the moan of the wind as it moved through the canopy of the trees. He looked up into the sky. Although the sun was a blaze of glory in the heavens, it was still cold below. He sniffed the air and it smelled like snow. I don't think winter's done with us yet, he thought.

57

Afterword

GOD AND SANTA MARIA ARE DEAD

After Nicolas Ortiz escaped from prison in 1643, he was not heard of again.

* * *

At the end of Governor Pacheco's term of office, about December of 1644, the relatives of the eight men he had executed brought suits against the governor. The results of these suits are unknown.

* * *

In 1650, Alonso Baca discovered a plot of rebellion in which the Indians planned to kill or drive out of the kingdom every Spaniard and priest. The plan for Thursday night of Holy Week was betrayed when a group of Indians who had stolen some horses were overtaken and confessed to the plot. This revolt was quelled and many Indians were arrested. After an investigation by Governor Concha, nine leaders from the pueblos of Isleta, Alameda, San Felipe, Cochiti, and Jemez were found guilty and hanged.

* * *

On August 10, 1680, at most of the Indian pueblos north of Isleta, the Indians rose up in rebellion. After cutting off communication between the scattered settlements and putting the colonists to flight, the Pueblos killed approximately 422 individuals. Of the approximately 2,347

303

persons residing in Spanish households before the rebellion of 1680, there were only 1,946 left afterwards, 474 of whom were Indian servants. There were no individuals bearing the name of Ortiz, Perez, or Perez de Bustillo among the survivors.[1]

GLOSSARY OF FOREIGN WORDS/TERMS

(The words below have not "gone over" to English.
For example *Rio Abajo* but not Rio Grande)

Abuelos: Grandparents

Acacia: Locust tree

Adelantado: An honorific office left over from the Middle Ages

Adobe: Sun-dried mud brick; the average brick in colonial times measured 10 x 18 x 5 inches and weighed 50 or 60 pounds

Agave: A desert plant that looks very similar to yucca, having a dense cluster of rigid, fleshy leaves with spines along the edges and at the tips

Agnus Dei: Literally, "Lamb of God;" a wax medallion bearing the figure of a lamb, blessed by every pope in the first year of his pontificate and every 7th year thereafter

Agua Fria: Literally, "Cold Water;" a village west of Santa Fe

Several of the following, like most Spanish words that begin with "al", are probably of Arabic origin.

Alacena: A cupboard built into an adobe wall and covered with double puncheon shutters

Alamo: Poplar or cottonwood tree

Albacar: A huge space surrounded by a wall and connected to a castle. This is where a village population could find refuge with their livestock during an attack. This space is akin to the bailey, the walled enclosure in front of the keep in non-Moorish-influenced structures

Albayalde: White lead, ceruse; a skin cosmetic containing this substance; this cosmetic was also made from deer or elk horns burned until they were white and soaked with corn cobs for several days, the water being changed often; the horns were then finely ground and a little *romero* (rosemary) added which was thought to be good for *el aire*; melon seeds were added to combat wrinkles.

Albricia: Reward that by ancient tradition was owed to a messenger bearing good news

Alcalde: A mayor, magistrate, or justice of the peace; a civil official with judicial, executive, and legislative functions

Alcalde mayor or *justicia mayor*: A town's chief executive. He presided over local affairs, administered petty justice, settled minor disputes over land and water, supervised the use of Indian labor, rallied the local militia, announced governmental decrees, and helped the friars maintain discipline in the missions

Alcalde ordinario: Magistrate on the town council

Alferez: Ensign

Algerita: Desert Barberry. Shrubs and small tree-bushes of the middle and upper deserts

Alguacil: Sheriff, constable

Amole: Yucca root which has detergent qualities and can be used as a soap

Analco: A segregated zone in Santa Fe in which *genizaros* lived

Apaches de Nabaju: people of Athapaskan tribes who hunted, gathered, raided, and farmed like the other Athapaskans, but relied more heavily on farming; *nabaju* may refer to "large cultivated fields" (Gutierrez, xxvii)

Arenilla: Fine sand used for soaking up excess ink

Arroba: A weight equivalent to 4.26 gallons or about 25 pounds

Arroyo: Stream bed or gulch, most often dry

Audiencia: A high appeals court presided over by a president

Azulejo: Glazed tile of graceful blue-and-white designs

Baldachino: A structure in the form of a canopy placed above a throne

Barrio de Analco: *Analco*, in Nahuatl, means "on the other side;" in this story it refers to the other side of the *Rio de Santa Fe*. See *Analco*.

Belduque: Utility knife

Bizcochitos or *Biscochitos*: Sugar cookies

Bosque: Forest, woodland

Broccato: Brocade

Bufa (La): See *La Bufa*

Caballero: An honorific meaning knight or gentleman

Cacique: Headman; today, chief priest, the final authority at a particular locality on all matters Indian

Calabaza: Gourd, pumpkin, squash

Calidad: The various qualities that constitute the essence of a person or thing

Camino Real: Royal Road

Capilla: Chapel

Carreta: Cart

Casa real: Any government building, but more particularly, the official residence of the governor

Cedula: Royal decree

Celemin: A measure roughly equivalent to a peck

Churro: Sheep which originated in Italy; characterized by their short stature, they yielded wool that was double-coated and considered *lana basta y burda* or coarse

Chichimeca: A generic term of contempt picked up by the Spaniards from natives of central Mexico, meaning something like "dirty, uncivilized dog." By calling the Indians dogs, the Spaniards dehumanized them

Cicisbeo: (Comparable to the Spanish *Cortejo*). The professed gallant and lover of a married woman

Comendador: Knight commander

Comisario: Local superior of the Franciscan order having temporary delegated authority

Concho: Shell

Congregacion: The settlement resulting from the forced concentration of small, dispersed pueblos into larger towns so as to more easily indoctrinate the Indians who lived there

Convento: Priests' quarters or house; those subsidiary buildings in which the priests and lay brothers lived

Convento Grande: The principal house of the "Holy Gospel" diocese which retained its primacy In New Spain as the original Mexican province

Criado(da): Male or female servant respectively

Cruzada: A special tax raised by the sale of indulgences

Cruzado: An old Castilian coin of gold, silver, or copper, so-called because it had a cross on the obverse side

Cuirass: A piece of armor for the body, made of a breastplate and a back plate fastened together

Cuirassiers: The troopers armed with *cuirasses*

Custody: Dependent clerical administrative district

Dado or *Faneja*: A broad finish of talc and earth applied to the lower wall of an inside room with a *zalellita*, a small piece of sheepskin about 6" square; this wainscoting was also called a *regla*, and the resulting protection, the *guarda polvo*

Definitor: An officer whose duty it was to decide points of discipline; these officers, collectively, were known as a *definatory* whose job it was to advise the father *custos*

Del Paso: The Pass later to be known as "El Paso"

Derecho: A share of water; the annual amount of acre-feet of water to which a watering participant has a right; the amount needed to cover one acre with one foot of water

Derecho de pernada: The right of a feudal lord to deflower the bride of one of his men

Despensa: Storeroom

Dios Mio: An exclamation meaning, "My God"

Disciplina: A scourge of rawhide or sisal

Don: Spanish title used before a masculine Christian name; the origin of the term is obscure; supposedly, it is the contraction of the words, *de origen noble* (of noble origin); others have suggested that it is from the Hebrew, *adonas* (meaning "Our Lord").

Dona: Spanish title used before feminine Christian name

Duque: Duke

Encomendero: Estate holder; holder of an *encomienda* grant which allowed the individual to collect and use tribute that otherwise would have gone into the royal treasury

Encomienda: Unit of entrustment; a grant to certain individuals to collect tribute from Indians

Espanoles: Those credited (by their own description) with pure Spanish blood (or *pureza de Sangre Espanola*)

Entrada: The formal entry into a new land

Estancia: Cattle ranch

Estrado: A room or section of a room for receiving or entertaining guests

Euskara: The Basque language

Fanega: A dry measure varying from 1.5 to 2.6 bushels depending on the locality

Fata Morgana: A well-known mirage of a city that sometimes appears in the Strait of Messina off the coast of Sicily

Fogon de campana: A corner fireplace so-called because of its bell shape

Franchone: Derogatorily applied to those foreigners who roamed over Spain as beggars, peddlers, knife grinders, castrators of animals, etc.

Fray: Friar

Fuero: Medieval town's royal charter of privilege

Gaban: Greatcoat with a hood worn for hunting and traveling

Gamuza: Chamois; leather softened with the root of *cana agria* which contains a large amount of tannin, or with boiled animal brains, rather than tannic acid which is extracted from oak leaves

Garbanzo: Chickpea

Gavache: A derogatory term applied to an individual from the Gevaudon, an exceedingly poor section of France

Genizaro: From the Turkish Yeni, "new," and Cheri, "troops." The term was applied to Plains Indians who were captured as children and brought up in colonial communities

Gente de razon: "people of reason," or rational beings

Gesso (or *Yeso*): Gypsum

Gevaudon: A portion of the Auvergne in France

Guardian: Local superior of a *convento*

Hacienda: Farmstead

Haldudo: Full-skirted

Harquebus: A firearm having a matchlock operated by a trigger and supported for firing by a hook; an old form of portable gun used before muskets were invented

Hermita: Hermitage

Hidalgo: A contraction of the Spanish words, *hijo de algo*, literally, "son of something;" the sense is the "son of a somebody;" this was the lowest rank of Spanish nobility with an approximate equivalent to the English "squire."

Hita (female) or *Hito* (male): A corruption of the word *hija* (or *hijo*), meaning child; a term of endearment

Hombres ricos: The rich and powerful moguls

Iago: Diego, Jaime, and even Jacobo, meaning James; Saint James is the patron saint of Spain.

Jerga: A coarse, woven, black and white wool carpeting or fabric so inexpensive that traders used it to wrap bales of goods; sackcloth

Jornada del Muerto: Literally, "Dead Man's Route;" apparently named in reference to the fugitive, Bernard Gruber, a Sonora-based German peddler accused of distributing along with his wares certain mysterious little slips of paper and claiming that "whoever should chew one of these papers would make himself invulnerable for 24 hours." Imprisoned in 1668, he eventually escaped, only to die in the forlorn and shimmering desert stretch south of Socorro later to be known by this name. (Kessell, pp. 211-15)

Justicia mayor: Senior judge (See *alcalde mayor*)

Kiva: A male lodge house and ritual chamber, circular or square, usually subterranean

Kuba Rumia: In reference to "The Christian Tomb," the designation given a curious structure in Algiers about whose origin there has been much speculation.

La Bufa: A promontory crowned by bare, greenish rock near the southern end of the great central plateau which separates two chains of Mexico's Sierra Madre

La Canada: Today's Santa Cruz

La Cienaga: The marsh or marshy place

La Cieneguilla: The Little *Cienaga*

La Concepcion: A term ascribed to a church or a town memorializing the Immaculate Conception of the Blessed Virgin

La Nuestra Senora de los Angeles de Porciuncula: Our Lady of the Angles of Porciuncula; Portiuncula is the village about two miles from Assisi where St. Francis, in 1208, received his vocation and which he made his headquarters

La Nuesta Senora de Piedad: Our Lady of Mercy

Las Milpas de San Miguel: See *Milpa*

Las Navas de Tolosa: The Plains of Tolosa where the Moors, in 1212, suffered their disastrous defeat at the hands of King Alfonso VIII of Castile

La Tetilla: Small nipple; a 7,206 foot peak 14 miles from Santa Fe on *La Majada Mesa*

Maize or *Maiz*: Indian corn

Mangonel: A machine formerly used in war for throwing large stones

Manta: A piece of cotton cloth six palms square; in 1642, it was reckoned in price at six *reales*; the term is also used in reference to the blanket made from these squares.

Mantona: Shawl

Maese de campo: Field marshal similar to our field rank of colonel

Mayordomo: Overseer

Mesa: Tableland, plateau

Mi bon compano: Literally, "my good companion;" taken from the Italian, *buon compagno*

Mihrab: A prayer niche in a Moslem mosque which points to Mecca

Milagro: Votive offering

Milpa: *Maize* field; the word is also the Mayan term for the slash and burn technique.

Montante: A broadsword with large *quillons* requiring two hands

Montellina: A variety of *mantilla*

Moradore: An individual who maintained rights to Indian service rather than tribute

Mozarabe: A Christian living in Arab territory

Mulato: An individual of mixed Spanish and Indian ancestry

Mudejar: A Moor living under Christian rule

Nueva Espana: New Spain

Nueva Vizcaya: New Biscay; the central swath of New Spain between *Nueva Galicia* on the south and *Nuevo Leon* on the north

Ojo del Perrillo: "Little Dog Spring;" a small, slow flow of water in the desert stretch below Socorro named in reference to the little dog that led the Spaniards to it.

Olla: Bulging, wide-mouthed pot or jar

Paraje de Robledo or *Cruz de Robledo*: The Robledo campsite

Parciante: Ditch member having rights to water from the *acequia*

Pastore: Shepherd

Patio de Armas: Defensive courtyard

Pedrero: Stone-throwing gun

Peninsular: Having to do with the Iberian Peninsula

Peralvillo: A place near Ciudad Real where the Holy Brotherhood executed its prisoners

Petronel: Fifteenth-century portable firearm resembling a large-caliber carbine

Picacho: Top, peak, summit

Picote: A coarse goat's hair cloth, so rough that it pricks one when touched

Piloncillo: Little cones of raw sugar as hard as rock

Pinon: The large nutlike seeds of the *pinon* tree

Portal: Portico, porch

Porteria: *Convento* gate

Portero: Gatekeeper

Posole: Stewed hominy

Prenda: A pledge, gift, jewel or highly prized object

Procurator-general: A person authorized to act for the clerics in supplying the missions

Punche: A low grade of tobacco raised in New Mexico

Puto carbon: A male whore or complaisant cuckold; the worst of insults

Quemado: Literally, "burned;" referring, apparently, to an area burned off by Indians or to an ancient lava flow

Quillon: Either arm of a transverse piece forming a guard for a hand between the hilt and the blade of a sword

Quivira: A mythical kingdom for which the Spaniards searched, said to abound in gold, silver, and rich textiles

Rancheria: Loosely grouped cluster of dispersed huts of nomadic Indians

Real: A coin valued at an eighth of a *peso*

Real patronato: Concessions of royal patronage codified in a series of papal bulls

Regidore: Alderman or councilman

Reredo: An ornamental wood or stone screen or partition wall behind an altar

Retablo: A raised shelf above an altar for the altar cross, the altar lights, and flowers

Riestra: A tied string of chilies

Rio: River

Rio Abajo: Downriver sector of the Rio Grande Valley

Robledo: A point on the Camino Real 20 leagues north of El Paso recalling the burial there of Pedro Robledo the first colonist to die in New Mexico

Sala: Drawing room

Sal petrae: Saltpeter; a salty, white mineral used in making gunpowder

Salon de coronas: Meeting room decorated with crowns

San Antonio de Padua: St. Anthony of Padua; Padua is the oldest city in northern Italy

San Lorenzo: St. Lawrence, the first Spanish martyr

San Nicolas de las Barrancas: Saint Nicolas of the Ravines. The name of the Gomez *estancia* located downriver in the vicinity of today's Belen

Sant': Saint

Sargento mayor: An officer of field rank like our major

Siete Partidas: Seven branches of laws and customs based in part on Roman law

Soterano: From *soterrar* meaning "to bury;" root cellar

Seignioro: A feudal lord

Seigniorial: Having to do with a *seignior*

Sierras: In Spain, the word applies to high, saw-toothed mountains; it was appropriately transferred to the Southwestern ranges by the Spanish colonists.

Stoa: A portico or roofed colonnade

Syndico: A person who managed the business affairs of the church

Tipi, Tepee, teepee: A cone-shaped tent, usually of dressed skins, mounted on poles meeting near the top

Tia: Aunt

Tortilla: Cornmeal cake

Travois: Two poles trailing behind a single dray dog or horse to support baggage

Triunfo envidado: A game of cards predating and similar to poker

Vara: A variable measure equal to about 2.8 feet

Vaquero: Herdsman; so-called, said Fray Jeronimo de Zarate Salmeron in 1626, "because they subsist on the cows (*vacas*)" (Gutierrez, p. xxvi)

Vega: Fertile plain

Villa: Town, city; Santa Fe was the only one in New Mexico during this period.

Visita: A preaching station without a resident priest, but which was regularly "visited" by a priest who conducted services there

Zaguan: A double-doored and covered entranceway, wide enough for a wagon to pass through

Zapata: The carved decoration on a square ceiling beam or *viga*

ACKNOWLEDGEMENTS

A number of books were helpful in developing the cultural and historical background for this novel. The following were essential:

John A. Crow, *Spain: the Root and the Flower* (1963)

Fray Angelico Chavez, *Origins of New Mexico Families: In the Spanish Colonial Period* (1973)

Alfonso Griego, *Goodbye, My Land of Enchantment*

Paul Horgan, *Great River: the Rio Grande in North American History* (1984)

Cleofas M. Jaramillo, *Shadows of the Past*

John L. Kessell, *Kiva, Cross, and Crown: the Pecos Indians and New Mexico, 1540-1840* (1979)

George Kubler, *The Religious Architecture of New Mexico: in the Colonial Period and Since the American Occupation* (1990)

Donna Pierce and Marta Weigle (Editors), *Spanish New Mexico, Volumes I and II* (1996)

Mark Simmons, *Coronado's Land: Daily Life in Colonial New Mexico* (1991)

And, most especially:

Ramon A. Gutierrez. His work, *When Jesus Came, the Corn Mothers Went Away: Marriage, Sexuality, and Power in New Mexico, 1500-1846* (Stanford: Stanford University Press, 1991) was used throughout this study. Excerpts are reprinted with permission by Stanford University Press.

The following abbreviations are used in the notes which are grouped within a given paragraph:

C   Horgan, Paul. *Conquistadors in North American History.* New York: Farrar, Straus and Giroux, 1966.

CL   Simmons, Marc. *Coronado's Land: Daily Life in Colonial New Mexico.* Albuquerque: University of New Mexico Press, 1996.

CM   Gutierrez, Ramon A. *When Jesus Came, the Corn Mothers Went Away: Marriage, Sexuality, and Power in New Mexico, 1500-1846.* Stanford: Stanford University Press, 1991.

GR   Horgan, Paul. *Great River: The Rio Grande in North American History,* Hanover: Wesleyan University Press, 1984.

KCC   Kessell, John L. *Kiva, Cross, and Crown: The Pecos Indians and New Mexico, 1540-1840.* Albuquerque: University of New Mexico Press, 1987.

LC   Chavez, Fray Angelico: *La Conquistadora: the Autobiography of an Ancient Statue.* Santa Fe: Sunstone Press, 1975.

RA   Kubler, George. *The Religious Architecture of New Mexico: In the Colonial Period and Since the American Occupation,* Albuquerque: University of New Mexico Press, 1990.

RF   Crow, John A. *Spain: The Root and the Flower.* New York: Harper and Row, Publishers, 1963.

SF   Levine, Frances. *Down Under an Ancient City: An Archaeologist's View of Santa Fe; and Sanchez, Joseph P. The Peralta-Ordonez Affair and the Founding of Santa Fe, in Santa Fe: History of an Ancient City,* David Grant Noble (Editor). Santa Fe: School of American Research Press, 1989.

NOTES

1
His Lordship the Governor

1 Council of Trent (1545-1563)
2 RF, p. 126

3
Francisco Gomez and the Baggage Train

1 C, p. 209
2 Meaning for three generations
3 KCC, p. 186. These are actually the titles listed as belonging to his son, Francisco Gomez Robledo. Gomez Robledo likely inherited some or all of these from his father, Francisco Gomez.
4 CM, p. 105
5 The non-capitalized form, "pueblo," is used for the architectural unit. The capitalized form, "Pueblo," is used for the tribe, for the village name, for an individual member of any Pueblo tribe, and for the culture characteristic of Pueblo tribes.

5
Custos Juan de Salas and Santo Domingo

1 RA, pp. 74-5
2 KCC, pp. 105, 108
3 KCC, p. 109
4 CM, p. 98
5 "For proclaiming and defending Catholicism as the one and only true religion, and for promising to convert the infidel in newly conquered territories." These concessions gave the king "the right to establish all ecclesiastical institutions in the realm, to present to the Holy See nominations for all ecclesiastical appointments and benefices, to establish diocesan boundaries, to collect and reapportion church revenue, and to review (and even veto) all communications between the pope or the general of the religious orders and clerics." CM, p. 95
6 RA, p. 56

6
Nicolas and Maria

1 RF, p. 178

2 Kua'p'o-oge or O'gia p'oghe meaning "the place of the shell beads near the water," or the "bead water place."
3 SF, pp. 9-18

7
A Place as Parent

1 CM, p. 57
2 A corruption of the word *hija*, meaning daughter
3 CM, p. xviii

8
The Adventus

1 CM, p. 99
2 CM, pp. 99, 119
3 RF, p. 93

10
The Controversial Fray Juan de Vidania

1 RF, p. 118
2 CM, p. 230
3 CM, p. 230
4 Defined by Fray Jose de Vera as "when both candidates are of illustrious and respected families and in order to conserve the fame and respect of their families, and that the maiden not be forced to marry a man who is not her equal, a consanguine wishes to marry her so as to protect her reputation."
CM, pp. 244-45, 334
5 CM, pp. 334-35

12
Difficulties at Jemez

1 Spanish women in marriage retained their maiden name.

13
The Martinez *Residencia*

1 "*Quien toca la puerta de esta mission?*" ("Who knocks at this mission door?") To which he would receive the expected reply: "*Yo, buscando mi salvacion, penitencia, penitencia*" {It is} "I, seeking my penance and salvation.").
2 KCC, p. 156

14
The Egyptian Day

1 Her Christian name was Gertrudis de los Angles. Being but a slave, she had
no last name. She spoke of Juana and Simon Perez de Bustillo as "mother"
and "father," and was referred to by them as their "daughter." She was
addressed as a child (*tu* rather than *usted*) and would be forever infantalized.
The family of the Perez de Bustillos had total control over her person, as they
did their other thralls, power and authority that would continue until she
married.
2 Malachite; a green mineral that is an ore of copper and is used for
ornamental articles
3 A coarse woolen fabric used for sacks, packing, tents and wagon covers
4 Mostly heavy buckskin jackets or *cuera de anta*

15
A Plum to be Picked and Eaten off the Vine

1 "Goodbye?" "Thank you?" "What?"
2 "When?" or "Later"
3 The four "S's" they say all true lovers ought to be are *sabio* (knowing), *solo*
(single-hearted), *solicito* (diligent) and *segreto* (discreet)

16
A Fit of Pique

1 Dominguez, Fray Francisco Atanasio. *The Missions of New Mexico, 1776,*
translated and edited by Eleanor B. Adams and Fray Angelico Chavez
(Albuquerque: University of New Mexico Press, 1976, 65), as reported by
Donna Pierce in *Spanish New Mexico, Volume I, The Arts of Spanish New
Mexico*, p. 69.
2 CM, p. 115
3 CM, pp. 115-16

17
The Hapless Fray Antonio Jimenez

1 He was, by extension, distantly related to the Perez de Bustillos' clan. His
wife was Maria Romero. His brother-in-law, Matias Romero, was married
to Isabel de Pedraza. Gaspar's sister-in-law was the daughter of a Juan de
Pedraza and an, as yet, unidentified member of either the Archuleta or Perez
de Bustillo families.

18
The Evil Counsel and Counselor

1 It was, for Nunez, a maternal title that had been given to one of his early
  forebears, a Martin Alhaja, who had, in 1212, engaged in the climactic battle
  of *Las Navas de Tolosa* (The Plains of Tolosa). Alhaja had placed at the
  entrance of a defile the skull of a cow by which to mark a strategic pass in
  the mountains. Until then but a humble shepherd, he was ennobled by King
  Alfonso VIII of Castile for the assistance he had given the combined forces of
  Navarre, Aragon, and Portugal against the Moors. It was he who had changed
  his name to "*Cabeza de Vaca*." He did so to memorialize the origin of his
  improved social status.

19
The Ladies of the Altar Society

1 Wife of Alonso Varela; their *estancia* was at La Cienaga
2 Perez de Bustillo, widow of Asencio de Arechuleta
3 Perez de Bustillo, widow of Hernando Ruiz de Hinojos
4 Wife of Antonio Baca
5 Wife of Diego Santa Cruz
6 Wife of Simon Perez de Bustillo
7 First wife of Pedro Lucero de Godoy
8 Wife of Francisco Gomez
9 Widow of Pedro Marquez; their lands were at La Canada.
10 Perez de Bustillo, wife of Blas de Miranda, their lands were in the valley of
   Taos
11 Wife of Andres de Peralta
12 Widow of Juan Marquez
13 Wife of Francisco de Anaya II
14 Wife of Diego Marquez; they lived at their *estancia* at Los Cerrillos
15 Wife of Pedro Varela de Losada; they lived in the Sandia district
16 LC, p. 65
17 SF, pp. 34-35

23
The Venerable Fray Nicolas Hidalgo

1 CM, pp. 76, 209-10

24
The Governor's Lackey

1 RF, p. 190
2 CM, p. 115
3 The X, *"el Sabio,"* "The Learned," 1252-1284

28
A Private Extinction

1 CM, p. 61

31
Angry Words
1 GR, pp. 359-60
2 They were made illegal in 1639 as characteristic of prostitutes
3 His right to deflower the bride of one of his men

32
In Antonio's Garden

1 Made with dried leaves of mint, lavender, rosemary, sweet basil and musk oil
2 KCC, p. 95. Some historians, notably Hallenbeck, have identified the river
  Baca discovered as the Mississippi. It was Baca's survey that "gave New
  Mexico her claim to the territory now embraced by western and northern
  Texas, and which Spain, and afterward Mexico, recognized as a part of
  New Mexico up to the time this region was taken over by the United States."
  (Cleve Hallenbeck, *Land of the Conquistadores*, The Caxton Printers, Ltd.,
  Caldwell, Idaho, 1950, p. 111.)
3 Their paternal grandfather, Juan de Vaca, the explorer, who had been with
  Vasquez de Coronado; and father, Cristobal Vaca, the settler, who had been
  with Onate
4 These socks did not provide comfort, warmth, or protection and their utility
  is unknown. Used by both Indians and Spaniards throughout the colonial
  period, these stockings remain an anomaly of the New Mexico experience, an
  unexplained artifact of colonial days. CL, pp, 8-11

35
The New *Custos* and Governor

1 *Hijos de algo* or *Hijos-dalgo de Solar*, the "Sons of Something" of the lands
  owned by them; the origin of the term, with the sense of "The Son of a
  Somebody," is obscure; it was the lowest rank of Spanish nobility.
2 The date was June 24th when all running water was in and of itself believed
  holy. This tradition may stem from the celebration of June 24th as the
  birthday of St. John the Baptist. The celebration of his birthday forms

an exception to the celebration of the festival of saints on the day of their deaths, because John was believed to have been sanctified in his mother's womb, so he came into the world sinless. (Butler, *Lives of the Saints*)

3 CM, p. 60

4 Stewing pan

37
The Rosas *Residencia*

1 An ancient elm between Gisors and Trie where French kings and Norman dukes negotiated their differences

2 The tree was revered by the Pueblo Indians because of its fit into their origin myth in which a tree struck by lightning would contain an obsidian arrowhead that would be Oak Man' heart and protection.

3 SF, pp. 27-8

4 CM, pp. 178-79

5 KCC, p. 159

6 Rather than gray; the blue honored the Immaculate Conception

7 RF, p. 222

38
The Honorable Francisco Gomez

1 *Encomendero* of Santa Clara and Jemez; Herrera's wife was Ana Lopez del Castillo, Granddaughter of Ana Perez de Bustillo

40
The Encounter at Isleta

1 To gaze blankly at the ceiling

43
Dimly Lit but Full of Shadows

1 Two of these individuals, Juan Ruiz and Pedro de Chavez, were also members of the Baca clan. Juan Ruiz Caceres was married to Isabel Baca, while don Pedro's mother, dona Isabel de Bohorquez, was Baca's sister.

2 Antonio de Salas, who was one of Rosa's guards, held the *encomienda* of Pojoaque Pueblo. He was a member of the *Cabildo* of Santa Fe in 1639. A stepson of Pedro Lucero de Godoy (*El Viejo* ?), Salas was married to Maria de Abendano, daughter of Simon de Abendano and Maria de Villanueva. Maria de Villanueva was Antonio Baca's sister.

47
A Substitute Husband

1 Maria testified (1) that she had been guilty of adulterous relations with Rosas over a period of four years; (2) that after her husband returned from New Spain, Rosas had urged her to run away with him; (3) that Rosas had even urged her to kill her husband, offering to provide her with the means to commit such an act. She further stated (4) that she had gone to Rosa's home on January 9 of her own accord and that no one had forced her to do so. In fact, Rosas had summoned her, and had threatened that if she did not come, he would go to her. Finally, she swore (5) that no one had in any way influenced her testimony or induced her to testify falsely.

50
Caught, Convicted and Condemned

1 A former visitor general, and himself a bishop of the secular or diocesan clergy. Sometime before May 23, 1642 he had been appointed archbishop of Mexico and on June 9 he had been named viceroy of New Spain, governor of Mexico, captain-general and president of the *audiencia.*
2 Church *and State in New Mexico 1610-1650.* The University of New Mexico Press, pp. 115-167
3 Statement of the Constable of Castile, Grandmaster of the Knights of Santiago, at his own execution in 1453
4 RF, p. 159

52
Say Nothing to King, Rook or Earthly Man

1 The description of the torture Nicolas endured is an echo of that inflicted upon a slave by Alejandro Mora, CM, p. 185

53
A Nicely Set-Out and Well-Provisioned Spanish Column

1 His wife was an Archuleta, daughter of Asencio de Arechuleta and Ana Perez de Bustillo

55
Correcting the Uncorrectable

1 CM, pp. 220-21
2 CM, p. 177

3 Maria's verbal and written pleas before Fray Vidania and the ecclesiastical
   judge are a combination of the complaints made by Maria del Rosario
   Martin in 1785, CM, p. 216; Maria de las Nievas Miera y Pacheco regarding
   her defilement by Josef Trujillo, in 1805, CM, pp. 219, 222-23; and the words
   of dona Maria Manuela de la Luz Romero in her suit against Mariano Baca,
   CM, p. 224
4 "Unfortunate Frailty," the lament of dona Maria Luisa de Aragon regarding
   her daughter, CM, pp. 213, 224
5 CM, pp. 231-32
6 CM, pp. 231-32
7 The request for compensation by Palonia Varela is that made by Ines Garcia
   in 1736, CM, p. 218
8 CM, pp. 218, 225
9 CM, p. 220
10 "Solace her Evil," the rejoinder of Sebastian Lujan to the accusation by
   Juana Rodriguez, CM, p. 220

11 Inspired by the words of Fray Juan Alvarez, ecclesiastical judge re: Juana
   Trujillo, 1705, CM, pp. 233-34
12 CM, pp. 211, 220. "Dry loves" (anal intercourse)
13 CM, Honor and Virtue, p. 209

57
Afterword

1 CM, p. 133 (See *In the Dust of Time* by this author)

www.ingramcontent.com/pod-product-compliance
Lightning Source LLC
Chambersburg PA
CBHW011403010726
47495CB00009B/2762